MAGIC REVERSED

Book I of the Celtic Bestiary Tales

MAGIC REVERSED

Book I of the Celtic Bestiary Tales

KENNETH McINTOSH

CANDLEWOOD
YOUNG ADULT

Magic Reversed: Book I of the Celtic Bestiary Tales

CandleWood Young Adult
Vestal, NY 13850
www.candlewood-books.com

IngramSpark 2020 paperback ISBN: 978-1-62524-817-6

Author: Kenneth McIntosh.
Cover design by Ellyn Sanna.
Interior design by Camden Flath.

A NOTE TO THE READER

A while ago, a headline in a newspaper captured my attention: REVEALED, IRELAND'S REAL-LIFE ZOMBIE SCARE. No, I was not reading one of those trashy tabloids that populate the grocery-store checkout lane; this was real news about Irish archaeologists who had discovered skeletons, buried in the 700s, with stones in their mouths. "Experts believe," the story read, "that the locals did this to stop the dead from returning to walk the earth."

That raised my curiosity, and I was soon pursuing the walking dead as they left their trail of carnage across the medieval landscape. I came across an ancient Gaelic phrase—*neamh mairbh* (pronounced "nave mare-vh)—that roughly translates as "living dead." Next, I found the old Germanic word *draugar*—the "after-walkers" (in other words, bodies that walk after their death). I discovered that both Celtic and Germanic cultures had all manner of stories about the living dead that terrorized the British Isles during the Dark Ages.

I learned several fascinating details as well: that the living dead had a run-in with the Irish super-hero Finn McCool, for example; also, that they could be killed by piercing their unbeating hearts with yew stakes; and last, that some of them came out of a magical cauldron. In fact, there's an ancient Celtic silver vessel called the Gundestrup Cauldron with images beaten into its sides that show what appear to be dead warriors being dipped into a cauldron, then emerging as the undead.

The story you're about to read takes place during the terrifying days when the undead walked the British Isles. The descriptions of zombies in this novel—and most matters of mythology, culture, and traditions—come from my study of folklore and history. I'm not saying, of course, that there really was a zombie apocalypse back in the Dark Ages. But then again, given the way that legend and historical facts can blend together . . . well, who knows?

1

SLAVERY

The Kingdom of Northumbria
Year 610

"Don't stare at me, boy."

Shite. She's caught me watching her again.

My face hot, I tear my eyes away from Freya as she rides past. She's the oldest daughter of the man who holds me slave, and I've no right to be looking at her at all—and definitely not with eyes filled with longing.

Freya pulls on the reins, drawing her mount to a standstill in front of me. The mare blows air out her huge nostrils and dances restlessly. I step away, not wanting to be trampled should Freya decide to put her heels to her mount's sides. Last week, she rode her mare straight at me as I was carrying a bag of grain over my shoulder. I ended up sprawled out flat on the ground, the sound of her laughter in my ears as she rode away.

Freya has been alive sixteen summers, the same as me, but she always acts as though she's far older. She pretends to have such dainty manners, such dignity, as though she were a jarl's stately wife instead of a thane's young daughter. Ever since her mother died a few years ago, she's had to rear her two wee sisters and tend her father's household—but that's no excuse for the way she acts. She may be beautiful, and I may not be able to keep my eyes off her—but I hate her.

And yet at the same time, I can't stop thinking about the way she looks. Her long hair is the color of ripe wheat, and she wears it in fancy slender braids that hold back the thick strands falling loose around her shoulders. I've never heard a kind word fall from her mouth—not to me, at least—but still, I have to admit her lips are sweet and curved, just begging for a kiss. If the Angles' goddess of love and war were to appear, I can't imagine that she'd be any lovelier than her namesake.

The deep-hued gown Freya's wearing today makes her eyes seem even bluer, like the blue of the ocean on a summer day. The dress is made from some thin shiny stuff her father got from traders, and the morning drizzle makes the fabric cling to her curves.

I spend way too much time thinking about those curves.

I'm smart enough now, though, to keep my face blank, my gaze carefully fixed on the gray sky, waiting for Freya to be on her way.

"Why aren't you working?" she snaps.

Because you stopped me, you numpty wench. Still looking at the sky, I try to move around her so I can go back to lugging the boulder her father wants hauled up the hill.

"Look at me when I speak, boy!" Freya snaps. "Don't stare into space like the witless clod you are."

I'm flummoxed now. If I look at her again, she'll scold me, and if I *don't* look at her, she'll be equally peeved. I can't win.

Before I can decide which course of action will lead to the least trouble, her father's voice bellows from behind me, "Slave, why are you talking to my daughter?"

I turn and see Aedgar striding across the field, his face red above his heavy beard. A big man with meaty shoulders and ponderous belly, he has a nose like a potato and wild eyebrows that hang over his beady eyes like the two wings of some outlandish bird. I don't know how he sired a daughter as beautiful as Freya.

"Has he dared to offend you, daughter?" he shouts. "If he has, I'll cut off his bollocks and serve them to you on a plate."

Freya turns away from her father, and I see her yank a small bone comb from her hair. Before her father is close enough to see what she's doing, she lets it drop on the ground between us, and then she calls, "I dropped my comb, Faeder. I was just asking the slave boy to pick it up for me." Her blue eyes meet mine, but I can't read their expression.

What game is she playing now?

"Then why haven't you picked it up, slave?" As I turn to face Aedgar, his huge fist cuffs me across the side of my head.

I stagger and fall back against Freya's mare. The horse nickers and steps sideways, while I try to keep myself from falling under her hooves. My arms flail and I feel the brush of Freya's skirt against my face.

"Careful, boy!" she hisses in my ear. "Don't get too close to me!"

I manage to regain my footing, then stoop to pick up the bit of carved bone from the mud where it landed. With my eyes downcast, I hold it out to Freya.

She leans down, her hand stretched out. When I glance up at her, I can't help but see straight down the neck of her gown. I suck in a breath and try to keep all expression from my face, but I can tell by the smug look on her face that she knows the effect she has on me.

Then she sniffs and draws back. "I can't put that back in my hair. It's filthy."

At that, her father gives me a kick in the backside that sends me lurching forward. This time I manage to avoid the horse, but I go down on one knee. "You heard my daughter!" Aedgar bellows. "Take her comb down to the river and wash it."

I scramble to my feet and take off running. The river Wear flows through the valley below the hill where I've been working, but it's not a mere jaunt away. It curves around the village of Escomb, and today, mist crawls up from its banks like a grey blanket unfolding itself over the fields that lie between me and its flowing water. I plunge through the fog, knowing that if I'm not back fast enough to suit Freya and her father, I'm likely to get more than a kick on my backside or a cuff across the head.

When Aedgar first bought me as his slave four years ago, I'd hurl myself at him every chance I got, kicking, biting, swearing. And every time, I got nothing for my trouble but a beating. My eyes were constantly swollen and black from Aedgar's fists, my back was striped with purple welts from his whip, and my head was struck so many times that my brains rattled. For weeks on end, I went around in a daze of rage and pain, barely able to think.

A century ago, when the Anglefolc's ships first swarmed onto our shores, Aedgar's ancestors set out to conquer us and take away our land. I was born far to the north, though, beyond the great wall the Romans left behind, and I grew up thinking I was safe—until the night the Angle raiders descended on DunCollum and stole me from the village where I'd lived all my life.

Weeks later, I was bitter and banjaxed from all the beatings but still determined that I'd not give in to my captors. I dreamed about my ma and da, and the rest of my friends and family. I plotted ways I could escape and make my way back home. I refused to bow my head to Aedgar or the other Angles, no matter how often I was beaten.

And then one day, I pissed on Aedgar's door, thinking he'd never know who left the yellow puddle on his doorstep. He found out of course—I still wonder if it was Freya who saw me and tattled—and then he tied me to a stump and pounded me with the flat of his sword. By the time he was done, the world had gone black. When I came back to myself, night was falling, and I was alone, propped up against the stump. My sides and belly were covered with deep welts, like a plowed field, and I knew my back must be even worse. I couldn't stand up straight for a week, and I burned and shivered for days after that, so sick with fever I truly thought I might die.

I learned my lesson that day. Aedgar is like a mountain of flint. You can throw yourself against it all day, but it's not going to move a bit. All you'll get for your effort is a load of hurt dumped on you. So now I curse inside my head, and I hold my anger in check. He still finds reason to hammer me now and then, but mostly I've learned to stay out of his way. No matter how I hunger for the Gaelic words of my childhood, I speak in Englisc, I do my work, and I keep my head down.

Except when Freya rides by.

I reach the river at last, gasping for breath as I kneel and dip the comb into the water. I despise Freya for treating me this way—but I despise myself even more because I almost enjoy it. When I hear her snippy little voice, it breaks the terrible monotony of my life. Running back and forth to suit her whim, though, it's hard to remember

I was born a free man of the Scoti. She strips away my dignity even more than her father's blows do.

It wasn't always like this. For years, I barely noticed her; she was just a skinny, little blond girl sticking up her pointy nose whenever I walked by. But last winter, something changed. Every night as I slept in my shed, I no longer dreamed of my family and home; instead, I dreamed about Freya. And while I shivered through the winter's cold, snuggled up to a cow and some geese for warmth, she slept snug and warm inside her father's house.

Since then, as the months have passed, it's just gotten worse, this strange thralldom she's put on me, more powerful and painful than that with which her father holds me. She infuriates me every time she speaks to me—and at the same time, I'm helpless to stop the sheer swelling want of her.

I know of course that the distance between us can never be crossed. And yet, she doesn't ignore me. I look up from my work and find her gaze on me just as often as she catches me watching her. And sometimes, like today, she even seems to seek me out.

Now, torn between longing and anger, I trudge back up the hillside, across the plowed fields that were forestland before the Angles came. Freya's still waiting where I left her, but her father has moved away to talk to another man from the village.

Silently, I stand in front of Freya and hold out the clean comb. She leans down from her mount, but this time, I refuse to let my gaze wander inside the neckline of her gown. As she takes the comb from me, though, her hand brushes mine. My heart leaps, but so do other parts of my body.

"Oh, my," she says. "What's that you have in there? Did you grab a fish from the river and stuff it in your britches?" My entire body is so hot with embarrassment and lust that I'm sure the mist against my skin must sizzle. She giggles. "Your face has turned as red as your hair!"

"Freya!" her father bawls across the hillside, and for once, I'm grateful to hear his voice. "Don't waste your time with the slave boy."

"Yes, Faeder," she calls back to him and picks up the reins.

I watch as the mare trots down the hill, back to the village. I'm waiting for the moment I know will come, and sure enough: Freya twists in the saddle to give me one last backward glance. The expression on her face reminds me of the way a cat looks at a mouse.

"Don't stand there gawking, slave!" Aedgar hollers. "Move!"

He slaps a gloved hand on the grip of his seax. His favorite weapon, it looks like an overgrown version of the cleaver my ma used to cut a joint of meat. "If you don't get six more stones up this hill by sundown," he yells, "I'll slice you to pieces."

Oh, dry your arse, Aedgar. I keep my face expressionless, despite my thoughts. Aedgar gives his seax another slap, then walks away. I turn back to the stone I was heaving onto a wooden sledge when Freya interrupted me

I can't think how her father came up with the idea that he needed to build a stone altar to appease his gods. Aedgar's brain is about the size of a mouse's diddy, but once a thought squeezes itself into the tiny space, it never escapes. A few weeks ago, a traveler from the south brought with him a tale of dead folk coming out of their graves to eat the flesh of the living. The man had heard the story from a trader, who had heard it from a farmer, who heard it from his wife's cousin. Everyone except Aedgar knew it was just one of those stories that travel back and forth across our island, but for some reason, Aedgar took it seriously. He decided he needed a shrine to earn his Thunder God's protection—and then he lit on the idea that he could use the stones from an old Roman fort to build an altar. Of course, his slave is just the one to do the work.

As I bend my back to hauling at the stone, I give a snort of laughter. Aedgar, big hulking man that he is, is terrified by the sort of stories children tell to scare themselves around the fire. Back when I was growing up, the elders sometimes told us tales about the living dead—the *neamh mairbh* we called them in our tongue—but my da told me it was all just blarney. My ma, though, would say to me, "But remember, Finn, just in case—if you're ever facing evil, a branch of yew will ward it off. The yew tree has the power of life and death." My brother and I used to make ourselves make-believe swords of yew and run through the forest, pretending we were killing neamh mairbh . . .

But my da and ma, my brother, and everyone else I love are all far away, and the days when I had the freedom to laugh and play are long gone. In the end, I care not so much as a flea's arse why Aedgar is building his altar. All I know is I have to lug his stinking rocks for him. And by Woden's swollen bollocks, it's hard and ghastly work. My thoughts make me shake my head at myself, half ashamed that I even curse like one of the Anglelfolc now. What would my ma and da think of me if they knew?

Pushing and pulling that manky block of stone, my body goes back to normal, and after a while, I manage to let Freya slip from my mind. My muscles fall back into the labor's rhythm, and my mind goes looking for the sound of my mother's voice. It's trick I've learned to help me endure the long days of labor. While my muscles work, my mind runs free, listening again to all the things Ma used to tell me—pieces of advice, things she wanted me to remember, stories about the Faerie folk. "You're one of them, Finn," she used to say. "You have Sidhe blood flowing in your veins." Remembering, I smile a little. *Too bad, Ma, but I have no magic powers. They'd come in handy about now if I did.*

When I reach Aedgar's altar in its circle of moss-covered oaks at the top of the hill, I dump the block and stretch my back a moment, my head tipped back. It's only a few days past Beltane, and usually by now the morning mists should have cleared, and I'd be feeling the sun warm on my face. Instead, the sky overhead seethes with black clouds. As I watch, the thunderheads pile up even thicker, until it seems like night has fallen, stealing away the day.

But I can't stand here looking at the sky, no matter how odd it looks. There's work to be done. I bend and use all my muscles to lift the stone onto the altar. I'll need to hurry down the hill again for another stone if I hope to get five more up here before sundown.

Each block of granite is as long as my arm and twice as heavy as a man—and every last one has to be heaved onto the wooden sledge, then hauled with a rope up this cursed hill. Even the giants from the old stories would have broken their backs hauling these loads. You would think by now I would have become accustomed to the pain in my back and the sting of the rope biting into my hands. Well, I guess I have.

Almost.

Last week, I was so fed up with my life that I beat one of the giant stones with my fists when no one was looking. I yelled like a madman and pounded my knuckles on the rock. Now my hand's still swollen and purple, and my knuckles are ugly black scabs. I didn't cause the rock any pain, of course, but I think I broke a bone in my hand. Proper eejit I am sometimes. Hitting that rock was pretty much like trying to fight Aedgar—a fecking waste of time

As I hurry down the hill, the clouds are like raven feathers, hanging low over my head. Something seems wrong, something that makes me shiver. Then I realize what it is: I can't hear any birds singing. Usually, I hear jackdaws and rooks jabbering while I work, but they've fallen silent now. There's not a note from a lark or a thrush, and the very leaves on the trees hang limp and still. It's like someone whispered, "Hush!" to the entire world.

But I've reached the old stone wall, and I have work to do. I pick up a stout stick to use as a lever for the next block of granite. *By Thunor's arse, this stone is heavy!* With a final heave, I manage to shove it onto the sledge.

As I bend to grab the rope, something catches at the corner of my eye, a flicker of shadow off to the left where there's nothing to cast any shadow, only empty hillside. I straighten and peer into the darkness. *What* is *that?* There's an odd flitting darkness, like something coming and going through the hedgerow between the fields. And then—nothing.

Must have been my imagination.

I put it out of my mind and go back to work, moving faster now, but there's not much use in trying to hurry a block of granite. By the time I reach the top of the hill, I know I've lost nearly half a day, and I still have to get four more stones placed on the altar. My stomach growls loudly, and it's hard to think of anything but my next meal. All my hard labor makes even stale porridge seem delicious.

As I trot back down the hill, though, I catch a whiff of something that takes away my appetite. It's not any of the normal smells of earth, manure, and cooking fires; it's something foul, like dead flesh. A sheep, maybe, hidden by a bush where no one saw it, rotting now . . .

A scream interrupts my thoughts. I stare down the hill, trying to see through the mist into the valley. The thatched roofs of the village are only dark shadows, and there's not another human being in sight. I wait a few breaths, uneasy but knowing it's none of my business— probably a man beating his wife or two women quarreling—and the Angles won't thank a slave for sticking his nose into their private affairs.

Then another scream rises through the fog, filled with so much horror that my skin prickles. This time I recognize the voice.

Freya?

I drop the rope and run down the hill, across the fields, through the cow yard, my feet sloshing and sliding in the muck, and then through the village's outer wall. There's Aedgar's house ahead of me, and from inside it, I hear Freya scream again.

I lunge forward—but I hesitate at the door. Slaves aren't allowed inside their master's house without permission. To enter now could be a good way to get my head separated from my shoulders.

But I hear children crying inside, and then Freya screams again. *To Hel with my head.* I jerk open the door and step cautiously inside, uncertain what I'll find.

At first, I can't see anything at all. The windows are only slits, the air is smoky, and the hearth fire is small.

Then my eyes adjust to the darkness, and I see something that can't be real.

That thing can't *possibly* be real.

2

THE WALKING DEAD

I blink, but the thing is still there. And now I see that Freya is backed into the corner of the room, her two little sisters clasped one beneath each arm. Her eyes are so big with terror that they look black, all the blue swallowed up.

A man—what must be a man—looms over her. The only man I've ever seen who looked like this one, though, was one month dead. The thing wears what must have once been common working clothes, but they're faded and filthy, not much more than tattered rags. Through the shreds of cloth, I catch a glimpse of what looks like the long bones of a leg, a twist of green intestine, a rib showing white between gray clots of flesh. A few strands of black hair cling to the thing's lumpy scalp. The stench comes off it in waves, and I gag.

The thing turns its head toward me, and I see its face. The mouth is a skull's bony grin, and the bloody eyeballs have no flesh around them. The nose is altogether gone.

I stagger back. I want to run out the door, run and never look back. I'd rather move all the stones in Angleland than face this thing.

And then I look into Freya's wide eyes. I straighten my shoulders. *All right. Think. Don't just stand there staring.* My eyes dart around the room, looking for something I can use as a weapon.

There! Aedgar's spear is hanging on the wall. I grab the shaft, yank it down. The foul creature just stands there as I raise the spear.

And then I hesitate. I've never killed a man. I've wished to kill folks a mickle lot of time, but to actually do it is another thing.

But is the thing actually a man? It smells like Fenris' reeking rear. No *human* smells like that.

I drive my arm forward, shove the spear through the thing's chest. Its hide is tough as leather. I grind my teeth and push harder; the blade punches through the ribcage and out the back.

But the thing doesn't fall. Instead, it turns toward me, as though I'd merely tapped it on its shoulder—and then it howls. Its eyes are balls of rotting jelly, but I know they're staring at me. Before I can react, it leaps at me. In one tiny corner of my mind, I'm thinking that it jumps the way certain spiders can, suddenly, without the normal use of sinew and thew. The rest of my mind is simply stunned, frozen, unable to think at all.

It knocks me down, and bony hands reach for my neck. I try to squirm away, but the thing is too strong for me. Slimy fingers fasten around my throat. The rank smell is so thick that it sucks any air I might have been able to squeeze into my lungs. For an instant, everything turns dark, and fear flows through my veins like ice water. This thing is going to strangle me. I'm going to die.

And then, the hands around my throat drop, and the thing lets out another howl, this one so awful that every hair on my body stands up. It's not a sound that could come from a human throat, not even from someone demented, and it's like no animal cry. No, this is a screech that comes straight from the underworld. The ghoul holds up its bony hands as though they've been burned and wails again.

And then, *thud!* The noise is like a very large egg being cracked. When the creature falls to the floor, I see Freya standing there behind it. Her eyes are wild, and a brass pot swings by its handle from her hands. When I glance down, I see she's smashed the ghoul's skull. Something thick and gray is splattered across the floor.

Freya and I stare at each other. I swallow back the bile that's rising up from my gullet and scramble to my feet. "That should take care of it." I try to give her a shaky smile.

Before she can answer, the fiend springs up, a rattling bag of bones that jumps and jerks with a black, ferocious energy. It whips its arm back, but I never see the blow fall. All I see is Freya flying across the room.

She sprawls against the wall, her face as white as milk. Her sisters are crying, crouched in their corner, and the sound of their whimpers draws the monster's attention.

"No!" Freya's breathless cry is fierce.

The thing pivots back toward Freya, and then it makes another spider-leap. I can't see Freya now; she's hidden beneath the broken bones that twitch and jiggle as I watch, as though they're fitting sockets and joints back together. I punch my arms in the air and shout. Maybe I can at least distract it long enough that Freya can roll free of it.

"Out of the way, slave!" shouts a voice behind me.

I'm accustomed to obeying that voice; I drop to my knees. A blade whistles through the air—and the thing's head flies across the room. It rolls along the stone floor, trailing strands of gore in its wake, and then it's still. Aedgar steps past me, something black dripping from the blade of his seax, and reaches down to his daughter.

As he pulls her to her feet, Freya gasps. "Faeder!" She points a trembling finger behind Aedgar. He turns, and his eyes bulge.

The thing is still on its feet, even though it's headless now. It's bent over, all the bones cracking and snapping, while it runs its bony fingers back and forth across the floor. It's looking for its head.

This can't be happening.

At that instant, something opens up in my mind, like a door cracking open to let in understanding. Of course—this wight is one of the *neamh mairbh*, the walking dead. The old tales were true after all. I hear again my mother's voice inside my mind, and I look around the room, my eyes searching frantically. I have to find what I need before the thing locates its head.

There! In the room's far corner, Aedgar's unstrung bow leans against the wall, a long flexible shaft made of yew. I leap across the room, avoiding the creature as it scrabbles across the floor with its searching bony fingers, and snatch up the bow. Summoning all my strength, I thrust it into the thing's back, alongside the spear shaft that still pokes out between the ribs.

The bones fall with a rattle onto the floor. For a moment, they shake with a horrifying violence, but after a moment, they only jiggle gently. They jitter a moment longer, while the hip bones tap up and down on the stone floor, once, twice—and then they all are still.

Freya pulls herself to her feet and rushes to scoop her sisters into her arms. Aedgar is staring at the stinking bundle of bones, a dazed look on his face. I know he has seen his share of death and battle, but I'm pretty sure he's never seen anything like this.

I'm shaking now, worse than the creature did before it fell still, but I know something else needs to be done. "The, the—the—" I shake my head and try to halt my stammer. "The head," I manage to say. "It—uh—it needs to go." I motion toward the hearth, where the banked fire smolders amid the pile of peat and wood.

Aedgar blinks at me. "You should have built that altar faster, boy." He doesn't sound angry; he just looks gobsmacked, even more slow-minded than usual. Clearly, he's not going to do another thing until he recovers his wits, so I swallow and try to bring myself to pick up the broken skull. My hands hover over it—and then Freya gives an impatient sigh and pushes me aside. She grabs the strands of black hair and flings the head into the fire. The look on her face makes me think, *Never get on her bad side.*

Aedgar lets his seax fall from his hand. As he collapses with a thud onto a stool, he glances at me again, and this time, I can see a flicker of thought in his beady eyes. It's time for me to leave, before he can think any more. I have entered my master's house unbidden, and I have taken hold of his bow. Either of these actions could mean my death. Without another word, I duck out the door. Aedgar and Freya can clean up that sack of rotten bones by themselves.

News moves like wind through the tiny hamlet, especially news like this. For the rest of the day, the villagers come to gather around Aedgar's hut, thanes and freemen alike, stepping around the piles of sheep shit and sending the chickens clucking out of their way. After years of captivity, I've learned to sit as quietly as a clod of dirt, unnoticed, and I make use of this skill now, sitting cross-legged on the ground, listening.

The dark clouds have lifted, giving way to streaks of blue and white. I glance up at the sky, glad for light and clean air. I reckon by the sun that the day is waning, and I'm wondering if Aedgar is going to remember the stones he said I had to carry before nightfall.

Before I can decide whether I should get my rump off the ground and climb the hill to fetch a chunk of granite, a rider gallops through the gate in the outer wall. Both man and horse look ragged with exhaustion, their skin soaked with sweat—but at least their skin is alive and hale. The man leaps from his horse and shouts something I don't catch, his voice as scratchy as an old saw blade. Whatever he said, it sends the Anglefolc running to hear his news. I follow after them, hanging back so they won't notice me.

The man is panting so hard he can barely speak—with fear or exertion, I can't tell—but he manages to gasp out that he is from a village less than a day's journey away. They were attacked last night by the same foul creatures as that thing that's still on Aedgar's floor lies. The folk from the neighboring burgh are scattered. Most of them are dead.

"Eaten," the man says, his rough voice flat like a stone. "The things eat the flesh of those they kill. I saw one gnawing on a man's arm as though it were a chicken bone."

After that, horror spreads in waves through the village, as the man's story is repeated again and again. When it reaches the jarl, Lord Wulfstan, he calls at once for a meeting in his great hall. I watch as men, women, and children find their way between the carved wyrms that flank the lord's door. I'm left outside, of course. Slaves aren't welcome at village meetings, only thanes and freemen.

Then a man sticks his head out. "Slave," he calls to me, "you have something to do with this. You come too."

When I step into the long, shadowy enclosure, I see a large fire in the center. My clothes are still damp, and I'm grateful for the warmth, but my nose wrinkles at the thick smell inside the hall. The odors of cooked meat, peat in the fireplace, the sweat of working people, and sweet mead spilled during countless celebrations all mix together. It's nothing so bad as what I've smelled today, though.

As my eyes adjust to the shadows, I see that the men, women, and children stand with their backs against the walls, their attention focused toward the seat at the far end of the hall. Lord Wulfstan sits there, enthroned between carved posts topped with wolf heads, wearing a bearskin beneath a vest of polished brass scales. His black beard is braided in knots, and his dark eyes glint like embers.

Wulfstan rules over all the freemen beneath him and answers only to the king. Unlike Aedgar, a man of brute force but little brain, Wulfstan speaks with careful cunning, and his watchful eyes miss very little. I always think that Wulfstan must have a dozen thoughts he keeps hidden for every word he speaks—and at least half of them might be useful.

Now, Wulfstan taps his long spear on the wooden floor, calling the assembly to attention. "We must speak today of the living corpses. We thank the All-Father that Aedgar arrived in time to slay the horror that attacked his daughters."

No mention of my role, of course.

"But," Wulfstan continues, "if we do not prepare ourselves, we may not be so blessed the next time we encounter these creatures. Elthric, a freeman from Aldershire, has brought more news of this strange danger that threatens us. Let us hear him, that we may equip ourselves for whatever lies ahead." Wulfstan extends his hand toward the gaunt disheveled man who stands near him, swaying on his feet from weariness. "Elthric," the jarl commands, "tell us what you have seen."

Elthric has long stringy hair and a wispy beard that hangs from his chin like a goat's. He clears his throat. "They came just after dusk yesterday." His voice is still raspy, like the voice of someone sickening from a chill—or someone who has screamed himself hoarse. "There were as many as would fill two or three longships. They looked like men—and women, even young ones—but their flesh was like the dead's. Rotted. Foul."

Elthric gulps, clears his throat again. "They ran like a pack of wolves into the village, but they were worse than any wolf. They spoke not a word of human language, but they screeched like— Like nothing I have ever heard before. No animal makes a sound like that."

Elthric shuts his eyes for a moment, as though gathering strength. "One ran straight at me, and I looked into its eyes. No soul shone there, not even an evil soul. Its eyes were like a dead man's. I thought I too would be dead, and I was so scared I pissed myself." His voice lacks any shame as he admits his terror. "But it ran by me and leapt upon another man, a friend of mine. It moved so fast, too fast for my eyes to follow it. By the time my gaze could focus, it was feasting—on my friend's face. It raised its head, only for a moment, and I saw blood and flesh clinging to its teeth."

Elthric's voice breaks, and he falls silent. The entire assembly is silent too, as each of us tries to absorb the tale he's told.

Finally, one of the men gathers his wits enough to call out, "Do they have weapons?"

Elthric nods. "Axes, scythes, pitchforks, clubs. And now—now they have likely taken swords and spears from our dead."

"Your warriors fought them?" Wulfstan asks. "They had time to reach for their weapons and defend their homes? What happened in the blood fray?"

Elthric shakes his head. "They are unstoppable. After the first wave had swept through the village, they turned back to those of us who were left. We fought them with every blade and cudgel we could lay our hands on. We stabbed them, hacked at them. We smashed their heads. We even sliced their heads from their bodies. They hardly slowed. They are so fast—" Elthric shakes his head. "Only a handful of us survived."

"*You* survived because you fled." Wulfstan's voice is harsh with scorn.

Elthric hangs his head. The Angles hate cowardice more than any other disgrace, but I can't blame the man. Better to run than let yourself become a dainty dish for one of the undead creatures.

"Do they show cunning," asks another man, one of Wulfstan's champions, "as warriors do when plotting battle? Did they fight according to some plan—or at the direction of a leader?" This is an intelligent question, in my opinion, and a more useful tack to take than blaming poor Elthric for being still alive.

"They know how to fight," Elthric says after a moment's thought. "Yet they do not enter a fray as one unit." He scratches his beard, staring into space as though he's calling to mind the details of what he witnessed. "There was one of them who acted as leader of sorts," he says at last, "but only in a rough way. Not as a jarl would command respect." He nods toward Wulfstan. "This leader was garbed differently from the rest, in robes and armor like the ancient Roman statues. I noticed once that he seemed from time to time, even in the midst of the fray, to pause and cock his head, as though he were listening to someone—or something—though there was nothing he could have heard about the clamor of the battle. He seemed to me like one of those puppets that dance from invisible strings. Almost as though he had no will of his own." Elthric shakes his head. "For the most part, the things fought like animals—faster than serpents, more vicious than wolves—but without thought. Without intelligence. In truth, they seemed more like an angry swarm of bees than any beast."

An armed man pushes to the front of the hall, then leans to speak in Wulfstan's ear. Wulstan leaps to his feet. "My guard here, Cedric, brings more news. He was sentry today, roaming the forests between Aldershire and our village, and he has seen the same foul monsters." Wulfstan waves his hand at the man beside him. "Cedric," he commands, "repeat your report so all can hear."

The man who steps forward now has braided locks and beard. "My lord, a throng of creatures like I have never seen—living corpses—are running toward us even now on the forest road. They are halfway here already, and at the pace I saw, they will arrive by nightfall. I nearly killed my horse racing to get here so far ahead of them."

At this, a buzz of voices fills the hall. Elthric blurts, "Flee! You must run for your lives! You cannot fight them. They will kill you—and then they will eat you."

A woman screams, children are crying, and men shout strings of curses. Wulfstan pounds his spear to silence all the voices. His face is as calm and cunning as always, and as the people turn toward him, the commotion stills.

"Send messengers to the king," a woman calls out. "Surely he can raise an army to defeat these monsters."

Wulfstan shakes his head. "The king's fort is more than a day's ride away. Even if we sent a messenger now, King Aethelfrith could not gather his warband in time to reach us. No, we must make our own plans—and quickly." His eyes sweep the gathered assembly. "What do we know about these creatures? They must have some weakness. What do the old tales tell us?"

The village wise woman speaks up now. "These things are the draugar, those who walk again after death. Our fathers' fathers' fathers knew them once upon a time." She is a tiny, bent woman, but her voice is surprisingly strong. "The draugar cannot rest in their graves as dead flesh is meant to do. Instead, they walk the earth with their bodies half decayed. The old tales told that they have twice the strength of mortals." She pauses for a moment, then finishes with a note of ghoulish drama. "They sustain themselves by eating human flesh."

A wave of horrified voices ripples across the hall. A man as old and wizened as the wise woman shouts, "We know the legends, woman! But the old stories never speak of hordes of draugar, such as we've heard tell today. They came back from the dead singly, not in whole tribes."

There's a murmur of agreement around the room, but the wise woman holds up her hand. "Recall the stories, old man. The draugars' bite infects the living. It changes normal folk into draugars themselves. After all these years, they have had time to spread their foul contagion—and meanwhile, they never die. They only multiply." Her voice is shrill with authority, but I suspect she's only making things up now. She doesn't really know the answers to our questions.

Wulfstan's eyes narrow. "And yet they can be killed. Aedgar has proven that." The jarl turns to Aedgar. "The monster was in your home—and you slew it. How? With what skill, what weapon did you do what none could do in Aldershire?"

Aedgar glances around the room, licks his lips, and then throws back his shoulders, his head held high. "Not every warrior has skill and strength to take off an enemy's head with one blow." The other thanes nod agreement. "But I have that skill, and that strength is mine. First, I put a spear through the beast, but that did not stop it. My daughter smashed its head with a kettle, and that did not stop it either. But when I cast off its head, then the draugar ceased its attack."

Elthric looks doubtful and shakes his head. "Some in my village also took off the creatures' heads. But that did not stop the monsters. Some dark life still moved their limbs, so that they sought and found their skulls—and then set them back on their shoulders. To sever their heads from their shoulders slowed them down but a mite. It did not stop them."

"Well," says Aedgar, "there is more to my story. After beheading the creature, I—" He hesitates, and I wait to hear what tale he'll tell to give all the credit to himself and none to me. "I sought another weapon, to doubly kill the thing. I ran my bow through its middle, and the monster fell at that blow. It never moved again. I suspect the things need to be twice killed before they stay dead."

I shake my head. What a bawhead! He should thank me for saving his daughter, instead of spinning stories that only prove his ignorance.

Excited discussion fills the hall. Cedric's voice breaks through it. "We must think carefully about this. How do we know it is a double blow that does the work? To hear Aedgar tell it, the thing was dealt a fourfold blow—first a spear, next a kettle, than the beheading, and finally the bow driven through it. Perhaps some particular combination of these attacks was what wrought the thing's death." Cedric frowns. "But what else might explain why Aedgar achieved what none in Aldershire could do? Surely, in such a fray, some creatures would have been struck over and over. And yet Elthric tells us that none ceased to move."

Wulfstan nods slowly, then turns back to Aedgar. "What other detail might explain your success? What about your fight with the creature was different from the slaughter in Aldershire?"

Aedgar puffs out his chest a little. "Perhaps Thunor looked on me with favor. After all, I alone in the village believed these draugar were coming, and I alone built an altar to the Thunder God to ask for his protection."

His voice is full of pride, but Wulfstan merely waves his hand in the air, as though he's not impressed. "I will not have us sit here on our arses relying on the gods' protection. There must be something else we can do." He narrows his eyes at Aedgar, as though he's sensed there's something else the thane's not telling him. "Think, man. What else made your fight different?"

Aedgar looks uncomfortable. "My great courage, my lord?" he ventures.

By Woden's pimply pizzle, the man's a fool. He'll have us all killed at this rate. My heart is beating hard, but I dare not speak up and tell Wulfstan what I know.

And then, Freya steps forward into the firelight. "My lord," she says, her eyes shining like a cat's, "you should ask someone else your questions."

"And who is that, my dear?" Wulfstan smiles down at her, as though her gold hair and proud, straight back have diverted him, if only for a moment, from the serious matter at hand.

Freya raises her hand, as though she's a queen, and points it straight at me. I feel my face burn as she continues, "The slave boy was the one who— Well, I suspect he may know something. He had—by chance—unlawfully entered our house, just as the thing attacked me."

Liar.

I meet her eyes, and I know she sees my thought written across my face, but her voice is just as cool and steady as she continues, "Who knows what mischief drove him—and yet, by some good fortune, when he saw the thing, he seemed to know what to—what my father should do. The slave was the one who— Who handed my father the bow which he drove into the thing."

Wulfstan points his spear tip toward me. "Speak up, slave, and tell us what you know."

Even now, when I'm as terrified as all the others of the undead horde that's speeding toward us, I'm nearly as worried that my smallest mistake will earn me a broken limb or welted back from the Anglefolc. I move nearer to the jarl's chair and bow my head to show my respect. Behind me, I hear the crowd's impatient buzz as I suck in a breath and choose my words with care. "My lord, I know but a little . . . hearsay. Old stories my people told."

Wulfstan waves an impatient hand. "Tell what you do know, then. We haven't all day."

"Yes, my lord." I gulp back my nervousness. "My people call these things the neamh mairbh. Our tales sound much like your legends of the draugar. As a child, I heard tell that the fiends' victims arise from death to become undead themselves—unless the bodies are burned to ashes."

"Your words sound strange," a villager interrupts. "How do you say that phrase?"

I sound out the Gaelic word: "Nave-mare-vh. In your tongue, it means the 'walking dead.'"

"Why did you give the bow to Aedgar, and why did it stop the draugar?" asks Cedric. "What is special about that weapon?"

I long to tell the truth—that I first attacked the monster, that I did it to save Freya, and that I delivered the death blow—but contradicting Aedgar would only earn his wrath. As much as it eats my pride, I would be wise to go along with his lies. "My mother told me stories of our heroes, and how they could defeat the neamh mairbh by piercing their hearts with weapons made of yew. I have heard my master say, on a number of occasions, that his bow is made of the finest yew wood. And so—"

"Why yew?" Wulfstan interrupts.

I shrug. "I do not really know, except—well, a holy man who came to my village. He told us of Iosa, the nail-riven god who died on a pole made of yew wood. And then Iosa came to life again. But even before that, before the priest came, my mother always said that yew is the wood of life and death. She said the walking dead cannot bear the yew-wood thrust."

The wise woman stirs in a corner. "There is some truth in the slave's words." She tips her head toward me, and the bone plugs in each earlobe sway and dangle. "Yggdrasil, the great trunk that holds the three worlds together, is a yew tree. That is why yews can live forever. That is why they stay always green through the winter— because the everlasting force of Yggdrasil lives in each one of them. The Great Yew is the axis on which our world turns. Potions made from its bark may heal the wasting disease, and yet a greater dose will make a fast and cruel poison." She nods her head. "It is as the slave boy says—yew holds within it both life and death. Even the draugar must succumb to the tree's great magic."

"Enough then!" Wulfstan pounds his spear. "No more talk! Our foes are on their way, and we must act. Each man, woman, and child who is able, be at it then! Make yew stakes. Shape them like daggers and swords. The men who are our best warriors, practice the head-taking slash, so that we may have opportunities to drive the yew stakes into the creatures while they are down. We will form a shield wall where the forest road enters our village. There we shall meet these walking corpses." He rises to his feet and lifts his arms high. "Even if they come from Hel itself, we will defeat them!"

The hall explodes in cheers and war cries, but in the midst of it, Freya steps forward again, her hand lifted. Wulfstan calls for order once more, then waves his permission for Freya to speak.

"The slave knows more than he's telling," she says. "When the draugar grabbed the boy's throat, the creature dropped him quickly, as though it had been burned. The thing seemed to not like the feel of the slave. As though something in him—some charm or magic—guards him."

The villagers' heads all turn toward me, as if I were some strange thing they'd never noticed before. Aedgar mutters a curse, but Wulfstan motions to him to hold his tongue. "Well, boy," the jarl asks, "what is it that protects you from the fiends? What secret powers have you against them?"

Silence hangs over the hall, as each person waits on my words. Only the fire crackles. I draw a breath. "I don't know. Truly, my lord."

"We have no time for lies!" bellows Wulfstan. "Out with it—or I'll take the time to flay you." I see by the fire in his eyes that this is no idle threat. I've got to come up with an answer. I frantically search my brain.

"Well, there is something my mother used to tell me. But—"

"Tell us!" the chieftain barks.

"She said I am descended from the Sidhe, the Faerie folk. The Sidhe are our gods, who are now driven underground. They are, well, like what you call elves. She said the Faerie blood protects me from evil."

Wulfstan lets out a bark of laughter. "Aedgar, that's a rare slave you have here. Descended from the magic folk." He scowls at me. "If you have elves as kin, why would they stand by while you became our slave? You'd think they'd come to rescue you." He leans forward and growls, "Boy, I have no time for children's stories. Tell me or—"

"Wait!" the wise woman calls out. "Whatever the truth, this boy may be of help to us. Let us tie him to the horse post where the road leaves the forest. That way, the horde of draugar will see him first. If—for any reason—the boy can turn away the undead, then they will be slowed in their attack, and we shall take advantage of their hesitation. If the boy is telling lies—" She shrugs. "Well, then the walking dead may pause to take him for a meal.

Either way, he slows the draugar's advance and gives us an advantage."

Her words are met with shouts of agreement. "Thunor's bollocks," I mutter under my breath. I glance left, then right—*there!* An opening in the crowd. I lunge for freedom, and then—

Oomph! My head just banged into a chain-mailed chest, and now gauntlet-covered hands grab me. "Insolent slave!" A thane slaps my face, then shoves me forward.

"Take him out," Wulfstan orders. "Bind him to the post."

As I'm dragged out the door, I twist my head to look back over my shoulder at Freya. Her blue eyes meet mine, and I hope she can tell what I'm thinking now: *Whatever gods there be, let them curse the moment I went to help you. You may be the loveliest thing I've ever seen, but you have a serpent's heart.*

3

BAIT

The sun goes down, and I lose feeling in my bound hands. I'm shivering and I can't tell if it's from the chill and drizzle or from fear. Neither Aedgar nor Freya has said a blinking word to me since the village meeting. I'm just property to them, fit only to be used in whatever way will benefit them most. Unfortunately, serving as bait is my current usefulness.

Women from the village have smeared bloody slabs of beef on my skin and clothes, in case my own blood isn't quite tasty enough for the rotting ghouls. As the blood dries, it tightens my skin. I want to itch, but my hands are tied.

At first, I struggled against the cords that tie me to the horse post, but now I've accepted that there's no escaping, not that way. I lean back against the post and try to think. I search through my memories of my childhood, looking for something that will help me now. Instead, I find the old sorrow rushing over me, the well-worn longing for my home.

My people's ways are different from the Anglefolc's. Our land had fields, as do the Angles, but we also had large plots of forest, where oak and ash and alder joined their branches in a green canopy, while hazel and willow leaves fluttered brightly over streams and little falls. Trees and water—how we loved them both!

The night around me feels unreal, as though I'm caught in a nightmare. I can't wake up from this terrible dream, so instead, I let my thoughts drift next to memories of my parents. What would they want me to do now? Would they expect me to pray for protection?

But my parents' faith was always strong, and mine is not. My father Dugal often tied clooties—strips torn from our worn-out clothes—on the branches over a spring or stream. He believed the fluttering rags would catch the blessings of the well goddess. My mother Deirdre—solid and fair, with hair as red as a fox—tossed leftover bread to the ravens, to honor the Morrigan, the Power seen in everything green and fair, the one who also held the mysteries of darkness and death.

But back then, Brigid was the one I always loved most, queen of the Sidhe and bright goddess of the hearth. When I was a young child, whenever I was afraid or sad, I would whisper all my troubles to Brigid. I pictured her bending down to rescue me, her hair even redder than my mother's.

"Brigid," I call into the night. "Brigid! Help me now!"

The wind sighs through the trees above my head. I try to convince myself it's an answer to my prayer—but if it is, it does me little good, for here I still stand, tied fast to the post, waiting to be eaten. Prayers have never done me any good.

I blink away tears. The Angles have taken so much from me, and now, hung up like meat, I have nothing left at all, only the past that still lives within my head. I refuse to let fear and sorrow wash away my memories, because if I do, then I will go to my death without anything at all. If I have to die tonight, then I will leave this world with my head filled with sweet images of home. The past is my only refuge now, the days when I took for granted that life was a lovely thing, full of laughter and love.

So I reach for a memory to distract me—my father's voice, telling tales of the hero Cuchullain as we sat at night around the fire. Cuchullain, said my father, could lop off the heads of three enemies with one swing of his sword.

"I could use your company tonight, Cuchullain," I say softly. My grin is shaky, but still it's a grin, and I am proud of it.

My mother told other tales, gentler stories of the Sidhe. What I told Wulfstan was true: my mother often said to me, "From my mother's mother, Finn, you've got Faerie blood in your veins. Someday, when you need it most, you'll find there's magic in you." Looking back, I'm not certain if she said it in earnest or in jest. At the time,

I took for granted she spoke the truth. I puffed up my narrow chest with pride, and I made stories in my head about my Faerie kin, the lords of the underground realms. Brigid was a part of those stories too, the Faerie queen who ruled that magic world where I too belonged. Back then, when I was a young boy, the fey world of magic and mystery was as real to me as the cows in the field or the stew in my bowl at night.

Magic blood. I shake my head. Wulfstan was right: if I had Faerie kin, they would have rescued me long ago. They're not likely to come riding into this moonlit clearing now, all slant-eyed and lovely, and set me free. No, I'm not expecting any help, not from the Morrigan, not from Cuchullain, and not from the Sidhe or their queen. I'm on my own, just me, the post, and the death-filled night.

Standing here like this, tied to a post, makes me think of the post that stood in the center of my village. That post was cross-beamed, placed there by Priest David, a follower of Iosa the Nail-Riven, who came to our village with his family, all their belongings in a single ox cart. David had strong shoulders and a ready grin, and we welcomed him. When he asked our chief if he could be a part of our dun, the chief handed him the branch of holly that gave him the right to join our ring-fort.

Priest David's family became like kin to my own. We heard tell that the Iosa-Followers in the southern part of the isle—those sent from Rome—did not allow their priests to marry. None of us could understand why on earth anyone would make such a foolish rule. David's wife and children were a happy bunch, always laughing and making jokes. His son Micheal was my special friend. I admired him greatly because of his ability to fart entire tunes. Oh Micheal, he was gifted, there's no denying. I'm grinning now, just remembering his musical talent.

Priest David tended his own small field, but when his work was done, he carved a tall wooden cross, then painted it with scenes of Iosa, his god-hero. Our village chief, delighted with this bright art, asked that the cross stand in the center of our ring-fort. Gradually, that post became the center of our life. In my mind, I hear again David's voice as he stood by the post on an evening, telling us tales of the Threefold God and of Iosa, whom David also called the Criost.

Now, as I stand here strung up on a post like Iosa, the night around me is very dark. A breeze sends little whispers through the leaves, and somewhere far away an owl calls to its mate. I shiver, from cold and fear, and turn back to my memories, searching for yet another memory to take me away from this moment.

I remember a fall morning when the air was bright and brisk, cold water pouring in a flood over my head from Priest David's hand as he performed a birthing ceremony. He spoke the holy words that made us kin to Iosa, and afterward, we stood in a line, wet and shivering, our faces bright with joy. My father was one of the few in the village who didn't become family with Iosa that day—he wasn't ready yet, he said—but I remember how Da smiled at the look on my mother's face, the way he kissed her head. Then David raised his hand over us in blessing and gave us each a talisman as keepsake of the day: a cross-carved stone disc.

My memories turn dark now, though, darker than the night around me, because less than a moon-cycle after the birthing ceremony, the Angles raided our village. They poured over our ramparts in the night like an evil tide, lingering only long enough to scoop up everything they saw of any value—and me. Our guards had barely shouted the alarm before the raiders were gone into the night again. I heard my father's heels pound across the ground, louder even than the horses' hooves, but he was not fast enough on foot to catch the raiders. Face down across a horse, I had my last glimpse of my family, their faces white and terrified, my mother screaming, her arms outstretched to me. Five days later, the raiders took me to the slave market, where I was bought and carried west, then traded to Aedgar in exchange for one of his fat sheep. That's all my life was worth, now that I was a slave.

So much for the power of the Three-in-One God. Iosa helped me no more than the Morrigan and Brigid did. I will not pray to him now, for he betrayed me.

But I still wear David's pendant around my neck. I keep it because it is the only thing I can hold and touch from my life before the Angles. Standing here, bound and helpless, I feel the familiar weight of the disc against my breastbone.

But I am no longer kin to Iosa, and unlike Iosa, I do not offer up my life willingly on this post—not for the people who have held me captive, not for Aedgar who has given me nothing but blows, and certainly not for serpent-hearted Freya. But what choice do I have? This is how my story ends, dying as bait to protect the people I hate. Eaten by a rancid pack of moving corpses.

Life's a stinking heap of shite, it is.

I can't see what's happening behind me in the village, but the damp night carries the sound of voices. Wulfstan shouts orders, and if he's afraid, his voice does not betray it. I hear his firm commands as he forms the villagers into two lines. The first line will be the shield wall, where the village warriors—men and boys older than ten and a few shield maidens—stand close ranked, with round shields of wood and cowhide locked together, yew spears sticking out from between the shields. Behind this front line, Wulfstan forms another row: women and children, along with the elders will be the second line of battle. Only those too young or too old to stand will not clutch a weapon made of yew during the coming fight.

They move closer to me, and I see the flickering light of their torches lighting the clearing where I stand. Wulfstan shouts, "Remember, even if these draugar come from the mouth of Hel, we have greater powers. The Hammerer and the Furor fight for us. That is why we have conquered this land. The old stories tell of our heroes who vanquished enemies as foul as these we face tonight. We are as strong as our ancestors!" The villagers cheer, but Wulfstan is not done yet. He raises his voice over theirs and bellows out, "This day we behead the fiends! We impale their shriveled hearts with swords of yew! And then we will burn their stinking carcasses!"

He lets the villagers cheer now, and I have to acknowledge his wisdom, filling the people with heady crowd-fever that drives out their fear. But they're eejits, every one of them. If they're such great warriors, why do they have a Scoti slave as their first line of defense? But they seem to have forgotten that I'm even here. Ungrateful turds.

I stand there with my back to them, looking into the darkness. If the undead troops hadn't been heading toward our village before, they certainly will now, after the racket everyone's making. Might as well shout out, "Come and get us!"

As the cheers finally die down, Wulfstan again lifts his voice. "In every fight there are losses. Know that whoever dies tonight with weapon in hand, face to the foe, will go straight to the Mead Hall of the Gods. Fear not death, for you will enjoy forever the pleasures of the immortals. In the gods' mead hall, our kinfolk wait to welcome the greatest among us." The crowd shouts again, and Wulfstan waits for them to quiet, then continues, "Our people will make ballads of our triumph this night. They will sing of our glorious deeds for generations."

At the moment Wulfstan utters these words, a horn sounds from the woods ahead. I suck in a breath. I know a sentry has spotted the enemy.

"Now!" shouts Wulfstan. "With Thunor! With Woden! To victory!" The entire village yells behind me. I hear the clank of the warriors' chainmail as they jump up and down, battle lust coursing in their veins.

Wulfstan gives one more command: "Remember, hold rank! Don't break. Fight as one! Our foes are formidable—but their brains have rotted." The trees rustle, and I see something shift within the shadows, something paler than the night. "Victory!" yells Wulfstan.

"Victory!" scream the villagers.

But I'm not paying attention to them now. A pale shape has emerged from the darkness. It stands still and silent, not more than ten steps from me. Then another figure is beside it—and then suddenly there are dozens of them, a long straggly line. At first sight, in the moonlight, they look like a bunch of regular people—men, women, and children with gray skin and ragged clothing. They hold clubs, farm implements, knives, and axes. I see the glint of one or two long blades.

The wind moves through the trees, and it carries their stench to my nose, a smell like rotten meat, shit, and stale piss, all mixed together. I choke back the puke that rises in my throat.

The first to come out of the darkness is taller than the others, and he wears rusted metal like the armor that the old ones say the Roman centurions once wore. A corroded helmet covers his head, and in both hands he grasps a wide-curved axe. He turns his head, and I see that one of his eyes hangs by a string of exposed nerves from its socket, dangling over his cheek.

Sweet Iosa, have mercy. The old prayer rises unbidden into my mind, an automatic response to the terror.

"Aaaa-yah!" The scream comes from behind me. An Angle warrior hurtles past me and throws himself onto the walking dead. He has disregarded Wulfstan's command to hold the line, but the berserker madness has come over him. Through the darkness and fog, I see his seax swing in savage arcs. A gray arm flies off one of the corpses, and the undead howl with what sounds like a single voice.

More warriors catch the blood frenzy and hurl themselves forward. From my post, I watch clubs and wooden rakes, axes and swords, all rising and falling as though they're reaping some dreadful harvest. Blood sprays across my face, and I flinch. The walking dead have surrounded the Angles, hacking at them with their crude weapons.

"Together, charge!" Wulfstan yells.

Now that the berserkers have surged past me, I am no longer useful as bait. Instead, Wulfstan sends in his first line of defense to support his other men. The human wall thunders behind me, then smashes against my arms as they charge past the wooden post. The fog has dropped between the trees, and all I can see through the shifting mist is a whirl of blood and weapons. Here a spear flashes dimly, there an axe cleaves. A stick slams through a walking corpse, a rake slashes a villager's face. The fog trails around it all, giving me only glimpses, never enough for me to see exactly what it is happening.

The walking dead push the villagers back, nearer to my post, and now I can see one of the undead, its head half-severed and hanging off its shoulder, staggering as it tries to right its skull. Behind it, the armored leader suddenly looms out of the fog. A shield maiden of the village, yew sword in hand, lunges at it, but her sword slides off its armor. The ghoul-warrior twists, so fast that all I see is a blur, and smashes his axe into her shoulder. She stumbles, slips on the blood-slick ground, and falls. The battle roils over her.

I stand in a sea of furious movement, the only still point in the mayhem. The battle surrounds me, but somehow, no blows fall on me. I cannot see beyond the circle of violence that hems me in, but I am certain of one thing: the undead prevail. With each breath I take, I hear fewer human voices, while the howls of the neamh mairbh rise ever louder, until my ears ring. Some of the undead have stopped fighting now. Instead, they have dropped to their hands and knees to begin their feasting. One is crouched at my feet, bent over the shield maiden I saw earlier. I hear the crunch of bones, the splat of her intestines on the ground, and my stomach heaves.

Now that the frantic rush of the battle is subsiding, I am once more aware of my own danger. Soon, I know, the wights will notice me—and then I will be their next feast. Panicstricken now, I twist against the cords, until my wrists are wet with blood. I am like a fox caught in a trap; if I could I'd bite off my own hand to set myself free.

"Hold still, boy."

The voice comes from behind me. I can't see who is speaking, but I recognize the cross tone. *Freya?*

She's sawing at my bonds with a blade. As my wrists fall free, I twist around to look at her. Her blond hair has come lose around her shoulders, her face is spattered with blood, and her eyes are wide. She's panting, fast and hard, like a dog that's been running on a hot day.

"Run!" she gasps. "Before they get you, you fool!"

But something holds me frozen by the post. "Why did you free me?"

Her laugh is high pitched, a breath away from hysteria. "I got you into this. I'll get you out." She tosses her head toward the forest. "Go."

"But what about you?"

Her crazed laughter makes the goose bumps rise along my neck. "I've sent two of the stinking creatures back to Hel tonight, and I'll send more there before I'm done. When I can't fight any longer, I'll rise to the Mead Hall of the Gods holding these." She gestures with the long yew spike she holds in one hand, then lifts the blade that's clutched in her other fist.

I know I should run, but something keeps me from fleeing. The villagers are my enemies, but they are human.

As much as I hate them, how can I leave them to be eaten by the living corpses?

How can I leave Freya, even if she's ready to go to the Mead Hall of the Gods?

"You're free, damn you, run!" Freya jabs her blade toward my face. I stagger backward, and she whirls away from me. The fog closes around her, but I hear her battle scream as she enters the fray again.

I hesitate another moment. But there is nothing I can do to stop the slaughter—and even if I could, the only thanks I'd be likely to get would be a beating or a kick. I look around me, dazed by all that's happened. The undead near me are absorbed with their terrible meal. No one notices me.

I'm free.

The realization comes over me slowly. I can go home. Like a ghost, I slip away into the fog.

A cold drizzle chills me as I run from the trees into the fields. The fog hides the moon's face, only a pale shine slipping through now and again, but I can make my way in the dark. I have worked these fields for long years, and I know the location of every bush and stone and ditch. I slip and stumble over muddy furrows, my skin burns when I run through nettles, but my pace never slows.

And then I come up short, smashed against something that looms up suddenly in front of me. The rancid stench tells me what I've run into, and I bite back a scream. As I jump back, the living corpse seems to leap just as quickly away from me, howling.

Through the darkness I see a fallen warrior on the ground. He is still slashing feebly with a yew sword, but the ghoul is beyond his reach. The thing turns toward it and raises its scythe. I know the warrior is a dead man.

I grab a rock from the ground and jump at the ghoul. The stone crashes against its skull, and I yell, "Take that, ya foul Hel-born wight!" The fiend staggers for a moment, the top of its skull crushed, but then it turns. Its single eye fixes on me, and it lunges toward me. Faster than a lightning flash, the fetid smell smothers me as the living dead thing lunges for my throat. Bony fingers wrap around my neck.

And then the creature leaps backward and howls, as though my skin has burned it. I shake my head, too dumbfounded to know what I should do next. Before I can decide, the neamh mairbh staggers and goes limp, the spiked end of a yew sword protruding through its wasted belly.

"Got him." The man on the ground chuckles and then falls back against the wet earth, as dead as his opponent.

I shake my head again, gasp for air, and run on. The smell of blood and rotting flesh fades away, and I no longer hear the distant sound of screams and howls. The night air is sweet again with the scent of soil and growing things, and the only sound now is the call of an owl, the soft whisper of the wind, and the faint trickle of water running in a ditch. I'm too exhausted to run any further, and I let myself drop into a walk.

The longer I walk, the more unreal the night seems. Could all that have really happened? Perhaps I drank a mickle lot of mead and now I'm sleeping it off, my head full of crazy dreams. But my wrists hurt. In fact, I hurt all over, and now that I'm no longer so terrified, my stomach churns with hunger. No, the night is real.

I trudge on and on, with no thought of a destination except to get as far away from the village as I can. By the time the sky turns gray with dawn, my legs are shaking, and I can barely propel myself forward.

And then I stop walking and look around me. By Woden's great rank arse, I'm heading right down the road to Aldershire—where a whole other tribe of the undead might still be feasting on the bloating corpses of the villagers, for all I know. Bloody Hel. What was I thinking?

I haven't been thinking, that's the problem. I've been too scared to think, but it's about time I started.

There's a good-sized wooded stretch between the villages, land so uneven and thick with old forest that even the Anglefolc didn't have the strength to burn and fell it. That forest is my only hope. If I can escape between the ferns and oaks and alders, let the green cover my tracks, the woods will be a great living shield against the walking dead.

Stumbling from weariness, I shove my way through a long hedge of tightly woven bushes, and then I'm in the old forest, pushing against wet leaves and bracken, moving deeper into the green shadows. Vines and webbed tree roots seem to reach out to grab and yank me off balance, but they're ordinary living things, not monsters from Hel. My pace slows. The forest's mossy green arms enclose me; the wet leaves wipe the smears of blood from my face.

At last, I can walk no further. The moss is soft underfoot, softer than my pallet in Aedgar's shed. The green woods seem to swirl around me, and I can hold myself upright no longer. I let myself drop, and instantly I am asleep.

I'm so exhausted that for a long while I'm aware of nothing at all. And then, suddenly, I jump awake.

Something wet and slimy touched me.

4

EASY PREY

I scream and leap to my feet, my fists up. I hear a yelp, and then fur brushes against my bare legs. I search the shadows—and then I grin.

Just a dog. A collie like the sheepdogs back home, black and shaggy with bright eyes and a white stripe on its chest and snout. It's not much older than a puppy, its back no higher than my calves. With a soft woof, it drops its haunches to the ground, then sits and looks at me with dark shiny eyes, its butt wiggling back and forth.

"Oh, no." I shake my finger at it. "Go away! I haven't food for myself—never mind a freeloader. You'll bark and give us both away to the ghouls."

The dog just stares at me intently, then gives a little whine. Its tail flops back and forth.

"Oh, pish. Leave!"

I pick up a stick and throw it at the dog. The silly creature dodges, then runs after the stick, brings it back to me, and drops it at my feet.

"Thunor's balls, ya stupid mutt, get outta here! Go! Go home."

But then I realize its home was probably in Aldershire—and who knows what awful things have happened to its owner, what horrors it's smelled with its keen nose and seen with those big eyes.

Damn.

"Go away!" I push at the mutt's snout, then grab a rock and throw it at the animal. The dog whines, but then it comes panting back to me. It licks at my bloody leg.

I sigh. Screw the three pimply old Wyrd Sisters; some fates cannot be avoided. I have a dog.

"All right then. I give up." The dog seems to understand. It rolls on its back at my feet, its legs splayed out so I can scratch its belly. "All right, you're a boy, I see. You have a name?"

Oh Hel, I'm talking to an animal now as if he's going to answer me.

"Very well then. I'm giving you a name."

He's a strong-looking dog, sleek and well muscled. He deserves a name that's noble, manly, strong.

"Artair," I tell the dog. "Your name will be Artair, after the great king of old."

The dog wags his tail. He seems satisfied with his new name.

"Right. Now, Artair, we need to find food—and water. I'm starving and so thirsty I could drink a barrel. Shh, though. We need to be quiet about it."

Artair prances around and jumps up on my legs—but he doesn't bark.

We strike out into the woods. It must be nearly midday now, but the green tangle of branch and vine is so thick and interlaced that beneath the trees it's still dusk. Thick ivy wraps around the tree trunks, adding its darker green to the softer light that filters through the trees' leaves. Wood doves make their sighing moan, and somewhere in the distance a cuckoo calls. In the places where sunlight reaches the forest floor, wild garlic grows like white lace spread out between the trees. The walking dead seem far away; in fact, they seem impossible.

I notice a cherry tree, and I strip off a handful of tiny hard green balls and toss them in my mouth. They're nowhere near to being ripe, and they taste like pish—but I'm so hungry that I swallow them down. I've only gone a few steps, though, before I regret eating them. They're so green that they make my stomach churn and cramp.

Artair and I push on through the forest. It's so thick now it seems like one huge green spider web of vegetation. We stumble across a brook, and Artair splashes into it, lapping up draughts with an eager tongue. I lean down and cup my hand into the clear water, and then I too drink and drink.

No longer parched, my stomach feeling better, life is already looking up. With the sun shining in long slants through the leaves, the scent of green things in my nose, and my new companion at my side, my heart lightens. For the first time since I was tied to that post, I'm convinced that I'm going to get away. Everything is going to be all right after all. I just need to figure out where I am exactly, and then I can make my way home.

But just as I'm thinking these happy thoughts, a twig snaps. I freeze. Something is out there, something larger than a squirrel or a hare, something hidden in the leaves— and it doesn't sound like it's too far away. Instantly, fear flows through my veins again.

I hear the rustle of something moving. If I can't see it, then it can't see us, I reason. If we stay still, maybe whatever it is will move on by, never knowing that we were here.

And then Artair barks.

Stupid dog. I crouch closer to the ground, peering through the leaves. I catch a flash of brown, but it doesn't look like animal fur. And then I see the quick glint of metal, as though for an instant, sunlight caught the flat side of a knife.

Whatever's out there is moving slowly, stealthily, creeping closer to my hiding place behind a thick holly bush. It's stalking me.

But the neamh mairbh don't stalk their prey like this. Do they? I put my hand on Artair, trying to convey the silent message that he needs to hold still, stay quiet.

The dog isn't paying attention to me. Instead, he's wriggling through the leaves, straight at whatever is out there. He barks again, then growls and stands his ground. He may not be very well trained, but he has courage, I'll give him that.

While I'm still trying to decide what to do—slink away through the undergrowth while the dog has whatever it is occupied, or go to the dog's rescue—I hear a voice that makes the breath go out of me in a loud *whoosh*. I know that voice all too well.

"Call the dog off, boy," calls Freya. "I don't want to have to hurt it."

I leave the prickly shelter of my holly bush, and there she is, standing in a band of sunlight. If I didn't know her voice, though, I'd hardly recognize her. Her skin and clothes are streaked with mud and soot, and her hair is tied back in a single knot, woven with leaves and bits of bracken that hide the bright gold. She blends in with the tree trunks, only the bright blue of her eyes shining out from the layers of dirt and ash. In her left hand, she carries a bow, and on her back she wears a quiver of dark fletched arrows. Her short seax hangs at her waist.

Artair growls.

Freya reaches for an arrow and nocks it. "Call off your bitch if you don't want me to put an arrow in her."

The dog barks at her again.

I jump forward and grab the mutt. "Don't shoot!" I shout. "And it's a he—his name's Artair."

She sights along the arrow, and her blue eyes narrow. "That's a Welsc name. Artair fought against my people. So your dog is my enemy."

I sigh. By Thunor's arse, why is this female so crazy?

"Girl," I say, "I've seen you kill walking corpses—so why are you worried about a pup? Besides, he's friendly."

"Call him off." Her voice is like iron, as sharp as the tip of her arrow.

"Artair, come here!" Artair bounces back to me. Apparently, he's decided it's all good fun. I pat his head. "Good boy."

Freya lowers her weapon and turns her blue squint on me. "You look ghastly."

"You aren't exactly dressed for a village dance your-self." Out here in the woods, after only a day of freedom, I find myself acting like my true self, rather than the slave she thinks me.

She doesn't seem to be paying any attention, though. "You're a fool," she announces. "You ate green fruit that could very well be poisonous. You should be thinking of the trials that lie ahead, not traipsing through the forest as though you haven't a care in the world. You need good food, to get your strength up."

There's so much craziness in what she just said that I don't know what to answer first. "Where am I supposed to get this good food?" I say. "And Hel, girl, what do you know about the trials ahead. What trials? Can they be any worse than the trials that lie *behind*? Because let me tell you, being a slave wasn't exactly my idea of fun." I'm so pissed that I'm spitting my words, but it feels good to be angry, to be angry and to let someone *know* I'm angry. "And what are *you* doing here anyway? Why are you out here traipsing through the forest? Do you even have a plan?"

She tosses her head. "I've been trailing you all afternoon, boy. The great wild boar of Asgard would be no harder to track than you are. Stomping and crackling, chatting up that creature as though it were a man instead of a beast, splashing through streams, bumbling and fumbling like the gormless clot you are."

"Who asked you to follow me?" I snap. "What do you want from me?" If she's here to take me back to her father, she can think again. No girl alone in the woods, even an armed girl, is going to take away my freedom again.

She sniffs. "You should be grateful I followed you. Without me, the undead would be feasting on your lousy carcass before nightfall."

I don't think she's protecting me from the living corpses out of the goodness of her heart, so I ask her again, "What do you want from me?"

For a moment, I think she might be about to cry, but then she squares her shoulders and presses her lips tight together. "You're coming with me," she says then, "to avenge my father's sword arm. I command you to."

I give her an evil grin and shake my head. "You don't own me any more, Freya. I'm free now."

"Free from a wooden pole, where you'd be dead and eaten if I hadn't cut you loose. You're still my slave."

"Thunor's arse I am!"

Her eyes widen, then narrow again. "Don't talk to me like that. I have sensitive ears," she says primly. "And besides," she adds, "I can put three arrows in your guts before you could run away."

The girl is a loon. I shake my head at her, too exasperated to find the words to tell her what I'm thinking.

In reply to my negative head motion, she nods her head in an exaggerated way. "Yes, boy, I own you. And I can kill you any time I want. Faeder told me that the day he bought you."

"Freya." I raise both my hands. Over the past couple of days, I've seen people die. I've watched while rotting dead people attacked people—and then I've seen the grisly creatures feasting on human flesh. But with all that, I think maybe Freya is the maddest, most terrifying thing I've ever seen. It's hard to take her seriously—except the iron tip of her arrow is pointing straight at my belly.

I give her a sickly grin. "Hey, Freya," I try. "Let's slacken the tension a wee bit? We're just two people in the middle of the woods. There are flesh-eating fiends crawling the countryside. We'd be better off uniting forces, don't you think, rather than pointing arrows?"

Freya's square shoulders don't relax at all. "You're defenseless. I have weapons. You're going to obey me."

"Oh yeah?" I've had just about enough. Bad enough that the undead may kill us all, bad enough that I'm on my own in the middle of a forest, bad enough that I've been a slave for years—but this girl is just more than I can stand. "Well, you know, Freya, you can take that arrow and—"

Her fingers tighten on the nocked arrow. I suck in a deep breath and try to calm myself.

"You can take that arrow," I continue in a softer voice, "and your bow and just set them down, because I'm not going to hurt you and neither is Artair. He's a nice dog, and he'll probably just lick your hand if you don't threaten him. You don't own me anymore, let's get that straight. But that doesn't mean I won't help you."

"Swear?"

"On my father's dirk."

"You don't have a dirk, and I don't know your father."

Woden's arse! "You said to swear, Freya, and that's how my people—"

"I don't like your way," she interrupts. "Swear by Thunor's hammer."

I sigh. "I swear by Thunor's hammer, Freya. I won't hurt you and I'll do what you want me to do to help you."

Her shoulders slump. She puts the arrow back in its quiver. It occurs to me that the girl has been through a lot in the last couple of days. I feel just a tad softer toward her—but then Artair whines and pushes against my leg. He's not exactly warming up to Freya, and I don't blame him.

"Now," I say, "what do you mean—'avenge my father's sword arm'? And why are you following me?"

She drops the bag on her back. "Eat first, then talk. You can't think if you don't eat right."

"Eat right?" I shake my head in pure wonderment. "Your household hasn't given me a decent meal in bleatin' years! You get beef, I get slop. Why the sudden concern for my well-being?"

She reaches into her bag and pulls out a ham. "I need you to be stronger. We're changing your rations."

Bloody Hel. "We? I don't see any 'we.' I just see you."

"You swore by Thunor's hammer you'd do whatever I say."

"I said I'd help you. I didn't say I'd be your slave again." My mouth is watering as I look at the ham, but this girl is almost more trouble than the undead.

Freya lifts her nose into the air. "Fetch me firewood."

"Fetch your own wood."

She puts a hand on one hip and caresses the hilt of her short sword with the other. "Do we really have to go through this again, boy? Do I need to remind you which one of us has the weapon?"

I sigh. "Hel, I'm fetching your grotty fire wood."

"Good boy."

"That's how you talk to Artair, not to me," I warn her. "Come on, Artair. At least *you're* good company."

It doesn't really take long to gather firewood but I bide my time, waiting for my boiling anger to calm down to a mere simmer. When I finally return, the sun has sunk behind the trees. Freya sits straight as the pine tree behind her. She's motionless, hardly breathing, with her eyes wide open and nostrils flared, her bow with an arrow across it in her lap.

"No sign of the undead?" I ask.

She shakes her head.

"Won't the fire draw them?" I ask her.

She shrugs. "I am a freeman's daughter. I prefer my food hot."

I'm not going to bother to answer that, so I just drop the firewood at her feet.

"Arrange them in a standing cone," she says.

I sigh loudly, but I stack the wood in a neat circle, leaning against each other in the center. I've decided that I have far greater dangers to worry about than Freya acting like a queen. Besides, one of us has to be sensible.

Freya produces a flint and steel from her pouch, and then a scrap of wool for starter. Unless she always carries a fire starter with her, this girl clearly didn't just take off running into the woods, the way I did. She strikes stone to metal, sparks fly, and in minutes we have a fire. She hacks off a couple of chunks of meat, then skewers them with green sticks. As though she's royalty bestowing some magical wand on me, she hands one of the sticks to me with a gracious bow and a tight-lipped mouth. While she places her chunk of ham in the fire, I gnaw at mine. I haven't had ham in so long that I'm not willing to wait for it to be charred over the fire, not even to make Freya happy. Artair puts his nose on his paws and looks up at me intently, whining softly, so I pull off pieces of meat for him. He wags his tail in gratitude.

"All right," I say, when my stomach feels more contented than it has in some time. "I want some answers from you. What are you doing here? What happened to the village after I—after I left?"

She wipes her mouth daintily with a piece of cloth. Has the girl actually packed napkins? "You are a slave. Why should I impart any information to you?"

"Hel's bum, girl, can't you see there's no slaves and no owners now, not with the undead out there? We're just humans, and if we want to help each other survive, we'd better stick together." I examine her face in the firelight, and for the first time, I realize that her eyes are bright with unshed tears. "What happened, Freya?" I ask more gently. "What did you mean when you spoke of your father's arm and vengeance?" But even as I ask the question, I think I know the answer. Aedgar must have died in the battle. "I'm sorry, Freya. Your father—"

She interrupts me before I can finish my sentence. "My noble father fought the draugar bravely. Four of the fiends lost their heads to his great swinging blade. He sent the walking dead back to Hel's gate. They shall rue the day that—"

But I'm sick to death of the flowery way highborn Angles talk, and this time it's me that interrupts. "Bollocks, Freya. Just tell me what happened."

She gives another one of her snooty little sniffs, but this time, I realize she's doing it because she's on the verge of tears.

"Tell me, Freya, for Thunor's sake!"

She clears her throat. "Then my father most bravely called out the fellest of the foes, the leader, tall and adorned in the garb of an ancient—"

I interrupt her again. "Yeah, yeah. The Roman guy. And then what?"

Her straight spine slumps a little. "My father's arm was outstretched, ready to swing his mighty blade again. But the draugar was fiercer than the hounds that rush after a rabbit. It had a blade of its own, and its arm was faster than a hawk that swoops to its prey. The–the thing—it—" She breaks off.

"It cut off your father's arm?" I hazard to guess.

She doesn't say anything eloquent this time, just nods up and down, staring into the fire.

"He lives?" I'm surprised. Few men would live after a wound like that, but Aedgar, for all his faults, is a strong man.

She nods again. "My father and I were fighting back to back. He fell atop me, and the draugar chieftain went seeking another foe. I crawled out from under my father's body. The blood—" She looks down at her skirt, and I realize that the dark stains on her clothing are not only mud and soot. "My father wanted to die, to go to the Mead Hall of the Gods. He ordered me to leave him, to let him bleed until there was no more blood in his body. And then he begged me. But—"

She wipes at her eyes with her fist. "I couldn't let my father die. It—it was not his time. So I pulled him out of the village into the wood."

I look at Freya and shake my head. The girl is stronger than she looks; I'm not sure I could have dragged Aedgar that far. The man is shaped like a barrel, and his weight must be at least twice Freya's.

While I'm thinking all that, Freya is continuing her story. "My two sisters came to us, with my old nurse. She put a hot blade on the wounds, to seal them, to stop the bleeding. He was in agony, but he held his tongue so the draugar would not find us. His heart is strong as an oak, his gaze fierce as—"

Yeah, yeah, I'm thinking while she continues with her hymn of praise to Aedgar. He's still the same bastard that beat and starved me. But I can see that Freya is still struggling not to cry; apparently, even snakes have hearts.

"I have sworn myself to a cause greater than death in battle," she tells me now. "I have decided to revenge the loss of my father's sword arm. I shall hunt the draugar till every last one of them is rid from the earth."

I can't keep myself from laughing as I clap in mock applause.

She glares at me.

I try to put on a straight face. "So, Freya, how many of the undead did you kill today? How many will you send back to their graves tomorrow? And what is your glorious battle technique?"

I'm being sarcastic, but Freya's too full of puffed-up pride to notice. She holds up her quiver of arrows. "I've two dozen fresh arrows—all made from yew wood."

"Good idea."

"And I am creating my second weapon now."

I glance around. "And what's that?"

She points a finger at me. "You."

"Bloody Hel!" I shout so loud that Artair wakes and barks. "It's okay, boy," I tell him. "It's just this crazy girl talking out of her hind end again."

"I'll not be insulted by a slave."

I laugh again. "Remember, Freya? No slaves, no masters anymore."

"But you swore by the Hammerer that—"

"I swore I would do what I could to help you. But I'm no weapon."

"Oh yes you are!" Freya leans forward over the dwindling flames, her blue eyes glowing. She looks like some magical creature of the woodlands, with the leaves in her gold hair, her face covered with mud. "A draugar took you by the throat," she says, "but it had to release you. You were tied to a tree as bait—right in front of the battle line—and you survived without a scratch. From a distance, I watched while you struggled with another draugar. You should be dead, boy, you should be dead ten times over. And yet, here you sit."

"Right. Finn the slayer of the walking dead, that's me." I give her a little bow. "How great is your luck, oh fair one, that you have me with you." I laugh.

"Hush, slave." The iron is back in her voice. "My father got a good deal when he bought you, though we would never have known if the undead had not attacked us. I don't know what magic has been said over you, or what charm you carry, but I know useful property when I see it. You're going back down that road with me—and together we will wreak vengeance on the draugar."

"No, Freya." I'm not laughing anymore. "I am going home. Four years I've slaved in that pile of excrement you call your village. I've been beaten and kicked and treated like an animal. Four years without my ma, my da, my sister and brother, without my own people. I've not had one word about their safety or whereabouts. And now I'm going home, Freya. If you want to kill me, fine. I hope those walking corpses hunt you down and chew on your sweet meat till you're nothing but gnawed bones."

For a moment, her eyes go wide, and her pink lips fall open. "Well," she says finally, "you have proven yourself to be a lout." She turns her nose up and sits still, unspeaking, for so long that my thoughts start wander.

In the faint flickers of firelight, even covered with mud and blood, Freya is still beautiful. I drag my eyes away from her. Artair barks and jerks, chasing a squirrel in his sleep.

"You're being unreasonable" Freya says into the quiet. "Your mind is unsettled. We'll talk again at breakfast. Then you'll understand that I'm right."

"Not likely."

She shrugs and sits staring at the fire.

I stare into the fire too, fuming. She's like all the Anglefolc, treating me as though I'm nothing but a tool, living and breathing only for her convenience. I'll sneak off with Artair before dawn, I decide, and we'll head north through the forest, toward my clan. I'd much rather have the dog for company than this serpent-hearted girl.

I glance at her, and I can't help but notice the way her face looks in the flickering light. Instead of planning my getaway, I find myself imagining what it would be like to touch her hair . . . Did she really follow me all this way merely to use me for her purposes? Wasn't there any other able-bodied male who could have helped her?

Will she ever stop thinking of me as a slave? Could she think of me as . . . well, as a friend?

Freya is still lost in her thoughts, still gazing into the fire's glowing embers. She's leaning back on her hands. When I lean back too, the fingers on my left hand aren't so far from the fingers on her right. I shift slightly toward her. After another moment, I shift again. I've altogether stopped planning my escape. All I can think about now is Freya's hand. Her little finger is only a hand's breadth away from mine. If I spread my fingers a little wider—like this—my finger grazes hers . . .

"Don't!" She screams so loud that she must have woken the entire forest. A rook caws, and Artair jumps up barking. "Don't," Freya hisses. "Ever." She whips her dagger from its sheath and rolls closer to me. "Touch." The dagger presses against one of my more sensitive parts. "Me." I can feel her softness pressed against my body, but I'm much more aware of the sharp point she's pushing against my tunic.

"Sorry!" I squirm out from under her, my knees raised to hold her off from me.

"Touch me again, slave," she says, "and I swear by Woden's good eye, you'll no longer be a man by the time I finish with you."

We stare at each other, both of us breathing hard.

"Do I make myself clear, *slave*?" she whispers.

"Yes." I'd like to regain my dignity, but I can't think of any way to do that. My face is so hot that I know I must be the color of a ripe apple.

"Good." She puts her dagger back in its sheath, then settles herself as far from me as she can get and still be near the fire. "Swear by the Aesir that you'll never touch me again."

"I swear!" Why would I want to touch her? How could I have let myself forget, even for a moment, her slimy serpent's heart? "Never again," I promise, and then I turn away from her and put my head down on Artair's warm side.

I pretend to fall asleep, but I lie awake a long time. Why do my fears about the undead seem so small and trifling now? Right now, all I can think about is Freya.

I hate her. Serpent girl.

"Wake up, boy!" Freya's lips are against my ear, sending a shiver through me. "They're almost here," she hisses, and I forget all about the feel of her warm lips touching me. I suck in a breath, and the stench of rotting flesh fills my nose.

While I'm still trying to gather my wits, Freya throws more wood into the dying fire, so that it crackles and leaps. Then she jerks me to my feet. "Back against the flames," she says. "That way the fire will protect us from behind." She hands me her short sword. "Chop at their necks. They don't like to touch you. While you distract them, I'll finish them." She waves an arrow at me.

Artair is barking frantically, and I can scarcely breathe, I'm so terrified, but Freya's calm and cool. As I square my shoulders, preparing myself for a fight, an odd thought occurs to me: apparently, I have the power to upset Freya more than the draugar do.

The dog is bouncing back and forth at the edge of the dark forest, growling, his hackles bristling. I feel a moment of sorrow for him. Artair and I have only just met, and I fear he's about to give his life for me.

Within the forest's darkness, branches crack. Leaves rustle, as though shaken by a storm, and then a shrill cry splits the night. It's followed by another and then another, like the high-pitched wail of cats fighting—except the draugars' screams don't come from warm throats that breathe and swallow. These creatures are like nothing living.

And now I can see the flicker of their pale bodies through the trees' dark knotwork. As they emerge from the forest, at first glance they look like ordinary people, like folk who might say, "How are you?" and "What's the news?" But as they come nearer yet, I see the green rot that tinges their flesh, the ooze of yellow fluid from gashes on their bodies, the glimpse of muscle and bone.

Bodies should sleep where they're planted in the earth. They're not meant to rise up like this, as though some dark force has claimed them for its own purposes.

I touch a finger to the amulet around my neck, and I find myself whispering a prayer to Iosa. And then the creatures screech, as though they have a single throat, and they leap at us. I step forward, in front of Freya, and lift the blade in my hand.

Artair jumps forward and sinks his teeth into a corpse's arm. The creature flails around, trying to shake him off, but Artair is holding on tight, snarling between his teeth. *Swish!* An arrow hisses past my ear, and then it appears in the monster's belly, the yew sunk up to the fletching. The neamh mairbh screams and spins around, then drops to the ground.

Another ghoul swings a pitchfork at Artair, but he dodges and clamps his jaws on its leg. *Thwack!* An arrow goes through the fiend's eye. It grabs at the shaft, trying to pull it out. *Whump!* Another arrow hits its chest, and it falls.

Then there's a big one in front of me, naked and ugly as anything I've ever seen in my entire life. I mean, these things are all ugly, but this one is really—well, he must have been a poxy sight when he was still alive. All the while I'm thinking this, I'm also trying to figure out the best place to sink my blade into it. It screams, and its club whistles past me as I duck just in time to keep my skull from getting smashed.

I grip Freya's blade in both hands and take a swing at the monster's neck. The blade sticks like an axe in a big hunk of firewood. I try to pull it back, but creature lets out howl and smashes me with the side of its arm. I stagger, trying not to lose my balance and fall against Freya behind me; I don't want to push her back into the fire. The hulking ghoul bares its teeth and snarls, its rotted canines protruding from yellow-green gums, and then it lunges toward me, jaws snapping.

I swerve, leap sideways. The wight's teeth tears off a piece of my tunic, but my flesh is still intact, thank all the gods. But now it's leaning over me again, my blade still stuck in its neck. I swallow, take a breath, and prepare to die. Before the big ugly one can lean forward for the kill, though, another one—a female—lunges at me with an axe. I fall to the ground, roll to my side, and the blade smashes into the ground beside me. I've lost track of Freya and Artair now; all I can do is worry about my own skin. Desperately, I pull up my feet and then kick out at the female. She drops back, but now the big one has grabbed me around the neck with its long bony fingers. I choke, gag—and it drops me as though I were a burning coal.

What makes them do that?

I don't have time to puzzle over it, though; I shake the hair out of my face and look around for Freya. She's no longer by the fire; instead, she's backed up against a tree—and I can see her quiver is empty. Her yew bow swings in front of her, her only weapon now, and the draugars are still coming at us, faster and faster, like angry hornets pouring out of a burning nest.

"Freya!" I scream. "We've gotta run!"

"Can't!" she yells back at me. "We're surrounded." She tosses her hair behind her shoulders and laughs, then pierces a ghoul with her bow. "I'm going to the Mead Hall of the Gods, boy!" Her laughter peals above the noise of the battle, and I feel the hairs along my arms lift.

I duck as a corpse takes another swing at me with its axe. The blade whistles next to my ear and smashes into a tree trunk. Freya yanks her bow free, then thrusts it into the ribcage of another ghoul. It crumples to the ground, and she pulls out her bow again.

Her blue eyes glitter in the light from the fire, and as her arms thrust back and forth, I'm pretty sure she's humming one of Aedgar's battle songs. The creatures are dropping around her, but I know she won't be able to fight them off forever.

I struggle toward her. Freya glances at me and curses. "Stay back!" She stabs another draugar with her bow, catches her breath, and shrieks, "Follow my orders, boy—and I'll let you be my slave in the next life!"

"Like Hel," I mutter, lunging toward her.

But there are five ghouls coming at Freya from five different directions now, and I'm not going to get there in time. Artair has disappeared beneath the swarm of fiends, and weapons are coming at me so fast that I don't know which way to jump. "Sweet Iosa," I whisper, "have mercy on us."

Suddenly, the world flashes white—and everything seems to freeze.

5

STRANGE COMPANY

It's as if the sun came out in the middle of the night. I blink, trying to understand what's happening. The knots of branches and vines are like an enormous black spider web against the light. And then everything is black again.

Wham!

Thunder? The noise is so loud that the ground shakes beneath my feet—and then there's another flash of light. The neamh mairbh howl and hide their eyes, as though the light burns them.

Then, above the din, comes the sound of a woman's voice, chanting words in my own mother tongue: "I bind unto myself today the flash of the lightning, the whirl, the shock of the winds."

The undead shriek, as though the words hurt them. They fall back, away from Freya and me. The voice continues, even stronger than before: "Against all Satan's spells and wiles, against the knowledge that defiles."

Freya looks as bewildered as I feel. We stare at each other across the fire-lit clearing—and then a woman steps into the light.

She's older than my mother was the last time I saw her, but not so old as my grandmother. A cowled green robe falls around her short plump shape, and she holds a shepherd's crook in one hand, an oil lantern in the other. Before either Freya or I can say a word, she hooks me with the crook. "Come along!" she shouts to me, then leans to wave the lantern in front of Freya's face. "Don't stand there staring, girl. Step lively!"

She's speaking Englisc now but with the same accent as mine. "Shall we go?" She asks politely, then yanks me toward her with the crook. "Best make our way while the revenants are in shock."

"Wait!" I look around the clearing, searching for a glimpse of Artair. "Come here, boy!"

I don't expect to see him—the draugars must surely have killed him by now—but then I feel his wet nose press against my hand. "Artair!" I lean down to hug him, and his tongue swipes my cheek.

"No time for that!" the woman shouts over her shoulder as she pulls me along. "Hurry now!"

The undead surge weakly toward us, but then, *Wham!* Another bolt of lightning, this one paired immediately with a thunderclap, strikes a tree on the other side of the fire. A spurt of flame leaps up from it, and the ghouls fall back, howling.

"Nasty creatures, those revenants," our rescuer calls over her shoulder. She's marching through the woods with a sprightly step, her head held high, her eyes sparkling as though she's out for a brisk stroll in the fresh air. I stumble along after her, too exhausted from the battle to ask any questions. Even Freya seems subdued, as though all her battle joy has drained away.

We press through the woods, leaving the leap and flicker of the burning tree behind us. The round little woman passes easily between the trees, as though she sees some invisible path, but the undergrowth catches at my clothes and scratches my face and arms. Beside me, Freya trips over a tree root and nearly falls. My hand shoots out to catch her, but then I remember—I'm not supposed to touch her—so I let my hand drop to my side. Freya shoots an evil glance at me as she scrambles to regain her footing.

"Why aren't you helping me, boy?" she whispers, but I'm too bewildered to do more than roll my eyes at her contrariness.

Despite the fast pace the woman sets us, I know how fast the neamh mairbh can be. Their howls echo through the night, and they seem to be drawing nearer.

The woman cocks her head, as though she's listening, and then she turns and hands me the lantern. "You two follow the path. I'll catch up soon enough."

"But you're unarmed," Freya protests.

The woman chuckles. "No time to argue, I'm afraid." She makes a shooing gesture as she pushes past us. "Get on with you—and hurry it."

I swing the lantern around, and by its light, I see a faint path winding through the trees ahead of us. "Come on," I say over my shoulder to Freya. The little woman doesn't look like much of a warrior, but somehow I have confidence in her.

As we push on through the forest, I hear the woman's voice calling through the night: "Against the heart's idolatry, against the wizard's evil craft, against the death wound and the burning, the choking wave, the poisoned shaft, protect me, Criost, till thy returning."

But the shrieks of the walking dead are even nearer than before. They must be almost upon the woman. I have to stop and look back.

The moon has risen high in the sky, and by its light, I catch a glimpse of the woman through the trees. She's standing with her back to us, facing toward the fiends, her arms upraised as though she's leading a choir of singers. As she chants her song, the Scoti words falling sweet and firm into the night, mist rises from the ground all about her, hiding her from sight.

A moment later, she emerges from the fog, dashing toward Freya and me. Behind her, the fog thickens, grows so dense that it's like a white wall closing us in from behind. "Keep moving!" In a flash, the woman has caught up with us. She grabs the lantern from my hand and takes the lead again. Ahead of us, despite the mist that presses behind us, the path lies clear in the moonlight.

"Revenants are bad with sudden light," she whispers to us, the Englisc words barely louder than a breath. "Their rotten eyes can't handle it, I suppose. And they're entirely befuddled by mists." She's striding along ahead of me again, Artair prancing happily at her side. "Their brains aren't fully resuscitated," she says softly over her shoulder. "But we can't linger. We'd best use this opportunity to put some distance between them and us."

Behind us, the unearthly cries grow fainter. The woman pushes us to go even faster, and soon all I hear are the normal sounds of the forest at night.

The moon is no longer high in the sky, but through the trees I can make out a sheer rock face in front of us. Before I can wonder if we'll be trapped here between the forest and the cliff, the woman grabs at a bush with her crook and pulls aside the leaves. "Come along, children," she says. "Don't bump your heads." Then she walks straight into the rock and disappears.

It's an entrance to a cave. I step inside and find that the ceiling is so low enough I have to stoop. Freya follows me, but Artair stands at the entrance and whimpers.

"Come!" I call softly, but he clearly doesn't want to obey, so I grab him and haul him inside.

Meanwhile, our guide has pulled the concealing bushes back in place over the entrance. "Follow me," she whispers, the lantern lighting our way from her out-stretched hand.

She's short enough that she can walk without stooping, but Freya has to bend her head, while I'm forced to slump along. I soon have a crick in my neck, and the sides of the tunnel seem to press around me. The air is cold and smells of wet stone and soil. The lantern's flame flickers, and I feel oddly breathless, as though we've used up all the air inside this crack in the earth.

Then, just as I think I can't take any more of this, a breeze tickles my face. A few breaths more, and we step outside into the moonlight. I stare around me at a clearing ringed by ash and elder.

"Here we are!" Our guide chuckles and claps her hands. I see that firewood is already neatly stacked inside a circle of fallen tree trunks. The woman bends, and fire from her lantern spills onto a pile of kindling. As flames leap to life, she motions toward the logs. "Have a seat," she says, as though she's a thane's wife welcoming us into our home. Freya and I glance at each other, and then we take a seat beside each other on a log. Artair settles at my feet, and the woman plops down on another log. She lets out a sigh of contentment.

I can see her more clearly now in the firelight. Her face is round and dimpled, and her dark eyes sparkle, as though she's constantly on the point of bursting out in laughter. In the center of her round bosom is pinned a silver brooch—it's a square cross atop two crossed swords—and she carries a leather pouch strapped over one shoulder. Beneath her robe, I see now, she has more layers of clothing, so that only her hands and face are exposed.

"So." She looks from Freya to me, and then she gives me a wink. "In a wee bit of trouble, weren't you?"

I nod. Beside me, Freya shifts a little—I hope my arm didn't brush against hers—and then she bursts out, "Who are you? Did you do magic back there? Are you a witch?"

I have questions of my own. "Where are we? What is this place?"

"Of course you are full of questions." The woman smiles. "I am Sister Sima O'Donahue, missioner from the Abbey of Saint Brigid in Cill Dara—that's in Éire—at your service. You can call me Mother Sima." She turns to Freya and adds, "That's 'shee-mah,' dear."

"It means 'treasure' in our tongue," I tell Freya. Tonight, this woman proved to be indeed a treasure. Without her, we'd surely all be lying dead right now. Or else—I shudder—we would have joined the ranks of living dead.

"As for this place—" Mother Sima waves a plump hand around the clearing. "I have friends throughout Albion who keep places like this. Food and firewood is kept here for travelers. We will be safe here from the revenants, at least for a little while."

"But are you a witch?" Freya asks again. "You chanted strange words back there—a magic spell that drove back the draugar."

"Oh dear me, no." Mother Sima shakes her head. "That was Saint Patrick's Lorica, spoken in the Scoti language. It's a strong prayer against evil, but it's not a spell. I was simply making a humble request of the Good God."

Freya looks as skeptical as I feel.

Mother Sima settles her wide haunches more comfortably on the wooden seat, plucking at her robe so that it falls smoothly over her knees. "And you, my dear?" she asks Freya. "Who might you and your brave companion be?"

Freya lifts her chin. "I am Freya, Aedgar's Datar, of the shire of Escomb, in the Kingdom of Northumbria."

She turns toward me, and I know she's about to tell Mother Sima that I'm her slave. Before she can, I introduce myself. "Finn MacDugal, from the village of Dun-Collum in the Kingdom of Dalriada."

Mother Sima nods. "I likewise am born to the Scoti tribe. No doubt we have clan in common." Then she turns her gaze toward Artair. "And your four-footed friend? What do you call him?"

"Artair. I just adopted him." I touch Artair's head and grin. "Or I guess he adopted me."

"Ah, Artair," says Mother Sima. "A good strong name for a strong brave friend. I saw how he defended you against the revenant." Her smile broadens as she looks back and forth between Freya and me, and she clasps her hands together against her heart. "I see that you two are sweethearts."

I'm so appalled by these words that I bark out rudely, "Hel no!"

Freya looks like she bit into a sour apple. "No, no, no!" She tips her nose even higher toward the sky. "He's my slave," she says primly.

"Oh." Mother Sima's smile fades a little, but her eyes are shrewd as she continues to look back and forth between our faces. "Well then, if the very idea upsets you, I apologize. But the two of you look—well, never mind."

Freya has inched a few inches further away from me on the log. "Why did you save us, Mother Sima?" she asks, changing the subject. "And why were you there at that exact moment, when we needed you?"

The woman plants a hand on each knee. "There's no mystery, my dear," she says comfortably. "I set aside time to be still each day, to hear the voice of the Spirit. She led me to you."

Freya scrunches up her brow. "I don't understand what you mean."

I understand a little, because of Priest David, but I have still more questions. "If you are from Eireland, how did you come to be in Angleland?" Priest David told us of women who gave their lives to God instead of to a husband, but he said they lived together, in one place, like a little village of holy women. He never said anything about them wandering around the countryside all alone.

"I am here because of my mission," Mother Sima says.

"What's that?" Freya is eyeing Mother Sima as though she's trying to figure out the slot inside her head in which the woman belongs: commoner or thane, slave or noble, those are the only types of people Freya knows.

"My promise to serve the Threefold God," Mother Sima explains. "The Creator, Iosa, and the Spirit."

Freya frowns; she's never heard of Iosa, I know.

"When I was a young woman," Mother Sima continues, "about the same age as you two, I chose to give my life to Iosa. Many of the Scoti now follow Iosa, and I joined a community of men, women, and children who were all his followers. As I grew older, the leaders of our community saw in me certain traits. A particular sort of strength. They told me I was given these abilities to battle against the forces of darkness. As a sign of my identity, I wear this cross." She touches the silver brooch on her chest. "It is my sigil, a seal on my very soul that I am both a warrior and a follower of Iosa."

I'm thinking that she's a funny sort of warrior, with her good-natured smile, her short round body, and her little plump hands. Freya's gaze is fixed on the square silver cross with its two swords upraised behind it, and she looks more impressed than I am. "You mean that's what you do?" she asks. "You journey here and there, fighting against things like these draugar?"

"Is that what you call them in Englisc? Draugar?" Mother Sima gives a nod. "That's a good word to add to my store of knowledge. And yes, I am called to defend others against these walking dead." She's no longer smiling. "And against other such fell creatures that spill out into our world."

"You're a monster killer?" I ask. "But you're a woman."

She looks at me, and her eyebrows rise. "Women can have a warrior spirit." She turns toward Freya. "As do you, my dear. I saw how you fought against the revenants."

Freya smiles and sits very straight. "My mother—she is now in the Mead Hall of the Gods—was a great shield maiden. She fought beside our men and put fear in the hearts of our foes. I carry her legacy."

"Ah." Mother Sima's gaze is wise as she examines Freya's face. "That is a source of pride for you, I can tell. And," she adds, "it must at times make your life difficult. It is hard to always be strong. We can never let down our guard, can we?"

Freya only shrugs, but I see an emotion I can't identify flicker across her face. Looking at her, I narrow my eyes, trying to see a little further into her than I have before.

She squints back at me, and I know she would have me think that she is always strong and fierce, no matter what she may hide inside her heart.

I pull my attention back to Mother Sima as she says, "The mothers and fathers of my community sensed dire doings in the Island of Albion. The Threefold God spoke to them and revealed that there is a champion, a hero-warrior—someone who can stop this horror. This person could be anyone. Whoever it is might not even know. So the elders sent me across the water between Éire and Albion, to seek out this warrior. That is my mission here."

Freya nods, as though she knows exactly what Mother Sima is talking about. "It's him." She points her finger at me. "He must be the person you're seeking. There's something special about Finn."

"Ah," says Mother Sima again, "and yet you say he's not your sweetheart?"

Freya makes an impatient motion with her head. "He's not special like that. He's stupid and weak, and he's—well, he's an utterly *worthless* slave who won't do anything I tell him. But—there's something that saves him every time from the draugar."

Mother Sima looks at me, her eyes narrowed and her head cocked to one side—and then I see her eyes widen. She shrugs. "Well, we shall see. These things reveal themselves with time."

I hunch my shoulders. "I'm not your slave, Freya," I mutter, "and I'm not some great champion against the undead." I turn to Mother Sima. "I'm just Finn— a free man—and I am going home to my family. I'm not interested in fighting any more battles against the draugars—so please tell this serpent-hearted girl to leave me alone."

For the first time since I met her, Mother Sima frowns. "Young man, you must treat Freya with the respect she deserves."

"By Thunor's great arse." I sigh gustily. "Not you too."

Mother Sima's draws herself up. "Finn, such language is not appropriate for use around women. You must learn to hold your tongue when you are angry."

Freya nods. "That is so true, Mother Sima."

"Enough!" I jump to my feet. "Come on, Artair, let's find someplace to sleep—away from nagging females with their sensitive ears.

I duck back inside the hillside, into the cave. It's dank and dark in here—not a good place to sleep at all—but I'm too proud to go back to the circle of firelight where I can hear Freya and Mother Sima still chatting. I slide my backside down against the stone wall and settle myself on the floor of the cave. Almost immediately, I realize I'm sitting in a puddle of fetid water. My breeches wet, I shift around until I find someplace dryer, and then I lean my head back against the rock. Artair presses against me, and I stroke his muzzle. "Good boy, Artair. How about you and me go home? My family and clan will welcome us and life will be good again. Sound good to you, Artair, huh?"

He licks my hand, and I smile in the darkness. "All right then, we'll leave tomorrow."

As soon as I close my eyes, I see the tangle and turmoil of bony limbs against my lids. I try to find something to think of that will drive away the images of rotting flesh and dangling eyeballs, bulging intestines and grinning skulls' teeth.

The circle of huts within the larger circle of the hill fort. The smell of wood smoke and green grass. My mother's smile.

Home . . .

When I wake up, every bone in my body feels sore and stiff. I stagger to my feet, then make my way toward the daylight, hobbling along as though I've suddenly aged a lifetime. Then the smell of frying ham fills my nose, driving away any thought I had of bidding farewell to Freya and Mother Sima. *Maybe after breakfast.*

The little clearing is filled with that peculiar light that comes just after dawn. Mother Sima is crouched over the fire, holding a sizzling skillet over the flames. I catch a glimpse of eggs frying next to the ham, and my step quickens.

The two women turn toward me. Freya is whittling a stick, and she holds it up for me to see. "I'm making new arrow shafts from yew. And I'm sharpening yew-wood sticks—like daggers—for you to use the next time we meet the draugar. You're not very skilled with a blade."

"Don't start, Freya," I grumble. "It's too early."

"Good morning, Finn," Mother Sima says cheerfully. "Does life look a bit better this morning?"

I shrug, my eye on the frying pan, and she chuckles. "Would you like some breakfast? I'm steeping herbs in hot water, and there's milk back in the cave."

The three of us hunker down over the food, and for a while, there's a blissful silence that's broken only by the sounds of smacking lips. Artair puts his nose on his paws and follows each movement I make with earnest eyes. Once my stomach is full enough that I can feel generous, I share bits of ham and eggs with him.

At last, we lean back on the logs. "Mother Sima," Freya asks, "what do you carry in that satchel?" She points to the leather bag that hangs from the woman's shoulder.

Mother Sima reaches into the bag and pulls out a small square object, not much broader than my hand. It's a book, I realize, a little like the one Priest David carried, from which he read the words of Iosa. This one, however, is decorated with silver-and-enamel designs of fabulous creatures: dragons, unicorns, mermaids, and something with a lion's body and eagle's head and wings. Even Artair seems interested in the book and lifts up his snout to sniff at the cover.

"A book?" I run a finger over the cover. "What is it?"

"*Bestiarium,*" Mother Sima says. "In Latin, that means 'Bestiary.'"

"What's that?" Freya asks. "Why do you carry it?"

"Officially, this book doesn't exist," Mother Sima says. "It's my community's secret, our hidden weapon against the fell creatures of darkness. Can I trust you two to tell no one that you have seen it?"

I nod and so does Freya, her eyes on the woven pattern that loops across the book. The Angles don't have shiny written texts like this, and I can tell she's awed and fascinated. "Why is it a weapon?" she asks. "What does it do?"

Mother Sima opens the book, revealing pages that are illumined with images so bright they look like they might leap off the vellum. "This," she says, "is a listing of all the creatures that do not belong to this world. For most people, these things are only rumors, creatures from old stories told to children. But they are real, these things, though they live in the realm that lies next to ours. Most of the time they stay on their side of the between-world, but sometimes—" She lowers her voice. "Sometimes they slip over."

I'm filled with a powerful curiosity to look at each page of the book, but I would hate to touch it with my mud-caked hands.

"Like the draugar?" Freya asks, and Mother Sima nods.

"Are they all evil?" I ask. "Foul, fell things?"

She shakes her head. "Some are good, some bad, and most can go either way—like humans. Every creature made by the Threefold God has its purpose. Like the unicorn." Mother Sima turns the page to reveal a white steed with a long golden horn. It's so lifelike I half expect it to whinny and shake its mane. "It is a fearsome beast," Mother Sima continues, "so that in the faraway land of the Ethiopians, it may even kill an elephant with its horn. And yet, when it rests its head in a maiden's lap, it becomes so docile that a huntsman could take and capture it. This is a testimony to the power of Mary, the mother of Iosa, she who was so pure and whole that the Child of God could be born from her."

Freya must have no idea what Mother Sima is talking about, but her attention is caught by just one word that Mother Sima spoke. "What is an ella-font?" she asks.

"Ah! That is a wonder indeed." Mother Sima turns more pages until she comes to the image of a huge creature, its size shown by the little people around its feet. The beast has two deadly horns that stick out on each side of a long, long nose like a vine. On its back is a little tower with archers and men holding flags in it. "Though it is taller than an oak and stronger than an ox," Mother Sima says, "the elephant has bad joints in its knees. If it falls over, it cannot be lifted except by one of its companion elephants. This teaches us that we humanfolk—who are like the mighty beast in many ways—must live in good fellowship with our neighbors. We rely on them for help when we are in trouble."

It's an amazing book, sure enough, but I'm wondering if every beast really has some tidy little message for humans, the way Mother Sima seems to think.

"Tell us some of the other creatures in the book," Freya asks.

Mother Sima leafs through the book, careful to touch only the edges of each page, and reads aloud: "Centaurs, chimerae, demons, dracaenae, goblins, giants, gorgons, griffins. And—" She flips ahead in the book. "This. Does it look familiar?"

Freya and I lean forward to see. "The draugar," Freya gasps. The picture is so realistic it's frightening.

Mother Sima studies the page, her lips moving as she reads the text to herself. After a moment, she glances up at us. "Yes, but this is in Latin, so the word here is 'revenant.'"

"What else does it say?" I ask. "What does it tell you about the undead?"

She squints at the page, as though she needs to focus her eyes before she can decipher the tiny marks on the vellum. Then she reads out loud, translating as she goes: "'Revenant, also called the Living Dead and the Walking Dead. Reanimated corpses. Reported since the earliest civilizations, occurring in Africa, in the lands around the Great Sea, in the Far Isles, in Gaulic and Germanic lands, in Éire, Albion, Cymru, Dalriada, and the land of the Picts. Persons who are murderers and haters, practitioners of the dark arts, return a peculiar sort of life to the corpse by means of incantation. In some lands, a magical cauldron or other device may also reanimate dead flesh. All revenants are vicious, filled with a terrible and furious hunger. They retain nothing of their soulish intelligence, and they cannot speak with a human voice, yet they are agile and faster moving than mortal humans.'" Mother Sima points with one stubby finger at each word as she reads it. Now her finger hovers over a note someone has scribbled in the margin. "'Voyagers to the far Western Islands across the sea have brought stories of revenants that are slower in their movements. These are said to walk with an odd shuffling gait.'"

Her finger returns to the straight lines of letters that march across the page, and she continues reading. "'Some surmise that the lessening of rational capacities causes a corresponding increase in the animal nature, such that these behave, as beasts do, by instinct and raw ferocity. Others, however, believe that they possess a peculiar energy that has nothing in common with any breathing creature. They must dine on the flesh of living humans to sustain themselves, leading some to suspect that the fire of warm flesh and blood serves to maintain the vital force within these ghouls. So long as this foul vitality remains within them, they cannot be killed, despite injury that would fell a normal man. Those who survive the bite of a revenant suffer a fate worse than death, for thus they are transformed themselves into one of the undead.'"

Mother Sima looks up at us again. "The moral lesson of the revenant—" she starts to say, but I interrupt her.

"Can't we skip that part? How about something more useful—like how can the living defend themselves against the undead?"

Mother Sima gives me a stern glance, but her finger moves lower down the page, and she reads, "'The revenants can only be felled by three means. Firstly, prayer, especially the invocation of the Blessed Archangel

Michael. Secondly, a yew stake through the heart. Thirdly, burning. Once felled, the remains must at once be cremated or buried with charm stones in their mouths to prevent them from reclaiming their dark vitality.'"

Mother Sima looks up again. "There is one more thing in this book that may be useful to us," she says, "and it is this that points me toward the next step of my journey."

"What is it?" asks Freya.

"A list of authorities on each creature. People who have experience with the particular thing." She points to several names stacked at the bottom of the page. "This one—right here—might be of help to me as I work to end this plague."

I lean over the book to see the name she's pointing to, and then I spell out the letters in my head.

I look up at Mother Sima. "Really?"

I've heard stories about this guy. Some say he's crazy, others say he's a demon. Some say he died long ago, some say he'll never die, and other says he never existed at all.

"Who?" Freya demands, and for the space of one breath, I can't help but feel a little smug that I have been taught to read the script, while she has not.

I read the name aloud. "Merlin."

6

THE DARK FOREST

"I've heard of him," Freya says. "He was the sorcerer who helped the Welsc to fight against my people."

"Defeat your people," I correct her. "But that was a hundred years ago. No man could live that long."

"Perhaps he has supernatural vitality," says Mother Sima.

"Like the undead?" I ask.

She shakes her head. "No, something different. A force that keeps his flesh from growing old. Or maybe the Merlin who fought with the Welsc was another man with the same name."

"I've heard he's a demon," Freya says. "His mother lay with a demon. They say he has horns like his father."

Mother Sima chuckles and shakes her head. "I think we can safely dismiss those stories as mere fabrication."

"No," I agree. "He's just a crazy old lunatic. He lives a day or two's journey from my home fort. There was a man from my village who came across him in the woods. He said Merlin lives like an animal—and when he tried to talk to him, Merlin couldn't say a single word that made any sense."

Mother Sima's smile doesn't fade. I'm starting to find her constant humor just a little annoying. "If you're hoping Merlin can help you fight the undead," I tell her, "then you really are daft. Why go into the wild places looking for a crazy man when it's warriors you need? My people have kept the Anglefolc on their side of the Roman wall for a century. We'll do the same with the neamh mairbh."

Of course Freya can't keep silent now. "My people, the Angles and Saxons, have kept the Scoti barbarians on *their* side of the Roman wall for a century. Our warriors will stop the draugar." She lifts her head high. "And I shall help them."

I find myself noticing the way the growing daylight catches the gold in her hair. Even filthy, the serpent-girl is more beautiful than she has any right to be.

Mother Sima looks thoughtful. "I've been gathering news from here and there. The revenants have utterly destroyed village after village. The creatures are as many as the fall leaves in a great forest. Our people"—she looks at me—"and your people"—she looks at Freya—"are all warrior-folk. We know how to meet our foes bravely, with strength and courage. But the undead are stronger and faster than any mortal—and they are ravenously hungry for human flesh. No band of human warriors can ever prevail against them for very long."

A pair of swallows flits into the little space where we sit. I watch as they dip and swoop, and then fly up into the sky again. They're a lovely sight, but they give me a thought that fills me with dread. I turn to Mother Sima. "Is there any chance the undead will climb over the top of this stone hill where we're enclosed? Then they would drop down into the middle—and we would be trapped."

Mother Sima shakes her head. "Not likely, dear. They lack the cunning to find the entryway through the cave, and their brains are too dull to form another plan. Besides, the rock walls are jagged. Even with the revenants speed and strength, I've never heard of them scaling such a craggy stronghold."

I frown. "Some of them do seem to have a sense of direction." I'm thinking of the tall ghoul who wore the Roman armor. "They have a sort of purpose to their movements."

"Yes." Mother Sima nods. "I have noted that as well. It is as if some malignant force guides them. If I could discover what that is . . ." Her voice trails off as she drifts into thought.

"How did the undead start?" Freya asks. "The wise woman in my village said they have always been here— but now, as time has passed, they have multiplied."

Mother Sima shakes her head. "They have always been here, but whatever dark magic from the other realms created them, it was a rare thing. They were few and far between, not like the hordes we face now. This plague started in the Summer Lands near Avalon and spread from there into the Saxon lands of Sussex, Wessex, and on up into Englisc Northumbria. When they reached Hadrian's Wall, they spread along it clear to the Isles of Bride." Mother Sima shakes her head again, and her face is completely serious now, without a hint of her usual smile. "They must be stopped," she says, "or this entire green island will be emptied of the living. Scoti, Saxons, Angles, Picts, and Cymry—it matters not. We shall all be carrion for living corpses. And that," she concludes, "is why we must find Merlin. We need a greater wisdom than our own."

Freya nods thoughtfully. "This may be the best way I can avenge my father's arm. By joining our forces with yours in your fight against the draugar."

"Our?" I shake my head. Now that Freya has Mother Sima, she won't need my help. I'm finally free to go back home—why should I turn aside for a wild-goose chase after a mad man in the forest? I get to my feet. "You two do what you please. I'll be on my way now. Artair and I are going to my home."

Mother Sima looks up at me for a moment, and then she says, "Very well, boy. Be on your way then."

I'm surprised she's not going to argue with me. It feels a little odd to say goodbye and walk away, after all that's happened. But I think again of the green hill fort and my mother's smile. "Thank you, Mother Sima," I say. "Thank you for coming to our rescue. The followers of Iosa shall be proud of you, I am certain."

I'm trying to sound serious and noble, but when I turn to Freya, I can't keep the same tone. "You're a pain in the arse, Freya, but you're beautiful, I'll give you that. I hope the neamh mairbh don't eat you before you have a chance to grow up and get some sense."

I turn toward the tunnel in the rock. "Come on, Artair."

Then I remember something and spin around. "I'll take these," I tell Freya and grab two of the yew branches she's whittled into points. And then I duck into the tunnel, Artair running ahead of me.

Behind me, I hear Freya, shout, "Stop! You can't leave, boy. Come back this instant!"

I don't even break my stride. "Shove it up your arse," I mutter.

"Finn? Listen to me." This time it's Mother Sima's voice I hear. The words, spoken in the familiar Gaelic, sound so much like my mother that I hesitate. "Come back, Finn, and listen to me say just one thing. Then, if you still want to journey on alone, I will let you go."

I stand still in the darkness. As though sensing my indecision, Artair has left me and is already bouncing back into the sunlight. I sigh. "All right." I turn around and follow Artair. "I'll listen."

Mother Sima looks up at me from her seat on the log, but Freya is standing now, one foot stamping up and down, two spots of red glowing on her cheeks as she looks at me. I can't help but give her a grin when I see how angry she is at the thought of me leaving.

"You're right to seek your kin, Finn," Mother Sima says. "May Iosa, Brigid, and Patrick bless you for it. But think a moment. I am seeking Merlin—who lives just a hurley-ball's throw from your village of DunCollum. Why shouldn't we journey together? We are bound to run into revenants along the way—and we'd be better off fighting them as three. So, by your leave, why don't we walk the road beside you just as far as your home? Then we'll fare you well and be on our way."

I look back and forth between the two women. Their company is about as welcome as a pimple on my bum. But . . . oh, she does have a point.

"All right," I tell them. "We go together. But Freya, no telling me what to do. I'm no more your property than the forests and mountains are, you hear? And Mother Sima, I'll not be putting a bridle on my tongue for the sake of your sanctified ears. I'm a free man, and I say what I please."

They glance at each other, and then they both nod. I can tell they're only humoring me—but what can I do?

Freya insists on tipping and fletching her arrows before we start on our way, so the sun is at its midpoint in the sky by the time we leave. We go back through the tunnel, which is as dark as night even at midday, and then we peer out through the tangle of leaves that hides the opening.

"Anything?" whispers Freya

Mother Sima cups her hands around her ears to listen. She sniffs the air, then glances down at Artair. He's eager to be out in the open air, and clearly, he too smells and hears nothing that worries him. "They're gone," Mother Sima announces at last. "Let's go."

In the bright of day, I can finally get my bearings. We've walked a long way through the tanglewood, and now we need to find the road that leads northwest toward Glas Cu. It's nine days' journey or more to Glas Cu—but from there, it's only a day further to my home fort.

We walk quietly, not speaking, for most of the day, past the gentle hills and well-cleared fields typical of most of Angleland. Here and there, we pass through small patches of forest, left by the Angles to provide habitat for game. It's a rare clear blue day, the air bright with sunshine and birdsong. Artair runs back and forth, ahead and behind us, treating us as though we're a small flock of sheep, and we can't help but exchange smiles at his antics. It's hard to believe this is the same land where the neamh mairbh are wreaking such awful destruction—except that each farm we pass is deserted and empty. There are no workers in their fields, and sheep and cattle are ambling aimlessly, unherded. Now and then we hear a cow lowing, longing to be milked, but for the most part, the farms lie silent. I don't want to look too closely, for fear I'll see more signs of the slaughter that claimed the folk for miles around.

Toward dusk we come onto a wider dirt road, one that has patches of stonework laid down centuries before when the Roman legions were in the land. We walk abreast, Artair circling our company. The broad road makes the three of us seem very small.

Normally, this time of year, the road would be packed with travelers, but not today. Have the walking dead claimed everyone? Or are there living folk somewhere, hunkered down behind their stockades, afraid to come out? My thoughts cast gloom over the sunny day.

We trudge onward, growing more tired and grimy with every step. Sweat trickles out from Mother Sima's wimple and streaks her face. I find myself wondering idly why she wears the thing. Is it because she's wed herself to Iosa? It seems like Iosa wouldn't mind if she took it off when she got hot.

I'm sweating too, and Freya's perspiration draws lines through the mud that still cakes her cheeks. We all smell like pigs. "I hope the neamh mairbh aren't drawn by smells," I say. "If they are, we're surely done for."

"I do not smell, boy." I can tell Freya's tired by how half-hearted her denial sounds.

On we plod, not speaking any more. I try to imagine what Ma and Da will say when they see me. What will Fiona and Brecken look like after all these years? Will they still recognize me?

And then, Mother Sima and Freya both stop dead in their tracks. I start to ask them why—and then I hear it too, the rumble of noise from the other side of the hill that lies ahead. Mother Sima points silently to a copse of hazel and linden, and we dash into the trees, then crouch down amid the tangle of vines and leaves. I wrap my arms around Artair, who whines almost silently, tiny breathy sounds so low I can barely hear him. Mother Sima tightens her grip on her shepherd's crook, Freya nocks an arrow on her bowstring, and I take the yew dagger from my belt. A flock of wood doves flies up from the road, a burst of wings that makes me jump.

And then I hear . . . hoof beats? The neamh mairbh don't ride horses—or do they? How many skills do the walking dead retain from when they were alive? And would a horse let such a foul creature sit on its back?

I don't know the answer to these questions, but as the riders crest the hill, I'm relieved to see they're clearly human. I let out the breath I've been holding. "Thank you, Iosa," murmurs Mother Sima.

The company of riders keeps pouring over the hill, a dark tide of score after score of horses.

"So many," Freya whispers. "It must be the king's war band!"

She leaps up from our hiding place and dashes toward the road, Artair barking at her heels. Mother Sima and I follow, waving our arms and calling to the men to stop.

They're riding so fast they don't even see us. Their hooves are like thunder, their steeds tall, powerful horses, so much larger than the ponies I'm used to. The warriors wear armor—scale and chainmail; leather, copper, and iron—and they are as tall and strong as their horses. Their red and blond braids stream back from their fierce faces, and a thrill runs through me at the thought that these warriors will defend us now.

And then, as they gallop by us, I see the bloody rags around their heads, the filth and blood that cling to their faces and necks. Their armor is dented, their spears broken. Some carry shattered swords, and the helms of others hang in pieces over their heads.

Freya turns to me and shouts, "This is no charge—it's a retreat." Her eyes are bright with something that looks suspiciously like tears. "They've been beaten."

"Are these really King Aethelfrith's champions?" I know they are, but I wish she could give me another answer.

I see her swallow, then set her shoulders square and firm. That motion, so familiar to me now, reminds me of what Mother Sima said to her last night: *It's hard to be strong . . . to never let down our guard.* I almost wish I could take Freya's hand—but I remember all too clearly the sharp poke of her knife against my private parts.

The three of us turn to watch the company ride southward, the thunder of their hooves diminishing, until they are black specks that disappear at last over the crest of a distant hill.

"So," says Mother Sima, "Northumbria's hope is defeated. The kingdom's strongest horsemen are fleeing for their lives." Her voice is matter-of-fact, and she squares her shoulders in a gesture very similar to Freya's. "Now we must rely only on the Threefold God to show us the way to save Albion."

I can't imagine how the four of us—a plump old woman, a snippy young girl, one loyal dog, and me—have much hope when the king's war band failed to defeat the undead. I don't have the heart to argue, though, so I silently fall in step with the others as we continue on our way.

The sun is sinking toward the west, casting long red beams across the land. Swifts flit in and out of the trees, and a woodpecker taps in the distance. The roadside is white with clusters of wild garlic. In the distance, I hear sheep and their lambs calling back and forth across the fields. We trudge onward, toward Glas Cu.

When night falls, we make camp in another copse. Mother Sima says we dare not light a fire, not here, but she helps us make beds of moss beneath the branches, then hands us portions of smoked beef she pulls out from her satchel. We huddle together, passing around a loaf of bread and a horn of mead. *What else does she have in that satchel?* I wonder idly. There seems no end to the useful things she pulls out of the leather bag as needed.

The mead warms my blood and comforts my heart. Our clearing is enclosed within a wall of tall oaks and elms. Oak and elm are powerful trees, according to my people's beliefs, and I hope they will guard us with their sturdy presence. When I tip back my head, I see that their branches form a lacework that's darker than the blue-black sky above them. I let out a long sigh and let myself relax. An owl hoots some-where in the night, hunting its supper. Artair looks up, then goes back to gnawing a cow's hoof he found along the road. Who knows what the mutt has been through in the past few days, and yet there he lies beside me, perfectly happy simply because he's beside me, gnawing on an old hoof.

For just a moment, I wish I were a dog.

Mother Sima chants softly, "De profundis clamavi ad te, Domine; Domine, exaudi vocem meam. Fiant aures tuæ intendentes in vocem deprecationis meæ."

When she's done, the silence settles around us once again. "That was lovely, Mother Sima," Freya says after a moment. "What do the words mean?"

"I'll sing them in Englisc," the nun replies. "Out of the depths I cry to you, O Lord, Lord, hear my voice! O let your ears hear to the voice of my pleas."

Listening, I feel both sad and angry. Priest David sang these same words, standing by his cross. My mother loved them, and repeated them to me whenever I felt glum and out of sorts. But there's no comfort left in those words for me today. Instead, they seem to mock me with their memories of long-ago happiness.

"It's lovely," Freya says. "Did a bard write that? Some-one from your tribe?"

"He was a bard and a great war chief," Mother Sima answers. "It is a song of David, king of the Hebrew tribe. He wrote more than a hundred songs like that."

"Do you know more of them?"

"Oh, yes. All of them, both in Latin and in Gaelic." Mother Sima turns toward me. "Finn, you must know some too, don't you? Will you sing with me?"

"I do, and I won't," I mutter in reply.

"I know some songs," Freya says. "One is called the Rune Poem, because each line starts with a letter from our alphabet. My mother taught it to me as a child. Would you like to hear it?"

"Of course," says Mother Sima.

Freya sings, her voice like a soft bell pealing into the deepening darkness. The song is an Angle poem I've heard before.

> *Wealth is a comfort to all men;*
> *yet must every man bestow it freely,*
> *if he wish to gain honor in the sight of the All Father.*

> *The auroch is proud and has great horns;*
> *it is a very savage beast and fights with its horns;*
> *a great ranger of the moors, it is a creature of mettle.*

> *The thorn is exceedingly sharp,*
> *an evil thing for any warrior to touch,*
> *uncommonly severe on all who sit among them.*

> *The mouth is the source of all language,*
> *a pillar of wisdom and a comfort to wise men,*
> *a blessing and a joy to every nobleman.*

Listening to Freya sing those words, I almost forget how angry she makes me. Her voice calms and comforts me even more than the mead did. I settle down on my bed of moss, listening as Mother Sima and Freya take turns singing quietly: now a psalm, then a ballad and another psalm, and then a tragedy about a warrior maiden and her lover. I let my heavy eyes sink shut.

I wake from my drowsiness when the singing stops, and Freya announces that she has to step into the brush before she goes to sleep. Mother Sima offers to go with her, and Freya demurs, but she takes her bow and arrows with her as she disappears into the woods.

I lie on my back, looking up at the darkness, listening to the soft rustle of the wind through the leaves above my head. What an odd few days it's been—but here I am, a free man. I owe the neamh mairbh credit for that.

"Feel better now?" Mother Sima asks me softly. "Not so angry?"

"I suppose."

"Can I ask you something, Finn?"

"All right." I'm wondering what's coming next. More talk about Freya and me being sweethearts?

But instead she says, "You are not a follower of Iosa—and yet you wear a cross around your neck. Why?"

I sigh. "My mother followed Iosa, and I wear it in her memory. But Iosa did nothing to help me when I most needed it. He let me become a slave—so either he doesn't care or he isn't real."

"I'm sorry," she answers softly. "I hope you will find love someday. And then you will know happiness, despite all you have suffered."

I snort. "My loves are in DunCollum. Ma, Da, my brother and sister, my whole clan, they are the ones I love. They are all I need to be happy. And soon I will be home." My voice is loud and firm, and I know I'm telling myself as much as Mother Sima.

"I hope it will be so," she says.

Freya returns, and I take my turn in the woods. When I come back, Mother Sima is snoring softly, and Freya's breath is soft and even. I settle down on my mossy bed, and Artair presses against me, keeping me warm despite the night's chill. I fall asleep almost immediately, dreaming of a voice that sings a song so sweet that my heart is filled with joy.

The days of our journey blend together. I know each step brings me closer to my home, but I feel as though I will walk on and on forever, never reaching anywhere. On our third day, we take a short cut through a field, pushing our way through the tall grass. I'm the one who suggested the shorter route, but afterward, my arms and ankles burn like fire from the nettles. Mother Soma and Freya seem immune to the sting, so I stomp along, muttering complaints and curses to myself, wishing I could blame them for sending me through the nettles. I'm starting to think that freedom—so far at least—is not a whole lot better than slavery.

The hills are high and steep, and by the end of every day, my calf muscles are aching. I fall asleep almost instantly—and then I wake up and do it all over again. We see no sign of the undead, at least, and I feel protected by the dense forestland. Gradually, my legs become accustomed to hours of climbing and descending, and my heart lightens. This is more like the land where I was raised, and I feast my eyes on the red-brown trunks, the dark green of leaf and needle.

At last, after days of endless up-and-down trudging, I see ahead the ancient Roman wall that separates Pictland and Scotiland from Angleland. The horizon lifts upward above the stone barrier that stretches from west to east as far as the eye can see. Now I know I'm well and truly almost home, and my eyes fill with tears. I saw the wall many times in my childhood, but as I look at it now, it still amazes me that there was ever a time when people had the time and energy to construct such a thing.

The wall was built to keep the Picts from what was then Roman land, but now I fear it will keep us too from crossing over. The Romans cleared the forest away to prevent surprise attacks on the wall, and the trees have never grown back, so we walk on open land as we approach the line of stones. For the first time in several days, I feel exposed, as though rotting eyes might glimpse us here.

When a hawk screeches high above my head, I jump. For a moment, I thought it was the eerie call of the undead.

"There!" Mother Sima calls and points ahead to a low point where the wall has crumbled to shoulder height. Several taller stones are still in place here and there, dark against the sky, but there's room enough for us to crawl between them. A faint path leads there; no doubt wayfarers have used this crossing point for years. We head toward it, walking quickly. Some urgency seems to grip us all, and as we draw nearer the crossing point, we begin to run.

A murder of crows rises in front of us from the wall, then falls back, bickering among themselves. We're close enough now to see why the birds gather here. What I thought were stones still standing along the broken wall are actually three bodies spread out atop the wall. We will have to climb over them to get across.

We scramble up the stones—even in the midst of my sick horror, I'm surprised by how nimble Mother Sima is—and then we are atop the wall, a level space wide enough that four men could stand abreast to defend it, edged by crumbling waist-high ramparts. We pause before we step across the bodies, and I see Mother Sima murmuring a prayer. I swallow back the sour liquid that rises in my throat as I look down at the bodies.

Two of them are men, wide shouldered and muscular, dressed in leather-and-chain armor. One still holds a shield, splintered, and the other holds tightly, even in death, to the hilt of a broken sword. Between them lies a young girl, her long red hair a tangle around her freckled face, a wooden spike clutched in her hand. My sister would be about the same age now, I think as I stare down at her, but after a moment, I cannot bear to look at her anymore. The side of her face, the entire side of her body, has been gnawed away.

How could there be a God, any god, who would let a child die like this?

"They died nobly," Freya says softly. "They deserve a funeral pyre, a torch to send them to the Mead Hall of the Gods."

Mother Sima frowns and glances over her shoulder. "We're vulnerable here," she murmurs. "We need to get off the wall."

I go down on one knee beside the red-haired girl and touch her hand. I cannot leave her like this, with her remaining eye dull and open to the crows' greedy bills.

And then, as I kneel so close to her, that single eye shifts toward me. "She's alive!" I gasp, but I know she can't be, not with half her head gone. Before I can make sense of what's happening, the girl pushes herself upright. She pulls her half-eaten lips back from her teeth and shrieks, then lifts her wooden blade and slashes at my neck.

I have just time to fall backward and pull out a yew stick. She swings again, and I block her stroke with my stick, then kick up at her with both my feet. She falls— and then jumps up again, faster than any mortal could.

Mother Sima's shepherd's crook catches the girl's weapon and pulls it from her hands. As she stoops to grab it, I lift my yew blade to stab her.

But staring up at her, I can't complete the thrust of my arm. She's a neamh mairbh, she's trying to kill me—but she still reminds me of my sister.

As I hesitate, the girl grabs her sword and swings it downward toward my face. At the same moment, a huge pair of armor-covered arms grabs me from behind and whips me around. One of the warriors who a moment ago lay dead at our feet now holds me by the neck—and then he lets out a howl and drops me as though I've burned his fingers. I drop over the side of the wall, feet first into a hazel bush.

I'm scratched but otherwise unharmed. As I untangle myself from the branches, I hear *phwit! phwit!* above my head. Freya has loosed two arrows, and as I watch, the red-haired girl flies backward, while the armored man falls over the side of the wall and lands with a thump beside me in the bush.

I push myself away from his rotting flesh and scramble back up the wall. As I reach the top, I see the other dead warrior stir, his hand reaching for his weapon. "Watch out!" calls Mother Sima. Freya whirls around, then drives a third arrow straight downward, between the warrior's metal chainwork, into his chest. He slumps back onto the wall, dead once more.

Freya and I stare at one another, panting. "We should cut off their heads," Freya says. "To be sure—"

The thought of severing the girl's red head from her body makes my stomach jolt, but I know Freya's right. But Mother Sima shakes her head. "No," she says. "There's another way. But we must be fast. We're exposed here." She shoves her crook into the warrior's armpit, hooks him on it, and then drags him to the edge of the wall. With a powerful twist of her arms, she lifts him up, then pulls her crook free and lets him drop. She gives me a grim smile and says, "Don't stare at me, boy. It's not so different from tatting—only I use a bigger hook to pull bodies instead of yarn."

Freya picks up the girl's feet and drags her, then gives her a shove over the side of the wall. We scramble down after the bodies. "Cover them with dirt and branches," Mother Sima commands. "Whatever you can find."

Freya and I hurry to obey her, and when we're done, the bodies buried beneath mounds of stones and dirt and hazel branches, Mother Sima reaches into her pouch and pulls out three green stones, then wipes the dirt away from each dead face. One by one, she pries open their jaws and places a stone within each mouth, then shrouds their faces with dirt and branches once again.

"What's that?" Freya asks. "What did you put in their mouths?"

"Stones from the Isle of Iona," Mother Sima says, "from the beach where Blessed Colmcille first set foot on the island. He prayed that whoever carries one of these green stones from that shore would be blessed."

I'm not convinced. "You really think that will keep them from rising again?"

"Oh, yes." Her face is as calm now as though she'd just risen from a prayer instead of battling against the ghouls. "The blessing of the saint will release their souls to the next life—and prevent any evil from claiming their flesh again."

"Will the All-Father welcome them to the Mead Hall of the Gods?" Freya's voice is smaller than the one I'm used to hearing.

"The Creator Father loves all that He has made," Mother Sima replies.

Freya cocks her head to one side and frowns. "Are we talking about the same Father?"

I shake my head and start toward the woods that lie north of the wall. I'm not interested in their discussion. But I can't help wondering, just a little, about the neamh mairbh. Are they still human? Do souls still linger in their rotting flesh, or have their souls gone somewhere else—to Heaven or the Mead Hall of the Gods or some other realm—while another dark spirit controls their bodies? Is even God—or the gods—confused by the undead?

There's no point wondering about things that have no answers. I hear Mother Sima's voice behind me, no doubt telling Freya all the answers she thinks she knows, but I plod forward, across the open land to the forest that lies ahead.

I cross a stretch of land where the first bright blossoms gleam yellow against the brown gorse, and I push my way through the spiky bushes toward an open place ahead. When I reach it, I stop a moment to rub the new scratches on my legs and arms, and then I look back, one last time, at the great stone serpent that crawls over hill and valley in both directions, as far as the eye can see.

"Why did you go *that* way?" Freya asks me.

She and Mother Sima have followed a sheep path through the gorse, and so of course they arrive beside me unscathed. I scowl, and she tries to smother a giggle.

"I was merely taking the shortest route to the roadway," I say with great dignity.

The land here is wide and open, and there's little we can do to hide ourselves until we reach the forest. I'm grateful when we enter the shadows cast by Pictish pines.

The air is colder now. I am gladdened by it, for it's another reminder of home. The woods have fewer lichens and ferns than there were to the south, and I know it won't be many more days until we reach Glas Cu. Soon after that, heading toward the direction where the sun sinks behind the trees each night, we'll reach the path that will lead us into my homeland of Dalriada.

Day after day, the sky is blue and the sun warm on our heads. Getting this many clear days in a row is almost as odd as the plague of the neamh mairbh. It's hard to even believe that the undead exist when the world seems like a place of sunlight and birdsong. When we see a herd of shaggy, long-horned cattle, though, there's not a sign of their owners, only an empty hut around the next curve in the path, and we realize that the undead have passed this way before us.

At last, we leave the forestland behind us and walk between cultivated fields that lie untended. Ahead, stands an immense and stately stone-walled town. We have arrived at Glas Cu.

When Kentigern—a great champion of Iosa—arrived in this wild region only decades ago, the Picts, those fierce tattooed people, embraced Kentigern's stories of Iosa. Soon homes sprang up around his religious settlement. Tradesmen build their shacks around the houses, and then stone walls were built to defend it all. I've been here many times before, on trading trips with Da, but I still feel a thrill of wonder now, looking at the town. So many houses all in one place!

Mother Sima has bits of jewelry she plans to barter for fresh supplies, so we proceed on toward the fortified town. As we draw nearer to the walls, I see the river Clyde rushing in a great stream along its stony course, with the drawbridge lowered across it. The ramparts stand three times the height of a man, massive piles of stones with walkways on top of each. Men in leather jerkins pace atop the defenses, bearing long sharp spears. Now we're closer yet, and I can see the blue tattoos on their cheeks and their flowing capes of bright plaid. Beyond the wall, I see the peak of the little wooden tower that tops the stone church of Saint Kentigern. The copper circle-cross rises taller than any other point of the settlement.

We join a small band of raggedy people on their way to the drawbridge. It's been so long since we were in human company that I feel odd. I am no longer a slave, and I can look at these folk as a free man with my head held high—but at the same time, I am no longer the boy I was when I was last at Glas Cu. I have a strange sense that I'm neither one thing nor another, an invisible person.

They are a motley bunch of women and children, clad in drab colors with their hair unkempt, led by a clump of monks in tattered brown robes. The Pictish tongue is much like the Gaelic spoken among my own people of Dalriada, but all the words are slightly different and funny sounding, so as I listen, I have to strain to catch the meanings. One of the monks croaks out words I recognize from the scriptures that Priest David read to us: "And I looked, and behold a pale horse: and his name that sat on him was Death, and Hades followed with him." The monk's voice is heavy with foreboding, and a chill runs up my spine.

A woman calls in response, "It is the end! Doom and Hades are unleashed. Repent! Doom is upon us!"

The crowd lets out a long, loud sound, as though it is a single dreary beast with a single groaning throat.

"Who are these people?" Freya mutters softly.

"They consider themselves followers of Iosa," Mother Sima answers, just as softly.

I can't help but be startled. The followers of Iosa that I knew as a child sounded nothing like these wretched souls. Priest David spoke only words of comfort and hope, not weal and woe. I sense the fear rippling through the crowd, growing greater with each word they speak, and soon they are jogging ahead of us like a herd of frightened cows.

We follow more slowly, across the enormous drawbridge—great rough-hewn logs held together by immense rusty bands—and through the town gates. The scent of the wet wind rising off the water brings back memories of visiting this place with my da. I almost expect to look up ahead and see him standing there, waiting for me.

He's not, of course, but as we walk into the town, we find it's packed to the gills with plenty of other folk. Every Pict for miles around has retreated to the fortified town. After days of quiet and few words, we're surrounded now by the babble of voices—children playing, old women gossiping, babies crying, young men and women flirting with each other. Not all are Picts; I hear my native Scoti spoken in snatches here and there, and even one or two words of Englisc. The whole of northern Angleland, all that survives, has been driven up across the wall and into this refuge.

For a minute I can only stand and gape at this throng of humanity: farmers in their rough wool garments that are hardly more than sacks covering their chests and loins; nobles decked out in brightly dyed plaids or imported fabrics of brilliant red, blue, or—rarest and most valuable—the royal Roman purple; members of the religious orders that follow Iosa, men in ankle-length wool robes dyed brown or green or left their natural grey shades, and women with only their hands and faces showing like Mother Sima. I see only a few Druids, the holy and learned men and women of my parents' old religion. Dressed in white with plaited circlets of oak in their hair and blue spirals tattooed on their cheeks, they move among the crowds with quiet gravity.

Mother Sima nudges me. "Don't stand and gawk, Finn. We've business to do here."

We proceed down a walkway of wooden slats set in the ground, a refinement that keeps down the dust and dirt. Sheaves of fresh straw are scattered across the walk and between the vendors' stalls. After the squalor of the Angle village and the horrors of a countryside blighted by the neamh mairbh, civilization like this is wondrous.

We find a mead brewer, his stall stacked with casks. He's a portly fellow with a round red face, and he smells deliciously of his wares. He has a face that's meant for smiling, but he's frowning now, his face tight and stern.

"Good day," Mother Sima greets him in Gaelic.

"What's good?" the man replies. "There's horror and death throughout the land. It may well be the apocalypse."

"You think so?" she asks.

He nods, and his frown deepens.

Mother Sima shrugs, as though the apocalypse is a trifling thing in her mind, and then she reaches into a pocket and pulls out a small brooch shaped like a broken circle and made of shining brass. The brewer examines it, then puts it in his own pocket and fills our horns with his sweet yellow fare.

We move next to a fishmonger, where we trade another bit of jewelry for dried fish. This man has a long face that looks as though it hasn't smiled in a decade, but his voice is jovial as he offers us the news, dreary though it is.

The surrounding villages have been abandoned and torched by the residents themselves, he tells us, in the hopes that the walking dead will go elsewhere if they see no humans. "Who knows what those creatures are," the man says, "but one thing I know—those blighters can't go long without people to eat. They must be starving and mad with blood fury by now. They'll be massing for attack." He nods his head, as though his prediction gives him a gloomy satisfaction.

"Will Glas Cu be able to hold them off?" Mother Sima asks.

The man shrugs. "The watchmen are constantly on guard, ready to raise the bridge and seal the town. We have months of supplies stored in case of a siege, and our warriors have an arsenal of weapons hafted with yew wood. But my faith lies elsewhere."

Mother Sima raises her eyebrows. "And where might that be?"

"Abbot Kentigern himself has committed to fast before the altar of our church until the plague is passed," the fishmonger tells us. "He will not eat until the undead are vanquished. He says that holy men have had visions of a rescuer—an unknown champion who will bring an end to this curse." I hear the note of confidence in his voice; this man's not afraid because he's totally convinced that Kentigern knows what he's talking about.

Freya pinches my arm. "What's he saying?" she hisses in my ear.

I forgot she doesn't know any Gaelic, so I translate quickly.

"A champion?" she says. "I wonder who *that* might be?" She stares at me pointedly, making her message clear, but I give her a scowl and turn away.

"It's good that you are here now," the fishmonger is saying to Mother Sima. "But be prepared to wait months—or years—for deliverance."

"I'm not staying in Glas Cu," I tell the man. "I've been a slave to the Saxons for four years, and now I'm going home."

He shakes his head. "If that's your plan, lad, your brains are addled. The only safe place now is behind these walls." He turns to Mother Sima. "At least you and the young lady will be staying."

But Mother Sima shakes her head. "We have an urgent reason to continue on our way."

"Well I wish you luck, Sister. And you, lad." He gives me a nod. "You and your wee lassie are a fine-looking couple of lovebirds. Awful sad to see you become supper for the flesh eaters."

I give him a glare, not because he thinks we'll end up eaten by the undead but because of what he said about Freya and me. *Why* do people keeping making that mistake? Can't they see we hate each other?

I'm so annoyed that I consider telling him I wouldn't put my bets on great-and-holy Kentigern saving them. As far as I'm concerned, the people inside these walls are all fish in a barrel, waiting for the reeking monsters to pull them out. But I bite back the words. If he's stupid enough to wager his life on a miracle, I hope he'll at least die happy in his delusions.

Mother Sima says a blessing on the man and his stall, and then we say goodbye.

"Where are we going now?" Freya asks. "Can we see more of the town?"

I don't blame Freya for wanting to linger here, but I know what Mother's answer will be.

"No, Freya, we must be on our way. I haven't much left to barter—aside from my sigil," she touches the silver cross and swords she wears on her breast, "and I'll not part with that. I have a few Roman coins, but who knows when we might need them? Anything we might wish for here—a cooked meal at an inn, a wash, or clean clothes—will cost more than I have. And we don't know how far away the monsters are." Mother Sima turns her face back toward the town gate. "We need to reach DunCollum before nightfall—and get Finn to his kinfolk."

As we leave the market, I savor the odors of fatty meat broiled on skewers, smoked fish from the river, and piles of oily fleece bundled together for carding into wool. The scent of perfume from a few stalls mingle with all the other smells, reminding me what human habitation is like in more ordinary times.

I can tell how reluctant we all are to leave by how slowly we're walking. I pause to look again at all the faces; old men with their gravity, children playing without thought of the looming threat, and all the young women with their lovely round curves under their dresses. I glance at Freya and catch her glaring at me.

What's your problem now, Snake-Heart?

Mother Sima prods me with her elbow. "You'll make more progress, lad, if you just put one foot in front of another—instead of standing there gawping."

I nod, and we leave behind the marketplace fragrances. As we make our way through the gate that guards the town's entrance, we're the only people going out; everyone else is hurrying to get in. I catch a couple of the broad-chested warriors watching us and then exchanging glances. None of them speak, but I know what they're thinking: *What are these barmy people doing leaving the safety of Glas Cu? Are they mad?*

Walking back across the bridge over the Clyde, I breathe again the smell of fresh water, and I look down at the bright ripples below me. The river is like a great living thing, and it comforts me somehow to know that this is one life the walking dead cannot take. Seagulls and other water birds wheel above the water, dipping and diving for fish.

Any sense of comfort I have disappears then, for it strikes me that soon we will be like fish swimming through dark waters, while the ravenous dead may swoop down and eat us at any moment.

When we reach the end of the bridge, the roads part: one way is the path we took to get here, and the other heads toward the westward sun—and my home. Without saying a word, we all three turn at the same moment to look back at Glas Cu, its tall walls standing proud and sturdy beyond the river, the ramparts bristling with bright banners and shiny helmets. Mother Sima—no doubt glimpsing the cross on the far-away church-top—makes the cross sign with her fingers over her heart. And then, we turn back toward the path ahead of us.

Mother Sima sets a brisk pace for us. Nightfall will be late, for the Solstice is drawing near, but the rumors that the undead are nearby have made her nervous. They've made me nervous too, truth be told, and I press forward willingly, eager to be out of the wild where we are more vulnerable to attack.

And I am even more eager to be home. As I walk, my stomach flutters, and my breath comes fast with both excitement and nervousness. The moment I have imagined for so many years is almost here.

The road soon narrows, becoming muddier and rougher, and then plunges into a thick forest. The tree canopy forms a dark tunnel ahead, and the shadows there make me uneasy. Without saying a work, Mother Sima motions us to walk single file—first her, then Freya, then me—just inside the trees, rather than on the road. I understand—if there are undead ahead or behind, they are less likely to see us before we can see them if we're sheltered by the trees—but it's hard not to trip over vines and roots. Nettles sting my ankles and calves, and clouds of midges hover around us. They seem to ignore Freya and Mother Sima, preferring the taste of my blood, and soon I'm scratching and slapping at them.

"Shh!" Freya hisses at me over her shoulder.

Night will not come until late today, but the sun has gone missing as it so often does near my home. A cold drizzle seeps down through the leaves onto our heads and shoulders, and wisps of fog trail between the trees. The shadows become even deeper and darker, until I can no longer distinguish oak from elm or ash from alder. Briars and twisty vines catch at my feet, and walking silently is impossible, at least for me; Freya seems to slip through the trees like some forest sprite, and even Mother Sima's larger girth glides like a ghost through the shadows. I follow them with a glum determination, but the dark forest has sucked all the excitement out of me. Instead, a heavy sense of foreboding is growing inside my chest.

In front of me, Freya stops so abruptly that I bump into her. For once, though, she doesn't snap at me for being clumsy. Instead, she whispers in my ear, "Listen!"

Now that I'm no longer snapping and crackling through the undergrowth, the forest is silent. "I don't hear anything."

"Exactly," Freya hisses.

I suck in a breath, realizing what she means: there's not a birdcall to be heard, no swift crackle of leaves as a squirrel runs past, and not a snort from a deer in the underbrush. The only sound is my own breath and the dismal *drip-drip-drip* of the rain falling from the leaves.

"Is it because we've scared them away—or is it the rain?"

I shake my head. "The rooks and crows wouldn't be bothered by either. They should still be making some sort of noise, bloody birds can hardly keep still for—"

"Ssh!" Mother Sima says over her shoulder and holds out a hand, signaling us to remain still.

And then I do hear something: a shrill voice and the sound of something snapping, like a branch breaking. Except that I'm terribly afraid that it's not wood I hear breaking but bone.

Mother Sima motions to us and we creep forward, easing from step to step so that even I manage to be silent. There's a huge stump ahead, an oak by the looks of it, and when we reach it, we huddle behind its enormous trunk, peering around it through the sliding scraps of fog.

I hear Freya suck in her breath sharply, and then she puts her hand over her mouth to muffle her gasp. She moves aside, so I can stand where she was, and now I see that three of the risen dead are crouched on their haunches in a small clearing just beyond our hiding place. Two are females, with rotting flesh that still looks sturdy enough, and the third is a bony, naked man with a long ragged beard. The bumps of his spine show black and bloody through the gray skin of his scrawny back. All three are eating something.

I can't tell if it's a boy or a girl, but it's a child. To them, it's just meat. They're eating like I might if I were sitting down to a feast after a long day's work—shoving pieces of flesh into their mouths, snapping bones and sucking out the marrow, their teeth making a horrible clacking noise as they chew.

I'm shaking all over, but it's not fear; it's rage. These monstrosities shouldn't exist. They have no *right* to exist. Before I even know what I'm doing, I burst out from behind the stump and dash toward the reeking things, screaming at the top of my lungs, "Ya bastards! Ya damn stinking corpses, go back to Hel where you came from!"

I've managed to take them by surprise, at least. I land with my yew stuck straight through the back of the skinny male before they've barely had a chance to look up from their dreadful meal. The thing falls flat underneath me, only an empty sack of bones, but now the two big females are lunging at me.

It's their unlucky day, because I'm suddenly filled with the fierce certainty that I am Finn the Chosen One, the killer of undead blighters, and I know what's coming next. The first one, stinking to high heaven, grabs my bare arms, then immediately throws back her head and howls, as though I've burned her. As she stumbles away from me, I pull my yew free, then stretch forward and shove it between her ribs. She shudders and falls on the ground, nothing but a heap of quavering, putrid flesh. I spin around, ready to meet the last of them as she comes at me with an axe. I duck, then slip on the bloody leaves beneath my feet and only barely manage to roll away before the second swing of the axe smashes into the ground beside me.

I leap to my feet and fly at the vile thing that's all that's left of what was once a woman. I have my stick pointed straight at her heart, but she's ready for me and kicks the weapon out of my hand. With one small, distant piece of my mind, I notice that her feet are long bundles of bones adorned with black and green toenails—and then one of those feet lands in my midsection and sends me sprawling. Winded, I gasp for air. The axe is about to descend again, I know, but my arms and legs have suddenly turned useless. I stare up at the thing and watch as she raises the axe high—and then *thwock!* Freya's arrow is lodged in the ghoul's chest. The half-rotted woman crashes onto the wet ground, like a side of old beef cut down from a hook.

Freya and I look at each other, breathing hard. Her eyes are bright, and we lift our fists into the air in unison. "Not a bad piece of work that! Did you—"

But before I can finish my question, a chorus of terrible shrieks rips through the silent forest—and a crowd of walking dead burst out of the trees in a great flood, the way ants do when you disturb their hill.

Shite!

Mother Sima lifts her crook in the air and her voice rises louder than the noise from all those dead throats. A column of something that might be fire cleaves the air in front of her, like a spectral flaming sword, casting spangles of light through the dark trees. The undead fall back, their bony hands covering their eyes.

Meanwhile, Freya nocks an arrow and shoots. An ugly tall blighter clutches at its chest, then falls facedown into the layers of dead leaves.

The axe that almost removed my head lies on the grass beside me, and I snatch it up, swinging wildly at the nearest dead thing. I have only a moment to notice that he used to be a young man about my own age, that strands of red hair the same color as mine cling to his rotting scalp, and then the axe has caught his throat and—*by Woden's grotty bollocks, I cut his head off!* The dead thing totters, spins slowly in a circle, and falls. Almost immediately, though, it's up on its knees, scrambling around as it tries to reclaim its missing head.

I don't have time to watch, because another neamh mairbh, this one a huge fat male with an iron-headed pitchfork, is coming at me. I swing my axe again, but it parries, then grabs the blade of the axe with its bare bony hand and pulls it from my grasp.

Gods rot it! The saggy putrid thing thrusts his three-pronged tool at me. I try to leap away, but two prongs catch my tunic and pin me to a tree trunk. I pull at the fabric, trying to rip free, but I'm pinned there like a slab of meat on a skewer.

I kick and twist, while the big corpse just stares at me, its rotting eyes empty of anything human. Then it throws back its skull and lets out a sound like stones rattling down a hill, and if I didn't know better, I could swear he's laughing at me. He grabs a rusty knife from the belt that sags around his rotting rolls of flesh and takes a step closer to me. It occurs to me that maybe he was a butcher when he was alive, and now he's planning to slice off the choicest cuts from my trembling body.

I look past him, searching for Freya amid the writhing mass of gray-fleshed bodies.

No! She's on the ground, two of the fiends crouched over her, and one of them has its hands around her neck.

Mother Sima is pushing through the bodies toward Freya and me, but she no longer has the miraculous sword-in-the-air. She whacks at an armor-covered corpse with her staff and it falls, but another of the undead shoves her from behind. Her head disappears from view, and the creatures swarm over her.

I feel suddenly very cold and very calm. Death is coming for all of us, and there is nothing we can do.

7

DESOLATION

"Yee-la-la-ahh!"

That's not the sound of neamh mairbh; that's a human warrior's battle yell.

Pinned to the tree, I twist my head, trying to see where the sound's coming from. Fortunately, the big ghoul coming at me with the knife has turned to look as well, or I'd be skewered by now.

A tall man bursts out of the trees. He's moving so furiously I can't get a good sense of him, only a blur of huge muscles and two swords that flash in silvery arcs, slicing into the walking dead like sickles taking down wheat. A rotting hand flies past me, followed a moment later by a severed head. This warrior moves nearly as fast as the creatures do.

I suck in a huge breath of relief as I watch him mow down the monsters attacking Freya. She scrambles to her feet almost immediately, her bow ready, and lets fly another arrow. Meanwhile, the undead crawling over Mother Sima have turned toward the newcomer, as does the big fellow who was about to run me through with his knife. With only a moment's hesitation, the corpses leap toward the warrior, moving in unison as though they heard some signal. I see a whirling flash of metal, and then there are only bit and pieces of the creatures lying everywhere. Arms and legs twitch, skulls jiggle, rib cages bump up and down, but they're in too many pieces to put themselves back together.

Our rescuer lets his arms drop, his two blades dripping with black blood. Freya is still staring at the mass of rotting body parts on the ground, her eyes narrowed, an arrow nocked in her bow, and I know she's not convinced the mass of creatures won't manage to rise up and attack us again. Mother Sima has pushed herself up on her elbow, and now she's rearranging her robe into more ladylike folds. I'm still pinned to the tree. Judging by the attention being paid to me, I must have gone invisible.

"In the name of the Threefold God," Mother Sima says in a breathless voice, "I thank you most heartily, sir." She pats her wimple back in place around her face and then smiles up at the man. "And to whom do we owe our gratitude for this well-fought rescue?"

As the man turns toward Mother Sima, I get my first good look at him. I guess he's seen around thirty summers—and he's several inches taller than the tallest man I have seen, a huge looming shape, with a crest of spiky hair that gives him even more height. The spears of hair are white against the shadows, probably molded with a mix of lime and lard. Dark blue patterns swirl around his arms' thick muscles. This man could be the great and terrible Finn MacCool himself.

"I am Nectan MacBrud, from Inver Ness, in the highlands." He speaks in Englisc with a Pictish accent. "It's a bright ray of luck on a wet day that I happened along this path just now, or I might not have the pleasure of this meeting. And who might you three be?" He has one of the longest noses I've ever seen, a chin like a chunk of rock, and dark hooded eyes that remind me of a falcon's. As he looks at Mother Sima, however, he smiles, and his face softens.

Freya leaps across the rotting arms and legs at her feet, practically kicking them away in her rush to get to the man. "I am Freya Aedgar's Datar, from Escomb in Northumbria." She looks a mess with sweat and rain running in lines down her mud-covered cheeks, her hair stringy with mud. I can't help but notice, though, that the rain also makes the fabric cling to the round breasts she's doing her best to thrust forward as far as possible, in case they might escape the man's notice.

The stranger—Nectan—gives her a small bow. "A shield maiden of the Anglefolc, I see." If he's impressed by her curves, he shows no sign of it. "You make good use of your bow."

Freya smiles, and her chest swells forward even more. "Thank you, sir. My mother was a great warrior woman. I do my best to be like her." She's staring up at the man, smiling, like he's made her forget all about the terrible ordeal we just went through.

Is anyone ever going to get around to noticing me?

Apparently not. Mother Sima dips her knee to the man. "Sister Sima O'Donahue, from the Monastery of Saint Brigid in Cill Dara, across the water on Éire."

Nectan nods. "A priestess of the Nail-Riven God, come over from the Fair Green Island." His smile grows broader. "I am not of your religion, but I respect those who serve Iosa. They make good neighbor folk, judging from the few I have met before." He turns to face me. "And who is this lad hung up on a tree?"

At last. But by Thunor's arse, this is not the best way to meet someone, with me pinned here by a farmer's rusty tool. I'm only glad I didn't shit myself when I thought I was about to die. "Finn MacDugal," I say through clenched teeth, straining to pull free of the tines that hold me fast. "From DunCollum in Caledonia."

Nectan's brow furrows. "DunCollum . . . Has your village been spared from the neamh mairbh?" Before I can answer, he asks, "You are Scoti, are you not?"

"Mother Sima and I are both Scoti," I say with as much dignity as I can muster. "We respect you Picts as distant kindred. I was kidnapped from my home years ago, but I have now regained my freedom, and I'm returning there to rejoin my clan. Have you heard news from my home?"

Nectan shakes his head, still frowning a little. "Not of late, no. I wish you well." He stretches out an enormous hand and pulls the pitchfork from the tree. Finally, I can step away from the wet tree and square my shoulders like a man.

"Finn is my slave," Freya says primly. "He just pretends he's free."

"Pish yourself, Freya!"

Nectan chuckles. "I think you're a long way from Angleland," he says to Freya, "to be claiming ownership of anyone. To my eyes, the lad appears as free as a deer."

I give him a grateful grin. I'm waiting for Freya to come back with some arrogant argument, but she just smiles up at Nectan and shrugs a little.

Artair has survived the battle as well, and now he's barking and running in circles around Nectan's legs. "Who's this then?" Nectan asks

"That's our dog Artair," Freya replies.

"*My* dog." I turn to glare at her, but she has eyes only for the Pict.

He kneels and puts out his hand for Artair to sniff; Artair seems to likes what he smells, for he wags his tail and then sits on his haunches while Nectan scratches behind his ears.

"I used to have a wolfhound once," Nectan says. "I miss her. I should get another one." He stands and turns back to us. "And how did you three get into such an awful fix?"

Freya points an accusing finger. "This boy just charged into the midst of the draugar—he cannot control his base impulses—and attacked them. If not for you, we would all be dead."

For a moment, there's silence, only the sound of the drizzle dripping off the leaves. "Hel," I mutter finally, "there were only three of them at first, and they were eating a child."

"You almost got us all killed." Freya has a tried-but-patient tone to her voice that makes her sound as though she's talking to a child. "We could have been turned—into those." She gestures at the broken corpses.

"Hush," Mother Sima says softly. "We'd best quiet down—or we might draw the attention of more of these things." For a moment her shoulders slump, and her face looks wearier than I've ever seen it. "I for one have no strength to fight again today."

I feel a twinge of guilt, but then Freya catches my eye, and the guilt disappears, replaced by the usual anger I feel more times than not when I look at Freya.

Nectan nods, but his eyes are moving thoughtfully back and forth between Freya and me. He turns to Mother Sima. "Do they always get along this way?"

Mother Sima just rolls her eyes, and Nectan bites his lips, as though he's holding back a grin. His face immediately grows more serious, though, and he says, "It is foolish to attack the walking dead, for any reason." His voice is matter-of-fact, without a hint of scolding, and I'm grateful at least for that. "They lack human intelligence but they operate with some other strange direction that makes them capable of setting traps."

Great, I think to myself. *Now I'm going to have one more person telling me what to do. It was bad enough with Serpent-Heart and the old clucking hen—but now I've got a warrior to lord it over me too.* I sigh and pull my attention back to Nectan. I have to admit he's a likable fellow, despite his fierce appearance.

"What are you doing out in the woods like this?" he's asking. "I thought all the people of the Lowlands had gathered for refuge in Glas Cu."

"I'm going to my home, like I said."

"And I seek audience with Merlin, in his Nest," Mother Sima adds.

Nectan raises an eyebrow. "Lailoken? You are indeed brave to seek audience with him. I've seen the mage from afar but never spoken to him. This meeting I would like to see."

"What about yourself?" I ask Nectan. "What are you doing alone in these wight-haunted woods?"

Sadness ripples across the big warrior's face, then disappears, leaving his face once more as grim and rocky as a mountainside. "The neamh mairbh took the life of one precious to me. I know revenge brings no one back, but there must be a way to end this plague on the island. There must be a way to return all the walking dead to the dust where they belong. And so I travel, always searching for an end to the curse."

"Well spoken." Mother Sima's round face has regained its usual cheeriness. "We are alike in this. We would be pleased if you chose to accompany us—first to DunCollum with Finn, and then, after he rejoins his family, I travel on to Merlin's lair." She meets Nectan's eyes, and for a moment, her plump face looks as fierce as his. "I believe that Merlin may have a word that will show us how to end this evil."

"Very well." Nectan gives his head a nod. "I'd be pleased to walk with you."

I can see how happy this makes Freya. I can't really blame her. The man's as tall and strong as an oak—and he seems kind and intelligent besides. Hel, if I were a girl I'd probably be lusting after him too. And it's not like I expect—or even want—Freya to have soft feelings for me. She has a snake heart. She treats me like a slave. She thinks she's better than anyone else. So no matter how beautiful she is—

Pish! Enough of these thoughts.

"We'd best be on our way," Nectan cautions. "There may well be other walking dead nearby." He gestures us to follow him, and we fall into line. This time Nectan's at the head, followed next by Freya, and then by Mother Sima. I'm still at the end, just like I was last time.

As we make our way silently through the forest—I'm getting better at not tripping over roots and vines—I'm thinking more and more about how Freya and Mother

Sima just forgot about me after the battle. Maybe I was foolish to leap into the clearing like that, but I did lop the head off a neamh mairbh. No one seems to have noticed how brave I was.

"Isn't he marvelous?" I hear Freya whisper over her shoulder to Mother Sima.

I can't hear Mother's answer, but she probably agreed with Freya. And they're not talking about me, of course. *Yeah*, I'm thinking, *Nectan's marvelous if you like men who look like walking mountains.*

We walk for hours, but as the light grows dimmer beneath the trees, it's clear that the encounter with the undead has delayed us. There's no way we're going to reach my home before nightfall. Seeing the trail between the trees is harder and harder, and even Nectan goes slowly now, hesitantly, as he tries to keep us from wandering off the path into the woods.

"We need to make camp," he says finally.

"Can't we press on?" I'm disappointed that we won't be reaching my home tonight, though truth be told, the undead have pushed from my mind all thoughts of reunion with my family. I'm not too happy about camping down out here in the forest where the walking corpses may find us.

Nectan just gives a single shake of his head in reply to my question, so I guess that's that. Freya starts gathering firewood, but Nectan stops her with a hand on her elbow. "No fire. We do not want to attract attention."

His hand on her arm has apparently driven all intelligent thought from her head. She gives him a dreamy smile and puts her own hand over the spot where he touched her.

We settle on the ground, and Mother Sima passes out dried fish. As we chew the tough salty strands, we pass around a horn of mead. I take a gulp of the fiery liquid, grateful for its warmth.

I notice that Nectan is sniffing the air, looking thoughtful. "Do you smell something?" I ask.

He nods.

My heart jolts a bit in my chest. "Are they near? The undead?"

He glances at me. "The undead? No."

"Then what do you smell?"

"You," he says. "The three of you. You smell like people."

Even Freya looks startled by that, and the silly look on her face fades a little. "Um, what else would we smell like? Are you saying we need a bath?" She looks worried now and gives her own armpit a sniff, then makes a face. None of us have had a chance to wash in many days. We must all be pretty rank. "I'm sorry," Freya says in a small voice. "I—"

Nectan waves his hand, cutting off her words. "I care not about your odors. But the neamh mairbh have keen noses, like dogs or wolves. They will track you by your scent."

I look at Mother Sima. "That wasn't in your book."

"Oh dear," she says.

"It's a problem easily solved." Nectan pulls out a horn hung from a belt around his waist. "Here, rub this over your skin." He pulls out the stopper and hands the horn to me. "When you're well soaked in this stuff, the neamh mairbh won't find you unless they blunder right into you. Their noses are sharp, but their eyes not so much."

I take a sniff, and then I pull a face and hand the horn back to Nectan. "Hel no. I can't put that stuff on me."

Freya reaches for the horn. "What is it?" She's ready to bathe in the stuff, I can tell, just to prove how much stronger she is than me.

"Hog piss," Nectan says.

Freya was about to pour some in her hand, but now she hesitates and glances up. I give her a grin. "Go ahead, Freya. Pour it on you. You can't smell much worse than you do already."

Nectan's voice continues over mine, as though I haven't spoken. "Hog piss," he repeats with a nod of his head, a note of satisfaction in his voice, as though hog piss were some expensive perfume he's proud to wear. "Mixed with whortle-berry and snake extract. It blocks human scent completely."

Freya's lips press tight together, but she tips a generous portion into her hand, then hands it to Mother Sima. Mother anoints herself without so much as a grimace.

"And now you," Nectan says to me.

"I'd rather be dead."

"The neamh mairbh could arrange that," the big man says quietly, "if they come across you asleep. The worst part is, you wouldn't *stay* dead. Like as not, you'd come back as one of them. And you will have led them to the rest of us as well."

I heave a giant sigh and hold out my hand. "Give it to me then."

We pass the horn back and forth between us, making sure our skin, our clothes, and our hair are all well soaked. By the time we're done, we small as bad as the reeking corpses themselves.

After that, there's nothing else to do but bed down for the night.

"I'll keep watch," Nectan says in the deep, quiet voice that seems to be his usual tone.

"I'll keep you company." Freya hunches a little closer to the man.

I settle myself on the ground. Artair drops down beside me with a tiny groan and rests his head on my belly. Beside us, Mother Sima is on her knees, murmuring.

When it sounds like she might be done with her prayers at last, I whisper, "Mother Sima?"

She sinks back on her haunches beside me. "Yes, Finn?"

"What was that burning thing you conjured up? When we were fighting the neamh mairbh?"

She's silent for a moment, and then she asks in an odd voice, "You saw that?"

I snort. "I couldn't very well miss it. It was like you had a sword made of fire." When she doesn't say anything, I ask, "Is it some secret weapon you have? And why did you only use it at first? Does it get used up so you can't use it anymore?"

After a long moment, she says, "That wasn't a weapon you saw, Finn. Not mine at least. It was the flaming sword of an angel fighting beside me."

Well, I guess that makes about as much sense as a flame-sword she keeps hidden inside her robe. I remember now the flashes of light she cast at the neamh mairbh the very first time we met her, and I ask, "Does an angel always fight with you? And what happened at the end back there today? Where did he go? Why wasn't he there when you needed him most?"

She sighs. "I don't know the answers to your questions, Finn. I only know that the Hosts of Heaven are great in number but not infinite. Nor can they be in all places at once. When I ask for their help, I never know when Beings of Light will come to my aid—or when they will leave once they have come. They are not mine to command. "

She pulls her robe around her, then lies back on the ground beside me. "But Finn?"

"Mmm?" I'm starting to get sleepy. It's been a long day.

"Most people can't see angels."

What's that supposed to mean? I wait for her to say something more, but then she starts to snore softly, and I realize she's fallen asleep.

But I'm no longer sleepy. I lie on the ground, thinking about everything has happened. As the full moon rises into the dark sky, I remember the last time I looked up at the full moon: I'd been sleeping in my shed outside Aedgar's house, and when I got up to take a piss, the moon was full, casting silver light over the sleeping village, so that for just that moment, it looked like a beautiful dreaming place instead of the Hel-hole it really was.

And now, just one cycle of the moon later, here I am—and everything has changed. It's hard to fit it all together inside my mind.

I roll on my side, trying to find a spot of ground where no stones or sticks are poking my arse. I've dislodged Artair's head from its resting place on my stomach, and he gives a complaining whine before he resettles himself against my side. I wrap an arm around him, and then for a long time, I just lie there watching Freya and Nectan as they sit silent in the moonlight. The moonlight glints like silver on Freya's hair, and by its light I can see the dark tattooed spirals that circle Nectan's huge arms as they rest on his knees.

After a while, Freya slumps a little to one side and her head falls on Nectan's shoulder. She murmurs as though she's sound asleep and dreaming.

I bet she's faking.

The dawn light wakes me. The gray air is like a cold wet hand against my skin, and my tunic and breeches are damp. Nothing new there, of course. Overnight, my nose has apparently become accustomed to the foul smell we all wear now, and I'm grateful for small favors.

The others are already up, and Mother Sima passes around our morning ration of dried fish. No one has anything to say, and we fall in line again, trudging along the trail once more.

Soon, I see light up ahead, where the forest has grown thin. Our trail meets a cart path that leads through a corridor of elm and ash—and my heart leaps as high as the trees' branches. I know this road. *I'm almost home!*

With each familiar landmark we pass, my excitement builds. There's the lightning-split elm where I hid once when I was playing hide-and-seek with Micheal. And here's the stream where Da would come to pray to the Goddess. There are his clooties, faded scraps of cloth fluttering from the branches over the water. Even the sound of the stream is familiar, and I realize that no other water in the world makes this exact noise, because no other water flows over these exact stones.

Everywhere I turn, I see something I recognize, trees and stones, places where the earth is humped, all nearly as familiar as my mother's face. Rooks and crows caw in the trees above my head, a lark launches itself singing into the sky, and on a nearby branch, a robin cocks its head, its tiny bright eye fixed on me. Even the birds are welcoming me home.

All the years of slavery fall off my shoulders, and I'm *me* again, the Finn who grew up right here on this land. My feet move faster and faster, until I'm running. The others are panting behind me; even Nectan, that great ox of a man, can't keep up with me now. If I could, I'd be flying.

And there's the corral, where Da and I felled saplings and made a wicker fence. It's broken in places now. I don't see any pigs.

No matter. Soon I can ask Da where the pigs have gone, because now I have come around the last curve of the road and there ahead are the grassy ramparts of DunCollum.

The earthen circle is just as I remember, the steep ramparts the height of two men, crested with pointed stakes to form the stockade wall. I run up the slant that leads to the gate, shouting, "Hallo! Hallo! It's me, Finn! Call Dugal! Call Deirdre! Tell them Finn's home!"

Now I've crested the ramp, and I'm over the bridge and through the gate. Home lies there before me, right there! I tip back my head to shout again at the guards in the towers, so they'll sound the call to let the village know I'm home.

The towers are empty

But two sentries are always on guard—always.

I dash past the first round houses. Their thatch is ragged, as though no one has mended it in years. No voices come from the houses, no smoke from cooking fires.

There ahead of me is my home, its round stone wall
and pointed thatched roof just the same as when I left it.
But the hide is missing that covers the front door. There's
just a dark hole there.

"Ma! Da!" There's a quaver in my voice I don't want
to hear

No longer running, I walk toward the doorway, my
steps slow. At the threshold, I hesitate. I don't want to look.

But I have to.

What I see as I step inside makes a sharp wail come
out of my mouth, as though someone just hit me in the
stomach. Half the ceiling has collapsed, and the floor
is strewn with straw and rush. The table stands where I
remember, and my mother's big wooden loom, but everything else is gone.

No one lives here. No one has lived here for a very
long time.

I turn around and go back outside, staring blindly at
the other round huts. All empty and abandoned.

I'm home in DunCollum at last. And I'm all alone.

The others join me, and we all stand silently for a
moment. I'm choking back tears, and when Mother Sima
puts her hand on my arm, I jerk away, afraid that any sympathy will tip me over the edge. I don't want to sob like a
baby in front of Nectan and Freya.

"I'm sorry, Finn," Mother says quietly. "Seems your
family's whereabouts is a mystery. We have no way of
knowing where they went."

Freya goes inside the house, then comes back out with something in her hand. "What's this?"

It's a sealskin pouch. I untie the wrap that holds it shut and pull out a dirk sheathed in tooled leather. Slowly, biting my lips, I draw the dirk from its casing. The blade is fine and slender, the handle made from bog oak carved with intricate knots.

"My father's dirk." I look up at Freya. "Where did you find it?"

"On a little shelf in the wall. Beside the hearth."

"A fine weapon," Nectan says in that slow, deep voice of his. "Perhaps your father left it here for you to find."

I can't keep the tears from rolling down my cheeks anymore. Why would my father leave his dirk behind? I slide it back into its scabbard, and then into the bag. With fumbling fingers, I tie the bag to my belt.

"Let's look around the village," Mother says gently. "Maybe we can find clues that will tell us where they've gone."

We wander between the huts. There's not a human soul, not a pig or cow or horse, not even a cat anywhere to be seen. Priest David's cross still stands in the center of the village, its bright paint now faded. I run my fingers along the wood, and inside my head, I'm remembering the day the cross was put there, the sun, the voices, the busy village. The memory seems more real than the silent abandoned village.

"What do you think happened?" Freya's voice is more subdued than I've ever heard it. "Was it war, do you think? Or—" She hesitates. "Do you think it was the draugar?"

I don't have an answer, I don't *want* an answer. With the back of my hand, I wipe the tears out of my eyes and try to make sense of what I'm seeing.

Mother Sima is no longer with us, but after a few moments, her stout shape comes through the huts toward us. "Finn," she calls, "I think you should come here." There's an odd tone in her voice.

I follow her to the edge of the village, the far side from the gate. A row of stones stands there, each as high as my waist, each marked with glyphs.

"These weren't here when I was a child."

She nods, as though she's not surprised, and then she points to one of the stones. "Can you read Ogham?" Her voice is very quiet, very gentle.

I kneel beside the stone and run my fingers over the tall line of glyphs, sounding out the letters as I touch them.

And then I know.

"Deirdre NicFergus. Wife of Dugal. Mother of Finn, Fiona, and Brecken. She rests in God's peace."

I repeat the words, dully, as though they mean nothing. Mother Sima rests a hand on my shoulder. "I'm sorry, Finn."

I shrug her off. "Leave me alone!"

She backs away, and joins the others who have followed us here. I know they're watching me, but there's nothing I can say, nothing I can do.

I've fallen into something dark and deep and empty. I haven't hit the bottom; I'm still falling.

Maybe there is no bottom to this hole.

"Lad." Nectan's deep voice pulls me back just a little from the void. "If your father had met his death unexpectedly, his dirk would have been with him—and it would have been buried with him, like as not. He must have left his weapon there in the house where you would find it when you returned. As a sign to you that he is still in the land of the living."

"And your sister and brother may well be with him," Mother Sima adds.

But I don't know what to think. All these years since the raid when I was dragged from my home, I've comforted myself that my last sight was my family's faces. They were grand, all of them, my mother too. They weren't hurt or wounded. They were grand.

And then I scream. It's a noise I've never heard come from my throat before, a wail from deep down in my belly. I fall on the face in the dirt and pound my fists on the ground, and the scream goes on and on, until my throat feels torn.

Finally, the scream is done. I sit up and pull out Da's dirk, and then I stab it into the ground over and over, as though the earth were an enemy I could kill. "I hate you all," I say between my teeth, but I'm not talking to Mother Sima and the others. It's the Anglefolc I hate, the neamh mairbh, Iosa, life itself. I hate them all.

The others are silent behind me. Maybe they've all gone away. It's fine with me if they do. I pull the blade out of the ground one last time and stare at it. *I need to see it spill blood.*

Without a thought, I slash the inside of my forearm. The blood I crave trickles out from a jagged line, but I want more blood than that, and so I draw the dirk across my skin again, deeper this time.

"Oh no, Finn, no lad, no!" Mother Sima is pulling at my arm, holding me down.

I try to shake her off again, but this time she won't let go.

"Get away!" I sob. "Leave me be!"

Artair whimpers and presses against me, but I don't care. I want them all gone, even the dog. I want to be left alone so I can disappear into that deep, deep darkness that's calling to me.

And then Nectan plucks the dirk from my fingers. "Your father didn't leave you his blade to be cutting yourself with," he says calmly.

"Shove off!" I mutter.

"Boy!" Freya gasps. "Your blood. Look at it."

I glance down at the blood spilling off my elbow. "What about it?"

And then I blink. There's something strange about my blood. Maybe I've lost too much blood already, and it's making me see things.

"By Belenos!" Nectan says. "In all my days I have never seen such a sight."

Tiny points of light, vivid as fireflies, sparkle in the stream of blood that pours from my arm. They blink and wink like little stars, except they're a vivid green, more green and bright than anything I've ever seen before.

"I've bled before," I say slowly. "This never happened before."

"Finn." Mother Sima's voice is soft and full of awe. "That's the blood of the Sidhe. You've Faerie blood in your veins."

My head jerks up. "Who told you that?"

Her brow wrinkles. "No one told me, son, no person. It's your blood that tells me."

My head bows again. "My ma used to say that," I mumble. "But I never saw this before."

"It's a message," Mother Sima says. "A message your mother gave you long ago. Sometimes messages don't reach us until the one who sent them is gone. Sometimes they only reach us when we are ready to receive them."

I glance up at her, trying to make sense of what she's saying. Now that my rage is spent, I just feel empty and exhausted.

Freya grabs my arm and I hear her give an impatient sigh. "Are you just going to sit there and bleed to death, boy?" She rips a strip from her skirt and wraps it tight around my cuts, staunching the flow of blood. Nectan hands me back the dirk, and I see a glittering line along the blade edge, like a tiny trail of green flame.

But he's right: I shouldn't have used my father's blade in a way Da would never have wanted. Slowly, with fingers that feel thick and numb, I wipe the blade clean on my tunic.

Then I just sit there, staring stupidly at nothing. The space of a breath could go by or an entire day, and I wouldn't know the difference. I feel as though time has stopped forever, and I'm caught here in this slow, terrible place I can never leave. Is this what it feels like to be one of the neamh mairbh, as though the soul inside you has been pulled out like a rotten tooth, leaving only a numb empty spot behind?

The wind picks up, and the drizzle turns to a harder rain, pounding like tiny hammers on the abandoned village. I still don't move, even though the rain is drenching me. What does a little water matter?

What does anything matter?

I assume the others have gone, probably to seek shelter in one of the empty houses, but then Mother Sima lifts her voice over the rain's clatter and says, "I would like to say a few words. For Finn's mother."

She can talk to the stones and the rain for all I care. She'll get no answers.

I lift my head enough to look behind me and see that Nectan and Freya are still there too, waiting in the rain. Why don't they have the sense to go inside? They huddle closer to me, while Mother Sima steps forward and uses her shepherd's crook to make a cross sign in the air.

"Sweet Iosa," she says, her voice firm above the rain, "you too tasted death. And you broke free from death and rose above it. We ask you now to bless the soul of this good woman. Comfort her son and renew the light of life within him. Protect her husband and her other children, wherever they may be." She waves the crook again and says, "In the name of the Father, the Son, and the Holy Ghost." Finn and Freya make noises that must be the Saxon and Pict words for "amen." I don't know. *I don't care.*

Mother Sima's words are no magic spell that makes everything all better. They do absolutely nothing, but I didn't expect them to. Slumped there in the rain, I'm still caught in this nightmare that is real.

Finally, Mother Sima says, "Finn, my grief for you is sky wide and ocean deep. Any other time, I'd stand here beside you all night long, keeping you company in your grief, until at last you could see a little beyond it. But these aren't normal times. The revenants could be just outside the wall—and if they're not, they'll find us if we stay here much longer. We have to move on."

"So go then," I mutter. "Leave me."

Nectan crouches beside me then, and his huge hand closes around my shoulder. "Finn, I too have known love and loss. My soul's gone cold same as you are now. But laddie, you have to get up and move. If we stay here, the walking dead will find us and make their supper. I'm sorry we can't allow you a proper time to grieve—but I'm certain your mother would nae want you throwing your life away for no purpose." His fingers tighten, and against my will, he hauls me to my feet. "Come now, Finn, you must put one foot in front of the other. Sure there'll be plenty of time to grieve when we're in a safer place."

Mother Sima takes hold of my other arm, and together they drag me away from my mother's grave. I let them pull me along; I have no will or energy to fight them. I'm an empty thing, trudging along, moved only by their will. Artair trots at my side, whining, while Freya follows behind us. No one speaks.

Mother Sima and Nectan steer me through the gate. Without a backward glance, I leave my home behind. There's only gray and fog ahead.

We stumble through the gray and drizzle into the thick forest west of the village. One part of me recognizes dimly that this is the dark, enchanted Caledonian woods. The rest of me doesn't care. Mother Sima and Nectan finally let go of my arms, and I trudge on mindlessly. The wind whispers like a ghost between the trees.

"Where are we going?" Freya asks finally.

"We follow the path to Merlin's Nest," Nectan replies.

"What is it? Why do you call it a nest?"

"It's a mountaintop hiding place," Mother Sima says. "And since the man who lives there bears the name of a small, sharp-eyed bird of prey—a merlin—his citadel is called a nest."

Their conversation continues, but I'm no longer listening. Their voices sound faraway, more distant then my memories of my family's voices. They don't matter to me.

Nothing matters.

As we go deeper into the forest, the path narrows until we can no longer walk four abreast. Mother Sima walks beside Nectan, and I drop back beside Freya. I can feel her glancing at me now and then, but she says nothing.

It doesn't matter. Nothing matters.

There's nothing in my head except a bright fine-edged memory of a day when I was herding pigs with Da. "Don't let the fat fellow get away, Finn!" I hear my father say. "Grab him now!" I lunged forward, landing on the hog, grasping it with my arms and legs while it ran away with me on its back. Da laughed so hard he had to lean against the fence, tears running down his face. "I didn't say to ride him like a horse, son," he gasped when I finally managed to get off the pig's back.

Then another memory slides on top of that one, and I hear Ma's telling me about the Sidhe. Her voice is as plain and clear as if she were walking here beside.

But Freya interrupts her. "I'm sorry, boy. I lost my mother too." Her voice is soft, gentler than usual. "I know how it feels."

I swing around and face her. "Don't try to comfort me, Freya." My voice is so hard and rough I barely recognize it. "For all I know, your people were the ones who killed my mother and destroyed my village. And if not for you and your people, I would have been with my family when they needed me. I'd know where they are right now because I'd be with them. Your people kept me from them all these years. You stole all the extra days I could have had with my ma." I turn away. "Shove your sympathy up your arse, Freya."

Freya says nothing in reply, only steps more quickly so that she's ahead of me now. It doesn't matter.

Nothing matters.

We walk on and on. The sun must have set above the rain clouds, because now the gray light has turned black. Ahead of me, Mother Sima tries to light her oil lamp, but the wick is too wet. It doesn't matter.

"We'll make camp here," Nectan announces quietly. "By the side of the road."

I don't care. It doesn't matter to me whether I'm trudging nowhere or lying like a lump on the ground. Nothing matters.

As I lie with my head on one of Mother Sima's leather pouches, my arm throbs. The pain gradually clears my head a little, and my thoughts sharpen.

If Da and Fiona and Brecken are alive somewhere, then why am I stumbling through the woods with this group of dimwits? By Thunor's arse, staying with them is just a good way to get myself killed. I should be on my way, looking for my kin, not off on some wild-goose chase after a wild man. For all I know, my family was part of the crowd back in Glas Cu.

The drizzle has stopped at last, and a warm summer wind has blown away the clouds. The moon's silver white light shines down on me. I stare back at it. The moon looks just the same as it always has. My mother is dead, my entire reality has changed—and yet there's the moon, the same as always. I'm not sure whether the thought comforts me or angers me.

As I lie there, feeling gradually warmer than I have all day, I see a dark shape stand up silently beside me. It's Nectan, of course; no one else would look like a great black giant rising from the forest floor. With only the slightest clink of metal against metal, he straps his two swords on his back and then disappears into the trees, as noiseless as a great cat. I assume he's gone to take a piss—or maybe stand guard in the trees where he can watch the path.

But then another form beside me stirs and rises. This time, it's Freya, her pale hair silver in the moonlight. She stands with her back to me, staring after Nectan; she must have loosened her clothes for sleep, because her blouse has slipped off one shoulder, exposing a pale curve of skin. I lie there, watching her, and I realize that the throbbing in my arm has managed to move to other parts of my body.

I'm about to ask her what she's doing, when she steps quietly away, toward the forest where Nectan disappeared. After a moment, I hear her calling softly, "Nectan? Nectan?"

And now it's just me and the moon again. I screw my eyes shut, trying to shut out the light, trying to sleep, but instead, all I can see in my mind is Nectan's huge arms closing around Freya, her pale skin against his swirling tattoos . . .

By the great gnawing serpent! Enough! I jump up and cinch my belt tight around my waist. Why have I been trying to fall asleep here on the ground with this poxy bunch? I should be on my way, away from the three of them. I make sure Da's dirk, my yew stakes, and my pouch are all firmly attached to my belt, and then I put my hand on Artair's back.

"C'mon, boy," I whisper. "Time to go."

At the path, I hesitate. I want to go back the way we came, away from Merlin's Nest, but the shadows and the moonlight have me confused, and I'm not certain which direction is which. "Hel," I mutter, "I'll just go in the opposite direction from the one those two love birds took."

It seems like a good enough plan to me, and so I start walking, driven only by the need to escape. Gradually, the path seems to grow narrower, branches reaching out to grab me as I pass, tangles of bracken wrapping around my legs with each step.

Artair runs ahead of me, snuffling through the leaves, as if a moonlit walk was just the thing he'd been wanting. I'm glad he's with me. If I were here in the darkness, all by myself, the trees creaking around me, tiny rustlings on all sides . . . Well, I'm just glad Artair's here. His wagging tail and pricked ears tell me he scents no undead, so that's a good thing too.

I trudge along, my head down, trying not to think. I don't want to think about Ma. And I don't want to think about Freya either—or Nectan or even Mother Sima. *I'm done with them*, I tell myself. *I don't need them.*

It occurs to me finally that I should figure out where I'm going, and I lift my head to find my direction from the moon. As I tip my head back, though, my feet catch in a snarl of roots, and I fall, sprawled headlong on the ground.

Shite. The fall sends needles of pain through my arm, and I have to bite my lips to keep from screaming. I pull myself up and look around me, trying again to orient myself.

But now I can't even see the path. The moon filters through the trees, turning their branches black, catching only slender lines of light here and there on a fluttering leaf. I twirl around, trying to see an opening through the forest, but there's nothing, only dark leaves pressing close around me.

"Artair?" He was here just a moment ago, he can't have gone far. "Artair!" I call more loudly. "Artair?"

There's no answer, only the wind whispering as it slips through the trees, and then the distant call of an owl.

The path has to be close by, I tell myself. *I can't have wandered far from it.* I plunge into the trees, back the way I came.

Except I'm not certain it *is* the way I came. Maybe I came from *that* direction instead. I switch my course again, walking faster, hurrying to regain the path, nearly running now . . .

And then I come to a stop and stand there panting. My arm is aching, my heart feels as bloody and bruised as my arm, but slowly, through the pain, I realize something: I probably wandered off the path a while ago, and now it will be sheer luck if I can stumble across it again.

I'm lost.

"Talk about eejits," I say out loud. Here I am, all alone in the middle of the Forest of Caledonia, with a bunch of rotting corpses out there somewhere. "Oh Hel."

What I'm feeling isn't fear exactly. It's more like everything that has happened to me, going right back to the day when Saxon raiders stole me from my home, has risen up inside me like a huge club that's beating me over my head. I've lost my family. Ma is dead, gone forever, and I'm not likely to ever find Da and the others either. My entire village is gone. There's no one left to remember the Finn I used to be.

So what difference does it make whether I'm in the middle of the forest—or back with Freya and the others? Either way, I'm all alone.

Tears slide out of my eyes, and then I can't hold back my sobs. They shake me so hard I feel as though my bones might come apart. I'm all alone, and there's nowhere to go. If I could, I would sink down on the ground and simply die here. I'm tired of walking, tired of fighting, tired of trying. I want to lie down.

But there are nettles all around my ankles. If I'm going to die, I don't want to do it in a bed of nettles. I stumble forward, looking for a better place to stretch out on the ground, but I can barely see through my tears.

And then, suddenly the darkness falls back, and the moon's white light is everywhere. I've come out of the trees, and ahead lies a gently sloping hill that's empty of trees. Three enormous stone pillars stand on the hill, topped by a huge flat stone, like a table for giants.

I recognize this place! Ma and Da brought me here when I was very small. We laid flowers around the stones, and Da prayed out loud. Ma whispered to me that between the great stones was a gateway to the land of the Sidhe. I remember the way the goose bumps pricked my arms and neck when I stood here, how certain I was that I could take just one step and be gone into the Faerie realm. I almost took that step, but then I turned and buried my head in Ma's skirts. She laughed, her hand on my hair . . .

Ma.

"Why?" I scream. "Why?"

I stumble up the hill to the giant stones, then tumble into a shallow pit between them. Sacred portal be damned. If there's another realm beyond this one, what good will it do me? I'd be just as alone there as I am here.

"Why?" I yell again.

Why was I stolen from my home? Why did I end up a slave to people who despised me? Why does the one Angle I almost—maybe— Well, the Angle who's the most beautiful girl I've ever seen, why does she have to have a serpent heart? Why does she like Nectan better than me? Why is there a plague of reeking corpses spreading out across the earth?

Why did Ma have to die?

The stones have no answer for me. They just stand there, tall and silent in the moonlight.

All my unanswered whys have left me hollow and empty, but now fury pours into the emptiness. I look up at the stone that towers above me, and I slam my fist against it. Pain bursts open inside my hand, but I don't care. I batter my hand against the solid rock again and again, until blood trickles from my broken knuckles, but it's still not enough to stop the pain and fury inside my heart. I scream again, my voice caught between the stones, and then I ram my head against the rock. The blow makes stars and blood-red flowers explode across my vision. Shaking, blind, and dazed, I fall back on the ground.

After a few moments, I become aware that blood is trickling from a gash in my forehead. I shove my hand across my face, swiping the blood out of my eyes. And there it is again—that strange, brilliant green twinkle caught on my bloody fingers. When I rub my eyes, tiny emerald fireballs flare across my vision. They flash out of sight, only to be replaced by new points of exploding green light, constantly appearing and disappearing.

Beyond the fiery green stars, the night whirls around me. The blow to my head must be what makes me feel as though I've drunk far too many cups of mead. On my hands and knees, I crawl out from between the stones, thinking vaguely that if I can grab some grass, I can use it to wipe the blood out of my eyes, and then I might be able to see again. When I move, though, the pain is worse, like a hand clutching at my guts. I rock back and forth on my hands and knees, while tiny green constellations explode across the darkness, and I know I can't fight any longer. I surrender to an entire sky of emerald torches the size of fireflies, all flaring and disappearing in random bursts of light. The lights swirl, whirl, catch me up and carry me . . .

"Finn!"

The woman's voice is very near. I roll over on my back and squint, trying to see. The dazzling green has gone now, and there's only the pale white light of the moon and the stars washing down over the hillside.

"I must have words with you, Finn MacDugal."

Something about her voice makes my breath catch and my heart leap. I push myself up on my elbows, then twist my head around, trying to see who's talking to me.

There. It's a young woman, just a few feet from me, but she's not like any other woman I've ever seen in all my days. Light radiates from her in bright lines spreading out into the darkness—and yet her body looks as solid and real as anyone's. As I stare at her, the wind blows gently across my face, carrying her scent to me, a scent like the smell of green growing things and apple blossoms.

Still dizzy, I stagger to me feet and turn to face her. The moonlight shines on her hair, turning it to a red flame that falls around her shoulders down to her waist. The curls move slowly, gently, as though they have a life of their own. When she meets my eyes, I see that hers are the same brilliant green as the Faerie magic in my blood. I've never seen a woman as lovely as she is, not even Freya, but even though this woman is young, not that much older than me, I could never feel about her the way Freya makes me feel. Looking into her eyes, I'm filled with an exultant, singing joy—and at the same time, I'm absolutely terrified.

"Do you know who I am?" Her voice is like the chiming of a hundred small bells.

I open my mouth, but no sound comes out.

"Can't you speak to me, Finn? You used to talk to me, when you were a little boy. When you were afraid or sad—remember?"

I suck in a breath. "Brigid?"

Her smile turns into a grin, and now she looks like a mischievous young girl. "I'm glad you remember me after all. We haven't spoken in so long, I was starting to think you had forgotten me."

She looks at me, still smiling, as though she's waiting for me to say something, but all I can do is stand there, staring at her. She's driven all the other thoughts out of my head—all the fear and fury, even my grief—and now there's only her. In the middle of the night's darkness, in the midst of my sorrow and the terrible loneliness, there she is, as warm and bright as the fire that always burned on the hearth at home. I don't know what to think or do. All I know is, I'm no longer lost.

"You *are* the man who is chosen," she says, as though she's answering a question I wasn't even thinking, not now at least. "You are the one can who rid our fair isle of the walking dead. I sent you helpers . . ." Her smile fades and a frown puckers her forehead. "But you mock them and flee their company. Why, Finn?"

I try to gather my senses enough to make sense of her words. "I'm sorry," I whisper at last. "I didn't know. I didn't know that—that you were the one who had sent them."

Her smile is back now. "I do not fault you, Finn. Few young men could live through the hurts you have suffered without their hearts growing hard and cold. But now you must change. You cannot fulfill your destiny with a heart of stone. Your heart must come alive."

Then she holds out her hand to me. "Give me your talisman."

I stumble a few steps closer to her, fumbling around my neck for the cord I wear around my neck. I drag it over my head, and with the talisman dangling from it, I hold it out to Brigid. When our fingers touch, I feel as though the points of green light in my blood all leap at once, and I swear I feel them fizzing through my veins.

She puts the pendant to her lips and kisses it. As soon as her lips touch the stone, it turns a blazing orange-white, as if it were iron within a blacksmith's burning forge. Her hands drop away from her mouth, and she looks at me, her eyes wide and dark.

"This is going to hurt, Finn. I am sorry, but there is no other way. Many years ago I gave birth to a great love that renewed these lands. Now it must spread from me into your heart, or else the walking dead will cover all the kingdoms of Albion. Now—" In a sudden fluid motion, she leans forward and drops the chord around my neck again.

When the glowing talisman touches my skin, pain shoots through me in a blaze of agony. The pain grows greater and greater, expanding inside me with an immense pressure, until I don't think I can bear it any longer. And then—

Something inside my chest bursts. I hear it shatter with the sound a boulder makes when a strong man crushes it with a hammer. The noise is enormous, echoing through the night, so loud that I press my hands over my ears to shield them—but I can't, for the noise comes from inside me.

I fall face down into the wet grass. Lying there, sobbing, I hear Ma's voice singing one of her songs. When I was wee, she'd come to my bed at night to give me a tuck-in and a lullaby, and her soft voice would drive away the shadows. I smother my sobs so I can hear her voice, and then, as plain as anything, I hear her laughter, the clack-clack of her loom, her voice telling one of her silly jokes. I hear her dashing around the house, chasing and scolding after us three children.

How can the world still be here when Ma is gone?

How could she die without me even knowing?

And then something odd happens to the loss and grief I'm feeling. It seems to stretch wider and wider, until it's broad enough to hold a host of other images. I see a war being fought, men, women, and children cut down, their blood spilled across the earth. I see dark, bone-thin people starving, their eyes like dull hollows. I see angry fists raised between friends, and a woman stagger when her man strikes her across the face. I see children crying bitterly, their clothes ragged and torn; a fox struggling in a trap, gnawing at its own paw; a deer lunging away from a wolf, spilling blood across the snow.

And then a scream rips across all these images, a long wail of utter terror, followed by another and another, then more and more, thousands of shrieking voices. It's the horror the living feel, I somehow know, when the neamh mairbh bite into their flesh. Behind the screams, softer, duller, I sense something else as well, an ice-cold despair, as hard and heavy as frozen stone. The only life within that stone is hunger, endless gnawing hunger, and I realize this is all that's left of a human mind within the walking dead.

Thousands of voices rise up, weeping, screaming, sobbing, and then the terrible chorus is swallowed up by a towering dark wave that spills through me. I'm left weak and trembling in its wake, but it's still not over: another wave rises up and crashes, and then yet another. The tremendous sorrow of the world passes through me again and again, until there's nothing left of me—no thoughts, no sense of my own body, nothing.

Then, even in the midst of the waves of agony, the far smaller hurt in my head and arm pulls at me, bringing me back to myself. Slowly, I become aware of the wet grass against my face, the smell of earth in my nose. After a moment, I manage to push myself over on my back, and I stare up at the sky. The moon has sunk lower now, leaving the stars shining even brighter. They seem to swirl in the sky—or is it me that's whirling down here on the Earth?

I push myself up with my bruised hands, but I'm too dizzy to try to get to my feet. I can only sit there, shuddering, squinting at the twirling lights. One of them is lower than the rest, larger, a luminous column beside me.

"Brigid?" I whisper, but all I can see are blurred and overlapping forms—a tree branch outlined against the sky, hair as red as flame, the tall gray stones, golden lines of light—all jumbled together. I drop my forehead on my knees.

And then I feel a touch on my head. A soft blanket seems to settle over me, shutting out the dizzy lights, and it calms me, quiets me.

After a moment, I can lift my head again. Brigid stands above me, looking down.

"The pain," I whisper. "How can anyone bear it?"

Her face is sad, but she leans forward and kisses my forehead. Her hair spills around me, and I smell her sweet, green fragrance. Warmth spreads out from her touch, quiet and gentle, and yet at the same time bright and strong. I feel it flow through my body and into my heart. The pain is still there, but now I'm strong enough to bear it.

"Brigid," I say at last. "I need to ask you something."

She tips her head to one side, silently giving me permission to continue.

"What's happening to me?" I blurt. "My mother used to tell me I'm descended from your people, from the Sidhe. And now—my blood—" But I'm too tired to continue; my wits are too slow and thick to shape my question.

Darkness closes around me, and I can no longer see Brigid. I hear her voice, though, coming through the dark like a faraway bell.

"Finn, did your mother ever in her life deceive you?"

Another dark wave comes toward me now, but this one lifts me, carries me, and its water is warm. I drift on it, deeper into the soft darkness . . .

"Finn?" Someone shakes my shoulder. "Finn? Can you hear me?"

I open my eyes, blink, squint into bright sunshine. I put up a hand to block the glare. A hazy face bends over me, and long bright hair skims my face. "Brigid?"

"Brigid?" It's Freya's voice, and she gives a little snort. "If you've forgotten my name, you must have hit your head even harder than I thought."

Something cold and wet brushes my cheek, and then I hear a soft whimper. I grope with my hand until I touch Artair's rough coat. "Good boy," I whisper.

"You had me scared," Freya says. "I thought you were dead." Her voice has an odd tone I've never heard before.

I shut my eyes again and lie still, trying to think.

"What did you call me," I ask after a moment, "just now?"

"What I always call you. 'Boy.'"

"No." I shake my head "You called me by my name. You called me 'Finn.'"

She sniffs. "I did not. You were delirious."

I smile. "I like the sound of my name on your lips."

She gives her head a little toss, and the tip of her braid tickles my face. "Time to put your head back on your shoulders, boy. My name's not Brigid, and the only name I call you is 'boy.'" She turns and shouts over her shoulder, "Mother Sima! Nectan! Artair found Finn! He's here."

Her loud voice rings through my head, and I screw my eyes shut. "Do you have to be so loud, Freya? My head hurts already without you screeching like a banshee."

"Ungrateful wretch," she mutters, but at the same time, she touches my forehead with fingers so gentle I barely wince. "What happened? Who hit you?"

My face gets hot. I don't want to tell her that I pounded my own head against the stone.

The stone. The night comes back at me, but I can't tell which parts were real. With shaky, feeble arms, I push myself up and look around—and there are the ancient stones, the open hill. That much at least was real.

I turn to look at Freya, squinting to bring her into focus. "You look different."

She glances at me, gives a little shrug. "I don't know what nonsense you're talking now, boy. I'm no different than I was yesterday. It's you who's turned into a mass of blood and bruises. Your brain must be soft as jelly."

I don't argue. I just continue to look at her, and she does look different, almost like someone I've never seen before. Oh, her hair is still pale gold, and her curves are just as sweet beneath her gown—but when I look into her face, I can't see the serpent heart I thought was inside her. Instead, her blue eyes are deep and soft with pain.

Who is this girl? I've thought she was nothing but a tasty piece of flesh I longed to touch—and at the same time, she's been nothing but a stubborn stone set in my path to trip me up, a hurtful thing I would have tossed away if I could. I never noticed until now the circles that have formed beneath her eyes like purple bruises, or the way her lips curve with laughter, even now when she's annoyed.

"What is it?" she asks. "Do I have a blob of mud on my nose or something?"

"No."

"Well, then—" Her long lashes sweep down, then up, and there's a hint of color across her cheekbones. "Stop staring at me."

Before I can answer her, Mother Sima is crouching beside me, her robe spilling around me as she goes down on one knee. "Oh Finn," she sighs. "Whatever happened to you, lad?"

"I'm thinking he had a fight with a stone," says Nectan's deep voice. "By the looks of it, the stone won." He points to a smear of blood on one of the ancient columns.

Freya's eyes flick toward the mark my head left when I battered it against the rock, and I brace myself for her sarcastic remark—but when she turns back to me, her eyes are sad.

I shrug. "I was an eejit."

"Well, we all have been that a time or two." There's a smile in Nectan's voice, a gentle humor that eases my embarrassment.

"It makes no difference how he did it," Mother Sima says. "I need hazel leaves for his wounds. Can you find me some, Freya?"

Freya jumps to her feet.

"I'll go with you," Nectan offers. "Keep an eye out for any walking dead."

When the two of them have disappeared into the forest, Mother Sima says softly, "You look different, Finn. Not like I've seen you before."

I give her a shaky, rueful grin. "Well, you've never before seen me after I smashed my head against a rock."

Mother Sima pulls a rag from her pouch and soaks it in a little mead, then gently rubs it over the gash on my forehead. It stings at first, and then it soothes. "That's not what I mean." Her dark eyes are bright with curiosity as she stares at me, searching my face. After a moment, she purses her lips and gives her head a little nod. "You've seen something, haven't you, lad? Something that's changed you."

"I don't know." In my mind, I see hair like flame and eyes as green as new leaves. Was she real? Or did my battered brain imagine her? "I don't know," I say again.

"What did you see?"

I hesitate, but what the Hel? I can't look any more foolish than I do already. "Brigid," I mutter. "I saw her. She shone . . . like fire."

"Ah." Mother Sima sinks back on her knees beside me. "Brigid." Mother nods her head as though everything makes sense to her now. "She is astonishing, isn't she?"

"You've seen her?"

She shrugs. "I always thought you might have a bit of mystic magic in you, Finn. Comes with the Faerie blood."

Her voice is matter-of-fact, as though it's the most natural thing in the world to speak with goddesses. She hasn't answered my question, though, hasn't told me if she's seen Brigid too.

She meets my gaze, her eyes bright with merriment, and I can't help but smile back at her. I see the wisdom carved into the lines of her face, the compassion in the set of her mouth, and I wonder how I could have ever thought she was nothing but an old clucking hen.

I want to help this strong, kind woman any way I can. I want to join the fight against the walking corpses, add my strength to hers.

"Mother Sima?"

"Yes, lad?"

"I'll do whatever has to be done to stop this plague on our land."

"Brigid *has* appeared to you." She gives me a grin.

I know she's right: dream or not, Brigid has changed me, and it's no longer hard for me to accept that I have a role to play in the battle against the neamh mairbh.

Freya and Nectan return with the leaves, and Mother Sima produces a small stone mortar and pestle from a pocket in her habit. I lie back on the ground and watch her, no longer even surprised by all the useful things she manages to hide within the folds of her garments. She crushes the leaves with the pestle, then pulls a small vial from another pocket and tips several drops into the mortar. I smell the tangy scents of agrimony and yarrow as she mixes the aromatic essence with the hazel leaves. She dabs the paste on me, first my head and my knuckles, and then the wound on my arm.

I close my eyes, breathing the healing odors. The pain is already easing, and sleep pulls at me. I drift away again, into the warm, dark sea . . .

When I wake this time, daylight is dimming toward dusk. The others must have dragged me in my sleep, because a thick canopy of leaves shields me from the sky. Freya and Nectan are standing guard a few feet away, talking softly to each other, and Mother Sima is kneeling nearby, her lips moving silently. Artair is curled up next to me, his head on my chest.

"Hiya, boy." He gives a soft woof and licks my face.

Freya sees that I'm awake and comes to sit beside me. "Are you feeling better now, boy?"

"I am."

She's plaited her hair into a circlet around her head. I know her hair must be as filthy as mine is, but the ring of braids makes her look like a queen with a narrow golden crown upon her head. Her face is as smeared with dirt as ever, though—and yet, she still looks different to me.

"Do you think, Freya," I say, "you could call me 'Finn' instead of 'boy'?"

She looks away, and for a moment, I think she's going to ignore me, but then she gives her head a quick nod. "Very well. But not when we're back home."

"Not *my* home," I remind her. I don't bother to tell her I have no intention of ever going back to Escomb.

She shrugs, then sits beside me, her hands in her lap, and I feel her relax. The angry tension she usually carries around her slips away, and after a moment, I hear her humming softly. Her voice is pure and sweet, and the Englisc song carries in it the solemn ring of icy winters, the blue-white cold of her ancestors' homeland. Our tribes began so far apart, and yet now, for good or ill, we share this island.

I feel something I can't remember feeling in a very long time. After a moment, I realize it's contentment. It feels good to simply lie here with Freya singing beside me. The walking dead are still out there, I know that, but now, this moment, is sweet and safe.

Despite my sense of peace, though, something is nagging at me, a thought that's as irritating as a mosquito. Finally, I ask, "Did you and Nectan—? Did you—well, are you lovers now? After you went to him in the woods last night?"

Her head snaps around, and the dreamy look is gone from her blue eyes. "What are you talking about?"

I feel myself flush. "I saw you last night. You got up and went after him."

Freya's hands turn to fists, gripping the folds of her gown, and she sits up straight and tall. "It's none of your business."

"No. I suppose not." I try to keep all expression out of my voice. I can't blame her if she's fallen in love with Nectan.

We're silent again, but the silence is no longer sweet and easy the way it was before. After a long moment, she says between her teeth, "He doesn't want me." She turns her head toward me. "Satisfied?"

"What?" Why would anyone not want Freya if she offered herself to him?

"He's not—interested." She looks down at her hands, and slowly, her fingers uncurl. "I don't care. The world is full of men. And it's not like I wanted to be his *lover*. Don't insult me like that! I just—I just wanted him to notice me."

"Well, if he doesn't *notice* you, Freya, there's something's wrong with his bits and pieces. *Every* man notices when you walk by."

She rolls her eyes. "Oh, I know. But that gets—boring." She gives me a tiny glance sideways. "I like the attention," she admits, "but I know what they really want. It's not like they want to talk to me, hear what I'm thinking. They just want one thing, and I'd be a fool to give that away."

I watch her face, the way her lips tighten for a moment, the tiny lines that pull together her pale arched brows. I've never thought what it would feel like to be on the other end of those admiring glances. I guess I've always assumed Freya just lapped up all the attention like a cat with cream.

"Truth be told," she says softly, "I'm relieved Nectan doesn't look at me like that. It's nice to think—well, that he could care about me out of friendship. That he doesn't want anything from me."

Her mouth softens again, and she sighs. "Anyway, Nectan is still faithful in his heart to Tristan, the man he loved."

"The *man*?"

Well, that changes things.

She nods. "They were companions but more than companions. They shared a bed." She turns to look at me. "Why do you sound so surprised?"

Some of my people's greatest heroes had warrior-lovers, so she's right—I shouldn't be surprised. "I don't know," I say. "I guess I just assumed . . ." I shrug.

Freya nods. "Me too. But there have always been men among my people who prefer to lie with men. They have the right to love as they wish, but they are still required to marry a wife and bear children. We can't afford people who don't reproduce. Nectan says it's the same among his people. He was brave to be faithful only to Tristan."

"What happened to him?" I ask. "To Tristan?"

"Nectan told me they had answered a call from the borderlands to defend the wall against the draugar. He and Tristan fought side-by-side, and they felled one draugar after another—but the dead kept coming. Finally, Tristan and Nectan prevailed, and the last of the creatures dropped lifeless on the ground—but Tristan had been wounded. He died in Nectan's arms. And then—" Freya's voice wavers, and I can see her swallow before she can continue. "Then Nectan did what he knew had to be done. He cut off Tristan's head and burned it. He didn't want his lover to become one of the wights."

We fall silent then, both of us thinking of Nectan. No wonder he carries sadness with him. He has borne far more than I have, I realize, and yet he is always good-humored. All my screams and wails, my slamming my hands and beating my head—well, it all seems merely childish to me now.

Mother Sima must have finished her prayers and gone out hunting, for she interrupts our silence by holding up a large, limp hare by its hind feet. "Supper," she announces.

Nectan whips a small knife out of his boot and begins to clean the meat. "Oh-ho," he says happily, "this is just what's needed to put you back on your feet, Finn, my lad. You'll soon be as pink and healthy as a newborn piglet."

I laugh, and then I lie there watching as the others prepare the meal. These three are my friends, I realize, the first friends I've had in many years.

When the meat is roasted, Mother Sima portions it out to us. "Eat up, Finn," she tells me. "You'll need your strength back by tomorrow."

I take a bite of meat. "What's happening tomorrow?" I ask with a full mouth.

"Tomorrow," Mother announces, "we're going to climb the heights to Merlin's Nest."

8

THE SORCERER'S LAIR

The smell of another roast hare wakes me in the morning. Freya's beside the fire, turning the spit so that the meat is brown and crackling on all sides. I lie still for a moment, my eyes on her face, thinking back on our conversation yesterday. She looks up and catches me watching her. Her face turns a little pinker, but maybe it's just the heat from the fire.

She removes the spit, slides the meat off, and then neatly trims off slices with her knife. "Breakfast," she announces.

The rest of us join her by the fire. You'd think I'd be tired by now of eating hare and more hare, with dried fish our only variety, but the meat tastes wonderful in my mouth. The early sun casts long gold beams through the trees, and a charm of goldfinches flutter between the branches of a nearby tree. They cock their heads and fix their tiny bright eyes on us, then break out into chains of trills and chirps, as though they can't help singing, despite their concern about these large strangers who have invaded their home. A red fox sticks his head out of the bracken, sees us, and then leaps back. I can't help but laugh out loud. Mother Sima cocks an eyebrow at me, and I say, "Did you see the horrified look on his face?"

She smiles. "It's *your* face that interests me more, lad. I don't think I've heard you laugh before."

Did I stop laughing four years ago when I was stolen from my home? And if that's true, why am I laughing now? The land's crawling with dead folks creeping around, devouring the living; my family's gone, my mother dead; and we're on our way to see a wizard who I reckon is almost as terrifying and dangerous as the neamh mairbh. To top all that, I have a lump on my head the size of a mountain, my arm is slashed, my knuckles smashed—all thanks to my own pure foolishness, of course—and I've gone so barmy that I more than half-believe I had a conversation with the goddess Brigid last night. I can still feel that ocean-deep well of sorrow she poured into my heart. And yet—

Well, that fox had the silliest look on his face. I can't help grinning again when I think about it.

"You well enough to walk, lad?" Nectan asks.

"Not just walk," Mother Sima puts in. "Climb. And he doesn't have a choice. We can't linger here any longer."

I take a few steps, then bounce a little on my heels. "I'm grand," I announce. Maybe my body's a bit bruised and battered, but somehow I feel better than I have for a long, long time. "Let's be on our way!"

Nectan knows the path to Merlin's hideaway, so he's in the lead. I walk just behind him, while Mother Sima and Freya follow. I can hear them chatting softly about nothing much, and I realize that something has changed in the atmosphere between us all. The dreadful fear and exhaustion have faded, and we march along with our heads high, as though we're off on some joyful adventure. Artair is full of energy too, bounding after squirrels and rabbits. The pain in my head has eased, my cuts and bruises don't hurt so very much, and I feel amazingly strong, as though I could walk forever.

We're in that region of Caledonia where the highlands greet the lowlands with a kiss. Da took me hunting here, the last few summers before I was taken captive. We camped at night in a tent made of hide, and as we sat by the fire, he told me stories from Eireland, our people's homeland. The memory makes me smile, bringing joy instead of sadness.

I can't help but wonder: *What magic did Brigid work in my heart?*

I think of Ma then, the way you might poke a wound to see if it's healed yet. And yes, the terrible pain's there, the sorrow and the loss. Still, there's something's different, even there, though I can't say just what it is.

As I walk, the answer slowly comes to me. I've been angry ever since those Angle raiders stole me; during the past weeks, since the coming of the undead, my anger has grown and grown. Now it's gone. I'm not angry anymore, at least not right now, with the sun on my head and the land bright and green all around. I'm sad—but the sadness no longer weighs as heavy on me without the extra load of rage.

We climb well-worn paths between oak and elm and the Pictish pines that pierce the blue sky like green arrows. Here and there we see pastureland in the distance between the trees, dotted with wooly long-horned cows, but most of the time we walk beneath a canopy of leaves. The forest seems gentler here, less dark and threatening, with more spaces for the light to shine between the trees.

The day is so bright and sweet, it's hard to believe any danger could be near—but just as the sun reaches the center of the sky's dome, we hear a clanking and rattling from up ahead. With a single swift motion of his hand, Nectan sends us into the forest, quietly and quickly. I scoop up Artair in my arms and wrap my hand around his snout to keep him quiet.

Crouched behind the shelter of an ancient fallen oak, we poke our head up enough to see the path we just left and wait for whatever comes. I'm pretty sure it won't be anything good.

The line of undead that comes trotting along the path appears to be some sort of monstrous war band. They are all males, broad and tall, and even covered with rotting skin and green strands of pus, they are a sturdy-looking bunch. They wear armor made of chain mail, leather, and copper scales, and they bear spears and axes. As they file past our hiding place, bony limbs slashing back and forth in that peculiar, faster-than-human gait, I count at least three dozen of them. What worries me most is how organized they look, almost like a human war band. How can their dim soulless brains be capable of such orderly behavior? I wonder, as I have before: *Is someone—or something—directing them? Do they receive orders they cannot help but obey?*

And then something else rattles past—a waggon, with branches woven in a crude cage around the bed. *Sweet Iosa!* Three people—three living people—are trapped inside the cage. A gaunt grey-bearded man and two young girls, naked and filthy, wail and shake the wooden slats that enclose them.

I pull out Da's dirk in my left hand and a yew stake in the right. My muscles tense, ready to dash into the road, and—

Wham!

Nectan's arms have slammed around me, pinning me in place. I squirm and twist, about to yell, but Mother Sima clasps one hand tight over my mouth, while the other shoves me down behind the log.

I'm always taken by surprise by how strong that dumpy little woman is.

I'm still trying to break free, but now Freya's hands are twisted in my hair, and the pain in my scalp forces me to lie still. Together, the three of them hold me fast, while the troop of neamh mairbh disappear from sight.

Finally, Mother Sima removes her fingers from my mouth.

"What're you doing?" I gasp. "Didn't you see? They had three people, three *living* people. We have to save them before the fiends decide it's meal time."

Mother Sima shakes her head. "We can't do it, Finn. We can't fight every battle if we want to win the war."

Outraged, I stare at her. I can't believe this. "You of all people, Mother Sima," I sputter, "didn't your Iosa say something about doing to others what you wish they'd do for you? Well, if I were those folks caught in a cage like three birds, I think I'd want someone to rescue me. Wouldn't you?" I twist around and stare up at Nectan. "Wouldn't you?"

Nectan tips his head gravely in agreement, and Mother Sima nods her head as well.

"Well, let's go then!" I'm ready to run after that unholy troop of corpses.

"But Iosa also said this," Mother Sima says. "'What king going to war will not consider the forces against him?'"

I make a disgusted face. "Bollocks, you just made that up."

"It's in Luke's Gospel, I give you my oath."

I shrug. "Who cares? I don't care what Iosa did or didn't say." I stare back and forth between them, but I see the same answer on all their faces. "Come *on*! We've beat the odds before and come out alive. Those people need our help. Are you cowards?"

Nectan puts a hand on my shoulder. "Finn," he says, his voice ever deeper than usual, "a true warrior knows to pick his fights. Did you see their armor? Their weapons? A host of seasoned warriors would think twice before attacking that band."

I twirl toward Freya, hoping at least she'll give me some support, but she shakes her head. "They're right, Finn."

After a moment, I sag. They *are* right, I realize, but I hate to admit it. "All right," I mutter. "Let's go then. Let's *hurry*. The sooner we can fight back against these walking corpses, the better."

We continue on our way, but my good mood has gone now. I can't stop thinking about those three people back there on that waggon. I understand why Nectan and the others think the way they do, but I don't care about being sensible and cautious. It's not right to leave those folks to be eaten.

Just as the sun begins its descent toward the west, we leave the forest behind us and climb into open land. A vast dark ridge towers above us, as if an enormous knife had carved away the side of the earth, leaving a long line of rock thrusting up into the clouds.

"Can we climb that?" Freya's voice sounds smaller than usual.

Nectan laughs. "Where I come from, we call that a hill. You should see real mountains."

"I used to hunt goats with my Da on ridges like this." I smile at the memory, and a little of my good humor returns. "We used to laugh and say the goats must have two legs shorter on one side to keep them balanced."

A faint path meanders back and forth along the craggy slope, like a long snake scaling the mountain ahead of us. We set our faces toward the mountaintop and begin the long climb.

Nectan lopes along the path with an easy gate, as though he were on level ground, and Mother Sima marches stolidly on and on, never hesitating. I'm doing all right, though my head is pounding now and all my other wounds are aching, but Freya is having a hard time of it. Her face turns red, and she gasps for air.

"The air is thinner here," I tell her. "Your lungs aren't used to it." I try to take her arm to help her, but she shakes me off.

"I can *do* it," she gasps.

The higher we go, the colder the air is. The bright sky is gone now, hidden by a layer of thick, wet fog, and an icy little wind fingers through my hair. Only tough, wiry grass grows along our path; otherwise, the mountainside is bare and bald, without even a patch of gorse. The wind gains strength and pushes us backward, as though Nature herself is doing her best to keep us away from Merlin's Nest.

I've heard stories about Merlin my whole life, impossible tales of magic and mystery. I believed them all when I was a child, and then, when I grew older, I decided they were nothing but stories made up for telling around a fire. Now I wonder: *How much is true and how much is only legend?*

Merlin the madman, Merlin the magician. What if *all* the stories are true?

We're all breathing hard now; we have to take two gulps of air to capture one good lungful. Our breath makes little grey clouds that hover around our faces, and Nectan's beard is silvered with ice. My fingertips are numb.

Freya comes to a stop and bends over, her hands on her knees, fighting to catch her breath. "Why does he live so high?" she asks, panting between each word. "He must truly be a merlin—only a bird-of-prey could live on such a high mount."

"He was once a Druid prince named Lailoken," Nectan replies softly, as though he thinks someone might be listening. "He fought for his king, Gwendalou, defending the fortress at Caerlaverock against the Saxons. He fought bravely, and the corpses of his enemies piled up at his feet. When it was clear that the invaders would triumph, he called down the mist to protect his clan folk, but it was too late. He watched as his beloved king dropped beneath an axe, and then he saw his own three brothers hewn down. Finally, when all his kin and clan lay slaughtered on the ground, and still the enemy pressed forward, he leapt into the waters of the moat and escaped from the Saxons' clutches. Driven mad by grief and guilt, he fled into the forest, and then here, to the mountain. He lives here to this day, with only the wild beasts as his companions."

"So he's a coward?" Freya puts her hand on her hips, clearly exasperated. "Why are we looking for this man? What good can he do us?"

"He is a great sage—a true seer," Mother Sima says. "Saint Kentigern himself spoke with Merlin, and the saint told me that he . . . well, Merlin may be barmy, but he knows things that no other mortal can tell. If anyone knows the way to destroy the undead, he will know."

I shake my head. "How can someone so full of guilt and sorrow have any answers to share?"

"Great souls are forged in solitude," Mother Sima replies. "They are born in wildernesses like this. Iosa himself spent forty days in the desert before he could receive the power of miracles and wisdom. Other heroes of the ancient scripture—Moses and Elijah—likewise lived in barren places before they were filled with power and knowledge."

Nectan nods. "That has always been the Druids' way. They spend long days in the forest groves, meditating alone, until the powers of nature become theirs. That is what the word 'druid' means—to become 'oak wise.'" He nods again and pulls some ice from his beard. "Sages have always found wisdom on the high places where sky and earth are wed."

"Is Merlin a magician?" Freya asks. "Could he turn us into an animal or a stone if we anger him?"

I might have laughed at her question once, but here on this dark slope, fog winding around us like serpents' ghosts, anything seems possible.

Mother Sima shrugs. "Those who walk in the light need not fear darkness, child."

Sometimes, I confess, the woman's cheerfulness can be a little grating.

"I have heard many strange tales of this man." Nectan's deep voice is calm and reassuring. "But I have never heard of him doing anything unjust. If he casts dread spells, I am certain they only fall where they're most deserved."

Freya doesn't look reassured. I'm not much comforted either.

The sky grows darker still, and lightning flashes, sending streaks of orange and red through the mist. Thunder rumbles and echoes off the mountainside. The fog and shadows, the storm-lit darkness, are like messages from the mountain itself, telling us to go back, to climb no higher. Even Nectan is shivering with cold, but we press upward. Artair keeps his nose to the ground, snuffling frantically at the unfamiliar scents. He's as scared and alert as we are, and he keeps close beside me instead of running up ahead.

At last, we pull ourselves to the top of the rocky crest. Below us is a small round valley, enclosed in uneven stone walls. Through the drifting mist, I see a waterfall like a long lacy line on the far wall. A stone round house stands near the falls.

"Merlin's Nest," Mother Sima says quietly.

We scrabble over the lip of the mountain and start down into the valley. The path is rocky and uneven, and several times we nearly fall when loose stones roll out from under our feet. As we descend, the fog closes around us tighter until we can no longer see more than a few feet ahead. We huddle together, and our steps slow as we make our way toward the sound of the waterfall. At my knee, Artair whimpers.

"What do we do?" I whisper. "Call out 'Yoo-hoo! Merlin?' Bang on his door?"

Before anyone can answer, a voice deeper than Nectan's booms out from the fog. "Ha! Hee! Ho!" The strange laughter is like thunder, and it sounds as though it comes from first one side of us and then the other, from in front of us and then behind.

We stop in our tracks and glance at each other.

"There!" whispers Mother Sima, pointing through the mist.

A figure slowly emerges from the fog. At first I get the crazy sense that this is no man but a walking tree. He wears a long robe of feather and fur, with odd pieces of bark and moss woven into it, so that it could almost be the forest itself gliding toward us. As he draws nearer, I see his large bare feet are so gnarled and dirty that they look like tree roots. His matted hair is plaited and coiled, and leaves and dry flowers are woven into the snarls. The wooden staff he carries is topped with a carved amber dragon that casts an orange-gold glow into the fog.

The only parts of this strange creature that seem human are his eyes. They're dark and twinkling, with a sharpness that seems to see straight through us. I look away, unwilling to meet his gaze for fear he'll work some magic on me.

Merlin. Merlin of many stories. Can this truly be the same magician who gave the legendary Artair victory over the Saxons a century ago?

The strange figure laughs again, and this time his voice sounds like a storm wind whistling across the mountainside. "Hoooo-haaaaa!" He stares straight at me, then points a finger at my chest. "The deliverer comes!"

I stare back at him, unable to look away. After a moment, the man throws back his head and laughs. "Ha! Ha! Ha!" The man's laughter is different every time; this time, he sounds like a raven clacking. "A fine set of champions you have gathered, Chosen One," he booms. "A holy woman from Éire, an Angle girl, and a giant Pict.

Ha! Hee! These are the folks you gather to save Albion from the walking dead?"

He's speaking only to me; he's not even looking at the others. I square my shoulders and find my voice. "Begging your pardon, sir, but I didn't choose any of them. They just—"

"Ho-ho-ho!" Now his voice rolls like ocean waves. "Didn't choose them? Didn't choose them? *That's* what you say?" He points his staff at me, and for a moment, I'm terribly afraid I might piss myself. "The chosen one *always* chooses his champions."

He swings his staff toward Freya. "Pretty one *she* is." The laugh that follows is like a horse's whinny. "Good hips too. She'll bear you a brood of little red- and blond-haired children, if I'm not mistaken."

"Umm, no sir. I mean, we're not—"

"We're not like that," Freya interrupts, but her voice quavers.

"Ohhh . . ." The mage makes a face and flaps his free hand at us both, as though we've exasperated him. At the same moment, I swear the amber dragon breathes out a wisp of smoke.

"Master Merlin." Mother Sima steps forward and bends her knee. "With your powers of sight, I'm sure you know why we've come." Her voice is as firm and cheery as ever. Does nothing faze the woman? "We have come to ask you how to end the horror that plagues our land. Where do these dead originate—and how can we undo their curse?"

He thumps the butt of his staff on the rocky ground. The dragon atop the pole flashes like a burst of lightning—and Merlin disappears.

We peer through the fog, and then we turn and stare at each other.

"Where'd he go?" asks Freya.

"There." Nectan points behind us.

We turn around, and there he is, robed in fog. His eyes are rolled upward in his head, hiding the irises. The white orbs look blind and strange, as though he's staring into his own head. Then, in a sing-song voice, he chants, "Where the Yeo twists under the Diamond Hall, there will the Dark God with his cold hand stir the raven's pot."

Freya and I exchange glances. Her nose is scrunched up in that look of hers that says, "You have to be joking!" Mother Sima, however, stares intently at the conjurer, as though he's making perfect sense.

"In they go," Merlin continues, "dead and rotted, head first into the pot. Plop! Plop!" He chuckles again, an eerie thunderous laugh, and then his ditty continues: "Out they come, walking dead, hungry for flesh. Splish! Splish!"

Mother Sima cocks her head to one side. "Really? No one has heard of the Dark God for centuries." She sounds mildly curious, as if she might be discussing a recipe with him and feeling skeptical about some ingredient he's suggested."

"No-oh-nooo." The wizard's voice rises and falls in an unpleasant way. "The Dark God sleeps—long, long—till now he wakes and finds the raven's pot. All ready now! A tasty stew of rotting corpses." He giggles, a high-pitched tee-hee that makes the hair rise on the back of my neck.

"Master sorcerer," Nectan says, his voice as unperturbed as always, "I am sworn to end this plague of horrors. Tell us how to finish the curse."

"Aha!" Merlin swings around and stares at Nectan as though he's just seen him. "How to end it, you ask? Oh, yes! A fine question, warrior of the Picts, a fine question indeed. How to put this horrible man-eating mess back into the stew? Wouldn't *that* be wonderful, were it possible?" He breaks into another crazed laugh, whirls his staff—and then he's gone again.

We turn around, peering into the mist.

"There." Freya sighs, as though she's getting tired of the wizard's shenanigans. She points through the fog at the glowing top of the mage's staff.

The amber glow comes closer, and the man looms out of the mist. He keeps walking straight at us, until he's uncomfortably close to Nectan, and then he leans forward until his nose is only inches from Nectan's huge beak. "Listen!" he whispers. "When the blood of the Riven God and the water of the Goddess of Avalon comingled flow into the raven's cup, *then*—" His eyes bulge out from his head and he leans still closer to Nectan. "Then the spell issss reverssssed." He hisses like a snake.

Nectan looks back at him with a level, unworried gaze. He doesn't even pull his head back but simply stares into the wizard's eyes, then gives his head a little nod, as though he understands.

I'd be terrified if that craggy nose were stuck up against mine, but I'm also curious. "Master Merlin," I ask, "what do you mean? And how can you know these things, up here so far removed from the world? Do messengers bring you news?"

"What?" he barks, whirling toward me so fast he takes me by surprise. "Messengers?" He pokes a finger at me, straight at my eye. I pull back, and he pokes at me again and again, while I back away, one step and then another.

"Enough." He gives me a crafty smile, then thrusts his staff up at the sky and looks at it thoughtfully. "I tell you what. The winds speak truth to me. The birds and creatures of the forest bring news from afar." He brings the staff down and stamps it on the rocky ground; the stone echoes like a bell. "The very earth reveals secrets for one who knows its language." He sticks his face toward mine, so close I smell his breath—an odd combination of sulfur and lavender. "You should spend more time outdoors," he suggests in a mild voice. "You'd be amazed what it will do for you."

Freya speaks up then. "Master wizard, did you say 'Avalon'?"

Merlin whirls away from me and makes a gesture with his open hand, as if to say *What of it?*

Freya lifts her chin, and I can't help but grin a little; no crazy wizard is going to get the best of her. "Well, isn't that part of the island overrun by the walking dead? If you want us to go there, how will we ever get there alive?"

"Oh! Ga! Gee!" This chortle reminds me of a bear's growl. "Smart girl you are. Oh yes!" Merlin swivels back to face me and gives me a wink. "She'll make you a happy man, that one."

"Well, no, sir—" I say, shifting back and forth uneasily. "I—uh—know your powers are great and all that—but, you see, she and I—"

"Oh please." The wizard waves his long fingers at me, as though I've bored him unbearably. Then he turns back to Freya and peers into her eyes. "Are you afray-ed?" He draws the word out, his lips curled back. "Hmm? Afraid those starving corpses will feast on your dainty flesh?" He shoves his face closer to hers. "Well? Are you? They could, you know. They might gnaw your soft parts until there's nothing left but bone and gristle." He draws back and nods his head. "That's possible, yes indeed."

Freya sways—he's gotten to her now—and her face is very pale. Mother Sima puts both hands on Freya's shoulders to steady her, and then she turns a stern look on Merlin.

"Oh very well." Merlin sighs as though Mother Sima has ruined his fun. "You'll need the very best steeds, of course. On foot you'll never make it." He lets out another odd chuckle; this one sounds a bit like a squirrel chattering, and then he turns to me. "No sir, you'd never make it. You'd be food for the slobbering corpses, every one of you."

With that, he turns his back to us and raises his staff. Then, in the most normal voice I've heard him use, he calls, "My children! I have need of you! Come!"

Suddenly, with a clatter of hooves, four massive stags emerge from the mist. Their red-brown fur is sleek, their shoulders and haunches thick with muscle. They stand taller than me, taller even than Nectan, and atop their proud heads they bear racks of enormous antlers that spread as wide as small trees. The arch of their ribs is vast, enclosing lungs that must be as big as a smith's bellows. On each deer's back is a saddle blanket of white wool woven with golden threads.

"Ohh," Freya breathes.

The deer look at us with enormous eyes that are soft and gentle. One stamps the ground with a hoof, and another snorts and tosses its majestic head. They're clearly ready to be on their way.

Merlin turns back to us. "Allow me to introduce my friends." He gestures at each deer in turn, saying, "Breth, Brochen, Brude, and Broca. They are the fastest and smartest rides in Albion. They have no fear of the revenants, and they will bear you where you must go. And now—" He lift his arms high, as if he's blessing us. "May earth, wind, fire, and water protect you on." With a final whirl of his robe, he floats away into the mist.

"Well," says Mother Sima, "let's be on our way then. Our audience is finished."

"Which way?" The mist presses so close around us that I don't have a clue where we are in relation to the mountainside.

"This way." Nectan points ahead, and we follow him, the deer tap-tapping daintily behind us.

In silence, we set our feet to climb the narrow rocky path out of the mountaintop hollow. The sure-footed deer follow us easily over the treacherous rocks, and then we're over the lip, descending the serpent-like switchbacks that crawl down the mountain face.

Going down is much easier than coming up. Our lungs suck in the thicker air, and the cold winds soften. My hands and feet begin to thaw. The mist grows thin, then disappears, and storm clouds no longer block the sun. A thrush sings, and I hear a wood dove's sighing notes, repeated over and over. I look at the good green land and sigh.

"That man was disgusting," Freya snaps. "And crazy."

I grin, glad to see she's back to her old self.

"And yet," Mother Sima counters, "he gave us the clues we sought."

"And four incredible deer," I point out. "Do you think we can really ride them?"

Nectan looks at the deer thoughtfully. "Let's have a try." He stretches his hand out to one of the deer.

Freya puts her hand on a sleek rump and leaps over the deer's back onto the saddle. She gives me a quick look over her shoulder, as though to make sure I'm impressed by her agility, and for a moment, I'm reminded of a day that seems so long ago now, when Freya sat astride her horse, looking down at me with such scorn as I carried rocks for her father. We've come a long, long way since then.

Nectan vaults easily onto another stag, while I bend my knee to make a step for Mother Sima. It takes her several tries to hoist herself onto the beast's back, but at last she's settling her skirts around her, while I struggle onto the last stag.

I've ridden a horse before, while working for Aedgar, but this is different. The back is narrower between my legs than a horse's, but I feel tremendous muscles ripple across the beast's wide chest and around its shoulders. It tosses its head, its antlers tilting like a tree that's buffeted by the wind.

"Now what?" I ask. "There's no bit or bridle. How do we steer these creatures?"

Freya leans down and puts her mouth next to the stag's ear. "Ha! Go boy, go!"

The stag breaks into a trot, and the other three follow with such speed that I lurch and grab a handful of thick hair. My bollucks bounce up and down, smashed back and forth by the beast's stride, and my head feels like its about to rattle off my shoulders. I tighten my legs around the creature's sides and try to hold on.

Freya gives me a sideways glance from her mount beside me. "Relax," she calls. "He's helping you, don't you see? He's not going to let you fall off."

After a moment, I realize she's right: every time I lurch one direction, the stag tilts the other way, adjusting its stride to counter my swaying weight. I still can't relax, but I'm no longer quite so terrified I'm going to fall beneath the pounding hooves.

The trees fly past us, and I realize how much faster we're covering the same path that we trudged on foot before. Artair runs alongside the deer, easily keeping up, for now at least, with their flying hooves. He probably enjoys not having to be constantly circling back for us slow humans the way he normally does.

Mother Sima throws up an arm and points ahead. "There," she calls, indicating a faint path that breaks away from the larger trail we're following. "That way leads south toward Avalon."

Freya clucks into her stag's ear, her knees pressing against its side to guide it, and it leaps onto the smaller trail, its brothers following behind. Freya is directly in front of me now, her skirts hiked up and flying out behind her, and I can't help but enjoy watching the way her round rump moves up and down with the movement of her mount. She gives me a glance over her shoulder, as though she's read my mind. I give her an innocent grin, which she returns with a suspicious frown, and then we're going too fast for me to think about anything besides holding on.

As we head south we leave the woods behind and gallop over grass-covered hills and fields. Soon, I see the Roman wall stretching far across the distant horizon.

Nectan swoops down one long arm and scoops up Artain onto his lap, while the stags run at the wall full tilt, never slackening their pace. I make out a notch in the wall, a place where the stones have crumbled, and the deer shoot toward the narrow opening.

Ahead of me, Freya's stag has already leapt over the wall, and I feel my own mount's muscles bunch beneath me—and then we're flying, impossibly high and long, and my arms are looped tight around the beast's neck. He lands smoothly, scarcely jarring me, then gives me a backward glance, as though asking me politely to ease my stranglehold.

South of the wall now, we're galloping across land the Romans cleared long ago. I can see for miles across the open land, and faraway, I glimpse a village, its roofs on fire, tiny figures running around it. My heart sinks. I long to turn my stag toward the village, to ride there as fast as I can and fight the walking dead—but I know my companions would not agree. And besides, I don't have a clue how to make my mount go one direction or another. All I can do is hang on.

As dusk falls, we reach a large river. "The Mersey," Nectan shouts, pointing at the fast, wide water. The deer slow to a walk.

"Can they swim across?" I ask.

Freya frowns at the river and shakes her head. "It's too deep and fast here. They'd never make it."

"We'll have to find another way to cross," Nectan says.

As we walk along the riverbank, Nectan suddenly halts and puts up a warning hand. "Look." He points toward the west.

I turn and squint into the sinking sun, and then my heart jumps into my throat. Coming toward us—still far-away but moving fast—is a gray, ragged group I know are walking dead men.

"Do they see us?"

Nectan shrugs. "Who can tell? Let's not wait to find out."

Our mounts seem to have already sensed the danger, for they veer away from the river, into a wheat field. The straw whips against my legs, and I hunch low over my mount as it picks up speed again. When I look over my shoulder, I can barely see the line of shambling corpses.

As I ride, I wonder, *What makes the undead decide to go one way or another?* Is it senseless and random, the way an entire herd will follow a single sheep that starts to run? Or is something directing their pillaging progress across the land?

As the sun touches the horizon, the deer bring us back along the riverside.

"There!" shouts Nectan. "A raft for ferrying across the river." He lets Artair down on the ground to trot beside us again as we make our way down the riverbank.

What I thought was a stroke of fortunate seems not so good after all. The closer we come to the raft that's tied to the bank, the worse the air smells. A cloud of flies buzzes in the air.

Thunor's arse! A body lies across the raft, so badly eaten and decomposed that it's impossible to see whether it was a man or a woman. For whatever reason, this is one corpse that's not going to be walking away. The rotting, gnawed flesh makes sour liquid rise in my throat. Freya puts her hand over her mouth, and even Mother Sima looks grim.

"What do we do now?" Freya asks in a muffled voice. "We can't ride on the raft with—with *that*."

"I'll take care of it," Nectan says quietly. He swings himself down from his mount and steps out onto the raft. Balancing himself on the bobbing wood, his legs wide, he draws one of his swords and then uses it as a lever to roll the body off the edge of raft. It falls with a plop and is instantly sucked up by the current and carried away.

Nectan looks up at us. "Shall we be on our way?"

The stags step willingly onto the raft, as though they understand exactly what we're doing and why. They shift their weight from side to side, responding instantly to the tilting surface beneath their hooves in much the same way my mount adjusted himself to my tips and turns. Artair, however, runs back and forth on the riverbank, whimpering, and he refuses to come when I call to him to join us on the raft. I have to jump off the raft, grab the dog in my arms, and carry him back with me.

On the raft, the terrible odor still lingers, and the flies are desperately looking for their meal. We swat them away, and then we grab hold of the ferry rope that extends across the river and pull ourselves along it, fighting the current that wants to push us downstream. It's hard work—but no worse than lugging Aedgar's stones. The rope sings as it glides through the slip holes in the raft, and we make steady progress across the river.

By the time we reach the far shore, darkness has fallen, but Nectan wants us to continue a little further before we make camp. Right now, I'd prefer the hard work of hauling ourselves along the rope to getting back on the stag. There's a pain at the base of my spine from jarring up and down, and my crotch and rump are aching.

Nectan gives me a grin, as though he can read my thoughts on my face. "Not much farther, lad. Then we'll rest for the night. But," his grin widens, "I can promise you that you'll feel even worse in the morning than you do right now."

Well grand, nice to know I have that to look forward to! I sigh and climb back onto my mount.

The stags walk slowly now, as though they sense our exhaustion, and the ride is far smoother than it was before. Just as the moon lifts its white face above the horizon, Nectan signals for us to halt and points to the fallen remains of a stone tower on the hilltop ahead. "There," he says. "We'll make camp there."

The deer step daintily through the gorse that covers the slope. At the top, stand the remains of an old Roman fort, sunk deep in an ocean of flowers. From here we have a wide view of the surrounding countryside, and we decide to risk lighting a fire.

Mother Sima produces her flint and steel, and Freya gathers tinder. Nectan and I find a dead tree lying on its side amid the flowers, and we drag it back to Mother Sima's fire. Soon, we're settled around the warmth, while the stags stand in a circle behind us. I can hear the steady sideways movements of their jaws as they munch on grass and flowers.

Mother Sima hands out dried fish, followed by a horn of mead, and for a while, we chew as steadily as the deer. Finally, when we've recovered a little energy, we turn to each other and begin to talk about the day's events.

"Who is this Dark God that Merlin spoke of?" Freya asks.

Mother Sima unclasps the leather pouch at her side and pulls out the *Bestiarium*. Nectan sucks in his breath and leans forward to see it better; books of any sort—let alone one as beautifully illuminated as this one—are rare among the highland tribes. For his benefit, Mother Sima explains what the tome is and makes him vow not to tell others of its existence. Then she carefully lifts the ornate cover and flips through the pages. "Ah," she says at last, "here we are."

She points to an image and holds the book out where we can all see it in the firelight. The drawing shows a dark-robed figure, precisely inked with tiny details, including wide sleeves and a hooded cape. The figure's right hand appears to be made of shining metal, and blue skin is drawn so tightly over its cheekbones that the face looks like a skull, bright embers burning from the eye sockets. A tangle of horns, dark and twisted, rises from its bald head. Two shadowy, ghost-like beings hover over its shoulders.

Mother Sima reads aloud: "'The Dark God, also known as Nuada, Llud, and Nudd. Once he lived among the fair and just powers, but now he is enveloped by darkness and corruption. Originally dwelt in Éire, King and chief Power of the Children of Danae (also known as the Faerie race), the Dark God was primal guardian of the Green Isle, having been given dominion there by the King of Kings before the mortal race inhabited that land. He is rumored to have been the consort of Danae, queen of the Faeries, before she gave herself in union to King Ériu, the Milesian, son of the Egyptian queen Scotia.'"

"Who *are* all those people?" Freya asks. "The book doesn't help me much when I've never heard of any the things it's talking about."

I've heard of most to them, but I know what Freya means: it's hard to make sense out of all the names and words. Mother Sima just goes on reading, as though she didn't hear Freya's question.

"'The Dark God fought against the Milesians but was betrayed by his fellows of the Faerie race who tired of his increasing greed and violent anger. In the midst of battle, the Dark God's subjects worked a spell against him so that he lost his Faerie powers, allowing King Ériu to cut off his hand. The Dark God then fled to Albion and settled in the region of the Sea Lakes. His Faerie powers then restored, he crafted a silver hand to replace his lost one. Brooding at his banishment, he became master of black and unspeakable arts by consorting with the dead, exploring vile regions of the underworld, and joining himself to demonic powers.'"

Mother Sima glances up, as though to make sure we're all still listening, and then continues. "'Feared for his mastery of the dark arts, the Dark God ruled Albion before the Romans came. With the conquest of the Briton tribes by Rome, the Dark God was no longer feared and was largely forgotten. Yet some who have sojourned in shadowy realms say he is not gone but waiting, biding his time to again take power as Principality over Albion.'"

"Oh great," I mutter. "Just what we need—an evil horned guy ruling us."

Mother Sima reads on. "'The Dark God is known for ruthlessness, violence, and utter greed, desiring only the increase of his reign by any means and at any expense to the innocent. He still possesses his Faerie powers, which give him the command of seeing, into the future and at remote distances, but he no longer hears the Great Song of Creation. He is skilled in all the unhallowed aspects of magic, potions, and plagues.'"

Freya makes a face. "We're up against *that*? I almost wish I'd never asked."

"At least we know our enemy." Nectan sounds as placid as ever, as though not even dark Faerie powers disturb him. Then he adds, "My people have a saying, 'If we know our enemy then we can kill him.'" Nectan may sound like the most peaceful man around, but he's not afraid of a fight, that's for sure.

"But what does the Dark God have to do with the undead?" asks Freya. "And do we even know he really does?"

Mother Sima tips her head to one side for a moment, thinking. "I suspect," she says finally, "that the Dark God is making a bid to regain his rule of Albion—and Éire after that. The revenants must have come from somewhere, especially in such numbers, and what better weapon for the Dark God to use against us? And we are weak. Albion has never been more bitterly divided and contested than now—Angles and Saxons, the Cymru, Picts, and Scoti all battle over her hills and valleys."

Nectan nods. "The best time to take a land is when its people are divided."

We all sit and stare at the fire. The sense of comfort I felt a moment ago is gone now, and despite the fire's crackling warmth, I feel a chill settle over me.

Another thought occurs to me. "Is *that* why the neamh mairbh seem to be following commands? As though they obey some purpose? Is the Dark God directing them?"

"Ah." Mother Sima narrows her eyes. "That would make sense. I have wondered about the way these creatures can seem to show intelligence at times and not at others. If the Dark God's magic directs them, then it is *his* intelligence we see." She squints thoughtfully at the fire. "Perhaps even their very existence depends on his evil will."

"Do you mean he brought them into existence?"

"Perhaps."

"But if the Dark God controls them," I ask, "why are there times when the undead seem just plain stupid and mindless? Like insects swarming over a piece of food with no purpose other than to feed."

"Even a powerful sorcerer like the Dark God," Mother Sima says, "cannot control all his monstrous spawn. Nor does he have any need to. He can leave them to spend much of their time wandering aimlessly across our land, following no command other than their need to consume flesh. They wreak plenty of destruction on their own—and then, when he wants them for some specific purpose, he picks up the reins."

None of this is particularly comforting, but somehow I feel better having the undead be less of a mystery. Nectan must be thinking along the same lines, because he says gravely, "Knowledge is our weapon."

"Then let's figure out more." Freya's eyes are bright in the firelight. "What did Merlin mean when he talked about the 'raven's cup'?"

"I can answer that one easily enough,' Mother Sima says. "Raven in the old tongue is 'Bran' and a 'cup' is a cauldron. He speaks of the Cauldron of Bran."

Nectan's eyes widen; clearly he knows what she's talking about, but I have only a dim memory of listening to my father's father tell a story about the Cup of Bran. Freya just looks puzzled. Her people know other stories.

"The book will describe the Cauldron better than I." Mother Sima turns the pages in her lap. "Here." She holds out the book so we can see the image of a strange being— half man and half stag—bent over an enormous copper kettle that's steaming above a bonfire. That stag-man is dropping tiny human bodies into the kettle as though he's making them into a stew.

"What's he *doing*?" Freya asks.

"Listen." Mother Sima begins to read again. "'The Cup of Bran, Cup of Cerridwyn, Cauldron of Rebirth. Bran the Mighty was born to a mother of the Children of Danae—the Faerie people—and a father of the Fomorians, the ancient hairy people who lived in Éire from the time of stone tools. Through arduous study of the magical crafts, he devised the Cauldron of Rebirth. This vessel has power to revive the life of human corpses stewed within it. They return to a semblance of life, save that they cannot make human speech and their flesh remains as decomposed as at the time of their immersion. The Cauldron is one source of revenants (see later entry).'"

Freya scowls at the page. "So the Dark God is dropping bodies into this cauldron?"

"Perhaps." Mother Sima turns another page and continues reading. "'Bran used the cauldron to reanimate warriors for the battle against the Milesians over the Isle of Éire, but the union of Danae the Faerie queen and Ériu king of the invading forces was of such strength that Bran and his army of living corpses suffered defeat. Bran the Mighty, foreseeing defeat, asked that his head be cut off and sent to Londinium in Albion, where it continued for centuries to serve as an oracle. After that, some chroniclers say the Cauldron of Rebirth was destroyed by the conquering race of heroes. Other sources tell of the sorceress queen Ceridwyn stealing the cauldron away to the Sea Lakes of Albion, where she dwelt in Avalon before the coming of the Holy Child to that place. However, the fate of the Cauldron is uncertain after the Milesian conquest.'"

"Avalon again," says Freya softly.

I've been watching the sparks fly up from the fire, but now I turn to Mother Sima. "And that is where the walking dead come from?"

She nods. "Some of them, at least. It all comes together: the Dark God is exiled to the south of our island where he seeks to regain power. The Cauldron comes to that same region after the current inhabitants of Éire—the men of the Milesian race—drive the Faerie people underground. Now the Cauldron has fallen into the Dark God's hands, and he has piled corpses into the vessel to create his undead army. And the army spreads and grows, as the undead bite and kill, infecting others with their plague." Her usually cheerful voice is somber. "It is like an enormous serpent crawling across our land. If we strike it here and then there, it does no good, for its length is too great to kill."

"Then we must cut off the serpent's head." Nectan's voice is matter-of-fact. "Destroy the Dark God, and the magic is undone."

Freya's brow wrinkles. "I'm trying to remember exactly what Merlin said. Wasn't it something like 'When the blood of the Riven God and the water of the Goddess from Avalon mingle and flow into the raven's cup, then the spell is reversed'? So does that mean the life will be taken from all the draugar, all at the same time? And what is the blood of the Riven God and the water of the Goddess?"

Mother Sima's face creases back into her usual smile. "Ah! That much is clear. I don't even need to consult the Bestiary." She looks back and forth between us. "Do you know anything of Holy Avalon?"

Nectan shrugs. "I have heard it is the ancient sacred hill, the place of magical apples and untellable blessings. It is surrounded by lake and marshland, with the holy town built on an island in the midst of the waters."

I nod. "My people call it Yns Afflon—Avalon—the place of the apples. It's also called Glasten Bury, the Isle of Glass."

"I have heard my people say," Freya adds, "that it is a frightening place, a place of powerful magic. A great evil dwells there."

"Your people *would* say that," I tell her. "That's because Avalon's strength opposes the invasion of your people."

"First it was a Faerie fort, where the Goddess Ceridwyn of the Sidhe held reign." Mother Sima's eyes are dreamy, as though she sees something beautiful and faraway. "But now the followers of Iosa hold it sacred as the place where faith in the Nail-Riven God first came to Albion. At the foot of the Holy Hill in Avalon is an ancient spring—and from deep in the mists of time it has been known as the well of the Goddess. Then Blessed Joseph of Arimathea came, carrying in a grail cup the blood of Iosa—the very blood that spilled from his spear-pierced side. Joseph poured the blood of Iosa into the well—and now it runs always red. It heals all who drink of it."

"And that, I think, is the answer to your question, lass," Nectan tells Freya. "The water of the Goddess is the spring at the foot of Avalon's Holy Hill—and now its waters are mingled with the blood of the Riven God."

"So does that mean we have to take water from this holy well and drop it in the Cauldron?"

"Yes," Mother Sima agrees. "I think that's it exactly."

"And that will end the plague of draugar?"

"That's what Merlin said."

"Well," says Freya, "that seems easy enough."

I shake my head. "We don't know where the Cauldron is. Merlin said 'Where the Yeo twists under the Diamond Hall.' But where is that?" I look at Mother Sima. "Do you know?"

She gives her head a little shake, but she doesn't look discouraged. "No, I do not. But as we head south, perhaps the answer will be given us. In the meantime, our course is clear—we must reach Avalon and fill a flask of water from the Holy Well."

We fall silent then, and weariness overtakes us. One by one, we stretch out on the ground and settle down to sleep. Nectan props himself against a tree, where he can keep watch from our hilltop refuge. I know he will sit there all night, guarding us against the undead—and then be up and ready to be on our way in the morning without a word of complaint.

I lie looking up at the night sky, Artair's warmth curled up against my side. A thousand tiny points of light wink down at me. The day's events rush through my mind, and I pick through all the pieces again, reassembling them in my mind.

A few feet away from me, Freya sighs, and her breath evens out into sleep. I roll over, and in the fire's light, I watch her sleep. She's curled on her side, the line of her hip dark against the fire. I've had my fantasies about those sweet curves, more times than I can count, but I never considered being her friend until the last day or two. As for something deeper—well, I've been telling myself I wasn't interested, even if it were possible. But I'm remembering now the way Merlin made the same assumption about our relationship that everyone else does. Merlin is a seer—so does that mean . . . ?

The unfinished question makes my mouth go dry with a strange yearning, but I push it out of my head and turn away from Freya. Mother Sima is on her knees a few feet away, saying her prayers to Iosa. I know she's probably wasting her time, but the sight of her solid body bowed in such determined prayer comforts me. I'm glad to have her on my side.

I'm glad to have Nectan and Freya on my side too. I know there are only four of us—well, five, counting Artair—going up against this Dark God, but I wouldn't choose any other companions. Despite our differences, we've forged something bright and strong between us. I don't know what I think about Freya, I still don't believe in Iosa, and the undead make my bones shiver—and yet I believe in our fourfold companionship. Maybe we'll fail in the end, but at least we will have tried. And at least we'll be together.

But my head is still full of questions. When Mother Sima finisher her prayers and settles herself near me on the ground, I push myself up on my elbow and whisper, "Mother Sima? Can I ask you something?"

She rolls over toward me, a round dark lump, her robe pulled tight around her for warmth. "Yes Finn, what is it?"

"You say I have the blood of the Sidhe in my veins. My ma said the same thing. But—well, there are so many stories in the world. How do I know which are true and which aren't? I grew up hearing stories of the Sidhe—the Children of Danae, we called them, or the Faerie folk. The bards taught that the fey folk dwell in an invisible land right beside our own, that they wield magical powers over the living."

"Yes," Mother Sima says. "I grew up with those stories as well."

"So are they true then? When Priest David came to my town, he said the Sidhe were just make-believe. He told us that Iosa the Nail-Riven was the only true story, and all the others were just legends that had grown up over the years. And yet your book—written in a monastery by priests of Iosa—talks as if the Sidhe are real."

"Yes." Mother Sima shifts a little, as though a rock is poking her. "Lad, this isn't an easy thing to explain. And it's late. We need our sleep."

"But I want to understand. How can we understand what we're doing, if we don't know what to believe? If we don't even know what's real and what isn't?"

Mother Sima sighs. "Very well then. I will tell you what I think, though I do not know all the answers either." She's silent for a moment, and I'm afraid she's fallen asleep after all, but then she says, "The ancient Hebrew scriptures speak of heavenly beings that dwelt on Earth in the ancient days. The holy writ says, 'The Most High assigned lands to each people, where they should live, and to each nation was assigned a heavenly being.' Later, in the Greek scriptures, the heavenly beings are called Powers and Principalities. At first, they were God's servants who ruled the Earth with justice. But back at the beginning of the world, some of these beings wanted power for themselves. Like us, they wanted to control their own lives, instead of surrendering themselves to the

High King of Heaven. Like us, they also experienced lust, and when they turned their eyes toward human women, they took them and bore offspring with them."

Her voice is soft and weary, as though she's struggling against sleep, but I push her a little further. "So—are you saying that Faeries are the same as the angels, the winged men our priest used to tell us about? And am I one of their offspring, from their union with a mortal woman? Is that how I come to have green sparkles in my blood?" She doesn't answer, and I raise my voice a little. "How can that be, Mother Sima? Do all my family have Faerie blood?"

She yawns. "What do you think, lad?"

I wish she'd give me straight answers for once.

After a moment, she seems to relent, though, and adds, "If you have Faerie blood, lad, like as not it came to you through your mother, passed down through the generations. Maybe your brother and sister have it too, maybe not."

I'm silent, absorbing that, and then I ask, "Are the Faerie folk good or bad then? I thought angels were good—but the Sidhe seem . . . well, unpredictable. Not exactly good."

"Are people good or bad?"

Here we go again. For every question I ask, she just turns it around with another question of her own. "Well," I say, "they're neither—I mean, they're both. It depends on the person. But even the same person can do good things and bad things."

"Well then." Mother Sima yawns again. "Why should it be any different with the Faerie folk—the heavenly beings?"

I decide to ponder that later. Right now, I don't want to let her fall asleep until I've asked one more question. "Mother Sima, if I'm the 'chosen one'—the one who's supposed to somehow bring an end to the reeking corpses—well, how will I know how to do that? I don't have a clue."

"You'll know." Her voice is so soft I barely hear it.

"But how? Where will the answers come from? And how will I know who's telling me truth and who's telling me lies?"

Mother Sima lets out a breath of laughter. "Finn, you have so many questions in that head of yours, you'd make a good student at Cill Dara. I hope that someday you can come to our monastery for a proper education. But in the meantime, see if you can take a few things by faith. You'll know what you need to know when you need to know it. That's how life generally works."

I open my mouth to ask another question, but she lifts her hand. "No, lad. Not another question tonight. I'm half asleep already, and you should be as well."

I sigh. "All right."

"Good night, Finn. May Iosa guard your dreams."

The next morning, we wake and are on our way again. I'm growing used to my mount's leaping pace, and I enjoy the way we fly across the land, the wind in my face, the hills and trees and fields streaming past.

Time seems to fly as swiftly as the stags' hooves, and the hours—and then the days—slide together. After three more days, we've still not sighted any of the undead, and our hearts are light and filled with hope. I'm dreaming of the fast and easy triumph that must surely lie ahead.

On the afternoon of the fourth day, we ride into land that's more mountainous and thickly wooded than any we've seen so far on our journey.

"We have reached the borderlands of the Cymry," Mother Sima tells us. "The people here have lived on Albion since before the Romans came—and they have never been defeated, either by the legions or by the Saxons."

Freya rolls her eyes. "Give us time."

I'm too fascinated by the land around us to pay her any attention. We ride between the broad trunks of ancient oak and ash, beech and alder. Their twisted roots are gnarled fingers reaching across our path. Soft green moss clings to every branch and root, like emerald fabric draped around each tree. Overhead, the sunlight filters through the layers of tree canopy, making each leaf glow as though lit inside with soft green flame. The shadows between the trees are deep and mysterious, and I feel that if I turn my head fast enough, I might glimpse almost anything among the shadows—the Faerie folk, some magical and lovely beast, a fantastic creature from Mother Sima's book.

The forest's deep green stillness settles over us, and as we ride deeper into the woods, we no longer talk among ourselves. Even the stags go more slowly, their hooves soft on the forest floor. And then—

Thunk!

The stag beneath me leaps and twists. I jump, my heart thudding, and look around, searching the shadows for whatever startled my mount.

And then the deer falls to the ground beneath me.

I leap off his back, and now I see: a spear shaft is sunk deep into his side. He pants and blows red foam into the dirt. For a moment, his great muscles struggle to push himself up again—and then he falls sprawled and limp across the path. He doesn't move again.

I still don't understand. I stare at him, as though I expect him to leap up again any moment. How could such a great and magical creature be robbed of life so suddenly?

Tears spring to my eyes. *I'm sorry, Merlin. I would have protected him if I'd only known . . .*

"Finn!" Freya yells. "Get on my deer! Hurry!"

I turn to look up at her, still confused. How can she expect me to ride away and leave the beast lying here in the dirt?

And then I hear a howl from the forest's shadows, and I see a flicker of gray limbs.

"Come *on*!" Freya screams, her hand held out to me.

I snatch up Artair in my arms, and we leap on Freya's mount. I barely make it—I wouldn't have if Freya hadn't hauled hard on my arm—and then I clutch tight to both Artair and Freya as the stag leaps into motion.

We're nearly flying, the hooves of the three remaining stags pounding on the path. I'm convinced we've escaped, and then we come around a curve in the trail—and find a throng of the undead waiting there.

Freya's mount trips over a bony leg, and Freya, Artair, and I fly over the stag's head, right into the midst of the grotty corpses. Freya immediately scrambles to her feet and grabs up her bow, while I pull yew stakes out of my belt.

"Dismount!" Nectan bellows to Mother Sima. "Everyone! Back to back."

In a moment, I feel Nectan's broad back pressed behind me like a wall, while Mother Sima takes her place behind Freya. Freya's stag has regained his footing, and now all three deer leap over the undead's heads. The beasts disappear among the green shadows, and I spare a thought to wish them well.

And then I turn back to the neamh mairbh pressed close around us. They're crouched, ready to leap at us.

Hel. What do we do now?

"Have courage," Nectan says behind me. "The battle belongs to the brave."

"Trust in God," Mother Sima adds, sounding far more grim than usual, "and may Patrick and Brigid preserve us."

The creatures leap, and there's no more time to think. I duck just in time to avoid the swing of a scythe, and then I lunge forward to stab a fleshy male in the chest with a yew stick. The hunk of rot collapses, spattering me with thick green slime.

I don't have time to wipe it away. At my side, Freya's arrows are flying. A ghoul that must have once been an adolescent goes down, tugging at an arrow in its throat. Before it can pull the arrow free, Freya nails it again, this time in the heart. Behind me, I hear the whistle of Nectan's two swords as they slash back and forth, and from the corner of my eye, I see that Mother Sima is whacking heads with her shepherd's crook. But I can't pay attention to the others anymore, because I'm weaving and thrusting, ducking and stabbing as fast I can. Just staying alive for one more breath seems like a triumph.

The stench from the corpses is so thick I can scarcely breathe. I gasp for air, dash the sweat out of my eyes, then focus on the half-rotted thing that's attacking me now. It looks like a child of no more than six or seven, and I hesitate, but then it tries to impale me with a rusty spike. *Not a child*, I remind myself and thrust a stake through its ribs.

The creatures are dropping all around us, but for every one that falls, three more seethe past it. They are so close around us now that Freya has no space to nock her bow; instead, she's stabbing at the creatures with a yew stick. I look over my shoulder to see how the other two are faring, and for a moment I can't see Mother Sima. My heart leaps with fear that she's fallen.

No! There she is! She's been pushed down to the ground, but at least she's on her knees, using her staff with both hands to ward off her attackers. Nectan gives a grunt behind me, and I know that despite his mighty strength, he too is flagging.

Like a nightmare, the battle goes on and one. The world around me is a blur of gray flesh, and I'm so weary that it hurts to lift my arm one more time. I only barely manage to step out of the way of a club that arcs over my head, and then, gasping for breath, I give a gray-haired hag a sluggish stab.

I'm too tired to keep on fighting. Any moment now, I'm going to be too slow to avoid a blow—and then it will be all over. I'll be impaled by some rusty farm tool—and I'll be corpse food.

A tall rotting fellow with huge bites taken out of his shoulder looms above me. He heaves a flail over his head and lets it swing. I try to duck, but my timing is off, and the flail skims the top of my scalp. The blighter pulls back his arm again, and I know this is it. This time when he swings the flail, it will smash my skull like an egg. And then—

Thwip!

The point of an arrowhead protrudes through the warrior's rotting chest.

9

PRISONERS

My undead attacker wavers on its bony legs, then falls forward. I barely manage to step out of its way before it crashes face first on the ground. Two more of the neamh mairbh leap forward to take his place on the pile of twitching corpses in front of me, but in the blink of an eye, they too have arrows sticking out of them.

Another arrow whistles past my ear. Luckily, it misses Nectan behind me. The undead throw back their heads and howl, and then they turn away from us. They howl again and charge into the shadows of the forest

The four of us turn to each other. We're covered with sweat and gobs of rotting flesh, but somehow, we've survived. Artair runs to my side, whimpering but unhurt.

"Who's out there?" Freya's collecting her arrows, wrenching them out of rotting chests, but she pauses now and stares into the forest. "And is it friend or foe?"

I swipe at the blood that's running down my forehead. "Right now any enemy of the undead is my friend."

Then, from further down the road, we hear the screams of the walking dead interrupted by the blasts of a horn trumpet, followed by the screech and clash of iron meeting iron. I'm ready to run toward the fray—after all, whoever is fighting the ghouls just saved our skin, so I figure we should do the same for them—but Nectan's hand closes around my shoulder.

"Wait, lad." His eyes are narrowed, his mouth hard. "I'd be happier if we—"

Before he can finish his sentence, the noise of the battle falls silent. Nectan glances at Mother Sima, then squares his shoulders and turns to face the sound of troops approaching. I can't figure out what his problem is, because I, for one, am glad to have reinforcements on their way.

Ranks of warrior march around the bend in the road, all wearing brass scale armor that shines and clinks with every step. They are light haired and square jawed, plaid capes fluttering over their broad shoulders. Some carry swords and large oval shields; the rest hold short bows.

A tall man leads the troops. He wears a gilded helmet topped with a red horsehair crest, and he holds a jewel-hilted sword, still smeared with the dark blood of the undead. He has a close-cropped reddish beard and mustache, the kind that demands daily attention to look so fine. "I am Aelwyn," he announces. "I command the battle troop of King Arthylwys. Welcome to Cymry." His words have a strange accent but they are close enough to my native Gaelic that I can understand them.

Mother Sima steps forward. "We are beholden to you for our lives, Aelwyn. I am Sima O'Donahue, of the order of Blessed Brigid in Éire."

Aelwyn smiles and tips his head to her. "The sisters of Jesu are always welcome among the Cymry."

I step up beside Mother Sima. "Finn MacDugal of the Kingdom of Dalriada."

"Our brothers the Scoti are also always welcome here." Aelwyn voice is as deep as Nectan's but I notice it holds none of the quiet humility that Nectan has. Instead, Aelwyn sounds like a man who's used to being obeyed.

Nectan steps forward as well. "I am called Nectan MacBrud, and I am from the highlands to the north." He bows slightly. "I am grateful for your rescue. My swords are at your service."

Aelwyn nods in return. "Well met. The Picts are fearsome warriors."

Now Aelwyn's gaze turns to Freya. She says nothing, only stares at the ground, and I realize suddenly that we might have a problem. The Cymry are known for their hatred of the Anglefolc; if she speaks, they'll recognize her as their sworn enemy.

I speak up before Aelwyn can say anything. "This maiden is . . . Catriona. She is from my village in Caledonia, but she is . . . timid and slow of speech."

Aelwyn's eyes narrow, and his gaze lingers on Freya as he says, "What brings you to travel the cursed land along our borders? Do you not fear the Cauldron Spawn?"

"Any sane person fears the revenants," Mother Sima tells him. "But our company is committed to free Albion from their curse." Her eyes narrow. "So you already know that the undead come from the Cup of Bran?"

Aelwyn only grunts in reply to Mother's question, and then he turns to his band of men with a swift motion of his hand. The men jog forward until they surround us. I glance at Nectan, suddenly sharing his unease. I can't help thinking we are now as much captive as protected.

"We march to Dinas Arthylwys," Aelwyn tells his men. "See to it that our guests arrive safely."

Something in his tone makes the small hairs lift on the back of my neck. As we fall in step with the warriors, Mother Sima says softly, "Reveal yourselves but sparingly at the king's hall."

Freya's sleeve brushes my arm. "Finn," she whispers, so low I can barely hear her. I turn toward her. "Thank you, Finn."

Even as uneasy as I feel, I can't help but smile. I want to give her words of assurance; I want to tell her that I won't let anyone hurt her. But we are marching too fast for conversation, and the Cymry are all around us.

Despite the weight of their armored tunics, the warriors keep a rapid gait. The four of us are still reeling from the battle we just survived, but we do our best to keep up. I have a feeling we don't have much choice.

We march and march, until my knees feel like jelly, but still we keep on. The scrape on the top of my head stings and throbs and all my other older wounds are aching, but I force my feet forward. The troop's pace never wavers. Here in the belly of the thick forest, it's hard to tell how much ground we've covered. The road simply goes on and on between the trees. The green twilight beneath the trees deepens, telling us that evening is falling.

At last, we march out of the forest into open land, and I see the torch-lit ramparts of an enormous circle fort. Its walls are three times the height of a man, and its length from end to end is four times that of my own home fort. Within this fort's outer wall stands a tower that's wider and taller than any I've ever seen.

Aelwyn gestures toward the fort. "Dinas Arthylwys, the mightiest caer in Albion. Here the king's army holds the Cauldron Spawn at bay. The other people of this island may fall—Saxons, Picts, and Scoti—yet the Cymry shall remain safe and free within these mighty walls."

"Pride comes before the fall," Mother Sima whispers in my ear.

I can see that the Cymry have military strength and discipline greater than any of the other people in Albion—but I have also seen the relentless force of the undead. I will grant, though, that the Cymry will certainly be the *last* to fall.

The soldiers march us over a drawbridge and through the fortified gates. Aelwyn dispatches most of the troops, leaving only a small detachment to accompany us. "For your safety." His smile bares his teeth.

Does he think we're fools? What danger could threaten us here in his fortress—except the Cymry themselves?

We proceed through a courtyard where vendors are selling fish and fowl and venison. I see the hanging carcass of a stag, an arrow still in its side, and I think with sadness of Merlin's magical creatures. They served us so well and were repaid for their loyalty so poorly. I hope the surviving three will find their way back to their master.

The guards escort us to the central tower, a mammoth structure that's filled with many rooms. We enter a long corridor with narrow slits along the outer wall, just wide enough for fresh air to enter; if the outer wall was breached, this tower could still be defended. Oil braziers are set into the interior wall, each an arm's length apart from the next, and their burning wicks light the long passageway. We march past a doorway, where I catch a glimpse of a great hall crowded with richly dressed men and women. In the flickering lamplight, they look like denizens of fairyland, but we do not linger long enough for me to see them clearly. The guards whisk us up a long length of steps to a second floor.

I've never climbed stairs that were inside a building before, never even been in a building that had floors stacked on top one another, and my head feels strange from all the layers of stone and wood around us. Artair whines and wants to turn around, but I pick him up and carry him. "Hush, boy," I whisper to him. "We'll be all right." I hope I'm telling him the truth.

As we climb, I glance over my shoulder at Freya; all this must be as new to her as it is to me, but there's no expression on her face. Her face is very pale in the shadows of the staircase, her eyes lowered. I wish there was something I could say to ease her fears—but I'm afraid too.

On the second floor, the warriors—our guards?—motion the women toward one room, Nectan and me toward another. "Wash and refresh yourselves," one of them barks at us. "We will wait and accompany you to the king's hall when you are ready."

I try to give Mother Sima and Freya a reassuring glance before we are parted, but neither of them catch my eye. Nectan has to duck to avoid hitting his head on the doorway's thick oaken beams, and Artair whines again, clearly uncomfortable with this enclosed space. The room holds two bed frames with blankets tucked neatly over the pallets of straw, and a fire leaps on a hearth. A basin of water is on the floor by the fire, towels hang on chairs nearby, and I see two strigils for scraping the dirt off our skin.

As the guards leave us, Nectan and I turn to look at each other. "Well, the Cymry know how to welcome guests," he says.

"Are we guests or prisoners?"

Nectan's grimace tells me he has already had the same thought. "Either way, we might as well take advantage of the chance to clean ourselves."

We strip and scrape the grime off our limbs, then wash with water from the basin. Nectan cleans the cut on my scalp. "Don't fret, lad," he says. "You're not bald yet. You've enough hair on your nob that no one will notice." He gives me a sly glance. "Not even Freya."

I change the subject by pointing to a line of clay bottles. "What do you think those are?"

He uncorks one, takes a sniff, then pours a little into his hand. "Ointment," he says. "To make us soft and sweet."

I open another bottle and breathe the scents of lavender and chamomile. When I give Nectan a doubtful glance, he grins. "Go ahead." He rubs a generous dollop of the stuff over his face, around his neck, and down his arms. "After so many months on the road smelling like hog piss, I've nearly forgotten how it feels to smell clean."

"After years of slavery," I tell him, "I've forgotten what the word 'clean' means."

It's a shame to put my filthy tunic back on over my clean body, but I have no desire to linger naked in our room while those guards are out there. We do our best to scrub some of the grime off our clothes, and then, once we are dressed again, Nectan's swords strapped across his back, we turn toward the doorway.

"Do you think we can open it?"

"I didn't hear the sound of a bolt." Nectan put his hand on the latch. "Only one way to find out." The latch lifts easily, and the door swings open.

Outside, six guards are waiting, lined up against the wall. "No weapons allowed in the king's hall," one says. We glance at each other, but Nectan says nothing, only unstraps his swords. The guard points silently to the sheath and pouch that hang from my belt; with reluctant fingers, I remove my dirk and the bag of yew stakes.

"You stay here, boy," I say to Artair and push him back inside the room. I don't want to have to worry about him while we go to meet the king. When the door closes on him, he yips a few times but then falls silent.

By this time, the women have emerged from their room as well. I stare at Freya; I'd nearly forgotten what she looks like beneath the layers of mud and blood she's been wearing. Her hair is damp and freshly braided, and when she steps closer to me, I catch a whiff of honeysuckle and roses. I give her a grin, and her cheeks turn pink, which makes my grin wider yet. For just a moment, I forget all about the danger around us.

The king's hall is enormous—twice the height and three times the width of Wulfstan's hall in Escomb. Blazing fires at each end warm the room, and long tapestries hang along the walls. Images of a fierce red dragon are woven into the hangings, the symbol of the great Artair, the Pendragon—Head Dragon—who lead the Cymry's victory over the Saxons.

"Close your mouth, Finn," Freya hisses at me, and I realize I've been staring around me gape-jawed. I've never seen a room as rich as this—or people as extravagantly dressed. Men, women, and children wearing bright plaids and shimmering fabrics are seated on benches by long tables. The women's gowns glitter with gold thread and jewels, and the men wear heavy gold torcs around their necks. Every last one of them seems to be talking, laughing, and gesturing, and the hall is filled with the roar of their mingled conversations. And the food—I've never seen so much food and drink all in one place. The tables are a little grimy, dull with layers of old grease—but the scents from all those heaped-up platters of meat and vegetables make my mouth water. Two men play a flute and a drum, while a bard with a hand-harp lifts his voice above the din. I feel as if I've entered Tir-Na-Nog, the land of the blessed.

But before I can gawk any longer, we're led to the head of the room, where the king sits in crimson finery with a circlet of gold atop his head. I have to admit I'm disappointed. From the power of his troops and fortress, I expected this man to look like the great Artair of legend—but Arthylwys is a grotty pile of flesh, larger sideways than he is upwards. To his left sits his wife, a small thin woman who looks a bit like an unhappy bird, all pointed nose and beady eyes. Next to her is a row of ladies, all chattering and laughing, while to the king's right is a line of warriors.

The small, piggy eyes of the king turn toward us, and he raises a hand. The noise of the revelry hushes, and the throng turns its attention to us. Scores of bright eyes are fixed on us, waiting to see what will happen next.

"Who might you be?"

Mother Sima curtsies. "Your highness, we are four—"

The king throws up his hand to stop her and makes a noise that reminds me of a hen's cluck. "I expect to be addressed by the warrior."

I know Mother Sima's not used to being treated with such disrespect—no Gaelic king would refuse to listen to a woman—but she bites her lips and steps back. Nectan takes her place and bows.

"Your highness we are four travelers from the north. Fortune has drawn us together in common cause against the walking dead."

Arthylwys says nothing, only continues to stare at us. His face holds no expression, and the silence grows so long that the crowd begins to shift uneasily. At last, he says in a flat voice, "Welcome to my kingdom." He waves his hand, and servants run to bring another bench to the table. "Sit and be our guests."

We do as we've been bidden. Servants set chunks of boar meat, pots full of rabbit stew, and horns of frothy mead in front of us. *By Thunor's arse, these people know how to lay a feast!* I might as well eat my fill; I have a feeling I may soon need all my strength.

The four of us eat silently, while the noise level rises around us once again. When there's a brief lull, Nectan asks the king, "Your highness, can you tell us more about the Cauldron Spawn? Any new knowledge will help us with our quest."

There's a strange odd pause, and I notice a few of the warriors exchanging glances. Then the king sniffs, and I hear the snot bubble inside his bulging nose. "I know little about the ugly things. They were all dead and buried before."

"Before what?" Nectan ventures to ask.

Arthylwys waves his knife vaguely. "Before they started walking around. Some of them are folks we know. Least we knew then when they was alive." He sniffs again, then turns his head and spits a gob of something thick and yellow on the straw-strewn floor. "Sickening thing, you know," he continues. "Seeing one's Aunt Gwendolyn walking around like that, all green and smelly, trying to eat other folks."

The king chugs down a beaker of mead, then lets out a belch. "I don't give the slimy things much thought. They're stopped easily enough with a few yew arrows—and the Cymry have the best bowmen in the world." He spears a chunk of meat on his knife, pauses to spit another slimy bogey on the ground, and then stuffs the meat in his mouth. "By Jesu, we're not only the best archers," he says through the mouthful of meat. I can see it, half chewed, between his teeth. "We're the best fighters. That's why the Saxon sons-of-bitches were stopped cold at our border. The Anglefolc turds, the Cauldron Spawn—" He waves a hand in the air. "It matters not to my warriors. It's easy shoot to them all." He burps again. "As easy as taking a piss."

He continues chewing, his fat jaws moving as rhythmically as a cow's, while bits of food spill out between his lips and cling to his moustache. As he reaches for a chunk of bread, his hand jars his wife's tankard, spilling mead across the table, but no one wipes up the sticky mess. Arthylwys stares at it blankly for a moment, then shifts his gaze to a point somewhere slightly above his nose. As far as I can tell, he's looking with great interest at absolutely nothing.

After a moment, Nectan reminds him, "You were saying about the Cauldron Spawn, your highness? What else can you tell us about them?"

The king swallows loudly, then wipes the back of his hand across is mouth. "Oh, yeah. They're not much different from the Saxons or the Anglefolc. Just move faster—and they smell a little worse." He guffaws. "And you have to burn the things or they don't stay dead. Sweet Jesu, those fires reek."

How is this kingdom so strong with a king who's a total pillock? I glance behind the king, where Aelwyn stands straight and tall, a grim look on his face. *Maybe Aelwyn holds the real power?*

Just as I think this, Aelwyn leans down and says, "Your highness, perhaps our guests would like to hear the bard sing his song about the Pair Dedeni?" The king looks blank, and Aelwyn adds, "The Cauldron of Rebirth?"

"Ah." The king nods. "Lovely tale. Yes, indeed." He claps his hands. "Bard Carwyn! A song for our guests. The one about the cauldron."

The bard smiles and bows, then plucks his harp as he sings, while the flutist and drummer accompany him.

Llasar Llaes Gyfnewid enormous was he.
Like the span of a tower his thighs were so wide.
Tall as three times the height of a tree
And stronger than steel the skin of his side.

The bard's song continues to describe the giant Llasar, who apparently lived somewhere in Éire, and then the giant's wife with her gigantic—well, attributes. There's all kinds of intrigue between the giants and a king of Éire, and lots fights, and the Cymry get involved in the story . . . I'm feeling heavy with meat and mead, and the tale is so long and hard to follow that my attention wanders. *What does this have to do with the Cauldron of Rebirth?*

The crowd in the room isn't paying much attention either, and it's hard to understand the bard's words over the hum of talk and laughter. Then Mother Sima prods me under the table and whispers in my ear, "Pay attention, lad. This could be important." I drag back my drifting mind and concentrate on the singer's words.

Pair Dedeni, great cauldron of gold.
Pair Dedeni, bubbling and churning.
The warriors of Éire mowed down and laid low.
Into the cauldron are thrown as it's burning.

Oh wonder! O glory! What a sight!
Corpses mangled and rotting!
What horror! What fright!
Out of the cauldron come leaping.

I take a draft of mead, and almost immediately, I wish I hadn't. The room is starting to look a little blurred around the edges. Mother Sima nudges me again, and I try my best to focus.

Efnysien feigns death among the slain.
The strong warrior lies still as a ghost
Among the raven's feast spread across the plain
Like a corpse with the dead host.

The sorcerer of Éire gathers the dead.
On a waggon piled with carcasses Efnysien is packed.
To the deep cavern the waggon is led.
Into the cauldron the bodies are stacked

Alive—still alive—the great fighter is thrown
Into the cauldron upended.

Magic reversed! The demon's spell undone!
Efnysien dead but the curse is now ended.

As the bard finishes, half-hearted applause ripples across the hall. Meanwhile, tables and benches, warriors and ladies, king and queen have all begun to twirl slowly around me. I've definitely had too much mead.

As I struggle to keep my eyes wide open and my head steady, the king leans across the table and stares at Freya as though he's just noticed her. "You're a pretty little thing. What's your name, darling?"

The warriors at the king's side also turn to look at Freya. She knows she's the center of attention, but she's no more able to reply than a calf could speak back to its butcher. She gives me a swift glance, then stares down at the table.

"Speak up, wench!" the king growls.

"Your majesty," I blurt, gathering my scattered wits, "Catriona is—shy. And she—she doesn't speak well. She's a little slow. She—"

"Shut up!" The king doesn't even bother to turn his head to look at me. "I've no interest in your lies. I want to hear the little bird chirp for herself." He points a fat finger at Freya. "Speak!" he bellows, as though she's an animal he can command.

"Your majesty—" Mother Sima says, but the king raises his fist in the air and silences her.

He turns back to Freya. "Speak, girl! Or I'll have your tongue ripped out." He mimes grabbing his own tongue and hacking at it with his knife.

"Your majesty," Freya says in a small, flat voice. "What would you have me say?"

"Englisc?" The king's tiny eyes narrow to mere specks. "You're a feckin' Angle bitch?"

The revelry has gone silent, and every head has turned to watch.

The king leans back and laughs. "Well, well. A tasty little piece of Angle meat has landed on my table." He holds out a hand to Freya. "Come here, Englisc bitch."

When Freya remains motionless, two of the king's guards step forward and drag her around the table. The king watches for a moment as she struggles in the grip of her two captors. His fat face is blank, and then a hint of a smile curves his lips.

Watching the expression on his face, the mead and rich food rise in my gullet, and I have to gulp them back. I'm shaking—with rage, not fear—and my muscles tense as I get ready to leap to my feet. Before I can, Mother Sima's hand closes over my arm. "Lad," she warns softly.

The king's jeweled hand reaches out and pulls the lace that fastens Freya's gown—and at the same moment, I shake off Mother's hand and leap across the table, screaming, "No!" I grab the knife he's been using to spear his meat and—

Everything goes abruptly and painfully dark.

By Woden's bollocks, my head hurts! Hel, where am I?

I open my eyes. I'm lying on the floor of the room where Nectan and I washed earlier. The fire is dying, but enough fuel remains to send faint flickers into the room's shadows. Artair is lying with his head on my chest, a worried look on his face.

"Hey, boy." I stroke his head. "What happened?"

He whines and licks my face—and then I remember. Freya!

I jump to my feet—only to drop immediately back on the floor. For a moment, I'm too dizzy to move, but then I crawl as fast I can to the pot in the corner. Once I've boaked up my entire dinner, I don't feel much better. My head is aching so badly that it has to be more than the mead I drank combined with all the old wounds on my head. Gingerly, I run my fingers over my tender skull and find a lump there the size of my fist.

But it doesn't matter. *I have to get out of here! Have to find Freya!*

I stagger to my feet again and fall against the door. It doesn't budge, no matter how much I shove my shoulder against it and pound on it with my fist. I scream in frustration, and then I put an ear to the door.

I hear footsteps and the clink of metal. The guards must be out there. And there's another sound . . . Mother Sima's voice. I can't make out words, but I can tell from the chanting lilt that she's praying.

Is she praying for Freya?

All at once, I'm wishing I still believed in praying. I'd do almost anything right now if it would help Freya.

But Iosa has never cared before—why would he care now?

I have to get out of here. I have to help Freya.

Shite.

10

OUT OF THE
FRYING PAN . . .

Iosa have mercy. Criost have mercy. Crouched on the floor, Artair clutched in my arms, I repeat the words again and again. There's nothing else I can do—and I *have* to do something.

And then, after what seems an eternity, the door swings open with a crash.

"Finn!" Nectan appears in the doorway. "Your dirk!" He tosses the sheath at me, and I catch it one-handed, then leap to my feet.

I dash through the door and find the guards crumpled on the floor. Mother Sima stands above them, her arm around Freya. Freya's eyes are so wide that the black pupils have swallowed up the blue. Her dress is torn, her hair pulled loose from its braids, and she sways against Mother Sima, a bloody blade clutched in her fist. When she sees me, she mumbles, "Finn." I've never seen her look so dazed. She lifts her chin, as though she's struggling to pull herself together. "We have to go. Now."

As shouts rise through the staircase from the floor below, Mother Sima nods her head. "That seems like a good idea."

Nectan flings his swords over his shoulder. I grab the pouch that holds the yew stakes. Once it and my dirk are fastened to my belt again, I feel a little better.

"This way!" Nectan leads us to another staircase at the other end of the corridor, and we stumble down the steep steps. Mother Sima has to push Freya along to keep her moving. I want to stop and ask Freya what happened, if she's all right—but I know we don't have time for that right now.

On the lower level, we find ourselves in a narrow dark corridor, where the air is heavy with the smell of onions and beef. We hurry after Nectan into the kitchen, where slabs of meat are roasting over a great fire. A servant girl turns the handle of a spit; when she sees us, her mouth opens, but Nectan puts his finger to his lips. After a moment, she nods—and then she points to a stone disc on the floor.

Nectan seems to know exactly what she means. He shoves the heavy stone aside, then points down into the hole that's revealed. "Let's go!"

He disappears into the mouth of a dark shaft. I follow him down a ladder, into a steeply sloping tunnel. Above my head, I hear Mother Sima pushing Freya after me, and then the scrape of stone on stone as Mother pulls the stone back in place.

Instantly, we're plunged into total darkness.

"I can't see a thing," Mother Sima whispers beside me. "Where are we?"

"It's a souterrain—a storage tunnel under the fortress," Nectan explains. "It will take us away from the fort. Just feel your way forward and keep moving."

We shuffle along the tunnel, stumbling now and then over objects that have been stored there—barrels and bags of vegetables, by the feel of them. The air is damp and smells of earth and mice. *Thunor's arse, I don't like this place!* But I'd go through a lot worse than this to get away from King Arthylwys and his warriors.

Artair trots at my side, sniffing. I hear a scuffle and squeak, and then he snaps his jaws at something. "What was that?"

"Mouse," Nectan says. "Maybe a rat. Keep moving."

Just as I'm starting to suspect that the walls are squeezing tighter and tighter around us, as though we're crawling through the belly of some foul serpent, dim light appears ahead. A finger of fresh air slides past my face.

And then we're outside, beneath a moonlit sky. We look around and find that we've emerged from the side of the fort's rocky knoll. The fortress walls are above us;

ahead, is a dark line of trees. There's the sound of distant shouts, and then the thunder of horse hooves over the drawbridge.

"We must get into the forest," Mother Sima says. "At once!"

We run as fast as we can across the stretch of open land, Artair dashing ahead of us. Dark trees close their branches around us like welcoming arms, and I breathe the familiar scents of leaves and moss. Fog curls between the trunks, and the shadows are thick. I've spent so much time in forests during our journey that they're starting to almost seem like home. I breathe a sigh of relief. *We made it.*

And then I hear hounds baying. *Shite. The Cymry are tracking our scent.*

We hurry faster, tripping over branches and vines, plunging deeper into the woods. When we reach a shallow stream, Mother Sima gives a soft, glad cry. "Praise Iosa! Wade downstream, everyone. The hounds will lose our scent in the water."

We stumble into the water, slipping and sliding on the stones. The water feels like ice on my toes, but I barely notice. My only thought is to get away from the warriors I know are following behind us.

At last, when my feet have long ago gone numb from the cold water, Nectan points to a shelf of rock, and we clamber up onto the stream's far bank. As we push deeper into the forest again, the sound of the dogs fades away behind us.

Our pace slows a little, but we continue walking. Finally, when our breath is ragged and our legs trembling, Nectan comes to a halt. "We've lost them."

"And we've lost ourselves," Mother Sima says. "We might as well rest a little."

We collapse together beneath the twisted canopy of an enormous oak. The fog is thick around us, like a blanket wrapping us in its folds.

"Now," I say, once I have caught my breath, "what happened? The last thing I remember is diving across the table at the king."

"One of the guards smacked you over the head with a club," Nectan says.

"You were being a fool, Finn. Like always." Freya's voice is faint, but I'm relieved to hear her sound more normal. After a moment, she adds, "But it was brave of you."

"During the scuffle," Nectan says, "I slipped away. I spent the next part of the evening skulking around the fort, scouting out escape routes. And then I waited for my chance."

"Eventually, Finn and I were dragged back to our rooms," Mother Sima says.

"What about Freya?" The nausea from the mead suddenly returns, and my stomach gives a sick lurch.

"Freya?" Mother Sima's voice is gentle. "What happened?"

Freya's face is only a pale oval in the shadows, but I can hear her fast, shallow breathing beside me. After a moment, she says in a small voice, "One of the guards threw me over his shoulder. Like I was a sack of vegetables. The king had me brought up to his chamber. And then they left me, for a long time. The door was locked shut, but I was trying to figure out how I could escape. I searched the room, behind the furniture, everywhere. The only thing I could find that might be useful was a hunting knife that had fallen behind a chest." She sucks in a long breath. "I stuck the knife inside my belt, behind my back, just as the king came back. He—he took off his clothes, like he was getting ready for bed."

I'm suddenly afraid I might puke again. I want to shout curse words, I want to run back to the fort and stick my dirk in the fat little toad that calls himself a king, but I force myself to stay quiet. *If Freya can bear whatever happened to her, then I can too.*

She's quiet for so long I think that's all she'll ever tell us, but then I hear a sound like a sob. "He—the king—he talked for a while, blabbering on and on in Welsc. I didn't understand a word of what he was saying. When he finally stopped talking, he—he grabbed me. Shoved me backward so I fell across his bed. He—he—he was panting like an enormous fat pig."

She makes the same sound again, and I put my hand out to touch her arm. "Oh Freya. I'm so—"

Freya interrupts me. "I twisted around so I could grab the knife and then—"

When she doesn't continue, I can't take it any longer, "Thunor's balls, Freya, what did you do?"

She turns to me, and in the dim light, I see the silver streak of tears across her face. Her shoulders shake, but I realize suddenly, she's sobbing with laughter. "I slashed the knife at whatever part of him I could reach. Turned out—" She chokes, giggles, sobs. "Well, he'll have no more heirs. I made sure of that."

"You cut off his—?" I gasp.

"Good job," Mother Sima says. "And then what happened?"

"He—he fainted." Freya wipes her sleeve across her eyes, and the hysteria drains from her voice. "There was a lot of blood."

Nectan picks up the story then. "I saw where they had taken Freya, and I was prowling around, trying to figure out a way to distract the guards. And then Freya came out, dripping with blood. The guards shouted and ran at her—but I knocked them on their heads with the flat of my sword. At that point, I decided we needed to get out of there as quickly as we could, before the other guards found out what had happened. We got ourselves back to the chambers where the rest of you were being held. I took care of those guards as well—and then we were back together again, the four of us."

Freya gives a sniff, and Mother Sima wraps her arms around her. For a moment, Freya tries to pull back, and then she goes limp against Mother's round bosom. "You were very brave, dear child," Mother Sima says. "Your mother would be proud."

At that, Freya gives a sudden sob I know isn't laughter, and her shoulders heave. Mother Sima strokes a hand over Freya's hair and murmurs something soft and gentle.

I'm realizing now something I was too stupid to grasp before: Freya lost her mother, just like I have. During most of the years I've know Freya, ever since her mother died of fever, she's been living with the same pain I feel now—and she's done the best she could to bear it courageously.

I wish I could wrap my arms around her the way Mother Sima has.

Freya's sobs finally ease. She sits up and wipes her sleeve across her face, then murmurs, "Thank you, Mother Sima." She gives me a swift glance and looks away, as though she's embarrassed to face me now.

Before I can think what to say to her, Mother Sima says, "Oh, we all need a good cry now and then." She sounds as if cutting off a king's manhood were just one of life's little frustrations.

"I have heard," Nectan says thoughtfully, "that Cuchulain—the greatest champion of all—keened and wept at times. Among my people, the greatest are those who are strong enough to give full vent to all their emotions, even the most painful."

Freya smiles a little at that and squares her shoulders. I wish I had Nectan's ability to sense just the right thing a person needs to hear.

I long to tell Freya . . . well, so many things, more than I can begin to put in words. I want to say that no man will ever threaten her like that again, because I'll protect her with my life. I want to say I'm so proud of her bravery, so impressed by her indomitable, fierce spirit. That I'm sorry for the way I've treated her, for the way I thought she had a serpent heart. That . . . well, it doesn't matter what else I would have told her, because my tongue can't find the words to say anything at all. I shift a little closer to her, though. And then I grab *my* courage and take her hand.

Her fingers close around mine. They're warm and slender—and suddenly, there's nothing at all in the world besides the way her fingers feel between mine.

"Listen!" Nectan whispers, bringing me back to our surroundings. "Do you hear that?"

At first, I hear nothing at all. I start to say so—*but no, wait, there's a distant chorus of howls coming through the woods!* Those aren't hounds howling either.

We leap to our feet. "They're coming from that way!" Mother Sima points. "Run!"

We launch into the forest again, stumbling on tired feet. The howls grow louder behind us.

Shite. Couldn't the fecking blighters give us just an hour of peace?

11

THE HILL OF WONDERS

Daylight is turning the sky gray as we run out of the woods. Ahead is an open plain with sloping hills. Nowhere to hide. Like rabbits chased by a fox, we sprint up the hillside.

"We can't run from them forever," I gasp.

"Blessed are those who persevere," Mother Sima pants. How can the woman quote scripture even at a moment like this?

"I say we stand and fight them," Nectan shouts.

"I'm with you!" Freya's frazzled braids are whipping behind her as she runs.

Before I cast my vote, I look back over my shoulder. Scores of gray, bone-legged wights flock up the hill behind us. "They're gaining on us," I manage to get out, "but we can't beat all of them."

"We won't beat *any* of them if we wear ourselves out running," Freya pants.

"She's right." Mother Sima stops running. "Stand your ground—and pray to Saint Michael for deliverance."

I'm just so sick of fighting the grotty things—but I have no choice but to take my stand with my companions. With a weary sigh, I turn to face the rotting throng that's loping toward us.

"Michael, Glorious Prince of the heavenly armies," shouts Mother Sima, "Defender of divine glory, Strength of God, Champion of God's people, save us now from the powers of darkness!"

Freya nocks an arrow and lets it fly. It plunges into the heart of a running corpse, and the ghoul drops on the ground, a tangle of flailing bones. Freya lets loose a second arrow, and another draugar drops.

The rest of them are almost on us, though. Mother Sima has her eyes closed, chanting the same prayer again and again. I grasp two yew stakes, and Nectan pulls his swords free of their scabbards.

At the same moment, the corpses throw back their heads and howl—and then they lurch forward. They're so close now I can smell the reek of their rotting teeth. I lift my arm, brace myself, and—

Aa-roo! A trumpet blast sounds from the north of us.

I turn and see a phalanx of horsemen coming at full gallop across the field. They wear brass armor and checkered capes. *Oh shite, shite, shite.* It's King Arthyl-wys' men. I don't know whether I'd rather face them or the ghouls.

The Cymry ride into the throng of living dead, thrusting and hacking with their long blades. The undead leap and swing, but they are outnumbered. The Cymry quickly overcome them.

"Run!" Freya urges. "They'll be after us next."

We turn and start back up the grassy hill, but we've gone no more than a few steps, when we hear the clomp of hooves just behind us. "Halt!" someone bellows.

It's Aelwyn. He gallops in front of us, his black charger prancing, its red plume swirling in the morning breeze.

We stand in a line, facing him. No one says anything, so at last I say, "Sir . . . we can explain . . ."

"Can you?" Aelwyn gives a ferocious grin. "I wonder—can you explain why the king seems to have misplaced his bollocks?"

"Is he—all right?" I'm worried that the man may have died from blood loss, and then Freya will really be in trouble.

"If by 'all right,' you mean 'still alive,'" Aelwyn says grimly, "then yes. He still lives."

I suck in a breath of relief. "Well, then we are—"

I really have no idea how I'm going to finish my sentence, so it's a good thing Aelwyn cuts me off with a brusque motion. "Do you know, boy," he says, "what happens when a monarch of the Cymry loses his manhood?"

I shake my head, waiting to hear what dire punishment is in store for us.

For a long moment, Aelwyn doesn't answer his question. I shift my weight, getting ready to turn and run, but Nectan breathes, "Wait, Finn. Wait."

Suddenly, Aelwyn leans toward me and shouts, "Well, I'll tell you! He's no longer king!" He looks down at me from his tall horse. "And do you know what happens when the ugly old tyrant has no heirs? Do you, boy?"

I shake my head. "Uh—no sir, I don't know."

Aelwyn throws back his head and laughs. "The commander of the royal armies takes his place!"

"You're the king now?" I manage to say.

"Not until we have a coronation," he replies, "but soon. And I owe you a great debt. You have delivered us from one of the worst kings Cymru has ever had. The man was the biggest fool I've ever had the misfortune to know. Under the reign of such a bewt, it's been sheer luck—and the skill of my warriors—that the undead did not destroy the kingdom. But now? Now you have paved the way for a brighter future for my people."

I try to adjust my thinking to this new turn of affairs. "You're not going to kill us, then?"

Aelwyn's laugh is softer this time. "Farthest thing from it!" He moves a little closer, and then he speaks directly to Freya in thickly accented Englisc. "Lady of the Anglefolc, by blood you are my enemy, but by circumstance I am in your debt. By your hand, my people have been saved from more years of unjust rule." His voice is gentle, his expression solemn now. "My forces are at your disposal."

Freya's eyes are huge. She glances at me, her eyebrows puckered in a frown, and I know she's not sure whether we should trust him.

Mother Sima settles the matter for us. "Well then, I thank Iosa for giving the kingdom to a good-hearted man." She sounds as calm as if Aelwyn had just caught up with us while we were out for a leisurely stroll through the countryside. "And I pray you will reign long and well. Now if you would, good Aelwyn, there is a boon I would ask of you."

"Name it then."

"We are headed to Avalon, where we will seek to further our cause. Could you grant us escort there?"

Aelwyn scratches his beard. "It's at least a three-day journey. And the way between here and there is mostly fields cleared by the Saxons—which means there are fewer forests for refuge. Worse yet, the Cauldron Spawn roam the land. All the living inhabitants have fled—or been eaten by the ghouls. Even for my armored warriors, this passage could be dangerous."

Mother Sima nods. "I understand. We will be on our way then, and—"

But Aelwyn interrupts her. "No favor is too great for those who have rescued our kingdom from such a king." He turns toward his men. "I seek twelve of you—with the swiftest horses, strongest shields, and fiercest swords—to foray quickly into the lands of the Cauldron Spawn, delivering our friends to Avalon. Who has courage to meet this task?"

Every last one of his men shouts, waving his weapon and clanging his shield. Aelwyn gives his fierce grin and says to us in an aside, "See the courage of the Cymry!" Then he calls out the names of a chosen dozen to ride with us.

"And I shall lead this adventure myself!" he announces. "My soul is bound to your safe passage. Besides," he adds more quietly, "I would like to see the Hill of Wonders."

Aelwyn orders that we each be mounted on horses he selects from his band. Once that is done, the larger force of the Cymry cavalry turns back, while the elite band of Aelwyn and his mounted warriors canter ahead of us toward our destination. As the morning sun rises above the horizon, we put our heels to our mounts and follow them.

The feel of the massive steed beneath me is another new sensation, far different from riding Merlin's stag. This is a warhorse, bred to carry a man with armor and weapons, and his back is so wide that the muscles in my thighs must stretch to accommodate its width. Few things—even the neamh mairbh—could halt this mount when he charges.

We leave the forest behind and wind our way between green hills. I clutch Artair in my lap, glad for the chance to at least catch my breath after all that has happened. The past day and night have been filled with such upsets and turnarounds that I feel dizzy.

And then the sunlight, the wind in my face, and the strong rhythm of my mount's muscles drive away my confusion. Beside me, Freya's golden braids fly out behind her, and all at once, my heart is filled with simple gladness. My friends and I have survived yet another round of challenges, and here we are, cantering together on sturdy warhorses, guarded by some of the strongest warriors in all of Albion.

After we've gone countless furlongs and the sun has passed its highest point in the sky, Freya pulls her horse closer alongside mine. "Do you believe Aelwyn?" she asks me. "Are these men really our friends? I have never known of a favor done by the Cymry for Anglefolc."

I give her a grin. "I've never heard of an Angle maid handing over the kingship to a Cymry warrior."

"I still don't understand what happened."

"According to custom, a king must be unblemished. The land depends on the king's virility for its strength. So a ruler who loses his—" I search for a delicate word. "His bits-and-pieces, well, without them, the land will suffer. So the king must surrender his throne."

"Did you know this would happen?"

I shake my head. "It never occurred to me. I thought they'd want to kill us after what you did."

She turns her head to look at me, then glances away quickly, as though she's still not sure if I'm shocked by what she did. After a moment, she asks, "But that still doesn't tell me—can we trust Aelwyn now?"

I shrug. "If he didn't mean to help us, what does he have to gain by heading into countryside thick with the neamh mairbh?"

She nods but still doesn't look at me.

"Don't worry, Freya."

She gives me a sideways glance, and this time her lips curve in a tiny smile. "All right," she says finally and then presses her heels against her mount. I watch her canter ahead of me, her head held high, her braids gleaming.

Mother Sima takes Freya's place beside me. "You did well to help Freya as you did, Finn," she says. "She's not always as strong as she would have you think. Your kindness has restored her confidence in herself."

Surprised, I turn toward Mother. "I didn't do *anything* to help her."

Mother Sima shrugs, wearing that smug smile that says she knows more than I do. After a moment, though, she changes the subject by saying, "Who would have thought events would turn out as they did? There's a lesson there to remember—just when things look darkest, sometimes even the most terrible things bring new hope."

I reckon she's right about that at least. I for one would have never suspected that cutting off a king's bollocks would end up like this!

Late in the afternoon, we come upon a dozen or so of the undead loping toward us on the road. Their rotting eyes stare at us from their skulls, their slack jaws rattle, and they lift their rusty weapons—but we charge through their midst as though they're not even there. They shriek and fall back from the warhorses, and we leave them behind without another glance. I laugh out loud, and Aelwyn turns to give me his wolfish grin.

The warriors talk little; instead, they constantly survey the land around us with a calm vigilance. Their mounts are equally focused, their great ears and noses pointed forward as they keep up their powerful pace.

When night falls, we make camp, while Aelwyn's men take turns standing guard. I'm too tired to think or ponder what lies ahead; I fall asleep quickly, but the walking dead haunt my dreams. When morning comes, I wake with tears on my face, though I can't remember the dream that put them there, only a terrible sadness that hangs over me as we go about breaking camp.

Throughout that day and the next, we pass through many groups of the undead. In our journeys to the north, we often came across them singly, but here they seem to all be gathered in what look a lot like troops. Their movements are more purposeful as well, as though the dark mind that guides them holds a tighter control over them here. Still, they are no match for the Cymry troops and their warhorses, and they give us no trouble.

At last, on the third day, we leave the hill country behind and canter across gentler slopes where the Saxons have plowed their fields.

"These are the Summer Shires," Mother Sima says. "The land is farmed in summer but abandoned in the winter." Her face puckers as she looks across the untended fields where farmers should be busy with spring crops. "But this summer they will lie empty if the undead cannot be stopped."

Her face brightens, though, as we ride through a grove of apple trees. "The Summer Shires are famous for their cider," she comments. "Pray that we will all drink it again when the plague has been driven from our land."

We ride on and on. Artair shifts his weight in my lap, getting restless. The shadows lengthen, stealing the light from the land, and the air is no longer sweet in my lungs; instead, I scent the stink of decay on the wind. A somber hush hangs over us now. There's not a lark in the sky, not a robin to be seen in the apple groves, not even the call of a wood dove. The only sound is the constant drum of our horses' hooves.

The sun sinks behind the western horizon. Our escorts' scale armor gleams dully in the gray twilight, and suddenly, they seem to me like a pack of scaly lizards. I shake my head to drive away the odd image, but I can't help but shudder. A chill creeps through my bones, and it comes not from the cooling wind but from a sense of foreboding deep inside me. I clutch Artair tighter, glad for his warm, breathing body.

Mother Sima pulls her mount alongside mine again. "Do you feel it?"

"Yes. But what *is* it?"

"We are near the lair of the sorcerer."

Fear leaps inside me. "The Dark God?"

She nods. "The source of the plague."

I suck in a breath. "Do we have to go this way?"

"It is the road to Avalon."

Our mounts slow a little as they climb a bare black hill where even the grass has been burned away. To the north, a line of charred trees thrust their broken branches into the gray sky, like skeleton fingers, while to the southwest, an enormous canyon splits the fields, as if a vast claw had ripped into the earth's skin.

Mother Sima points at the severed earth. "There. That is where the evil spills forth."

The gloom deepens as we pass the ruins of a town. Mostly it's just piles of stone, but here and there I see hints of long-ago Roman glory: the torso of a marble statue, a goddess naked to the navel with a crown of flowers in her hair; a tall column with leaves carved around its top; a line of arches in a crumbling wall.

Mother Sima says softly, "The abandoned town of Wells."

It's a quiet place. If the ghosts of ancient Romans linger here, they're silent and well-behaved, nothing like the walking dead.

We leave the ruins behind and continue on through abandoned Saxon farms until we reach a worn cart path that leads across the dead land. The clip-clop of the horses' hooves on the stones is like a slow and ominous drum. Even these powerful steeds are too weary now to canter. Their sleek sides are frothed with sweat, and their enormous lungs labor for breath.

Ahead of us, Aelwyn reigns in his horse and holds up his arm, pointing toward the west. In the dull red light that lingers there, I see the glimmer of lakes and marshes, a wide spread of water that lies like a mirror across the land ahead. As we ride closer, I make out an island rising from the midst of the waters, a tall hill as steep and round as the thatch roof on my home back in DunCollum. Against the bruised sky, the hill has a soft glow, as though it's lit from within.

Avalon! The sight seems to give us all a fresh burst of courage. Aelwyn and his men clap their heels against their mounts. They rise up in their saddles as their mounts surge forward with new energy, and the four of us gallop behind them.

We ride through apple orchards until we reach a road that runs along an embankment across the shallow water. The sense of heavy gloom lifts, and now I hear the normal sounds of a summer dusk: the sleepy twitter of birds in the trees, the *quack-quack* of ducks on the water, and the hum of bees in the buttercups and meadowsweet that grow along the road. Swallows dart and flash overhead, and the soft dark wings of a bat flutter against the evening sky. We have returned to the land of the living.

A new feeling flows into me: a quiet, glad feeling I can't quite identify. It's an emotion I haven't felt in a very long time, not since I was a child. It reminds me of the way I used to feel when my mother would drop a kiss on my hair as she walked by—or the way it felt to lie in bed, sleepy and safe, listening to the deep tones of my father's voice as he talked quietly with my mother beside the fire.

It comes to me then, the name of this emotion. It's peace.

Aelwyn urges his mount to go even faster, and our steeds keep up with him. The horses seem as eager as we are to reach the Holy Island. We fly past the fading glimmer of marsh and lake, and then a narrow bridge spans the last distance to the island.

A tall man in white robes steps out of the shadows and stands in front of us. We pull up in front of him, and he lifts a staff in greeting. His face is brown and weathered; dark red hair hangs looses over his shoulders, whipping in the wind.

I look around me. A line of stables for our mounts stands alongside the road on this side of the bridge; the hillside would be too steep for the horses, I realize. Ahead, the island is an enormous grassy mound, open to the sky.

I turn to Mother Sima. "The island looks undefended. How can it stand against the attacks of the living dead?"

"This is holy ground," she says quietly. "An unseen host protects it day and night."

I give her a skeptical glance. I don't see any angels guarding the island, but since she claims they're invisible, there's not much point in arguing with her.

And after all I've seen lately, I'm starting to think that most anything is possible.

The white-robed porter greets us in a low, grave voice and beckons us to follow him. We dismount, and several of the Cymry warriors gather up reins and lead the war-horses to a corral beside the stables. The rest of us follow the porter across the wooden bridge.

As I step across the boards, I have the oddest sensation: the air seems richer than any I've ever tasted, as if every breath is giving me an extra surge of energy. Even in the twilight, the hues of grass and water and sky seem strangely vivid, saturated with color. Everything glows.

When I look at the others, I can see I'm not the only one experiencing this sense of wonder. Mother Sima and Nectan, and Aelwyn, are looking around them with smiles and wide eyes. Freya looks less enraptured, but I can tell that even she is not immune to the magic of this place.

When I step off of the bridge onto the island, a peculiar tingle travels from the earth through my sandals into my feet and then up through my entire body. It's a little like the sensation you get sometimes during a lightning storm, when your body feels as though it has become a conduit for something wild and alive. Here on this Holy

Island, I sense that land, water, and air all possess a similar vital force, even when the skies are clear.

Another man dressed in a white cassock strides toward us through the entrance of the palisade. His long hair and beard are silver-white in the twilight. Like the porter, his skin is brown and his eyes dark. "Sister Sima!" he calls, his voice rich with gladness. "It has been far too long since we have seen you in Avalon!"

Mother Sima beams. "It has been far too long since I have seen Avalon—and far, far too long since I have enjoyed your company, Abba Yosef."

They hug and exchange kisses on the cheeks. Then Abba Yosef steps back and regards the rest of us. "Who are your companions, dear sister?"

She waves her hand at the Cymry who are standing in a row with their heads high. "This is Aelwyn, who will soon be king of the Cymry—and these brave warriors are his entourage."

Aelwyn falls on his knees in front of Abba Yosef and kisses the old man's hand. "I and my people are servants of the Culdees."

Abba Yosef takes Aelwyn's hand and lifts him up from the ground. Then the old man hugs the warrior. "I give thanks to Elohim for raising up a man of honor and integrity to rule such a great people." The white-robed priest turns to the rest us. "And who are you three?"

"This is Finn," Mother Sima says. "He was freed from slavery to fight against the plague of the undead."

She points next to each of the others. "Nectan is a strong warrior from the north. And Freya is a maiden of extraordinary courage."

The abba tips his head to us. "You are all most welcome." He turns back to Mother Sima and asks, "Are these three companions all servants of Iosa?" He smiles and bends to pet Artair. "Or should I say four companions, hmm?"

"They are all the Lord's servants," Mother Sima says, "but none of them knows it."

"Unwitting servants are oftentimes the best," Abba Yosef replies. "They have less pride to get in their way." He turns to look at a sundial. "I must go, for it is almost time for vespers. Please, all of you, proceed to our guest lodging. Rest yourselves, wash, take your ease. When the bell rings, anyone who wishes to join us in the chapel is welcome."

As we walk toward the guest quarters, Freya asks me in a low voice, "Why do their words sound so strange? They don't sound like either Saxons or Gaels. Or Picts."

Mother Sima overhears Freya's question. "The men and women in this monastery are descended from the Hebrews. After the resurrection of Iosa the Nail-Riven, Yosef of Arimathea brought Mariam the mother of Iosa, along with the friends of Iosa, Martha, Lazarus, and Mariam of Magdela, from the Holy Land to this place. The people who live here—the Culdees—keep the words and customs of that heritage."

"Both of those men are so thin," Freya whispers. "Like they don't get enough to eat. Do they starve themselves as part of their religion?"

Mother Sima shakes her head. "They are not like the Egyptian abbas who constantly fast. The men and women here are indeed weak from hunger, but it's not by choice. Although the angels guard this island, the walking dead have it under siege. The island's not large enough to support all the crops and cattle needed to feed its people. The Culdees will slowly starve to death in this holy enclosure if we do not stop the revenants."

A shadow falls across my perception of this bright and holy place. I had thought it immune to the plague of living corpses—but even here, their foul touch can be felt.

As we reach the guesthouses, low stone structures built against the curve of the hill, a gaunt woman in a green robe emerges from one and beckons to Freya and Mother Sima. Meanwhile, Nectan, Artair, and I follow a green-robed man to another building, where we are shown to separate rooms. Artair and I enter a tidy compartment that contains a pallet on a wooden bed frame, a stool, and a wooden shelf. A basin of water and a towel are on the stool, and a cross is carved into the stone wall.

I close the door and drop down on the bed. The mattress is stuffed with straw, and if feels like paradise after years of sleeping with the animals outside Aedgar's house. Artair jumps onto the bed beside me and rolls on his back. He looks as blissful about this unusual comfort as I am.

A knock sounds on the door, and one of the green-robed men sticks his head in. He holds up a folded pile of clothing. "We thought you might want fresh clothing after your long journey." He hands me the clothing, then retreats again and shuts the door behind him.

I take a look at the clothing—breeches, a tunic, and even a linen undershirt. I've never had clothes made of such finely woven fabric. After I wash myself, I step into the breeches, then pull the undershirt over my head first, followed by the tunic. The fabric smells of lavender and clover—and everything fits me fine, as though it were made for me. Once I'm dressed, I hardly feel like the same person. The thought crosses my mind that Freya might find me more to her liking when she sees me dressed like this.

When the bell tolls, calling us all to prayer, I hesitate. I do not follow Iosa anymore, and I have no wish to say prayers to him—and yet the bell tugs at something within me. Avalon is a strange and wondrous place, and I can't help but wonder how these men and women pray. Finally, my curiosity overcomes my reluctance. Leaving Artair in the room, I step outside and join the stream of people on their way to climb the steep hill at the center of the island.

We walk past rows of tidy stone huts with freshly thatched straw roofs. Some in the crowd are dressed in white or green cassocks, but others wear ordinary clothes.

Young children hold their parents' hands, while older ones run ahead.

Mother Sima falls into step beside me. She glances sideways at me, her eyebrows raised.

I give her a sheepish grin. "Don't get any ideas, Mother. I'm not won back to your faith. I'm just curious. That's all."

"There's nothing wrong with curiosity," she says mildly. "When we're curious, we are willing to learn something new."

The broad stream of people converges now onto a cobblestone street that leads up to the top of the immense hill. At the summit is a church, shaped like the great hall in an Angle village, a tall square structure with pale sides striped with dark beams. The walls are made from wattle-and-daub—willow branches woven tightly together and then daubed with mud mixed with white chalk—a building material I've seldom seen. I'm more used to small round buildings made of stone, and these tall square walls awe me. At the peak of the thatched roof is a tall pole topped with a wheel cross sheathed in gold. One last finger of light from the setting sun gleams like a spark on the gold cross—and then the sun is gone beneath the horizon. As night settles over us, the light spilling out from the church door seems to shine even brighter by contrast.

I step across the threshold into the church's glowing heart. The burning oil lamps don't seem to cast enough light to explain the radiance that fills the building. The soft gold light illumines the faces around me, so that each person seems to also shine.

The women take their place on one side of the church, the men on the other. As soon as everyone is in place, the people begin to chant, first the women taking a turn and then the men. They speak in a strange language I've never heard before, the syllables rolling back and forth between them as though they're tossing them from one side of the church to the other. I wish Mother Sima wasn't on the other side of the church were she can't explain to me what's going on

While the chanting continues—*are they reciting psalms?*—the church's interior seems to grow still brighter, and then brighter yet. When I look at the oil lamps, their flames are no higher than before, and yet the peak of the roof above me seems lit from some mysterious source.

As I'm squinting up at the ceiling, trying to decide if it's all my imagination, I realize that the building isn't only filled with light; it's also filled with thousands of voices, far more than the number of people standing in rows around me. The music from this vast throng of singers fills the building, sweeter than any human voices I've ever heard, and goose bumps run up and down my arms.

Out of the corner of my eye, something sparkles. I turn my head, but there's nothing there—only now I see a flicker of light move swiftly above me. Again, when I look directly at it, it disappears, while a gold glitter dazzles the opposite edge of my vision. The faces around me are lit up with joy, but they don't seem surprised or particularly interested in the spangles of light shimmering here and there through the air. *Am I the only one who sees them?* Or maybe they're just used to them; maybe this is what happens every time they gather in the church.

I have an odd feeling inside me. It's a little like the heady sensation I get after drinking mead, but I'm not dizzy the way mead makes me. Waves of energy seem to be pouring into me, as though I'm a cup filled up with light and song. At the same time, I sense sky and earth curving around me like a hug, holding me clasped between them. All misery, all fear, all sorrow is gone, and only joy remains.

And then the singers fall silent—both the ones I can see and the ones I can't—and a deep silence fills the space instead of music. No one whispers or coughs. Even the children stand quietly, waiting.

A white-robed woman steps forward in front of the assembly. She has the blackest skin and curliest hair I have ever seen on a human being. At the front of the hall, she stands before a gold box, head bowed in prayer, and then she stoops and kisses it. After a moment, she opens the lid and lifts out a cup. From the way she's acting, I'm expecting something of gold or silver covered with jewels—but it's just a plain wood cup, the sort that ordinary folk use.

The woman turns to face us, and Abba Yosef takes his place beside her, holding what looks like a small broom. He dips his brush into the bowl and flings droplets of water from it onto the heads of the nearest worshipers. Then he and the dark-skinned woman walk down the center aisle of the church, flicking water from the bowl onto the people on both sides.

It seems like a foolish thing to do—throwing water at people, the way my brother and I used to do on hot summer days—but somehow it doesn't look silly. When the abba and woman reach where I'm standing, I turn to receive the patter of water across my face. I suck in a breath, surprised by the warmth that flows through me.

Once Abba Yosef and the woman reach the back of the church and everyone has received this blessing of water, the abba returns to the front. He reads from the Gospel, familiar words I remember from when Priest David used to recite them. After that, he speaks to us for a while, but I'm barely listening. I'm too full of wonder at all that's happening. I had expected to be bored by the worship, but instead, I lose all track of time.

Finally, Abba Yosef holds up his arms and says in a loud voice, "Yahweh bless you and keep you. May Yahweh's face shed light on you and show you favor—may it be turned toward you and give you Shalom."

The crowd murmurs, "Amen," and then, like people waking from a dream, we file quietly out the door.

As soon as we are outside, I head straight for Mother Sima. "What *was* that?" I ask her. "What was going on in there?"

"This is the thinnest of thin places," she replies.

"What's that mean?"

"It's a place where the unseen and visible worlds meet and pass into one another."

I try to absorb that. My people have always believed that the visible world lives side by side with an invisible one, so that's not so hard to grasp—but I've never experienced anything like what just happened in this church. "What makes this place so—different?" I ask finally.

"As a child Iosa came and stayed on this island," Mother Sima said. "From then until now, his footsteps have hallowed its soil."

I give her a skeptical glance. Priest David always made it sound as though Iosa lived on Earth long ago and far away in a distant land. Even if Iosa did somehow come to this small island, I can't quite believe that a child's footsteps would make a place so peculiar. But I don't have any better answer to offer, so I ask grudgingly, "Is that why I heard those voices?"

We've begun to stroll away from the church, but now Mother Sima turns to look me in the face. "Voices?"

"The ones singing from the ceiling."

"Ah." An odd little smile flickers across her face. "You heard the angels. I should have known you would."

Is this something else my sparkling blood causes?

"What about the cup?" I want to know next. "Priest David used a cup in his worship back at my home—when I was young—but it didn't seem . . . well, it didn't make me feel the way I felt in there." I tip my head back toward the church.

Mother Sima nods. "That is another great wonder of this place—the cup of Iosa the Criost, Heaven's Champion. It is the very cup from which he drank on the night before his death."

I can't quite believe she's serious—but her voice is matter-of-fact. How can something so ordinary—even if it is what she says—have such power? I feel as though I might if someone told me a rusty horseshoe was actually a lump of Faerie gold. My eyes know better.

And yet there was definitely something strange and wonderful going on in that church.

Bells ring again from the tower, and a slow stream of robed men and women move toward a low building perched halfway up the hill. "It's time for supper at the refectory," Mother Sima says. My stomach is glad to hear that, and we fall in line behind the others.

Inside the refectory, slit windows let in the fresh night air, while torches fill the long room with flickering light. The straw scattered across the floor is fresh and clean, the long wooden tables spotless. Everything in the room is spare and clean and plain. It doesn't look much like the Cymry king's grease-grimed and sumptuous eating hall.

Nectan and Freya join Mother Sima and me, and Abba Yosef invites us to sit beside him at the head table. The robed men and women line up beside the tables and stand waiting for the food to be blessed. The same dark-skinned woman who held the cup during vespers now chants a prayer in that strange language. Then, with a shuffling of feet and benches, all of us sit down. Servers bring in pots of hot rabbit stew, and small portions are ladled out. Jugs of water are passed, and we fill our cups.

I'm not comfortable talking around Abba Yosef, and I sense Nectan and Freya feel the same. It's not that he's unfriendly or unkind, only that he seems to inhabit a higher plane than ordinary folk. Years of holiness hang like a cape around him, and I can't help but feel small and crude next to him. Mother Sima doesn't seem intimidated by him in the least, though, and she chats easily with him while she eats. They're clearly old friends.

Mother tells the abba about Merlin's prophecy concerning the power of the holy well's water to destroy the neamh mairbh. The old man listens silently and then says, "The Dark God is a demon not a man. More than that, he's a dark principality ascended from the lowest depths of the underworld. Even with our prayers and the protection of Saint Michael, Sister Sima, you'll be unable to match your power against his sorcery."

"Then we'll avoid a contest of powers."

"His cave is crawling with revenants," the old man warns. "There are as many of the risen dead there as there were once living humans in the Summer Shires. Even more, for they have flocked here from across all Albion."

"Well," says Mother Sima, "we'll just have to sneak past them." Clearly, nothing is going to discourage her.

Nectan swallows a bite of stew, then clears his throat and ventures to ask a question. "Abba Yosef, can you tell us where exactly we will find this wizard and his cauldron?"

"Merlin said something about 'where the Yeo twists under the Diamond Hall,'" Mother Sima adds. "Does that mean anything to you, Abba?"

The old man nods. "It's less than a day's journey from here. Follow the raised road that leads north, through the marshes, until you reach a great gorge. It winds between sheer rock cliffs, taller than you've ever imagined. The river that carved those cliffs runs between them still— the Yeo. Follow that—and the foul taste of the air. Both will lead you to the dark place you seek."

I have a question, and now I get up nerve to ask it. "Abba Yosef, why don't your Culdees destroy the cauldron? There's such—such power here."

The old man gives me a careful look, and he seems to see something in my face—I don't know what—that surprises him. After a moment, he says, "Purity of heart is to do just one task—and do it perfectly. Our calling on earth is to guard a treasure. We cannot leave here and put our calling at risk, even in the direst circumstances."

"We can't just walk up a gorge if it's packed with wights," Freya puts in now. "We'll never make it to the cauldron and its master. Is there only one entrance to the cavern?"

"Ah." Abba Yosef gives Freya a smile. "A good idea that. I explored around there as a child, before the Dark

God awoke, before that place was pure evil. The cavern is a magnificent creation of Yahweh, and I loved to investigate its depths. The room that Merlin spoke of—the Diamond Hall—is a place of splendid natural artistry."

He shakes his head. "Sadly, I imagine it is befouled now by the demon." He takes a sip of water, as though he's washing away a bad taste in his mouth. "At any rate, as I was saying—there is a way you can enter, one that I suspect the undead, with their limited intelligence, will not have found. I can only hope it's also escaped their master's notice."

He looks thoughtful, then continues. "When you reach the mouth of the gorge, take the side path toward the horizon where the sun sets. This will lead you along a bluff over and past the cave's maw. You'll see a path sloping down to a spot where a branch of the river flows under the hill. That is your entrance. It's very small—you will have to stoop to enter—but it leads into the cavern from another direction. One that may not be guarded."

"Very good." Mother Sima nods her head as though everything has been solved. "We shall sneak in the side entrance and take the Dark God by surprise."

Abba Yosef shakes his head. "It won't be that simple. The Dark God surrounds himself with a war band of the strongest and most vicious revenants, each of them guided by his magic. What's more, he possesses a seer's vision. Unless his attention happens to be elsewhere, he will know you are coming." He looks down at his plate for a moment, and the lines in his face seem deeper than usual. "I am sorry, my dear. But I cannot imagine how you will ever reach the cauldron, let along get the holy water inside it."

"With God all things are possible. You know that, Abba Yosef." Mother Sima's firm voice holds a hint of rebuke. Does the woman never know fear? "Mention us in your prayers tonight, Abba. We will be on our way in the morning."

A chill creeps over me, driving from my mind all the wonder and curiosity I've been feeling. I didn't realize how close we are to the final challenge. Until now, the confrontation with the Dark God was only a matter of discussion, more like a story than something real that would actually happen.

Abba Yosef stands and then taps on the table with his staff, signaling that the meal is finished. The Culdees stand together. One of them chants a benediction, and then all file out of the hall.

We follow them out into the cool night. Above our heads, the sky is spangled with stars, like beads of glittering water thrown out across dark fabric. The four of us walk together to the guesthouses, and then we bid one another good night, our voices quiet and subdued. I know we're all thinking of what the morning will bring.

Alone with Artair in my little room, I take off my new clothes, fold them, and then blow out the oil lamp.

The straw crackles when I lie down on the mattress, and I stretch out my arms and legs, enjoying this unaccustomed luxury. Artair jumps up beside me and plops down with a sigh, his nose on my chest.

I rub behind his ears. "Bet you never expected to have so many adventures, did you, boy?" He wriggles a little closer and licks my face.

After the long days in the saddle, I expected to fall asleep quickly in the comfortable bed. Instead, I lie there wide awake, thinking about tomorrow. Darkness fills my heart. I can't imagine any worse horror than the neamh mairbh—and yet I know the Dark God will be even more terrible. Even Abba Yosef believes we have no hope of triumphing over the evil sorcerer.

I know Freya thinks I have some uncanny power that will make me a victor in this battle. I've heard lots of talk about me being some sort of magic hero, and yeah, that's been pretty nice to hear. Makes me puff up a little inside and helps me feel like I'm not just some gormless slave. And I have to admit, I've had some amazing experiences I would never dreamed were possible a few months ago.

But deep in my heart, I don't really believe I'm special. Regardless of sparkling green blood and visions of Brigid, I'm just the same old Finn. Nothing much has ever gone right in my life over the past few years. Why should it be any different now?

I toss and turn on the crackling straw. Finally, Artair gives a grunt and jumps down from the bed so he can sleep in peace. And then, hour after hour, I stare into the darkness, listening to his soft snores.

I feel like a wee lamb being led to the slaughterhouse.

12

DESCENT INTO HEL

A sharp knock on the door wakes me. *Shite.* I barely fell asleep and it's morning already.

"I'm coming!"

I stagger to my feet, relieve myself in the chamber pot, and then pull on my new clothes. With the yew stakes and my dirk strapped to my belt, I'm as ready as I'll ever be.

Outside, the air is cool and foggy. A hush hangs over the island, as though it's holding its breath, afraid to see what the day holds. My friends stand waiting for me a few paces away, their bodies so cloaked in fog that they look like a shadowy row of ghosts. No one speaks as I join them, but Freya hands me a strip of dried meat and a horn of mead for breaking the night's fast. I have little appetite, but I know I'll need every bit of strength I can get.

While I gulp down the food and drink, Aelwyn emerges from his room and joins us. His face is grave as he regards the four of us, and then he gives us a deep bow. "Mother Sima, Nectan, Finn, and fairest maid Freya— I regret leaving you with your quest incomplete, but my men and I must be on our way home. Anything can happen when a kingdom changes hands, and I need to ensure that my people do not believe their new lord has abandoned them. In any case, I think there is little we could offer you in the challenge you face today." His lips tighten in a grimace. "I spoke with Abba Yosef last night, and I gather your success will require great stealth—something that a troop of soldiers is not well designed to achieve. I wish it could be otherwise."

"We understand." Nectan's deep voice is unafraid but somber, as though he carries a great sorrow on his shoulders.

Only Mother Sima smiles. "We go with the Threefold God," she says. "What more can we ask than to surrender ourselves to God's will?" I wish I had some of her peace of mind, but her words give me little comfort. Even Mother Sima seems to be implying that we may very well fail today if that's what God wants—and clearly, God's wants are usually far different from my own, or I wouldn't be where I am today.

"But we thank you, Aelwyn," Mother Sima continues. "You have speeded our journey by keeping us safe across the long leagues between Cymry and the Holy Island. May God grant you safe passage home." She stands on tiptoe to pull his head low enough that she can plant a kiss on his cheek.

The rest of us each in turn clasp him on the shoulders, speak words of thanks, and wish him well. As he turns to join his men where they stand ready to reclaim their mounts, even Artair lets out a farewell woof.

Nectan glances down at Artair. "We rely on stealth today. Perhaps the dog should remain here?"

I shake my head. "Artair has never let me down. I want him with me today."

"He is one of us," Mother Sima agrees. "He too has played a role in our journey together—and who knows what else will be required of him before we finish?"

Her words make me sad. Have I given my dog a death sentence?

Nectan nods, then pulls a horn from his belt. "We must wear the scent that will conceal us from the walking dead." He tips the poxy-smelling oil into his hand, then hands the horn to Freya.

Freya pours a dollop of the stuff into her hand. "We should camouflage ourselves as well."

I hate to dirty my new clothes. For so long I've worn the ragged, filthy garments of a slave; now, dressed in clean, fine-woven clothes, I feel like I am truly a free man again. But I know Nectan and Freya are right. And I'd rather be dirty than dead. When my turn comes to pour the hog-piss mixture into my hand, I slather it over me with a generous hand, and then I smear my clothes and skin with mud.

Freya has already turned herself back into a wild forest girl, her gold hair nearly hidden beneath twigs and leaves, her pale face stained green and brown from grass and soil. She gives me a critical glance. "You missed a spot." She dabs a glob of mud on the end of my nose.

She's standing very close to me, and our eyes meet. I wish I could bend my head and kiss her lips. Who knows if I'll ever have another chance? The moment hangs suspended, while I hover in indecision—but then she turns away, and the moment is gone.

"What's our plan?" I hear just the smallest waver in her voice.

"A very simple one," Mother Sima says. "We take advantage of whatever God gives us as it comes along. I trust the way will be given one step at a time."

That doesn't sound like much of a plan to me, and I can tell from Freya's face she feels the same. Nectan looks unperturbed, however, and I keep silent. I may not have much confidence in Mother Sima's God—but I've committed myself to following her, regardless if it makes sense to me or not.

Does that mean I'm prepared to die today?

I don't want to pursue that thought, so I'm grateful when I see Abba Yosef coming toward us. He holds a pottery container with flat, round sides. A leather strap winds through the two loops that flank its cork, and the shape of a square cross is stamped into its side.

"That's a pilgrim flask," Mother Sima murmurs. "The abbas and amas use them for carrying water on their journeys."

Abba Yosef lifts the flask up, holding it with such care and reverence that I know this container holds something more special than ordinary water for our journey. In a soft and solemn voice, the old man says, "When my namesake— Blessed Yosef, the uncle of Yeshua—came to this island, he brought a cruet that contained the blood of Yeshua—the one you call Iosa. The blood was taken from the wound in Yeshua's side when he bled on the cross-tree."

Abba Yosef pauses and makes the cross sign in the air over the flask. Mother Sima does likewise, and then the abba resumes his story. "When Yosef arrived here on this island, long years ago, he found the spring which those who lived here called the Well of the Goddess." He motions down the side of the hill, and in the morning light I can see what it was too dark to see last night: a spring rising from the green grass and flowing into a red-brown stream.

"Blessed Yosef poured the blood from that cruet into the well," Abba Yosef continues, "and its waters have come forth red from that day until now. So this—" He raises the flask higher. "This is the water of life, the blood of Yeshua mingled with the waters of Albion. This is the sacred fluid that can end the curse on our fair land."

His expression lightens, and he smiles as he steps closer to us. "I have wondered who should bear this holy flask. I took for granted it would be you, Sister Sima, but to be certain, I asked for Yahweh's guidance while I was in prayer last night."

He pauses—and then he takes me totally by surprise. "You, young Finn, are the one." He holds the flask out to me. "You are the one who must carry the flask and deliver its contents into the sorcerer's vat."

"Me?" My voice squeaks the way it did back in the days when I was first changing into a man.

Beside me, Freya gives a little snort, "He could have spared himself his prayers," she mutters to me. "I could have told him you were the one."

I hold the flask gingerly between my hands while Abba Yosef makes the cross sign with his fingers on my forehead. He lifts his hand over my head and prays in his foreign tongue.

"Amen," Mother Sima murmurs.

I sling the flask's leather strap over my shoulder and settle it securely against my side—and then I suck in a deep breath and square my shoulders. It doesn't really matter if I feel up to the job I've been given. I just have to do it.

The abba bids us farewell, and the four of us—plus Artair—turn to make our way down to the bridge. Our footsteps are slow, and I know we are all reluctant to leave the safety of this holy place. If I could, I'd choose to clean shit out of every outhouse back in Escomb rather than set forth on this mickle journey.

As we step off the bridge, I feel colder, and the sky darkens. That feeling of every sense being heightened— colors brighter, scents sharper, skin tingling—fades away.

We're back in the realm ruled by darkness. The fog is even thicker now, and each breath I take feels heavy in my lungs.

We hesitate for a moment, and I turn to look at my companions. Nectan's head is high, his spiky hair a proud crest atop his head, the blue spirals on his cheeks so dark they show even through the mud he's used as camouflage. He catches my glance and nods his head at me, his gaze as serene as if we were setting off on some happy outing together. Beside him, Mother Sima hikes up her robes a little for better ease of walking and then, with a little smile on her lips, lifts her shepherd's crook high. Clearly, she's ready for whatever comes. And then there's Freya, her bow in hand. She has that battle look in her eyes, and there's such fierce purity in her gaze that I can't help but suck in a breath, the way I might if I were breathing the cold clean scent of new-fallen snow. At my side, Artair whines, eager to be on our way. These four—and me—are about to go against legions of the walking dead and their war chief from Hel. I couldn't ask for better companions.

But it's like sending ants to kill a wolf.

Aelwyn has left us the same horses we rode coming to Avalon, and now we saddle our mounts and head northwest along the elevated path through the marshland. The great warhorses move sluggishly, as though they too are reluctant to begin this journey. As we ride, the trails of fog slither away like ghostly serpents, leaving behind a deep gloom that hangs like a shroud over the land. It's an odd darkness: the sun has only just risen, and there are few clouds in the sky, yet everything seems drained of color.

No one has spoken since we left the Holy Island behind, but now Nectan gives a grunt and lifts his hand in warning. Ahead, I see a tumbledown hut. Clustered outside it are a group of bony figures. They don't see us; their attention is all on something they're yanking back and forth between them. When I realize what it is—the body of a woman—I have to swallow hard to keep from puking. They're fighting over the limbs, tearing into them greedily, like starved people scrabbling over ham hocks.

A terrible thought occurs to me: do the neamh mairbh in this stripped and barren land survive by getting deliveries of new-killed victims from further afield? When they get a fresh body like the one they have now, is it like when farmers bring their butchered livestock to town on market day?

Eventually, if the undead kill everyone on Albion, will the ghouls die too—or will they just feel insanely hungry?

Who knows?

And who cares? If we're successful today, the undead will be destroyed. And if we're not, we'll be as dead as all the other living soon will be. I just hope I'm truly dead, not turned into a wight myself. As we turn and make a wide circle around the feasting ghouls, my thoughts make me shudder. Meanwhile, the stinking creatures never even look up from their meal.

Once we are back on our road, it leads at last to the crest of a low ridge. From here, I can see a long dark fissure in the earth. We've nearly reached the gorge that holds our destination, but I can feel no satisfaction, only a deepening dread.

The nearer we get to the gorge, the slower our horses' gait. It's almost the Solstice, but the land around us is sere and dead, bleaker than any winter could make it. The grass is brown, and every tree is leafless, their branches black and twisted as if burned in an awful fire or poisoned from their roots. The hillsides that should be green and lush are shades of gray. The strange gloom hangs over everything. Perhaps even more terrible is the utter silence. There is no wind, no cry of birds, nothing at all except the noise of our horses' hooves. It's as if every living, moving thing has been banished from this place.

Nectan points silently to the track that runs along the gorge, and we nod. We have to kick at our horses' flanks to make them ascend the trail; even these warhorses that would take their riders to the gates of Hel in battle are frightened here.

Soon we have crested the top of this great crack in the earth, and here at last we hear something—but it's a sound that makes the hair lift on the back of my neck: the grunts and shrieks of countless undead, rising to us from within the cave that lies below. Our steeds' ears twitch, their nostrils flare, and then they balk, refusing to go any further. We dismount and tie them to the dark and twisted branches of a yew, hoping the tree will give them some protection from the undead.

I give my steed a final pat on the nose and whisper in his ear, "Be safe." I'm reluctant to leave the horses fastened here, but I know that if we are successful, we will need them again.

"They too are in God's hands," says Mother Sima.

"Let's go." Freya's voice is tight with urgency. "Abba Yosef said we needed to keep along the rim of the gorge until we had gone past the cave."

We trot along the path in single file. I feel exposed; if any undead eye below glanced up, I fear they'd see us outlined against the sky. Artair runs steadily alongside me. His every muscle trembles, but his ears are pricked, his tail high. Poor dog, he's terrified, but his loyalty overcomes his fear.

Freya is the leader of our line, and now she makes a sudden gesture, cautioning us to stop. Ahead I see a line of ghouls, marching straight toward us, though they don't seem to have seen us yet. From behind me, Nectan grabs my sleeve and points at a ruined tower off to the side of our trail.

"Come on!" We hurry down the slope and hide inside the tower, hearts pounding.

On the path above us, the undead pass by with a clatter and clack of bones and rusty armor. They're all males, and they move together like disciplined soldiers, their faster-than-human strides in synchrony. Crouched in the tower, we glance at each other. This is a truly formidable group of wights, like none we've ever seen before.

They move so rapidly that the sound of their marching feet soon recedes into the distance. We climb back up to the path and continue on our way, running faster now. The screams rising from the gorge are louder than before, and we keep well back from the rim, hoping to avoid being seen by the ghouls below.

My legs feel like jelly, but when I start to flag, Mother Sima flaps her hand at me, motioning me to keep up my pace. *Thunor's arse! How can the woman keep running like that?* She's far shorter and plumper than I am, and it's not like I've lived a soft life these past years—but the woman puts me to shame.

Our path slants downward now, and Mother Sima calls softly for us to slow our pace at last. "We must be near."

We creep along, our eyes searching the hillside for the opening Abba Yosef described to us. Nectan and Freya are the first to see it, and together they point at a shadow that looks far too tiny to accommodate a human body. It doesn't seem possible that this can be what the abba meant for us to find.

As we get nearer, I see the shadow is indeed an opening into the hill, but it's only half my height. A stream flows swiftly and silently into the dark hole, as if even the water is afraid to lift its voice in this grim place.

At the mouth of the tunnel, we hesitate. We've hurried all morning to reach this spot, but now that we're here, no one wants to crawl inside. Dank, fetid air whispers out from it, like some foul creature breathing. The scent it carries is not the normal odors of wet earth and rock you'd expect to find in a cave. It's not the rotting sick-sweet smell of the neamh mairbh either; it's somehow even worse, even though I can think of no words to describe it. The odor is just *wrong*. It smells of something terrible and unnatural, something that has no connection to the earth.

Mother Sima stretches out her plump arms and gathers us all close to her. "The Lord is my shepherd," she says, and I recognize the words of one of the psalms Priest David used to recite. "I shall lack nothing." I try to find comfort in the words, but I'm too scared even to appreciate the fact that Freya is pressed close to me.

"Though I walk through the valley of death's shadow," Mother pronounces firmly, "I shall fear no evil."

I wish I had her faith. But I don't. I have only my determination to see this thing through, despite my fear.

When Mother Sima finishes the psalm, Nectan says cheerfully, "Right then. Let's find that sorcerer's pot. The sooner we find it, the sooner Finn can throw the holy water in it—and the sooner we can get this over with."

Mother Sima produces a small oil lamp from her shoulder bag, along with a cruet of oil, but I'm too terrified now to be either amused or surprised by the many and various things Mother carries concealed on her body. She could bring out a battleaxe or a side of beef at this point, and I wouldn't bat an eye.

Mother pours the oil into the lamp, then strikes steel and stone to light the wick. Freya makes the sign of Thunor's Hammer over her chest, and I check to make sure the straps of the pilgrim's flask are secure. Mother Sima holds up her lamp and enters the tunnel, and the rest of us follow after. Mother is short enough that she merely ducks her head to avoid hitting the rocky ceiling, but Freya has to bend at the waist, and Nectan and I are so hunched over that we're nearly on our hands and knees. Artair whines softly but follows close behind me.

Inside, the lamp casts a small, flickering light that's nearly swallowed by the shadows. The only path is through the streambed, and the shallow water is so cold that it numbs my feet. The wet walls press close around us, and I feel as though we're creeping down the slimy gullet of some terrible huge snake. The strange smell grows stronger.

The rocks above my head are rough and jagged, and I have to be careful to keep my knees and back bent, my head low, or I'll bang my poor ill-used noggin. As the dim light from the outer world disappears behind us, my muscles are already cramping.

Doesn't matter. You have to keep going. No turning back now.

We pass a narrow offshoot from our path, and we glance at each other, but Mother Sima shakes her head. "That's too tight for me to fit, I'm afraid. We'll stick to this one."

The passage twists and turns, and I can't shake the feeling that we're crawling through enormous intestines.

None of us says anything. Nectan, with his greater height, must be even more uncomfortable than I am, but he moves forward quickly, steadily. Mother Sima stumbles on the slippery streambed and goes down on one knee. Freya helps her to her feet, and we continue on.

Damn. I don't like how tight these walls are. Panic makes my chest grow tight, and I struggle to breathe.

"One breath at a time, lad," Nectan says softly. "That's all it takes—just one breath after another. Don't think about anything else."

Artair's warm tongue licks my hand. Comforted by the encouragement of these two friends, I try to focus only on my breath. No darkness, no narrow walls, no terrible smell burning my nostrils, just my breath: in . . . out; in . . . out; in . . . out.

Criost have mercy, Iosa have mercy. The familiar prayer whispers through my head with each breath.

Suddenly, the rocky ceiling so close above our heads is gone. We've come into a wide chamber, nearly as big as Wulfstan's great hall back in Escomb. The stream spreads out across the cave floor, leaving a dry pathway down the middle that crawls between strange pointed columns of stone. Long points of stone hang from the ceiling too, like rocky icicles. We've left behind the monster's intestines, and now we've reached its fang-filled maw.

The air here is fouler yet, the putrid odor of neamh mairbh mixing now with that other strange smell. We must be getting near to the creatures. I hesitate for a moment, but Freya tugs at my sleeve and pulls me forward.

We have to weave our way through the jagged points of stone that reach both up and down. The stone beneath my feet undulates in unexpected ways, as though we're walking across waves of stone, and it's hard to keep from stumbling. Above, below, to every side, ripples and drips of stone surround us. I have the dizzy sense that I'm floating in liquid, a liquid that's hard and sharp. Disoriented, I can no longer tell what's down and what's up. I can sense, though, that we're going deeper and deeper, and I feel the Earth's weight pressing down on me.

Breathe in . . . breathe out.

When we reach a place where several tunnels branch off into the darkness on each side, we come to a halt. "Which way is the cauldron?" Freya's voice is hushed.

Mother Sima shakes her head. "I don't know." I can't remember a time when Mother didn't have some kind of solution, and cold settles in my bones. If even Mother Sima is uncertain, then we are surely lost.

"If we follow the flow of the water," Nectan offers, his deep voice as tranquil as ever, "we'll know we're continuing in the same direction."

I'm glad to feel we have at least a little sense of where we're going, but before we've taken more than a few paces, we hear the sound of footsteps echoing from one of the other tunnels. Mother Sima immediately blows out her lamp, I pick up Artair in my arms, and we press ourselves into a narrow crack in the stone.

Peering over Freya's shoulder, I see four wights—males, armored and tall—emerge from the shadows. The one at the head of the line carries a smoking torch, and the others hold in their arms motionless corpses that look as though they've been dug up from their graves. Their skin is dry and leathery, nothing left of their faces but grinning skulls.

"They didn't eat them," Nectan whispers. "They must be intended for the cauldron."

"Then we should follow them." Freya breathes the words, so soft I barely hear her.

The neamh mairbh make their way between the stone teeth, and then they turn into another tunnel. We wait until we can barely hear their footfalls, and then we follow quietly behind them, feeling our way through the dark.

This passageway is high enough that at least we can all walk upright. It turns and curves, and I run one hand along the rippled stone to keep my bearings. A dim flickering light filters back to us from somewhere up ahead.

At the front of our line, Nectan stops and points at the wall. Distorted figures crawl and writhe along the stone face. My heart leaps in fear, and then I realize they're not actually moving—but even though they're only drawings pecked into the rock, they still send a shudder through me. The images are like nothing I've ever seen before: a procession of caped men with the heads of beasts and insects; enormous clawed lizard creatures walking upright like men; and, towering above all the others, cowled wraiths with gnarled talons for hands and long razor-like teeth. I shudder.

Are the real-life versions of these things waiting for us up ahead?

We're silent as we study the strange images, and then, just as silently, we continue on our way. We haven't gone more than a few steps, though, when I hear a sharp squeal behind me. I spin around, my dirk ready.

At first, I think there's nothing there—and then Artair growls, and I see waist-high shadows scabbering toward me.

Woden's balls! They're rats. Rats as big as pigs.

Freya lets out a tiny squeak, and I brace myself, ready to meet these giant rodents with my blade. They scuttle past us, though, and as quickly as they appeared, they're gone again, their naked pink tails slithering behind them.

I hear Mother Sima draw in a deep breath, then let it out. "I've never cared for rats," she says mildly.

Breathe in . . . breathe out. But it's not easy when the stench of the undead grows thicker with each step. Even worse is that other smell, the strange, dark smell that seems to crawl inside me.

Criost have mercy, Iosa have mercy.

We've reached a point now where the passage divides into two branches. We all pause, listening for the sound of footsteps from either side.

Nothing.

"Now what?" Freya whispers. "Which way do we go?"

As we stand there, straining our ears, I hear a new sound. This isn't the sound of the ghouls' footsteps, and it's not their wails and shrieks. This is something different, a deep thud and clack, thud and clack, again and again.

"What is that?" Freya whispers.

"It's the sound of demons dancing," Mother Sima murmurs. "The joyless veneration of the underworld."

"Let's go the other direction." Nectan points, then leads the way.

This passageway runs straighter, but the floor is more uneven, creased with deep fissures. Trickles of water make the rock slick under our feet, and here and there, the icy water rises high enough that we have to wade. We step carefully, trying not to slip or turn an ankle. To make our way even more difficult, the passageway is nearly pitch dark.

After a while, Mother Sima ventures to light her lamp again. The warmth of the small flame is comforting at first, but the flickering light illuminates pale shapes stacked along the damp walls—and with a creeping sensation across my skin, I realize they're human bones. Piles and piles of leg bones and ribs, arm bones and skulls, and all of them are scratched with teeth marks.

"This is the draugars' midden." Freya's voice is muffled, as though she's trying not to vomit—or cry. "It's where they pile up the garbage left after their meals."

Oh shite. I lean against a stone pillar, suddenly too sick to walk. Something tickles my hair, and I put up my hand—

"Stop, Finn! Hold still!" Freya's voice has an odd tone now, and my hand freezes. She's staring at my head, her eyes wide with horror.

"What is it?" I whisper.

"Just a bug," Mother Sima says, and Nectan brushes it off my hair. It falls to the floor with a thud, and in the lamplight I see a segmented body the size of my hand. It's landed on its back, its six legs wiggling, but it rights itself quickly and scuttles off into the shadows beneath the piles of bones. Long after it's gone, we still here its feet tap-tap-tapping on the stone.

Just a bug. Breathe in . . . breathe out.

We continue on, and my heartbeat slowly returns to almost normal. Then a sudden noise ahead makes it race again. Mother Sima instantly blows out her lamp, and Nectan pushes us down behind a pile of bones. We crouch there, barely even breathing, as footsteps come toward us. I'm trying not to think about enormous insects crawling over me in the dark.

Whoever is coming is carrying a torch. Its light shines full on Mother Sima's face for an instant, and she ducks down lower. I peer out between the bones of a ribcage and see seven neamh mairbh approaching. I can only hope their eyesight is as bad as all the others we've seen so far on our travels—and that Nectan's hog piss will do its job and mask our scent.

As the ghouls pass our hiding place, I recognize them. It's the four warriors we saw before—and the three bodies they were carrying, except now the leathery corpses are walking. They totter after the warriors, staggering like drunken people; it must take a while to get used to walking after being dead for so long.

Are they even aware of what's happened to them? Do they remember who they were when they were alive, really alive?

The wights disappear from sight, and eventually, the sound of their footfalls grows distant. "Come on," Nectan whispers. We leave our hiding place and continue on our way. Mother Sima relights her lamp and takes the lead.

After what seems a long while—but I can't really tell, for time seems to twist and writhe as oddly as the stone bowels we're crawling through—the passageway turns a sharp corner, and we find ourselves at the edge of an enormous chamber. The lamplight reveals a scene of eerie beauty: gleaming crystal tentacles of stone twist and interlace, from the floor to the ceiling. Mother Sima holds her lamp higher and illumines a vast crystal waterfall. I can't imagine what formed it; it looks as though a thundering cataract had suddenly been turned to stone by some magician's spell. The lamp's small flame catches at tiny facets everywhere in the chamber, and the rock glitters and flashes with purple-red sparks. Tunnels lead off from this great crypt in all directions, like spokes around the hub of a wheel.

"This is it," Mother Sima says softly. "The Diamond Hall."

She takes a few more steps, her lamp held up in front of her—and sure enough, in the center of the chamber is an enormous shining kettle, as tall as my waist, with bulbous curved sides. It glistens like brass—or gold—but there's no warmth to the metal's sheen. Raised designs circle it, distorted figures that echo the shapes we saw carved on the stone walls.

"That thing," whispers Nectan, "was not forged in our middle earth. It comes from elsewhere."

I'm not sure what he means—and yet, I sense the truth of his words. The cauldron is a cold, unnatural thing. Something about it makes horror creep through me, a cold and deadly sense of evil far worse than anything we've yet seen.

A bonfire's red flames leap and crackle around the vat. The odd stench I've been smelling is so dense here I can scarcely breathe. At first, I think the fire gives off the odor, but then I realize that it rises from the cauldron itself, as though something foul is being cooked inside the gleaming vessel.

Through my fear and nausea, I slowly realize: *This is it.* Everything relies on me now.

I hold the flask in my hands, leaving it still strapped around my shoulder, and look around the chamber. There's no one here but us. I suck in a breath and pop the stopper from the flask's mouth. All I have to do is cross the short distance that lies between me and the cauldron—and toss the water into it.

Can it really be that easy?

Freya gives me a shove, and I start to run. I'm almost there, my arm outstretched, ready to tip the holy water into the cauldron, when—

Aiiieee!

Neamh mairbh pour out from the mouth of every tunnel, floods of them. In an instant, they've leapt like gray spiders across the floor, and now a mass of them circles the cauldron.

I let the flask drop back on its straps against my side. There's no way through that wall of rotting flesh. I take a step backward and then another, my mouth dry.

But Artair is braver than I am. He growls from deep in his throat, his lips curled back from his teeth, his hair standing in a stiff ridge along his back. Suddenly, he races toward the ghouls and flings himself at them.

"No, Artair!" I leap to pull him back, but before I can reach him, one of the wights swings a scythe—and a high-pitched yelp echoes off the cavern walls.

"No, Artair, no," I whisper. My dog lies on the floor of the cave, a long, red gash along his flank.

I go down on one knee beside him, my face wet with tears. He looks up at me and whimpers, blood and viscera pouring from his wound.

No, by all the gods, no! Filled with a sudden rage, I yank out a yew stake and jump to my feet. When one of the undead swings its club at me, I'm ready for it. My stake sinks deep into its rotting guts. More of the ghouls are coming at me, a sea of bony limbs and shrieking skulls. I wrench my stake free and stab it into an eye, then jerk it free and jab again. *Take that, you fecking corpse!* I pull out Da's dirk and swing it with such strength that it slices through vertebrae and leaves a skull dangling from gray and bloody threads.

I give a scream of triumph and turn my attention to another neamh mairbh. This one holds a scythe, and I know he's the one that felled my dog. I've forgotten why I'm there; I'm too full of a vicious joy as I smash my dirk upward, catching him beneath his bony jaw. His skull flies off his shoulders, still howling. He totters, and then one of Freya's arrows catches him between the ribs, and he drops.

I give another battle scream.

"Finn!" It's Mother Sima, shouting to me over the undead heads. "The cauldron!"

My attention is fixed on another wight, my arm up. I know I can take this one just like I did the last. I'm the Chosen One after all—and these ghouls dared to hurt my dog. I'll make them sorry . . .

"Finn!" Mother Sima shouts again. "You're wasting time. We can't hold them off very long. You *have* to get to the cauldron!"

I shake my head, dazed. Finally, the battle rage recedes, and I remember the flask at my side. I glance down at Artair on the ground. *Is he already dead?* I can't tell, but I know I have to leave him here. I glance at my other friends, and I realize they're fighting for their lives. I may have already taken too much time.

With a sob, I push forward through the mass of rotting limbs, hacking back and forth with Da's dirk to clear myself a path. I've almost reached the cauldron, I can even feel the heat of the flames that burn beneath it, when I hear Freya scream my name in warning. I turn in time to see the battleaxe that's about to descend onto my skull. I jump out of the way, and now I'm even closer to the vat. I reach for the flask at my side, hoping that none of the precious water has sloshed from its open mouth. And then—

Crash!

One of the ghouls shoves a club at me like a battering ram. I stagger back, and at first I don't realize what's happened. I can't understand why my tunic is suddenly soaked with water.

And then I hear the rattle of broken pottery around my feet, and I understand. The ghoul's club smashed the flask into fragments—and the water of Avalon has all spilled out.

For a moment, I can only stand there, still swaying from the blow that broke the flask, while a terrible desolation sweeps over me. *I wasted my chance—and now there's no hope. No hope at all.*

But I have no time to linger in my despair. The same neamh mairbh is swinging its club at me again. I slide Da's dirk back into its sheath and grab a yew stake in its place. *I'll fight until I die!* That's my only thought as I step back into the fray, twisting and dodging, thrusting and slashing. The ghouls fall in a circle around me.

But for every one that drops, two more leap forward into its place. *Until I die!* Grimly, I shove a stake into a leathery chest. The corpse falls forward, burying my stake beneath its putrid flesh; I pull out another stake and meet another wight with my arm out straight.

The stake snaps against the undead warrior's metal armor, leaving me with only a broken stub. I shove it deep into a bloody eye, and hear the corpse's scream. As another of the rank creatures falls on me, I have another stake already in my hand. One more wight drops to the ground.

Dimly, I'm aware that Mother Sima is behind me shouting prayers at the top of her lungs, her staff whacking back and forth, and from the corner of my eye, I catch the flash of Nectan's swords. Freya's arrows are still whistling through the air like angry wasps, so I know that the four of us are at least still on our feet and fighting.

But we can't hold out forever against this mass of undead bodies. It's only a matter of time until we're bleeding on the stones like Artair. Sweat drips into my eyes, and I shake my head to clear my vision. *Until I die!*

A ghoul that looks like it was resurrected from a long-dead body comes at me, swinging a sickle from its skeleton hand. I plunge a stake into its broken cranium. It goes down, but before I can yank my stake out of its skull, another, fresher corpse launches its slimy flesh against me, pushing me out of reach. I fumble in my pouch for another yew stake.

The pouch is empty. I'm out of stakes. *No matter. I still have Da's dirk.* I yank it from its sheath and whirl around. *Until I die!* Another hunk of decomposing flesh drops.

But some of the fallen ghouls are scrambling to their feet now, rejoining the fight. The battle rage still drives me forward with a furious energy like nothing I've ever experienced, but for how much longer? There's only one answer to that question.

Until I die!

The battle rages on. My dirk swings back and forth, tearing at rotten muscles, spilling green coils of intestines, spattering black blood across my face. Then I hear Mother Sima let out a sharp cry, and I spin around, terrified by the agony in her voice. She's on the ground just behind me, her leg thrust out at a crazy angle from her body. A dark pool of blood spreads across the stones, pouring from a deep wound in her calf.

I lunge to stab the ghoul that stands over her, his broken blade ready to finish her off, but Nectan jumps behind the monster and decapitates it first. I kick the skull out of my way.

With a new rush of energy, Nectan, Freya, and I circle Mother Sima and fight off the endless onslaught. Bones crack around us like dead trees in a storm. Skulls fly across the cavern. Bits of flesh and gore are everywhere, and I have to fight to keep my footing, but my blade never hesitates.

And then, suddenly, there's a lull. Not a single wight is coming at us. Nectan's swords drop to his sides, and I hear Freya pant for breath. At our feet, Mother Sima moans, and I realize that even in her pain, she's gasping out prayers.

Freya goes down on her knees beside Mother, and I swallow back my horror. Mother's leg looks like it's nearly cut off. Freya rips a strip of fabric from the hem of her dress and binds it tight around the bloody leg.

A sound from across the cavern makes me turn, and I see more of the undead pouring out from one of the tunnels. At the same time, a few of the ones that lie around us are stirring back to life. Freya's eyes meet mine, and I see that she too has surrendered all hope that we will get out of this alive.

"I'm out of arrows," she whispers.

Nectan steps between us and this new wave of undead warriors. "Go!" he shouts over his shoulder. "Take Mother Sima and get out of here." He turns back to face our enemy, his swords lifted.

I don't want to leave him. "We'll all go down together!" I shout.

Nectan's poised and ready for the fight, but he spares me a single glance. "Go, Finn!" For a second, his gaze meets mine. "You are the Chosen One, Finn." His deep voice is as strong and steady as ever. "Go and be well, my friend. Run today so that you can fight tomorrow."

He's going to die here, I realize. He's going to give his life for me. My eyes fill with tears, but Freya yanks at my hand.

"Help me lift her!" She puts her shoulder under one of Mother Sima's arms, and I grab Mother's other arm. Together, we heave her to her feet. I look back at Nectan, longing to take my place at his side, but Freya reads my thoughts. "You can't, Finn!" she screams. "Come on!"

We drag Mother's weight as quickly as we can toward an opening. Her feet bump over the wights' fallen bodies, and she groans in pain. I look down and see a scrap of bloody fur. *Artair.* I'm amazed to hear a faint whine when I touch him. I can't leave him here; I pause just long enough to scoop him up with my free hand. His fur is wet with blood, and I feel the slimy flex of his guts in my hand. His scream of pain is so weak it's a mere whisper.

"Come on!" Freya hisses, panting from the strain of Mother's weight. I take as much of the load as I can on my own shoulder and push forward.

Joined by Mother's limp body between us, Freya and I reach the tunnel where we first entered the chamber. It's dark and empty, no sign of any undead. As we stagger between the stone teeth, I hear Nectan's battle cry behind us.

I turn back for one last glimpse of our friend, just in time to see him stagger. His swords drop from his hands, and he clutches at a spear that's lodged in the center of his broad chest. Over the sea of undead heads, his eyes meet mine. His gaze is the same as ever, firm and unshakeable, but but I know he's bidding me his last farewell.

"No!" I scream.

He shakes his head. "Go," he mouths—and falls. Countless neamh mairbh scrabble over him, and the chamber echoes with their triumphant screams.

"We have to go back!"

But Freya pulls relentlessly forward, even though she's sobbing. "We can't help him," she manages to get out. "It's too late. We have to go. The draugar are too stupid to realize we've gotten away." When I still hesitate, she swipes the tears of her eyes and glares at me. "Finn, Nectan would want us to go. Don't waste his life. Come on!"

Tears spill down my face unnoticed as we stagger along the slippery corridor. Mother Sima mumbles broken bits of prayers, Gaelic and Latin jumbling together. Artair shakes and spasms in my other arm. Only Freya's determination keeps me from turning around to die with Nectan.

Mother Sima falls silent, and her body's suddenly heavier. I hope she's merely unconscious, not dead, but we don't stop to check. When I slam my head into a jagged rock, I don't even pause, even though I feel blood trick from my scalp. *Nectan should have been buried with his weapons and jugs of mead*, I'm thinking dully, *while all of his clan folk sang his praises.*

We stumble into a tiny, narrow tunnel, like a black artery in the rock. There's no room here for us to go three abreast, so we pause to rearrange Mother Sima's weight between us. First, though, I thrust Artair inside my tunic, where my belt will keep him tight against my chest. He quivers very slightly; somehow, he's still alive. Then I get ahead of Mother Sima and put my arms under both of hers, dragging her while I shuffle backward. Freya picks up Mother's feet and carries them.

Before we've gone very many steps, I feel the tremor of Freya's muscles run through the body between us, and I know her strength is almost gone. I grit my teeth, blinking away the sparks of Faerie blood dripping from the gash in my head. At least my arms are plenty strong from hauling Aedgar's cussed stones.

Left foot, right foot; left foot, right foot. The words inside my head are my new prayer, the only prayer I have left. There's nothing but darkness all around us, nothing but darkness inside my heart. The weight of Mother's body grows heavier and heavier, and I continue my slow backward journey into the earth's belly. *Left foot, right foot; left foot, right foot.*

Inside my tunic, Artair spasms again, and I feel a flood of warmth against my skin. The smell tells me he's pissed and shat himself. I know it may have been his final death spasm, but I don't stop to check. If I let go of Mother's weight, I may not be able to find the strength to pick it up once more. I bang my head against jags of rock again, and then again, and the green glitter of my blood spills around me, the only illumination in the utter darkness.

And then I hear Freya gasp something, a word I don't understand until she says it again. "Light!"

I lift my head and see she's pointing past me. A breath of fresh air slides across my skin like a gentle cool hand. A few more painful steps, and I feel rain on my head. We're outside. We've escaped the cavern.

Freya and I pause. I know we have to get further away as quickly as possible, but we take a moment to catch our breaths. Artair is a damp, quiet bundle inside my tunic, and in the gray light, I can see that the strip of Freya's skirt has fallen away from Mother Sima's leg, leaving a mess of jagged bone and severed, bleeding muscle. I swallow hard and look away.

My eyes meet Freya's, and then, as though we've reached an unspoken decision, we pull Mother Sima up the slope to a small ferny hollow sheltered by a thorn tree. Freya sets her end of our burden down, and motions me to lower mine as well.

Once we have Mother resting on the ground, Freya says, "Give me your dirk."

"What?"

She repeats her command.

"Why?"

She points at Mother's half-severed leg. "If she stays like this, she'll bleed to death. Or an ill spirit will enter her leg and kill her."

"What are you going to do?"

"Cut off her leg." Her voice is matter-of-fact. "Give me your dirk."

"No! We'll go for help. Someone will be able to sew her back together."

Freya gives a snort of mirthless laughter. "I've seen too many battle wounds, Finn. If there's any hope of her surviving, I have to cut the leg off as cleanly as I can and tie her arteries shut." She glances down at Mother Sima, and I see the weariness and despair in Freya's face. "She may have already lost more blood than she can spare."

I hand Freya my blade. She bends over the mangled knee, then looks up at me again. "Do you know how to pray? To Mother Sima's God?"

I swallow and search my brain for the right words. During the past hours, my only prayers have been my breath, my willingness to die, and my commitment to walk step after step, but now I manage to pull out something else. "Criost have mercy," I whisper. "God have mercy. Iosa have mercy." I finger the cross pendant around my neck, and on impulse, on raise it to my lips. My vision of Brigid flashes through my memory, and I lift my head; for a moment, I might have caught the whiff of apple blossom and heard a distant chime of tiny bells.

"What is it?" Freya asks.

I shake my head. "Nothing." *Only my imagination.*

Freya makes the sign of Thunor's Hammer, then tears another strip from her dress. "I've always thought women's clothing was a nuisance," she says in a dull voice, "but this gown has come in handy more than once." She bends to her work, but I can't watch. After what seems longer than any of us can bear, I hear the rasp of metal against bone and then a final snap. Mother stirs and lets out a sharp cry, but her eyes don't open.

Freya wipes the dirk on her skirt and hands it back to me. "That a good sharp blade," she comments.

"Something else that's come in handy. Grand that your father left it for you."

Her voice is calm, her blue eyes very wide. I'm fairly certain she's gone completely off her nut, but she's still the bravest person I've ever met.

"Give me the dog now," she says.

Gingerly, I ease Artair out of my tunic, and Freya takes him from me. He's nothing but a bloody bundle of fur, his guts bulging through the wound in his side, but I hear the faint whistle of his breath. He's still alive.

I can't bear to watch as Freya stuffs his intestines back inside, but when I look away, my gaze falls instead on the piece of leg that's no longer attached to Mother's body. I lurch sideways and puke into the ferns.

"If you're done," Freya says, "you could help me with this." She's wrapped another strip of her gown around Artair's belly. "Hold it in place," she commands, "while I tie it."

Once she's done, she scrambles to her feet, and I see that her skirt hangs just below her knees now. Once upon a time, I would have been fascinated by the sight of her bare legs, but I'm too sad and weary to care. I pick up Artair as gently as I can and put him back inside my tunic. "We have to get back to the horses." I peer through the misty air. "They're that way, I think."

Freya nods, and we lift Mother Sima's arms over our shoulders, then once again heave her weight forward between us. The drizzle washes the blood out of my eyes, and the cool wet air against my face is a welcome balm. Even the gray gloom of this land is far better than the stench and darkness we've left behind.

We retrace the path we took earlier along the rim of the gorge; it seems like a lifetime ago that we were all walking here, the five of us together and in one piece. We've only gone a few paces before we hear the distant sound of a thousand dead throats wailing, followed by a trailing chorus that reminds me of a pack of hounds belling as they run after a deer. Freya and I exchange glances. We say nothing, but I know she's thinking what I am: the dark master of the neamh mairbh has realized we've escaped—and now he's sent his undead servants after us.

There's nothing we can do but keep going. We stagger along, step by weary step. Finally, I see up ahead the dark outline of the yew tree where we left our mounts.

But the horses are gone.

Freya and I set our burden down. For a moment, we simply stand there, panting, too tired to think what we should do next.

"We have to go back to Avalon," I say at last.

Freya nods. "But we can't carry Mother Sima any further. We'd have to leave her here." Her voice is very quiet.

I put my hand on Artair's limp bulge. "We have to try."

Freya shakes her head. "Think, Finn. We'll never make it. It's taken all our strength to get her this far. Besides, we can't keep bumping her along like this. It makes her leg bleed more—and she can't afford to lose more blood."

"We can't leave her here alone."

"No," Freya agrees, her voice so sad I can't bear to hear it. "We can't leave them. We can't let them die here alone." She blinks away her tears, then turns and studies the yew tree.

"Look," she says after a moment, "there's a crack here." When she turns sideways and squeezes through the space, she completely disappears. Her muffled voice emerges. "Come here, Finn. It's like a little room in here."

I follow her inside the yew's corded trunk, and find a round space surrounded by the many columns that form the tree. My mother told me that a yew is actually many trunks growing together. Even if the center dies, the outer ring will continue to grow. "A yew tree never dies," I whisper, echoing Ma's words. "It lets go of life in one place and sends it out in another."

"What did you say?"

I shake my head. "Nothing. Just something my mother used to say."

A faint light filters into this sheltered space, and I breathe in the sweet scent of wood and soil. This is a safe space, as safe as any we're going to find so near the Dark God's realm.

It's not easy fitting Mother's Sima's plump body through the narrow crack in the tree. She stirs and mutters as we pull and push her, Freya on the inside of the tree, me on the outside. At last, we have her inside, and we lower her to the ground. Freya uses Mother's leather satchel to elevate her stump of leg. I go back for Artair and lay him along Mother's side, close enough they'll feel each other's warmth. Then I pull my new undershirt over my head and bunch it up for a pillow to put under Mother's head.

"They're both breathing." It's the only hopeful thing I can think to say. It seems unlikely that either one of them will survive.

Kneeling next to my two wounded friends, a wave of weariness washes over me, and I long to fall back beside them on the soft soil of decayed wood.

"The fates have spun us a cruel fortune." Freya's voice holds no emotion, only a deadly weariness.

I stare down at Mother Sima, and my eyes blur with tears. I wish I'd told her how much I respect her, how glad I've been to be her friend. "Mother Sima was the wisest of our company, and Nectan the strongest. Why are they fallen, while we are left?"

"This may be the Gotterdammerung," Freya says, still in that flat voice. "Doomsday. Soon there will be more monsters than living souls. And then all Angleland will belong to the Dark God and his creatures."

She bends and presses a finger against Mother's wrist, then glances up at me. "Her pulse is very faint now. She doesn't have long." For the first time, her voice quavers, and when she speaks again, I can barely hear the words. "It was good to have a mother again."

I put my hand on her shoulder. "We should go for help. There may still be hope."

For a moment, she leans against my hand, but then she slumps down on the ground beside Mother Sima's body. "There's no point now. She's dying. I won't leave her to die alone."

13

THE DARK GOD'S PREY

I'm hunched up against the yew's ragged trunk, staring at nothing. I don't know how long I've been here. The misty rain has thickened and turned to heavy fog that's wiped away the rest of the world.

The fog is just one more enemy. If it would blow away, I could find my way back to Avalon and go for help. As it is, I'd be lost if I took more than a few steps away from the rim of the gorge. So I just sit here. I can't see more than a foot in front of me.

Everything has turned to nothing. Nothing to fight for anymore. Nothing to hope for. Nothing I'm afraid of now either. I'm dead inside. The hollow tree behind me is more alive than I am. I'm just an enormous empty hole.

Not quite empty, though. There's something awful in the hole that is all I am.

Guilt.

Nectan is dead, Mother Sima maimed and dying, and Artair a blood-soaked mess. Three companions gave their all so that I could destroy the Cauldron and end this plague of rotting ghouls—and I failed my friends. Like always, I couldn't stay focused. I let my rage push me around, as though being angry could justify me doing anything I wanted. Instead, all it did was distract me from my mission. My friends trusted me, and I let them down.

Chosen One. I shake my head in disgust. Abba Yosef and his prayers couldn't have been more wrong.

I should have been the one who died, not Nectan. Not Mother Sima and Artair.

I have never felt so all alone as I do now, sitting here in the fog, as though my guilt has wiped away the entire world, leaving only this gray nothingness. But then I remember: Freya, Mother Sima, and Artair are actually still close to me, and I should see how they are.

Before I can push myself to my feet, a voice calls, "Finn!"

The sound of my name comes out of the fog, but I can't see anyone. Just as I'm wondering if I'm so exhausted that I'm imagining things, I hear it again. "Finn!" The voice is like tiny bells chiming.

A shape materializes in front of me, moving closer through the fog. Hair like flame emerges from the gray air, tiny beads of mist clinging to the curls.

Brigid.

She comes close enough that I can see her clearly now, standing in front of me with her hands on her hips. "Why are you sitting there, Finn? Why are you doing nothing when your task is not yet complete?"

I stare up at her. "Don't you know what happened?"

"You lost a battle." She gives her shoulders a little shrug. "Why are you surprised? In every war, battles are lost. Did you expect victory would be easy? The Dark God and his undead are formidable foes. Yet the war must go on."

I blink up at her. What does she mean? Is she even real? Or are weariness and sorrow making me see things that aren't there?

"Wake up, Finn!" She snaps her fingers in front of my nose. "You don't have much time. While you sit here staring into space, the Dark God is putting the last touches on his final triumph."

I reach through the foggy air, half expecting my fingers to go straight through what looks like the image of a living woman. But instead, I touch the rough woven fabric of her skirt.

She sighs. "Finn, do I *look* like a vision? A ghostly apparition? Some brainsick fancy?"

No, she looks real. As real as me, as solid as the yew tree behind me. Actually, she seems *more* real than the rest of the world. Against, the white, drifting fog, she has a glowing, sturdy substance.

"What do you want me to do?" I stagger to my feet. "If you show me the way, I'll run to Avalon and get help."

Her eyes flash, and I know that's not the answer she was hoping for. I search for what else she might want me to do. "I'll bring Mother Sima's book with me," I offer. "I'll make sure the *Bestiary* gets to Abba Yosef."

She gives a snort that makes me think of Freya. The impatient look on her face reminds me of Freya too. "Finn, you are the Chosen One. Not some messenger or errand boy whose only task is running here and there. You have *work* to do."

I stare at her. She stares back at me.

"No," I whisper. "You can't be asking me to go back in that Hel-hole."

She raises her eyebrows and taps her foot.

"But there'd be no point," I protest. "Not now. I spilled all the holy water. I'd have to go back to Avalon first anyway to get more."

Brigid shakes her head. "When one route fails, you must look for a new route. There are other ways to defeat the Dark God."

For the space of a breath, anger flashes through me, and I can no longer meet her eyes. But then I remember: my anger has never gotten me anywhere. It's gotten me broken knuckles when I pounded a rock; it's led to my friends being attacked and even killed; and it's what made me hesitate when my only job should have been spilling the holy water into the Cauldron. I lift my gaze to hers again; her eyes are serene now, deep with peace and joy—and a love that asks only that I give whatever I have to give, even if I fail.

"All right," I say. "Tell me what to do."

She smiles. "You'll know when the moment comes."

Her words set off another spark of anger. "That's what Mother Sima said. And look where that got us! Look where it got Mother!" I stab my thumb over my shoulder at the yew tree behind me. "She's in there dying."

"Yes," Brigid says quietly. "And now you must act without the companionship of your friends. You are the one who has been chosen. You hold within you all that is needed."

I shake my head. "Do you *know* what happened? I failed. It was my fault. If you send me back, I'll just fail again."

"No." She shakes her head so vehemently that cascades of scarlet hair fly out from her head, shimmering in the fog. "Your past failures need not shape the future. Remember when last we spoke? Already since then you have changed. I see the changes. Your heart is no longer hard like a stone. Now, Finn, you must have the courage to go still further. It is time for you to change into who you really are. Trust your own spirit, the light that shines at your true center."

"No," I say miserably. "I'm not who you think I am. Any of the others would have been a better choice. They're the strong ones. Not me." I see Nectan's calm gaze so vividly in my mind that I have to choke back a sob. "I can't do anything without them. I can't do it alone."

"Who said you would be alone? You will carry your friends' love and courage within you for the rest of your life. All the Good Folk will be with you in spirit. The men and woman of Avalon will be holding you in their prayers. And the Light that shines through us all will never leave you. Your own small light is a part of the greater Light that never dims."

I try to absorb her words. I try to find comfort and strength in them. But all I can do is whisper, "I'm scared, Brigid,"

"Of course." She shrugs. "Even the heavenly ones cower when they behold the Dark God."

"Then how can you expect *me* to do it?" My voice is a wail. "I don't know how!"

"You already know how."

"No, I *don't*!"

"Yes, you do." She smiles. "Remember? One foot after another. One breath at a time. Until you die."

"Those were just silly things I kept repeating to myself," I mutter, embarrassed. "They were what kept me going down there in the darkness. But they didn't do me any good."

"Didn't they?" She raises her eyebrows. "You are here. You are still alive. And so are Freya, Mother Sima, and Artair. The Dark God is not pleased that those things are true. *He* knows that the war has not yet been won. But, Finn—if you delay much longer, he *will* triumph. Soon all places of refuge will be overrun with the undead. You must finish the task you were chosen to do."

I try to imagine going back into the dark tunnels all alone, my hands empty, with no plan at all except to simply keep going until I die. "I can't," I blurt. "I'm sorry. It's not in me."

"You are wrong, Finn. There is much greater power within you than you imagine. But you must win the battle inside your own heart before you can achieve victory for all Albion."

I feel a flicker of hope. "Do you mean—do you *know* that I'll succeed? Is my victory ordained by the fates?" It would be hard to believe, but if it's true, then I wouldn't have to feel as though everything were resting on my shoulders. All I'd have to do is muster up enough courage to jump into destiny's flow—and leave the rest up to God or the gods or the Wyrd sisters, whoever it is that's in charge.

But Brigid says, "I cannot glimpse around the next bend of time, Finn. I know only—as all in the Blessed Realm know—that you are the Chosen One." Her outline is growing misty, as though she's sinking back into the fog. I reach out my hand to try to hold on to her, but she's already gone.

I hear one last chime of distant bells, and then her voice comes to me through the mist. "Finn, *now* is your time to act."

I stand for a moment longer, staring into the fog. I suppose I'm hoping if I don't move, she'll come back. But the world is as chill and gray as it was before she came. I'd like to tell myself it was all my imagination. I don't have to go back down in the caves.

But I know she was real.

"Finn?" Freya asks from behind me. "Were you talking to someone?"

I turn around and find her standing in the split of the trunk, her face very white. Her expression scares me. "Mother Sima? Artair?" I brace myself for what she'll tell me.

But she says only, "The same. No better. Maybe a little worse." She clutches the tree's bark as though it's the only thing keeping her upright. "Who were you talking to?"

I shrug my shoulders. "It was—well, it was someone from the Otherworld. A woman who is—well, she's a queen there."

"You were talking to a goddess?" I can't tell if she believes me or not. Her face holds nothing but weariness.

I shrug. "Some call her that. But others say she's one of Iosa's Holy Ones."

"Was it my namesake? Freya?" Her voice holds a flicker of interest now.

"My people call her Brigid. Maybe she's the same as your Freya. I don't know." *I don't know who—or what—she is.*

"What did she tell you?"

I suck in my breath. "I have to go back." As soon as I speak the words, I know my mind is made up now: I'm going. Somehow, it's a relief to have stepped past all my excuses and fears. Freya is looking at me blankly, so I add, "Down into the caves. I have to end the Dark God's curse."

Freya's face was already as pale as I've ever seen it, but now it goes even whiter. "You can't, Finn. It would be madness. You'd be going to your death."

Until I die.

Well, if that's what it takes. "Freya, we'll all be dead anyway if the undead aren't stopped. I would rather die like this than sitting here waiting to be eaten by one those rotting wights."

She looks into my face, and I know she must read my determination there. "All right." She straightens and steps out from the tree's shelter. "I'll go with you."

For a moment, my heart leaps with relief. I won't have to do this alone after all. But then I shake my head. "No, Freya. You need to stay here with Mother Sima and Artair. I won't put you in danger again. This is my task. Mine alone."

A little pink flows back into Freya's face, and her face loses some of its weariness. "You are a mickle fool, Finn. You've got yourself all puffed up, thinking you're the great hero. Like you're the only one who's capable of killing a few draugar. Well, you're not even particularly good at it. I'm much better. You'll need me with you."

"No, Freya. You need to stay here." I'm relieved to see that I've made her angry. Now she looks more like her old self, and I can't help but give her a grin. "Anyway, you were the first to say I was the one to end the curse. You've always said that."

She scowls back at me. "Well, I was wrong." Her voice is shriller than I've ever heard it, and I'm horrified now to see that her eyes are bright with tears. "Finn, you can't leave me!"

I take a step closer, longing to pull her close to me. "Freya, it—it breaks my heart to leave you. But I have to." I give one of her braids a little tug. "And you need to stay here with Mother Sima and Artair." I slide my fist up and down the thick silky length of her hair.

To my astonishment, her hand comes up and clutches mine. "Then promise me you'll come back. Promise me, Finn! Come back to me!"

I open my mouth to make the promise. Of course, I'll come back to her. *Nothing on heaven or earth could keep me away from you.* That's what I want to say.

But looking into her blue eyes, I can't say anything less the truth. "I can't promise, Freya. But I'll do my best." My hand turns so that it clasps hers. "I want to come back to you. More than anything."

We stand there for a moment longer, our clasped hands raised between us, and for just that moment, I'm not thinking about the Dark God or his poxy Cauldron and undead hosts. The only thing in my mind is Freya.

"Then go." She lets go of my hand and steps back inside the shelter of the tree.

First, though, I have other farewells to say. I follow her inside and kneel beside Mother Sima. "Goodbye, Mother. All the nasty beasties and boggles in that book of yours wouldn't drag me from your side, but—well, I know you know how it is when Brigid tells you what to do. You'd understand why I have to go back." I put my hand on the curve of her round cheek. Even though I can see the faint rise-and-fall of her chest, she's so cold, as though she's already dead. I have to choke back a sob before I can continue. "I hope everything you believe comes true for you. I imagine the Nail-Riven One will be glad to welcome you when you come into his realm."

Next, I put my hand on Artair, and now, I can no longer hold back the tears. "Goodbye, Artair. You've given me so much—a grand companion you've been, as brave as any human I've ever known. I put you through so much since that day when you joined up with me— and you never once complained, never left my side. I hope one day we'll walk more hills and forests together. Even if it has to be in the Land of the Ever Young." I bow my head over him, my tears dripping into his fur. His side doesn't move under my hand. *Is he already running free in the Otherworld?*

"I'll stay with them," Freya says behind me. "As long as they need me, I'll not leave them."

I turn to face her there in the sweet-scented shadows inside the tree. "Be safe, Freya."

She looks back at me gravely. "While you are gone, I will not cease to cry out to the Aesir for your safety."

I give my head a quick nod and turn away before my determination wavers. But she grabs my arm and holds me for a moment longer. "Come back when you're done, Finn," she whispers. "Come back."

I give her a shaky grin. "I'll do my best, Freya." I hesitate, and for a moment, all I can think is how much I long to put my lips against hers.

She looks up at me for a long moment. Finally, she gives a sigh. "You are *such* a fool, Finn." And with that, she pulls my head down and brushes her lips against mine. Then she gives me a little push, and I stumble out into the fog.

I look inside the dark mouth in the stone. I walked the entire way back to the small entryway into the hillside with no other thought than the feel of Freya's kiss. Somehow, I managed to keep my course along the ridge without falling off on one side or wandering away into the fog on the other.

Now that I'm here, reality falls on me like one of Aedgar's stones slamming onto my shoulders. Last time I entered this small, dark hole, I was terrified because I didn't know what lay ahead; I'm even more terrified now that I know what to expect. I suck in one last breath of cool moist air—and then I crouch down and crawl into the darkness.

The same sick, unearthly smell hits my face, mixed with the reek of the undead. I'm back in the coiled intestines of this dark place, crawling deeper and deeper into the earth. It seems to take less time than it did the first time to reach the chambers filled with sharp fangs of rock. Shrieks from rotting throats echo back and forth against the stone walls, and soon, I have to press myself back into the shadows while the undead clatter past. I just have to trust that Nectan's hog's piss mixture is still doing its job.

The thought of Nectan brings tears to my eyes again, but I wipe them away with my sleeve. I don't have time for sorrow now. I have to stay focused. *Left foot . . . right foot. Breathe in . . . breathe out.* I step into the grand chamber where the Cauldron squats at the center.

The embers beneath the enormous pot give the only light to the enormous darkness that looms around me. I square my shoulders, suck in a deep breath.

Until I die.

The room seems to be empty, at least, the Cauldron unguarded. This is my chance then, though I have no idea what I should do next. *One step at a time*, whispers the memory of Brigid's voice in my mind. The only next step I can see is to get closer to the Cauldron.

Left foot . . . right foot. I make my way across the stone chamber, my sandals nearly soundless on the rock floor. I keep expecting to see a flood of wights pouring out of the openings that ring this enormous open space, but there's nothing. I'm still alone except for my own faint reflection in the pot's round sides.

It must be a trap. Why else would it be unguarded like this?

My skin crawls, as though a hundred hideous insects are creeping over me. But what can I do except keep walking, one step after another?

Oomph!

Enormous hands grasp me by the shoulders and lift me off the ground. I wriggle and twist, but I can't free myself. The hands snap me back and forth, the way a dog will shake a rat between its teeth, and the smell of rotting flesh makes me gag. Suddenly, I drop to the ground, and I hear something that makes my heart leap with joy: the familiar double-whistle of two swords swinging through the air.

Nectan! He's not dead after all. I spin around, a grin on my face. An enormous wight looms above me—but any moment now I'm certain Nectan will come up behind the ghoul and slash off its head.

The living corpse takes a step nearer. As it raises its two swords, I see the crest of spiky hair along its scalp. Tears of horror and grief spring into my eyes. "Nectan!" Staring into the gray and rigid face, I scream his name. He must be in there still, my friend, the kind and gentle man who is my friend.

But his eyes are flat and dead. No, not quite dead. They hold a gleam of hunger, and he leans closer to me, his mouth open as though he plans to take a bite of my face before I'm even dead.

Behind him, more neamh mairbh crowd into the hall. The stone chamber is like a hive of enormous angry bees now, but I can't pull my gaze away from Nectan's face. "Oh Nectan," I whisper.

The other wights are stamping their feet, clanging their weapons on the stone floor, and all the while, they're howling and shrieking. The stone rings with the terrible sound of hundreds of corpses, and the stench of rot is so thick that it's like something solid in the air, pressing hard against my face.

I'm reminded suddenly of the time when Aedgar beat me with the flat of his sword until my mind went into darkness. This is worse than that, worse than any pain I've ever felt. I long to disappear into unconsciousness, let all this go one without me being there to hear and see it—but I can't. I have to experience this with my eyes open, my heart pounding, and piss running down my leg. *Until I die.* That's the only thought I have left, the only thing I can hang on to.

Suddenly, on one beat, the clanging and screaming stops. For the space of another breath, the chamber still holds the echo of that terrible clamor. And then there's silence.

The neamh mairbh do something now I've never seen before. They stand still, their spines straight, like soldiers at attention. I recognize the ghoul with the Roman helmet standing at the front, as though he's the general of these undead troops. The corpse above me—*it's not Nectan, it's not, not really*—shoves me down on my knees, while the air in front of me grows darker, thicker, as though it's congealing . . .

A man—or something like a man—steps out of the darkness. It's taller even than the ghoul that was once my friend, half again as tall, and it's covered from foot to neck in a deep crimson robe that shimmers like a snake's skin. The robe's cowl is drawn back, revealing a bony cranium covered with tight reptilian skin. A tangle of twisted horns emerges from the crest of the narrow skull, and instead of a mouth, it has a narrow, gleaming fire-lit slit. Its eyes glow red as burning coals.

"You are the Chossssen One." If a snake could speak, it would sound like this. One red-robed arm raises, and a long finger points at me. The hand shines like burnished iron, and yet it flexes and moves as thought it's made of mortal skin.

I'm frozen, like a rabbit about to have its neck snapped by a wolf. If ever I was afraid before in my life, it was nothing to what I'm feeling now. And yet even now, some small part of my mind is working with a desperate cold speed, searching the room for anything I can use that will allow me to escape and carry out my mission.

You hold all within you that is needed. That's what Brigid said—but what did she mean?

While the wee clear-eyed part of me is searching for an answer, I notice two shapes drifting behind the glowing skull. At first I think they're wisps of smoke, barely visible against the cavern's darkness, but then I see they're like death heads. Instead of eyes, they have holes into terrible dark depths, as though they are windows into another evil reality. They weave back and forth slowly, like snakes twisting lazily in the sun, and I realize that somehow they both are emanating from the thing in front of me. They are part of it, and yet each holds its own grue-some existence.

"Ssscrawny. Pathetic," pronounces the horned skull. "Brainlesssss."

For some reason, the insults make that small rational space inside my head just a little larger. I suck in a lungful of air, and as foul as the air is, it helps to clear my head.

"Is this what they call a hero now?" The horned mon-ster makes a vile noise; it takes me a moment to realize it's laughter. "In past times, real men came up against me—Bran, Cuchullain, Artair. Not boyssss."

His metal hand shoots forward—like a serpent flash-ing to strike its victim—and he grasps my neck. His touch burns on my skin, and he leans so close I can feel the heat of the flame inside his slitted mouth. "Thissss island has gone to ssseed. It isss time for one ruler. It isss *my* time."

For a moment longer, he stares into my face, and then he lets me drop. "Kill him," he says, as though he's grown bored with me. "And when you are certain he is dead—put him in the Cauldron." But before any of his servants can move to carry out his order, he suddenly screams. The shining metallic hand flies up to his face.

An arrow is buried in the eye socket. The shaft catches fire and the feather fletching smokes.

Where did that come from?

The monster screams again, yanking at the shaft, and then it spins around and bellows like a bull in agony. The throng of undead in the room scream. The voices rise higher and higher, until the chamber is filled to the brim with gibbering and howling, and the booming, clanging crack of countless weapons hitting the stone floor.

And somehow, in the midst of all that uproar, a song springs into my head, a silly little ditty I heard somewhere recently.

Oh wonder! O glory! What a sight
Corpses mangled and rotting
What horror! What fright!
Out of the cauldron come leaping

I shake my head. My brains are truly addled now, if I'm humming to myself in the midst of all this. But while the tumult around me rises and rises, the tune continues relentlessly inside my head.

Alive—still alive—the great fighter is thrown
Into the cauldron upended.
Magic reversed! The demon's spell undone!
Efnysien dead but the curse is now ended.

And just like that, as I hear in my head the words the bard sang back in the Cymry fort, I know what my next step has to be. When a living soul was stewed in the cauldron, the magic was vanquished. So all I have to do is throw myself in the Cauldron—

And die.

My veins turn to ice. A thousand bright and shining images flower inside me—the faces of Da, Fiona, and Brecken; Mother Sima's smile; Artair's bright eyes; the look in Freya's eyes when she said goodbye to me—and then, through all the other images, I see Brigid's flame-bright hair and the peace and joy of her eyes. *You hold within you all that is needed.*

My life is what's needed to end the curse.

I look over the Dark God's shoulder at the Cauldron. It's only a few steps away, but the monstrous red-robed figure blocks my way. Behind him, a ring of wights have circled the evil vat. *Well, when you can't go around something, you just have to go over it.* The Dark God is still twisted and writhing in pain, while his undead troops contort and scream in some hideous echo of his agony.

For the space of a single breath, I hesitate—and I can't help but wonder: *Where will I go?* To the Land of the Blessed? To the Angles' Mead Hall of the Gods? To Iosa and his Holy Ones?

Or darkness? Absolutely nothing?

It doesn't matter. I was chosen to do this task.

Suddenly, everything seems very simple. It doesn't matter what happens next. It doesn't even matter whether I succeed. I just have to do this.

Let's get this over with.

The cavern echoes with moans and shrieks, broken only by the desperate clash of metal against stone and bone against bone, but the Dark God is snarling, starting to pull himself up to his full height again. *It's now or never.*

My muscles tense, I draw in a deep breath—*One breath at a time, lad,* says Nectan's calm voice inside my head—and then, before the Dark God can fully recover, I push myself forward with all my strength. My full weight falls against the monster.

He staggers backward, knocking down the ghouls behind him. Before he can regain his balance, I leap up and push against his chest with all my strength. He totters, then loses his balance and falls against the Cauldron, with me clinging like a squirrel to his scaly, red robe. His bony face is right in front of mine, and I'm breathing the foul burning scent from his slitted mouth. It's the same strange stench I've been smelling all along inside these dark caves, a terrible reeking odor like nothing that comes from the Earth. His burning eyes stare up at me, and he screams.

That scream is almost enough to make me let go of him. It stabs my ears like red-hot dirks, and I scream back at him in agony. But somehow I manage to hold on to him. I grab handfuls of his robe in my fists and pull myself higher, pushing at him with everything I have in me. Somehow, I have to get over his head and launch myself into the pot.

I feel the claw of his iron hand on my back, but I have no time now to pay attention to pain. I reach up and grab hold of his twisted horns. They're sharp against my palms, like some unearthly thorn bush, and I see the green spark and flash of my blood. He shakes his head back and forth, trying to free himself, but I'm pulling myself higher, higher—

He tips backward over the rim of the Cauldron, his hands clasped tight around me, and I know he's not going to let go of me, no matter what happens. *Guess I'll just have to take him with me then.*

We hover there for what seems an eternity. I stare past his head at the bubbling abyss that reeks like everything that has ever died since the beginning of time.

Iosa have mercy. Criost have mercy.

The Dark God twists beneath me, dragging his iron fingers through my skin. Before he can pluck me off from his chest, I grab the arrow in his eye and shove it even deeper. I shift my weight just a little higher . . .

Together, we topple over the edge. Down into the seething darkness.

14

AFTER

I've died.

I don't know what else has happened—*did I destroy the Dark God and his undead legions, or did I fail again?*—but I'm sure I must be dead.

I feel a faint sense of relief. Now that I'm dead, at least there's nothing else I have to do. No more fighting the undead. No more grappling with horned monsters. No more fear, no more anger, no more sorrow. I can just lie here in the darkness forever, listening to the only sound I hear, a faint whispering hiss.

In . . . out; in . . . out; in . . . out.

After a long time, it comes to me: I'm listening to my own breath.

But if I'm breathing . . .

My thoughts are slow, sluggish. I listen for a while longer to the in-and-out whisper of my breath, and then I finally realize: *If I'm breathing, I can't be dead.*

I'm alive.

And if I'm alive . . .

I sigh. That means I can't go on lying here forever. I'm kind of disappointed. It felt so good for a moment to have nothing I had to do.

I make myself lift my hand and grope through the darkness. My fingers move across cold wet stone. Up, down, around, with no break: I'm in a small round space not much bigger than myself. I stretch my arm overhead and find a gap in the stone, a round hole.

I push myself up on my knees and try to grab the edges to pull myself up and out. The ragged rock slices my skin like blades.

Shite. My fingers drip green spangles.

Looks like I'm not getting out that way. Once the pain subsides in my hands, I lift my head up and stare up through the hole. I see the blue-red glow of old embers and the faint glimmer of something round and shiny. Directly above my face, a black and jagged gap breaks the curved brassy surface of whatever it is. I can see through the broken hole, up into still more darkness.

I stare at it a long time before I realize what I'm seeing. I'm looking up at the broken Cauldron. When it cracked, it must have broken the stone floor beneath it—and I dropped down into this rock chamber.

But what about the Dark God?

And the neamh mairbh?

I kneel there, holding my breath, listening.

Nothing. Not a sound.

Are they dead?

Really *dead?*

I drop back from the hole, suddenly weak. *Did I do it? Did I do what I was sent to do?*

I feel no triumph, no sense of glad victory. Instead, a growing sense of dread creeps into my weariness. If I've succeeded in my mission, is it my destiny now to die in this stone bubble, buried deep beneath the earth where no one will ever know what happened to me? Will I die here of hunger, never seeing the light again, never seeing the faces of my friends?

My heart feels like a panicked rabbit leaping around inside my chest. I make myself take a slow breath, and then I hear the memory of Nectan's deep, kind voice: *One breath at a time, lad. That's all it takes—just one breath after another. Don't think about anything else.*

Nectan . . . For a moment, I'm tempted to surrender to the wave of sorrow that crashes over me, but then I hear another memory: *Promise me you'll come back, Finn!*

Crouched there in the darkness, I think of all the hundreds of expressions I've seen on Freya's face: the smug look of a cat tormenting a mouse; the wild fierce joy of the shield maiden; impatient glances at my stupidity; angry glares; laughter; terror; and last of all, the expression in her blue eyes when she bid me goodbye.

I want to see that face again.

If I have to, I'll push my way up through those blade-sharp shards of stone. What's a little more blood now, a little less skin? But first, I slide my hands back and forth around the stone walls that press so close around me. This time, I find a small opening, just large enough for me to squirm through. I hesitate. I'd almost rather slice my fingers off on the ragged stone above my head than squeeze into that narrow hole. But I don't know what's waiting up there. The neamh mairbh may have been destroyed along with the Cauldron, but the Dark God may still be there—and even wounded, he'll be stronger than I am.

Better this crack in the earth then facing him. I crawl on my belly into the narrow space of darker darkness.

Even when I'm stretched out flat on the ground, the rock is just above my head. The only way I can push myself forward is by hunching along on my belly, like a worm. The slender tube slants steadily upward through the rock, but I'm overwhelmed with the horrifying certainty that it leads nowhere. It's a dead end, and I'll never be able to squirm my way backward again. I will die with my face pressed into cold slimy stone. I will never see the light again. I will never see Freya's face again.

I've had a lot of bad moments. This one might be the worst.

There's nothing I can do but keep wriggling along. As I push myself further and further up the tube, jagged stones scrape at my head. At least now the sparkles dripping into my eyes cast a faint green glow through the darkness.

Then, just when I think my heart will explode inside me, the walls widen a little, then a little more. I can get up on my hands and knees now, and I crawl a little faster along the slanted tunnel.

Then, slowly, I realize the darkness is lit by something besides my green blood. A gentle light reaches me, and a tiny breeze carries the scent of growing things. With one last scramble over the rocks, I tumble out into an icy stream. Ahead of me is the light of day.

I've reached the same opening by which I entered the caves. I crawl out and stagger to me feet. Above me is the ridge that will lead me back to Freya, Mother Sima, and Artair. Overhead, the sky is bright and blue.

But when I reach the yew tree, it's empty. For a long moment, I stand staring at the space where I last saw my friends. The soft earth is bloodstained, and it still bears the print of Mother Sima's body.

Does this mean they are safe? Did someone rescue them?

Or did the wights carry them away?

Before I can decide what I should do next, I hear the *creak-creak-creak* of waggon wheels. I turn around and find an ox plodding slowly toward me, a broad-faced man on the seat behind the big beast. "Ho, Clover!" he says when he sees me, and the ox stops walking.

The man and I stare at each other. "You're not a wight?" he asks at last.

I give him a shaky grin. "No sir. How about yourself?"

"Not so I've noticed." He throws back his head and laughs, and I hear relief and delight in his voice. "You've enough dirt and greenish stuff all over you, I wasn't sure what you might be. But fact is, I hear tell the poxy creatures have all turned into dust. You wouldn't have seen me out here with Clover, not on this path, if I hadn't thought they were gone. Just can't quite comprehend it's true." He cocks his head at me. "You haven't seen any recently? They were thick in these parts."

I shake my head. "I—I think they're gone."

He nods. "The story going around is that some great hero jumped in a magic pot and died to end the curse, just like in the myths of old. They say the curse is lifted now. My brother came by this morning and told how he was facing a bunch of wights, thinking he was a dead man—when all at once, the plaguey things just crumbled where they stood. Nothing but heaps of dust." The man shakes his head in wonder. "And will you look?" He waves his hand at the grassy ridge. "The earth looks the way it's supposed to. And listen to that." He points up at a lark that's singing as it throws itself up at the sky. "Hel, the world even smells right again, like green things instead of shit and rotted meat." When he grins, I see a row of strong yellow teeth that remind me of a horse's. "Lad, I tell you the truth, I'd bust out singing if I didn't think it would make your ears bleed."

I grin back at him. I know what he means. One of my friends is dead, I don't know where the others are, and pretty much every bit of me hurts from one wound or another—but despite all that, the sun is shining, birds are singing, and life feels like it has a bit of hope again.

"So what's your story, lad? Where are you headed?"

I hesitate. "Well, it's a long story, I guess. But I'm on my way to Avalon now. I'm hoping to meet up with some friends there."

"Then hop up here, lad. I'm heading to Avalon too. Got a load of last year's wheat for the Culdees." He stabs a thumb over his shoulder at the waggon bed that's heaped with sacks. "We've not been able to get provisions to them for months now, not with those ghouls wandering about, so me and my neighbors all threw in what we could. I reckon the Culdee folk are getting pretty hungry."

I climb up onto the seat beside the farmer. For a while, I listen to his good-natured jawing, but after a while, my attention drifts. He doesn't seem particularly curious about me, which is a relief right now, and slowly, every muscle in my body softens until I feel as limp as one of the rag dolls my sister used to play with. The pain in my head and back and hands fades a little, and I slump back against the board, my legs sprawled out in front of me. The farmer's voice blends with the slow *clump-clump-clump* of the ox's hooves, the jabber of jackdaws in the trees as we roll past, and the squeak of the wheels turning around and around. The sun is warm on my shoulders, and for the first time in many days, I'm not afraid for my life. My head nods. I try to keep my eyes open, but finally, I give in and let myself doze.

"Rise and shine, lad!" The farmer gives me a shake. I open my eyes, blinking and confused.

Just ahead of us, the Holy Island rises up against the sky like the enormous roof of some great, green house. The white froth of meadowsweet spills along the path ahead, and cornflowers the color of Freya's eyes are sprinkled everywhere on the grass.

The waggon rolls to a stop as the porter comes out to greet us. When he sees me, he halts, a look of astonishment on his face. "Young man? You have the look of one I know to be dead."

I climb down from the waggon and walk across the footbridge. "It's me," I say with a grin. "I'm not dead after all."

This time, I'm the one who's astounded, because the tall, grave man grabs me in his arms and clasps me against his thin chest. Then he steps back and his smile is so wide I hardly recognize him. "You are very welcome here, lad. We can never express our gratitude for what you've done."

The farmer gives me a curious glance, but before he can ask me any questions, I thank him for the ride and bid him goodbye. I'm anxious to find out if my friends are here.

My skin is tingling, everything bursts with color, and all my wounds suddenly hurt a little less. My heart pounds as my eyes search the whitewashed buildings. I barely notice the crowd that has gathered or the excited buzz of their voices, even though I catch a word here and there: ". . . a miracle!" "He's the hero who . . ." ". . . not dead after all!"

I'm looking for just one face.

And then I hear my name shouted, and she's running down the hill toward me, her gold hair flying out behind her. Without a thought, as though it's the most natural thing in the world, I hold out my arms and she flies into them."

"Finn!" She pulls back a little and looks up at me, her eyes bright with something that looks a lot like tears. "You're not dead. Thank Thunor."

"Freya." All I can do is grin at her like a proper eejit and repeat her name. "Freya. Freya"

We look into each other's faces for a long moment. Finally, when I've looked my fill—at least for now—I remember that there's more I need to know. "Mother Sima?" I'm afraid to hear the answer, and I brace myself for sad news.

But Freya smiles and says, "She's healing. She's over there," she points at one of the whitewashed buildings, "in the infirmary. The leechkin here has amazing skills. She cut the bone better than I did—cleaner—and then she sewed Mother's skin so tight and neat she hardly bled anymore. I was afraid the leg would fester anyway, but the leechkin's herbs have kept the wound clean and healthy. Abba Yosef says her skills were handed down to her from the people who came here long ago from far to the east."

"How—how is Mother Sima? I mean—well, without her leg?"

Freya laughs. "Nothing slows that woman down for long. She's still weak, but she's told a carver here on the island exactly how she wants her wooden leg fashioned."

I let out the breath I've been holding. We've lost Nectan, but at least there's still Mother Sima, Freya, and me. If only Artair could have made it too. I'm about to ask where he's buried, when something cold and wet brushes against my hand, and I hear a familiar bark.

"Artair?" I go down on one knee, hardly able to believe my eyes. He jumps up, his paws on my shoulders, and licks my face until I laugh and squirm away.

"At least he took off a layer of dirt," Freya says. "I can almost see your skin."

I run my hand gently along Artair's side. The hair's been shaved away, showing dark stitches against pink, puckered skin. "He's almost healed," I whisper, looking up at Freya. "How can that be? His guts were hanging out. Is it this place? Some healing magic in the air?"

"Probably. I didn't think there was any chance he'd make it. But once the leechkin put her herbs and salves on Artair, he seemed a little better almost at once. And then as the days went by, he just got better and better." She shrugs. "Dogs do heal quickly."

"As the *days* went past?" I give Artair another pat and get to my feet. "Freya, how long have I been gone?"

"More than a week." She looks away and blinks, then dashes the back of her hand across her eyes. "We thought you were dead."

I lay under that mickle cauldron for days. It doesn't seem possible. When the farmer was talking about his brother, I was thinking all the while he meant the undead had only just disappeared the day before—but it was more than a week.

"I don't remember anything from that time," I tell her. "Only darkness." Maybe I almost *was* dead. I shake my head. "No wonder I'm hungry!"

My stomach growls loudly, and Freya laughs. "Come on." She grabs me by the wrist and pulls me after her. "You missed the midday meal, but I'll get you something from the refectory."

With Artair following close behind, we go into the refectory, and I sit at one of the long tables. Freya disappears into the kitchen, and I scratch Artair behind his ears while I wait. She comes back with a trencher piled with pease, curds, and oatcakes and sets it in front of me, then takes a seat across the table. For a while she just sits there with her chin cupped in her hand, watching me. I squirm a little beneath that steady blue regard, but I'm too hungry to mind too much.

And I kind of like it anyway.

Finally, when I've stopped shoveling food in my mouth, and the trencher is almost empty, she says quietly, "What happened, Finn? I looked for you. You—you were just gone."

I put down my spoon. "You looked for me?"

She nods, her eyes on the table. I drop some curds on the floor for Artair, and then I lean back, feeling more content and satisfied than I have in very long time. Suddenly, an image jumps out of my memory: an arrow deep in the Dark God's eye socket.

"Freya, that was *you*? You shot the Dark God in the eye?"

She nods again, still not looking at me. "I know I promised to stay with Mother and Artair. But," she glances up at me quickly, "I was sure Woden and the goddess Freya had already come for them. I knew Mother and Artair wouldn't mind if I left them before their death-hour, not if they thought I could help you. So I made an arrow out of a yew branch, and then I fletched it with a crow feather I found on the ground—and I went after you as fast as I could. I only had that one arrow, but—well, it was the best I could do. And then when I got to the Diamond Hall, the Dark God already had you." She shrugs. "So I took my best shot."

"Damn good one." I grin at her. "I wouldn't be here— and the undead would still be walking—if it weren't for your arrow." *Funny how all our small actions somehow added up to be enough.* "One step at a time," I murmur.

She looks up at me. "What?"

"Nothing. Just something Nectan said to me. I think he meant—well, that we just have to do the next thing, and then the next. All by itself, each thing wouldn't be enough—but you could walk from one end of Albion to the other, just taking a step at a time."

"Nectan." Freya says the word on a sigh, and a shadow passes across her face. "Is he really dead? I was hoping—"

I shake my head. "He's really dead. I saw him. He was one of the neamh mairbh."

Freya looks sick. "Oh Finn—"

"He must be dead now, though," I tell her. "I mean *really* dead. His soul will be in the Otherworld."

Freya blinks away her tears. "I hope he's with his beloved."

We're both silent, remembering our friend.

"What happened to you, Finn?" Freya asks at last. "I saw you topple into the Cauldron, taking the Dark God with you. I—I screamed and hid my eyes. There was a terrible noise, like an enormous stone exploding in a fire. The undead screamed and wailed—and then suddenly everything was silent. When I opened my eyes, everything had changed. The chamber was empty, and the Cauldron was tipped sideways. The cavern floor was covered with something that looked like ashes."

"That was the undead," I say. "All that was left of them."

Her nose wrinkles. "I didn't think of that. All I was thinking about was getting you out of the Cauldron. I ran across the chamber. I could see something thick and lumpy pouring out of the pot."

She grimaces, and I can hear her swallow. "It was yellow and steaming, like some sort of awful stew, and there was a terrible smell. I looked for your—your body. I found something that looked like a hand made of iron, but there was nothing else, nothing I could recognize. I thought—I thought you must have gone into that awful liquid and been—cooked."

She looks down at the wood table and traces the grain with her finger. "I looked everywhere for you in that chamber, Finn. In every last dark cranny and crack. I kept kicking through all those ashes, thinking maybe you were hidden beneath them. The fire that had been under the Cauldron was getting smaller, and I knew I had to give up. But before the light went out completely, I saw something."

She lifts her head, and her blue eyes meet mine. "Something terrible. At first I thought it was smoke from the fire. Only then I realized it was like two snakes weaving back and forth through the air. They hovered over my head for a long time. Like they were looking at me. Like they wanted to *eat* me." I reach my hand across the table and she grasps it tight. "They were real, I swear, Finn. I don't think I've ever been so scared."

"I know, Freya. I saw them too. Earlier. They came out of the Dark God."

"What *were* they?" Her fingers between mine loosen a little, but she doesn't pull her hand away.

"I don't know. They were part of the Dark God some-how. After his body was—gone, destroyed—well, those things, those wraiths were all that was left of him, I guess."

She nods, her face pale and grim. "They kind of slith-ered away into the shadows finally. And then the fire went out completely. Everything was black. I couldn't even see my own hand in front of my face. I sat there in the ashes and—Finn, it was about the worst moment of my life."

My fingers tighten around hers, and she holds on to me as though she'll never let me go. "Finally," she says, her head bent over our hands, "I got up and I crept through the dark, stumbling into rocks and— Well, somehow I got out." She lifts her head and glares at me, and now she looks more like her old self. "I thought you were cooked, Finn MacDugal, I really did."

I grin at her. "Well, I wasn't."

"But what happened to you? Where were you?"

"When I went into the Cauldron, I guess I broke it. I don't remember anything, though. The last thing I knew, the Dark God and I were falling into the pot—and then I woke up in a hole in the rock underneath the Cauldron. I couldn't climb out, and I thought I was stuck there forever."

I think about telling her that it was her face that made me keep searching in the dark for a way out, but I'm still not quite *that* brave. Instead, I ask, "How did you get Mother Sima and Artair back to Avalon?"

"When I got back to the yew, they both seemed—well, more alive, I guess. I no longer felt as though their souls were already wandering in the Otherworld. So I gathered a pile of dead wood and built a fire for a signal. I kept it burning all night—and toward morning, just as I was giving up hope, a group of the Culdee came rolling up in a waggon. The leechkin was with them, and she put herbs and fresh bandages on Mother's leg and Artair's wound. Then the Culdees lifted them into the waggon bed—and they brought us here. Along the way, we found Aelwyn's horses. Some of his men came and got them yesterday."

Her fingers tighten around mine. "Finn, I thought you were dead. All this time, I thought you were gone forever. Today, I was walking down the hill, feeling like I might never smile again—and there you were." Her eyes are bright with tears again.

I wish there wasn't a table between us.

Before I can answer her, Abba Yosef enters the refectory. Freya and I let go of each other's fingers and pull our hands back quickly. The old man's lips curve, as though we've amused him. "Ah, Finn," he says. "So it's true. You survived."

"Yes, sir."

I scramble to my feet, but he waves me to sit back on the bench. He takes a seat next to Freya. "I am glad to see you, young Finn."

"Thank you, sir. I'm—I'm glad to be here." I look at his wise, wrinkled face, and my mind is full of questions. "Sir?"

"Yes, Finn?"

"*Why* am I here? Why didn't I die in the Cauldron? I thought that's what would happen when I jumped into it. I thought that's what *had* to happen. So why didn't it?"

"Because you are not, young Finn, like most men."

"What do you mean?"

Freya snorts. "Finn," she says, "look at yourself."

I glance down at my hands and arms. In the refectory's dim light, I shimmer, as though I've rubbed firefly juice all over myself. Everywhere I bled—and I've bled so many places that I've lost count—tiny points of light blink like stars.

I look back at Abba Yosef. "My Faerie blood?"

He shrugs his shoulders. "I cannot tell you for sure. But yes, I believe so. You shattered that grim instrument of death with your living body, and you were not killed yourself. Something about you was so strong that it withstood the Cauldron's dark magic."

Freya's eyes widen as though she's just understood something. "You went into that pot thinking you were going to die, Finn?"

I nod and look away from her, embarrassed. "I remembered that song the bard sang back in the Cymry fort, about how the pot could be broken by a living body. In the story, the man who got in the pot lost his life, so I figured I would too—but once I'd spilled the holy water, it was the only way I could think of to destroy the Cauldron."

Abba Yosef nods. "The old legends always said that only life—true life—could destroy the Cauldron of Living Death."

Freya's eyes are wide as she studies my face. I squirm a little and try to think of something to distract her. "So what happened to the Dark God?" I ask.

The old man looks thoughtful. "I suspect, Finn, that when you destroyed the Cauldron, you destroyed him as well. He and his monstrous vat were so joined they had become one. One could not exist without the other."

"So is he truly gone? Forever?"

"Who can say?" The abba spreads his fingers wide, as though to demonstrate how little knowledge he possesses. "But I suspect the form you saw is gone forever. As for his malignant spirit—that I cannot say."

I think of those twisting, snake-likes shadows both Freya and I saw, and I shudder.

Abba Yosef gaze is serene. "Fret over the Dark Lord no longer, Finn. Whatever the future holds, today he is vanquished. Today is a day of joy, not fear." He smiles. "You did well, son."

My face turns hot. I know how badly I failed, over and over. My stupid anger cost Nectan his life.

The old man must have read my expression, because he says gently, "We all have faults, Finn. We do our best—and then we can only give our weakness to Yahweh along with our strength. In the end, the Lord of the Universe makes use of both."

He gets to his feet, and his eyes hold a twinkle. "I expect you young people might have things you want to discuss without an old man around. Perhaps I will see you later at vespers."

Freya and I stand up too to say goodbye to him. Once he's gone, we move around the table closer to each other. Looking at her, I feel suddenly awkward, because for the first time since she flew into my arms, I'm noticing how she looks.

The blue gown she's wearing is fastened at the neck with a bit of silver, and her gold hair is loose and combed on her shoulders. Every bit of her skin is so clean it seems to glow in the shadowy hall. Next to her, I feel like a tattyboggler, my clothes ragged and filthy, my hair knotted and stuck with twigs, and my skin covered with all kinds of grime I'd rather not think about. Even if there's a faint green twinkle almost everywhere on my skin and clothes, it doesn't make up for how minging foul I must look compared to Freya.

I shift my weight from foot to foot, searching for something to say. "What's that?" I ask finally, pointing to the silver brooch pinned to her gown.

She unfastens it and holds it out to me. It's Mother Sima's sigil, the square cross atop two swords. "She gave it to me," Freya says. "She said I'd earned the right to be considered one of Iosa's warriors."

"Even though you don't worship Iosa?"

Freya shrugs. "Mother didn't say anything about that." She pins the sigil back on her gown. "I do not worship Iosa, but I will wear his talisman with pride. It will always remind me of the three people who were my companions on the greatest adventure of my life. Mother Sima because she gave it to me. Nectan because of the two swords. And you."

"Why me?" I can't see anything about the silver sigil that has anything especially to do with me.

She reaches up and puts a finger on the stone I wear around my neck. "Because of the talisman you wear. As long as I've known you, you've worn the same square cross that's on Mother's sigil."

I put my own hand up to the stone cross. Strange to think that this bit of stone has been with me through so much. While the world's turned upside down around me, my talisman has remained the only constant, the only thing that still links me to my family and my past.

My family. Are Da and Brecken and Fiona still out there somewhere? *Will I ever see them again?*

"Finn?" Freya has an odd expression on her face, one I've not seen there before.

I pull my thoughts back from where they've wandered. "Yeah?"

"There's something I have to say."

"Yeah?"

While I wait for her to go on, I notice her face is very pink. Finally, she says, "Before my mother died, she made me make a solemn oath. She made me promise I would give myself in love only to someone who was my equal in strength and courage. She said to be my equal, he would have be the greatest warrior in all of Angleland." She smiles with a hint of her old pride, and my heart sinks.

I focus all my attention on the doorway where Abba Yosef disappeared, struggling to keep my feelings off my face. "I'm sure you will find him someday, Freya," I say finally, my voice stiff.

Her face floods with even brighter color, and she stamps her foot. "You are such a complete and utter galoot, Finn MacDugal."

What did I say wrong?

I stare at her like the numpty eejit I am. And then I start to grin. *Freya thinks I'm her equal?*

"So I'm no longer just a slave boy in your eyes?" I feel my smile grow wider. "Did I avenge your father's arm to your satisfaction?"

She sighs. "Just shut up for once, Finn, can't you?"

And then, I'm not sure how, she's in my arms. I don't know if she put herself there, or if I pulled her to me, but it doesn't matter. No matter how she got there, she feels just right. I don't want to ever let her go, but she pulls back a little then, just enough to tip her face up. My lips find hers.

After a long time, we step back from each other. Both of us are breathing as hard as we did back when we were running from living corpses. I'm not certain what I should say or do next.

Freya's gaze has dropped, and I realize she's looking down at me. I shift uncomfortably.

"Oh, my, Finn!" Her voice is filled with mischief. "There's that fish under your tunic again."

PEOPLE AND PLACES, HISTORY AND FANTASY IN THIS BOOK

Imagine if Finn could jump in a time machine and emerge in our twenty-first century world, either in the British Isles or in America. He would be overwhelmed by the strange mix of cultures, ethnicities, customs, languages, foods, and objects. Most readers of *Magic Reversed* are in a similar jam when transported back into the British Isles in the year 610. There were at least half a dozen distinct cultural and ethnic groups in the isles at that time, with a mélange of differing cultural ways. At the same time, a multitude of conflicts, treaties, and trades were going on between these factions. The following is a very brief guide to help orient you to the world of Finn and Freya.

Originally, the southern half of the British Isles was inhabited by a variety of Celtic tribes people who shared a common language known as Brittonic Gaelic—and hence they were known as Britons. They were conquered by successive waves of foreign peoples; first the Romans and then shortly after that by the Anglo-Saxons. Because of this, the Britons play no role in *Magic Reversed*. However, in our story the British Isles are still called Albion, which is the ancient Brittonic name for the land.

Finn is Scottish, but that means something different from what it does now. The Romans originally used the term Scoti (pronounced with long "o" and with the "i" pronounced like long "e": "skoh-tee") to refer to a variety of unconquered Celtic people. By the time of our story, the word applies more specifically to a confederation of clans originating from Ireland's east coast and then settling on the western shores of the land we now call Scotland. The Scoti empire is also known as the Kingdom of Dalriada (spelled variously in differing books, Dal Riata, etc). Two centuries after the time of Finn and Freya, King Kenneth McAlpine will lead the clans of Dalriada in a triumphant military campaign sweeping clear across the north of the British Isles, conquering the indigenous Picts and creating the nation we now call Scotland.

But in Finn's day, his people are relative newcomers to the British Isles; his grandparents would have colonized the land where his family lives. Their language and customs are still those of Ireland. Mother Sima is of the same background as Finn; although she is born and raised in Ireland, her Irish home is part of the same Kingdom of Dalriada.

At the time of our story, many of the Scoti are newly converted to faith in Iosa (Jesus, in the Scots Gaelic language, pronounced "ee-ah-sah," with accent on the first vowel). This is largely due to the efforts of a man named Columba who converted most of the Kingdom of Dalriada in his lifetime. The newly converted Scots still remember their old gods and goddesses, the Tuatha De Dana (pronounced like "two-ah day donna"), also known as the Sidhe (pronounced like "she") or Faerie Folk.

Freya is of Anglo stock, part of a larger cultural group known as Anglo-Saxons. In contrast to the Celtic Britons, Scoti, and Picts, the Anglo-Saxons are of Germanic or Scandinavian language and culture. The Angles came into northern England from modern-day Denmark, and the Saxons came into central England from modern-day Germany. In the twenty-first century, we still speak the English language (Angle-ish or Englisc), and we name the days of our week after Anglo-Saxon gods and goddesses (Wednesday is Woden's day, Thursday is Thunor's day, and Friday is Freya's day). This is because the Anglo-Saxons conquered most of England in the early 400s, about two centuries before Freya's time. In the time period of *Magic Reversed*, the Anglo-Saxons are proud and confident masters of the land, having subjugated or eliminated many local Celtic cultures centuries ago. They worship their gods and goddesses (Woden, Thunor, Freya, etc). Readers familiar with the Viking culture that arrived two centuries later will notice a great number of similarities between the Anglo-Saxons and their later Danish descendants.

Nectan comes from yet another culture: he is a Pict. The Picts are the indigenous Celtic people who live north of the great wall built by Roman emperor Hadrian to keep them safely in place. Neither the Romans nor the Anglo-Saxons and the Scoti have conquered the Picts at the time when *Magic Reversed* takes place. Today, we know very little about the Picts because we do not possess their writings. Their way of life disappeared when the Scots conquered them in the ninth century, so all we have of Pictish culture are a few words and numerous carved pictures in stone. Whatever this novel says about Nectan's background is, therefore, guesswork. Nothing is known concerning same-sex relations among the Pictish tribes, but it seems safe to assume they were similar to pre-Christian ways among other Celtic peoples, such as the ancient Gauls, who were described by classical writers as having many bonded love relationships between male couples. Ancient Irish legends suggest similar pairings of courageous "warrior lovers."

Our brave company travels down to the land of the Welsh (*Welsc* is the Anglo-Saxon word for these people) who live on the west coast of the English Island. In their own language, the land is Cymru (pronounced "come-ree") and the people are Cymry (pronounced nearly

identically). The Welsh are the indigenous Brittonic people of this land; in the twenty-first century, after 2,000
years of assaults by the Romans, Saxons, and Normans,
the Cymry still retain their ancient Celtic language. The
disgusting Welsh king who accosts Freya should in no
way be regarded as typical of this noble Celtic race; every
group of people has an occasional bad apple!

The magical land of Avalon is the present-day city of
Glastonbury, the annual scene of modern Britain's larg-
est rock festival. Marshes and lakes originally surrounded
the community, making the raised central hill essentially
an island; nowadays it is landlocked, but surrounding
regions can still be severely flooded. Avalon is the spiri-
tual heart of Albion; legend connects it with the Goddess, with a visit by Jesus when he was a little boy with
his uncle Joseph of Arimathea, and with the Holy Grail
brought there after Christ's death by Joseph. The Chalice
Well in Glastonbury remains a sacred site associated with
the Grail. *Magic Reversed* plays upon ancient legends that
Joseph of Arimathea and fellow Jews established the first
Christian church in England, the order of the Culdees,
protectors of the Grail and of the most ancient Jewish-
Christian traditions.

When our heroes arrive in Avalon, this novel moves
from the realm of history into the land of legends. But if
you climb up Glastonbury Tor (the great hill that over-
looks the land) and sit quietly on a summer day, you cannot help but feel that the country here is still very much

alive with the power of myth: there's something about Avalon that the rational mind cannot possibly explain. Some of that magic wove its way into Finn's story.

The adventures of Finn and Freya will continue
in the next book in the Celtic Bestiary series,
Freya and the Fire Dragon, coming soon.

ANOTHER EXCITING FANTASY FROM
CANDLEWOOD YOUNG ADULT

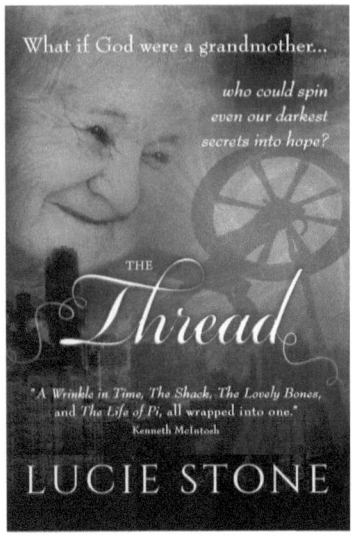

THE THREAD
Author: Lucie Stone
Price: $14.99
Paperback
Ebook Available
ISBN: 978-1-937211-78-3

Fifteen-year-old Callie follows a mysterious thread that pulls her through the night, deep into the terrible secrets of her own life. Meanwhile, Kirin hears his dead brother calling him, leading him to revelations that will change his entire world. Together, Callie and Kirin navigate a dark tide of old, long-buried evil that sweeps them both from their familiar reality and into a world they never suspected existed.

"If Madeleine L'Engle had collaborated with the authors of *The Lovely Bones* and *The Life of Pi*, the result might have looked a lot like this. Stone tackles the darkness of sexual abuse and murder, while offering a multi-faith roadmap to hope and healing."
—Kenneth McIntosh, M. Div., author of *Water from an Ancient Well: Celtic Spirituality for Modern Life* and *Magic Reversed*